THE LEGENDS OF THE ÄLFAR

RIGHTEOUS
FURY

THE LEGENDS OF THE ÄLFAR

RIGHTEOUS FURY

MARKUS HEITZ

Translated from the German by Sheelagh Alabaster

Jo Fletcher

New York • London

JF

Jo Fletcher Books
An imprint of Quercus
New York • London

© 2014 by Markus Heitz
Map illustration © 2009 by Markus Weber
English translation © 2014 by Sheelagh Alabaster
Originally published in Germany in 2009 by Piper Verlag GmbH
First published in the United States by Quercus in 2015

ISBN 978-1-62365-712-3

Library of Congress Control Number: 2014957508

Distributed in the United States and Canada by
Hachette Book Group
1290 Avenue of the Americas
New York, NY 10104

Manufactured in the United States

10 9 8 7 6 5 4 3 2 1

www.quercus.com

Dedicated to all who have a place in their hearts for life's scoundrels—as long as those scoundrels possess that certain something.

DSÔN FAÏMON

Map labels:
- THE HEART DSÔN
- AVARIS
- KASHAGÔN
- SHIIMÀL
- RIPHÀLGIS
- OCIZÌR
- WÈLÉRON

① ② ③ ④ ⑤ ⑥

① Status & Wealth

In Avaris there settled those álfar of high status blessed with wealth. Any wishing to reside in this radial arm had to have the support of all the other residents or else had to go.

② Sword & Faith

Wèléron fell to the warrior class and the priests and all who were involved with magic. But there were few powerful magicians among the álfar people. The magic in their blood did not permit for this.

③ Crafts & Knowledge

In Ocizìr the craftspeople sought their home and exchanged their skills amongst themselves. Different branches of knowledge fused to a unity and they founded schools and places of learning in order to perfect their skills.

④ Art & Death

In Riphàlgis there gathered the artists and they too collected together the various forms of artistry, creating a new art. Fascinated by the subject of death, they liked to utilise the materials that came with the ending of life.

⑤ Growth & Welfare

Shiimàl attracted those álfar who were skilled at farming. Huge farms were established where cattle and crops were raised in this one radial arm for supplying the whole realm.

⑥ Science & Death

Kashagôn is the home of the true warriors! Álfar, male and female, totally committed to the art of warfare came here and founded academies to train the hardest, best and most lethal of warriors.

Dramatis Personae

THE ÄLFAR
Nagsar and Nagsor Inàste, the Inextinguishables
Sinthoras, älf warrior, of the *Comets* faction
Demenion, politician (*Comets*)
Khlotòn, politician (*Comets*)
Rashànras, politician (*Comets*)
Yantarai, artist (f)
Timanris, artist (f)
Robonor, warrior and companion of Timanris
Timansor, artist father of Timanris
Hirai, his wife
Jiphulor, politician (*neutral*)
Helòhfor, soul-toucher
Caphalor, älf warrior (*Constellations* faction)
Enoïla, Caphalor's companion
Tarlesa, their daughter
Olíron, their son
Aïsolon, friend to Caphalor (*Constellations*)
Mórcass, merchant
The Humans
Raleeha, female slave to the Älfar
Kaila, female overseer of Sinthoras' slaves

Wirian, female slave to Sinthoras
Quanlot, slave
Grumson, slave to Caphalor
Longin, slave to Mórcass
Kuschnar, slave to Mórcass
Hasban Strength-of-Seven, prince of the Sons of the Winds (barbarian tribe)
Farron Lotor, prince of the Ishmanti barbarians
Armon, prince of the Herumite barbarians
Vittran, superintendant of the barbarian vassals

CREATURES

Munumon, king of the fflecx
Jufula, one of his favorites
Sardaî, thoroughbred night-mare
Linschibog, a fflecx
Gålran Zhadar, dwarf-like being with a talent for magic
Dafirmas, elf henchman to Gålran Zhadar
Rambarz, demi-troll henchman to Gålran Zhadar
Karjuna, an obboona female
Uoilik, prince of the jeembinas
Tarrlagg, overseer of the vassal óarcos
Gattalind, female strategist of the giants

MISCELLANEOUS

óarco: orc
fflecx: also known as alchemancers and poison-mixers. A black-skinned gnomoid people.
gålran zhadar: dwarf-like beings with a talent for magic
obboonas: a humanoid people also known as flesh-stealers
Tandruus: a tribe of barbarians
botoicans: a race with latent magic qualities, living in the west of Ishím Voróo
baro: an extremely rare wild predator
kimarbock: a male deer

wuzack: an artificial being created by the fflecx

jeembinas: a hybrid people, half-crab, half-human

Gramal Dunai: an eradicated tribe of barbarians

phaiu su: blood-sucking webs

cnutar: tripartite symbiotic creatures, able to merge or separate at will

Nostàroi: high-ranking älfar general

Herumites, Jomonicans, Ishmantis, Fatarcans: barbarian peoples

gardant: commander of a troop of guards

Phondrasôn: a subterranean place of banishment

Tark Draan: Refuge of the Scum (=Girdlegard)

schronz: (an insult) idiot, cretin

They are said as a people to show more cruelty than any other.

They are said to hate elves, humans, dwarves, and every other creature so much that the blood runs black in their veins and darkens their eyes in the light of the sun.

They are said to dedicate their lives exclusively to death and to art.

They are said to use black magic.

They are said to be immortal . . .

Much has been said about the Älfar.

Read now these tales and decide what is said true and what is not.

These are stories of unspeakable horror, unimaginable battles, gross treachery, glorious triumphs, and crushing defeats.

But they are also tales of courage, integrity, and valor.

Of friendship.

And of love.

These are the Legends of the Älfar

Unknown author,
preface to the forbidden books which transfigure the truth,
The Legends of the Älfar,
undated

Chapter I

Nagsar and Nagsor Inàste, the Inextinguishable Siblings, were looking for a home for themselves and their chosen companions.

They wandered hither and yon, surrounded by savage things, ugliness, and hideous creatures thrown in their path by the gods Shmoolbin, Fadhasi and Woltonn, in an attempt to destroy them. They named the place Ishím Voróo— Ubiquitous Horrendousness.

Epocrypha of the Creating Spirit,
1st Book,
Chapter 1, 1–7

Ishím Voróo (The Outer Lands), älfar realm
Dsôn Faïmon, Radial Arm Avaris,
4370th division of unendingness (5198th solar cycle),
summer.

Sinthoras was throbbing with anticipation, intoxicated by the thought of a new creative work. Everything told him to grasp hold of the brush, dip it into the paint and let his hand follow his imagination.

But it was too soon.

He stepped away from the easel to study the effect of the somber background wash. It covered the fine canvas perfectly and was now ready for a unique work of art.

He poured himself a glass of red and took a sip before placing it aside. Much as he usually enjoyed wine when painting, today it did not feel right. He was too animated.

"Excellent," he breathed, his eyes shining, his hands clasped tight to prevent himself from picking up the brush.

The repetitive sound of the vents filtering the air echoed through the high-ceilinged sunlit room. The substantial blue-tinted windows had hinged vents to provide fresh air. Shelves covered the walls to a height of five paces, with glass jars in varying sizes holding the liquid and solid ingredients, pigments, colors, and other mixtures he needed for his work. All were costly, and some were so rare they were nearly priceless. The topmost jars could be accessed only from a long ladder on rollers.

Head held high, Sinthoras circled the easel, impatient to start. His dark red robe with black and white embroidery flowed behind him like the surface of a lake. Here and there were paint stains, some old, some new—evidence of his creativity.

To keep his long blond hair clear of the palette and canvas he wore it tied back in a braid. This emphasized his slim features; the pointed ears showed that his beauty was not of a human kind.

Sinthoras walked over to the window and opened it wide. As the evening sunlight fell on the easel and on himself, his eyes immediately turned black and became two dark orbs. He took deep breaths.

Samusin is favoring me, he thought, as he felt the invigorating east wind against his skin. The strong breeze carried the smell of fresh blossom; a few white petals fluttered into the room, settling on the dark stone floor.

There was a knock at the door and it opened. "The god of the winds is with you," he heard an älfar voice say. "He has sent his lively east wind to inspire you."

Sinthoras turned and bowed to the red-haired älf standing at the threshold in a brownish-black cloak. "Thank you for coming to support my artistry with your own, Helòhfor. With your help it will be an extraordinary work."

Helòhfor stepped into the room, followed by two slaves in simple gray clothing. Their build suggested they were humans; the älf had made them cover their ugly features—you could hardly call them faces. Nobody with any sense of decency let one of their slaves appear in public unveiled.

One of them took Helòhfor's mantle, revealing a black silk robe with dark red decorations at the hem. The other, at a gesture from Sinthoras, placed a large case down next to a chair. Then, after sending the slaves outside, Helòhfor sat facing his host, forearms resting on the arms of the chair. "You are quite sure, Sinthoras?"

"Of course," came the answer without hesitation. "I am keen to see what happens when I combine my creative urges with the sounds of a soul-toucher's music."

"The effect will depend on the particular älf, but even I am not sure what will happen." Helòhfor directed his dark gaze toward Sinthoras, studying his face. "You might fall in a trance, you might be taken by the desire to fling yourself from the window, or you might crave the sight of blood." The soul-toucher looked at the canvas. "That you might complete a work of art is just one of many possibilities."

"To the task, Helòhfor!" Sinthoras' voice contained a mixture of request, command and longing. He had spoken out of turn, but had not been able to stop himself: he had been seized with the compulsion to create art that was superior to the work of any other painter—everyone should see that he was not only a warrior of great distinction but also an incomparable artist. "To the task," he repeated softly, and hastened to the easel.

He would let only a single color touch the canvas, but that one color would make the work perfect. Carefully he removed the lid of one of the pots and revealed the glowing yellow substance inside. With a shudder of excitement, Sinthoras took up a large brush and glanced over expectantly at the soul-toucher.

Helòhfor had opened the case and taken out his instrument. The body was made from a spinal column, with silver elements connecting the vertebrae. Valves were attached with silver wire and holes had been drilled into the pieces of bone. Murmuring softly, the älf inserted other items, fashioned from metal, glass or bone, into the openings. Finally he decanted a brown liquid into a wide-bellied flask, which he screwed to the instrument.

Sinthoras had been following every movement and it did not escape his notice how exact the adjustments were. Without long training given by a master of the craft no älf other than Helòhfor would ever be able to play this instrument—and certainly no other creature would stand a chance. The fluid used was said to be brain liquor extracted from cadavers; it was held to contain the dreams of the dead. Tonal vibrations activated the thoughts contained within and allowed the player to affect the audience.

"Prepare to receive the driving force of the dead and of death itself, Sinthoras. May Samusin protect your soul," he murmured, putting his lips to the mouthpiece and placing his fingertips on the tabs.

Helòhfor blew softly and a shrill tone slowly swelled. A gentle bubbling started in the liquid, increasing gradually to a rolling boil. Sinthoras saw steam swirling through the glass elements. As Helòhfor played, it seemed that several streams of air were circulating at the same time, creating brash, strident tones.

Sinthoras felt the hairs on his arms and on the back of his neck rise up and a sharp pain stabbed behind his eyes, blinding him. He gasped for breath. Suddenly the sounds changed and a strange melody emerged.

Energy coursed through his body; his fingers were surrounded by a blue light. As the east wind played on his features, his longed-for inspiration appeared.

Sinthoras watched himself dip the brush in the paint pot, watched the soft bristles absorb the color and watched his own hand carry pigment to canvas. He painted to the tones of the unearthly music—his hand, his soul and the east wind all in the power of the Divine.

The fine point of the full brush traveled slowly over the canvas, tracing a deep yellow line on the dark background. As the thin line grew fainter, Sinthoras was aware of the slight sound the paint made as it was transferred onto the wash.

The pigment was a mixture of molten, oily gold, a breath of black tionium and the liquid from a baro's spleen. It had a metallic shimmer, but there was life in this extraordinary deep yellow: the spirit of life made liquid and imbued with an unsettling radiance.

The fine bristles bent to the right in a sweeping movement and then they suddenly resisted. The line had faltered and had broken off—*incomplete!*

But Sinthoras knew what the work still needed. In his mind's eye he could see the finished article, and hear his name being called out, in both acclaim and in envy.

The tip of the brush hovered over the pot and dipped in and out. Only a tiny amount of yellow paint had adhered to it.

There is not enough! The mood of harmony shattered, forming an open wound out of which his inspiration poured. *Not enough!* His work was threatened. "Raleeha!" he shouted through the half-opened door.

To his own surprise, Sinthoras felt his soul follow where his voice was heading, as if he were hurling it away from himself while his body remained at the easel.

His summoning call flew down the corridor where paintings of stark beauty hung on the paneled walls, and forced its way through a wooden battle scene carving on a set of double doors.

He could see no further.

The right-hand side of the door was pushed open and a tall young human in a slim-fitting dark green dress hastened to his studio.

His soul swirled around her, following her steps.

For a human she was exceptionally beautiful; even elves would purse their lips and admit that she could almost match one of their own in beauty. That was why she was not made to cover her face. Around her neck was a leather slave collar with three silver filigree buckles, constricting her throat so that she could breathe only with difficulty. There were tears in her blue eyes and her black hair spread out behind her like a mourning veil.

Raleeha reached the half-open door through which light fell into the corridor, and behind which her lord and master stood. She knocked and waited for permission to enter—should she enter without waiting her life would be forfeit; he had stressed that. Raleeha's predecessor had paid for such a moment's thoughtlessness with her life, even though she had already served him for a division of unendingness. He was an älf and he would never forgive a human.

Sinthoras was fascinated to realize that his soul could read her expression: the tone of his voice had warned her of his anger and she was distraught.

The music in the chamber ceased as Helòhfor stopped playing, aware the master of the house was displeased.

Something pulled the artist's soul back and forced it once more into his body. The soul-journey was over and he had not been able to complete his picture—and it was *her* fault.

"Come," he ordered, his voice soft, intending to hide his displeasure from her. He would not show his anger: not yet.

Quivering, she opened the door and entered the room, dropping her gaze. She was not allowed to look at him, not unless he said so.

"Master, how may I be of service?"

"Raleeha, you were told to inform me if the pirogand yellow ran low," he said mildly, enjoying her increasing fear. She must be icy cold now. She had made a mistake and he was being civil to her—she must be assuming her fate was sealed.

She closed her eyes, shaking. "Kill me quickly, master," she begged, biting her lip to suppress a sob. "May the ancestors of the Lotor tribe receive me with mercy."

"The pirogand yellow, Raleeha." Sinthoras still felt intoxicated; even if his soul was no longer outside of his body, his mind was. He could smell Raleeha's fear and it was a sweet, enchanting fragrance.

"My mistake, master." She prostrated herself at his feet. "I thought the pot was still one-third full. My eyes must have misled me, master."

Sinthoras approached her. An älf's steps could never be heard unless he or she wished it. It was one of their wonderful gifts. His slender hand took her by the chin and raised her head. "Look at me." He pushed her head back so that her eyes swept over his form and she was forced to meet his gaze; the leather collar creaked.

Raleeha was robbed of the power of speech. He knew that his beauty caused her joy, suppressing her fear. This was why she had volunteered to serve him.

He took in every detail of her appearance, reproof in his cold black eyes. No other älf possessed such an attractive slave-human, it would be such a waste to kill her. But she had to receive a fitting punishment: She had to suffer, physically and mentally, for what she had done.

"You well know that this yellow is acquired only with the greatest difficulty, and in the most dangerous of circumstances. I had wanted to finish the piece today, that's why the soul-toucher came to heighten my genius for a unique work of art." His fingers still held her chin, the manicured nails pressing into her flesh. "But now I shall not be able to continue and the fault is yours."

"My failure is unforgivable, master," she said.

Her response was not feigned. He knew she was deeply dismayed at having failed her master. He stood aside to permit her a glance at the painting.

She trembled. "What sublime artistry—and now I have sabotaged this creation with my negligence!" She swallowed hard and a further tear escaped her eye. These were tears of shame, not of fear.

"Raleeha, until now I have been pleased with you," he told her, disappointment in his voice. "You are the first slave to know how to satisfy my needs. This is why"—the slim fingers released their hold—"you shall live."

"Master," she exclaimed in joyous bewilderment, bending to kiss the hem of his robe. "I shall never neglect my duties again!"

He touched her shoulder and she looked up him, gratitude in her eyes. Then with shock she saw a thin dagger in his right hand. He relished her terror.

"You said your eyes had tricked you?"

"Yes, master—"

"Then it shall only be your eyes that I punish, because the rest of your body, Raleeha, is innocent of fault and will continue to serve my purposes." Grasping her hair in his left hand, he stabbed twice with his right, piercing her eyeballs swift as lightning before she could blink.

The girl shrieked, but she did not flinch, accepting the punishment. Her eyes now destroyed, blood and clear fluid streamed down her cheeks in the tracks of her tears.

Sinthoras inhaled a deep breath of satisfaction. Releasing his grip, he wiped his dagger on her black hair before replacing it in the scabbard. "I shall expect you to adapt quickly, to find your way around my house as if you could still see," he said, loosening the middle buckle on her collar. "Go to Kaila for treatment. For today you are excused further duties. I hope you are aware of my leniency?"

"I am, master," she said, crying, her hands pressed to her eye sockets.

"Show me you deserve it. Out!"

The young woman rose to her feet, trying not to moan, her hands stretched out to get her bearings. It took her some time to find the door.

"If she'd been mine," came Helòhfor's voice behind him, "I'd have fed her to my night-mare."

Sinthoras turned round. The soul-toucher had taken his instrument apart and had packed it away. The case stood ready by the side of the chair.

"A normal slave would have forfeited her life and would not even have been worthy of being eaten by my night-mare," Sinthoras responded. "But she is of the Lotor family and in voluntary bondage. Her suffering pleases me more than her death would."

"You think she will forgive your action?"

"She thinks she brought it on herself," Sinthoras corrected with a smile. "*I* have forgiven her." Then he gave an angry laugh. "It is not my duty to understand her, Helòhfor. It is her duty to serve me."

The soul-toucher did not reply but called his own slaves. "And it is not my duty to understand you, Sinthoras. Your duty, however, is to pay me. Send the money to my house."

"Of course, my thanks for your performance—and let me say it was outstanding, an exceptional experience that I should like to repeat for the next painting." He turned away and crossed the room, heading for a different door. "Now you must excuse me. I must get more pirogand yellow."

* * *

Raleeha stumbled along the corridor to the slaves' quarters where her injuries would be attended. The pain was going straight through her brain. Her legs were unsteady.

"Kaila?" she called out in a strangled voice as she entered. "Kaila?"

"Yes, Raleeha?" She heard the overseer's sharply indrawn breath. Kaila was a human, like herself, but older. "No! By all that's unholy!"

"The master has been merciful to me, I deserved death," she replied swiftly, defending him. "He sent me to you to get treatment." She felt Kaila take her arms and lead over to a bench, where her legs gave way beneath her.

"The älfar know no mercy, Raleeha, least of all Sinthoras. Whatever they do is done from malice." There came a rustling sound, the sound of glass clinking, then liquid being poured. "The culin juice on these pads should prevent infection. Mind, though, it'll sting."

Raleeha cried out in agony when the sharp fluid touched her wounds, emotions raging within her. In spite of the pain, she was glad still to be alive. She would be allowed to continue serving her master. She had followed him of her own free will after seeing him painting near her home village. The piece he had been working on had produced a lasting effect on her and the gracefulness of his figure had attracted her in the same way.

Raleeha felt Kaila tie a bandage across her eyes to keep the healing pads in place. "What was it you did?" asked Kaila.

"I ruined his picture. He didn't have enough paint." She thought of the easel, of the wonderful creation she had been allowed to see. Her master had a unique talent, a very lively technique. Sometimes his temperament would get the better of him and he would laugh out loud or curse while painting; sometimes, if displeased with his own efforts, he might fling his palette into the corner. More than once he had destroyed a picture he had spent ages on.

Raleeha was entranced by all of his work, whether on wood, parchment or canvas. She always picked up his rejects and kept them with her own things in her chamber.

"So, because of some missing paint he cuts out your eyes?" Kaila spat the words out. "And you don't hate him for it?"

"No. How could I? It was my own fault." Suddenly she realized how cruel his punishment had been: she would never see his wonderful countenance again, would never again experience that joy.

Raleeha sobbed out loud in her despair.

Ishím Voróo (The Outer Lands), twenty-seven miles east of the älfar realm Dsôn Faïmon, level with the tip of the Radial Arm Shiimal, 4370th division of unendingness (5198th solar cycle), summer.

"Caphalor!"

The dark-haired älf turned his head to the left and looked up at the top of the black beech tree. The dark gray foliage swayed gently in the evening breeze. His friend, Aïsolon, sat hidden somewhere up there. Caphalor held a bow in his left hand; the other rested lightly on the quiver of long hunting arrows he wore at his belt.

"Shhh! I can see them."

He meant the deep prints left in the forest floor by the young baro. They had been tracking the creature since daystar-rise, and it wasn't making things easy for the two älfar. The baro kept going to ground in the grove and its coat made it difficult to see. But even the stupidest of humans couldn't have failed to notice these obvious tracks. Was the animal losing concentration after all this time, or was it trying to trick the huntsmen, luring them into a trap?

Leaves rustled and Aïsolon jumped down next to Caphalor. He also had a bow in his hands. "It's my first baro," he said excitedly. "I wonder how long it'll take to capture it?"

"It's a young one. Should get it with one shot." Caphalor drew out an arrow that had a coin-sized metal disk on the end. If he hit the right spot on the skull with that, the baro would be out like a light.

Aïsolon selected a similar arrow. "They're as big as óarcos and just as heavy. Baro teeth are said to be sharp enough to go through tionium armor."

"Scared, Aïsolon?" scoffed Caphalor jokingly as he placed the arrow against the bowstring.

"No, I'd call it being acutely aware of the danger," said his friend. "I've no wish to lose my immortality on a baro's fangs."

"Ah, you're still young, of course. An older älf would want to catch the baro with his bare hands." Caphalor gave a quiet laugh and moved forward.

Side by side, they made their way through the trees. Bow and arrow should work well, as long as their quarry deigned to show itself.

Caphalor and Aïsolon had been following the tracks of a kimarbock at first, but the baro had turned up and devoured their prey. The last time Caphalor had seen a baro had been at least thirty-seven divisions of unendingness previously, when he'd been hunting with a large group. Today it was just the two of them, so there was a good chance his would be the winning shot.

"Remember: we need to take it alive," Caphalor wanted to present his daughter with this rare beast. She had a way with the lower animals and could get them to do anything she wanted. She'd be pleased with the gift—even if her mother would not. But it was no use thinking about how angry Enoïla was going to be, they had to catch the damned thing first.

"Over on the left," he said, gesturing with the tip of his arrow toward a thicket. "Lob something in there to send it out."

Aïsolon found a suitably large branch and tossed it into the island of undergrowth.

There was an angry roar and the baro came raging out of its hiding place to within fifty paces of the two älfar. It really did look like an óarco, standing nearly three paces tall on its hind legs with scaly grayish brown skin, but it had a much more powerful lower jaw set with small, crooked and very sharp teeth. Its tiny deep-set eyes flashed as it glared at the huntsmen. This was not fear. The seven-taloned claws opened up, ready to take them on. A blow from that paw would feel like being slashed with seven knives at once.

"Whoa!" muttered Aïsolon, readying his weapon. "That's impressive."

Caphalor lifted his bow, drew back the string and shot before his friend could aim. The blunt projectile whizzed straight to the target, but the baro punched it out of the way; the same thing happened to Aïsolon's arrow, and then the creature rushed them. It looked like it was fed up with being hunted: time to turn the tables.

"And you want to take that home for your daughter?" Aïsolon asked in bewilderment. He swiftly nocked a new arrow, but once again Caphalor was quicker and this time the metal disk hit the creature exactly above the bridge of the nose.

Staggering, the baro shook its head and regained its balance, and then charged once more, kicking up leaves and mud as its powerful claws thudded against the soft ground. Aïsolon's arrow hit the scaled arm the beast was holding up to protect its skull and a furious roar filled with bloodlust echoed through the grove.

Caphalor discarded his bow and grabbed a cudgel. The scent of the baro was borne on the wind: a powerful, acrid smell of strength and youth. It obviously wanted to prove itself to these two attackers.

"Are you crazy?" Aïsolon drew back and shot arrow after arrow. The animal grew angrier with each hit. "We're going to have to kill it—"

"No!" Caphalor positioned himself in front of a tree, put down his belt quiver, threw off his mantle and waited for the creature to attack. He was relying on his speed and agility to get him out of trouble. Usually he would employ long, thin daggers, but an animal like this needed sheer unadulterated strength if he were going to have any chance of bringing it back alive for his daughter.

Eleven paces.

Aïsolon drew out a sharpened arrow. "Just in case," he said.

Caphalor did not bother to reply. The baro was hurling itself at him, arms outstretched, muzzle wide open in a roar and ready to snap. The stinking breath was hot, with more than a trace of the kimarbock it had devoured earlier.

The älf sprang vertically into the air, tucking his legs up under him and reaching with his free hand for a branch to pull himself up. He felt the shuddering impact as the creature slammed into the tree. Leaves cascaded past him. He looked down.

Blue blood was streaming from the creature's broken nose and there was a glazed look in its eyes. It appeared to have lost its sense of direction. Its smell had changed, too. Powerful anger had given way to fear.

And in a situation where you needed to keep a level head, fear was only of use to an älf.

Caphalor let go and jumped down onto the animal, which although reeling and stunned from the massive impact, was still upright. As his feet touched the creature's shoulders he delivered a two-handed blow with the wooden club.

The club broke in two and the baro screamed and sank down on its knees, arms hanging useless by its sides.

Caphalor sprang past the creature and gave it a kick with his heels. It uttered a sobbing noise and keeled over, landing on the soft leaf-covered ground, then swiveled round and tried to kick him.

At that moment a huge black shape arrived, hitting Caphalor in the chest and hurling him several paces backward. He somersaulted to absorb the impetus and jumped back onto his feet, drawing his daggers, ready to fight.

It was a third älf sitting atop a night-mare—which explained how he had been able to throw Caphalor aside—and he was stabbing at the baro with a long spear. The slim blade entered the animal's neck. The älf stood in the stirrups and pushed down on the spear shaft with all his strength, pinning the baro to the ground. The new arrival dismounted, landing gracefully at the dying creature's side.

"Oi!" shouted Caphalor angrily. "That was my prize!" He ran over to the blond älf who took out a knife patterned with delicate filigree and slit the creature's side. Taking a slender glass vial out of his robes, the blond älf held it up to the creature's wound, capturing the golden-yellow liquid seeping out.

"Your prize? It looked to me as if you were fighting for your life," the other responded over his shoulder.

"I needed it alive." Caphalor was furious. "I was about to catch it." He came to a stop, confronting his rival. "Then you turned up." He understood: the spleen of a baro was known to contain an ingredient of the rare and precious substance pirogand yellow. That had been the reason for his previous baro hunt, thirty-seven divisions of unending-ness earlier.

"I just saved your life," the älf retorted, continuing to fill the glass vial. "It was about to kick you. If it hadn't been for my night-mare those claws would have got you. You should be grateful, my friend, and go your ways."

Caphalor took in the black, hardened-leather armor of the blond älf. The delicate embellishments that flowed over its tionium plates marked him as an unmarried warrior with several decorations for bravery and battles won in the name of the Inextinguishable Ones. The fact that the älf was wearing war armor away from the battlefield told Caphalor that he set great store by titles and status. For himself, it would never have occurred to him to dress that way.

"*Your friend* is one thing I definitely am not," he said. "Because of you, I can't deliver the gift I promised to someone I love and they will be disappointed."

The final drops of the yellow substance collected in the vial and there was a smacking sound as the cut was allowed to close. The blond älf wiped the dying baro's greenish mix of yellow substance and blue blood from his hands with a bunch of leaves, stoppered the flask and stood up.

"I know you. You are Caphalor."

"Have we met?"

"You paid no heed. It was at a reception for the Most Brave. You were one of those that Nagsor Inàste chose to honor in the Tower of Bones." He nodded. "What a pleasure to be able to save such a noted warrior from the clutches of a dangerous baro." His expression showed that he did not mean what he was saying. There was contempt in his tone, and haughtiness, perhaps even envy.

Caphalor's anger grew: he was dealing with an arrogant, ambitious warrior—one who would do anything to gain the Inextinguishables' good opinion. "The baro would not have killed me. My *friend* Aïsolon had me covered, the fact he didn't shoot shows I wasn't in danger at all. Except from your questionable riding skills."

"As you wish. I'm sorry I killed your 'gift.' Get the cadaver hollowed out and stick a couple of gnome slaves inside to bring it to life. Nobody will notice." He didn't show a trace of remorse as he picked up the vial with its shimmering contents. "Fare you well. I must go and finish my picture."

Caphalor's right hand shot up and he twirled the dagger round to smash the handle against the thin glass.

The älf's reflexes were quick and he dodged—only to walk into a second blow. The delicate container shattered and the yellow substance sprayed out over the forest floor.

"What a shame." Caphalor gave a false smile and stowed away his daggers. "I'm sure it would have been an exceptional, sublimely beautiful painting."

The other älf stood in front of him, dirtied, still clutching the neck of the broken flask. Yellow droplets ran down his dark armor and fine black lines began to cover his face. It looked like he was about to explode with anger. "I shall not forget this," he swore bleakly, tossing the remains of the vial at Caphalor's feet.

"And I will not forget what *you* did," retorted Caphalor. He was sure he was going to be attacked now, the blackness in his opponent's eyes radiated unpredictable danger. Aïsolon appeared at his side, hand on his short sword.

The third älf turned and moved over to his night-mare, which was ripping great gobbets of flesh out of the dead baro with its fangs, then daintily separating meat from the scales. Its master swung himself up into the saddle and rode off through the grove away from the two friends. Sparks flew from its speeding hooves.

"Do you have any idea who that was?" Aïsolon released his grip on the pommel of his sword and started collecting the bows and the two quivers.

"No, should I?"

"His name is Sinthoras: he's one of the Inextinguishables' most ambitious warriors. He's an excellent fighter—excellent and arrogant in equal measure." Aïsolon handed Caphalor his things. "He's one of the Comets. They're determined Dsôn Faïmon should seize more land and win more vassals so they can go off and make war on the elves: Sinthoras has been touting his expansionist plans to them." His gaze traveled to where the night-mare and its rider had disappeared into the forest. "Personally, I think he must have left part of his mind on the battlefields. Despite all of the victories he's won, he's never been granted the Honor-Blessing."

So that's the reason for the envy. Caphalor glanced down at the half-eaten cadaver and the greenish mix of yellow pigment and blue blood on the black leaves. "I don't suppose we'll find another one. My daughter will be disappointed," he said quietly.

Aïsolon nodded agreement. "But we've got a great story to tell her."

Caphalor took a long look at the sharp claws of the dead creature. "Would it have got me, Aïsolon?" He bent down and cut off two of its toes as a trophy, then broke off the biggest of the teeth to take home as a consolation prize for his daughter.

The älf reflected for a moment. "Did I shoot or not?"

"You didn't even have the bow in your hands," Caphalor replied with a knowing smile. "Even if you had wanted to, it would have been impossible."

Aïsolon's face fell. "You noticed?" He sighed. "I thought I'd be more effective with my short sword. And no, the baro would have missed you, you don't owe Sinthoras anything at all."

"That's what I was hoping. I'd hate to have to feel any obligation."

Caphalor unstrung his bow and shouldered the weapon. "Let's get back and tell them what happened."

Aïsolon laughed. "I bet Enoïla will be glad we haven't taken the baro alive. Your daughter would never have been able to tame it."

"Oh yes she would," said Caphalor with conviction. "She's one of a kind, my daughter." They set off. "Has he been to see you about it?" he asked after a while.

Aïsolon let his eyes wander and took a deep breath. "Who do you mean?"

"You know exactly who I mean."

Aïsolon wiped away some of the baro blood from his glove. "I enjoy our outings to Ishím Voróo. It's dangerous, but I always know it'll be an adventure. Today was quite an adventure."

"So that means Sinthoras *has* been to ask for your support. He wants you to join the Comets?"

"Yes."

"Why didn't you say?"

"I don't like talking about politics, I avoid it wherever I can." Aïsolon looked his friend squarely in the eyes. "But since you've started: I belong to the Constellations, just like you do. And I share your opinion that we should look to our defenses and take stronger measures against potential threats from outside, but that doesn't mean we should embark upon an aggressive expansion of our empire. That would only give us more borders to defend: we won't be able to rely on our vassals and slaves for that."

Caphalor placed a hand on his shoulder. "Wise thoughts for someone who doesn't like talking politics."

"But there are so few now that think that way. The mood of the time plays into the hands of warriors like Sinthoras. The more rumors we hear about newly formed kingdoms, the more we question our strategy of defense."

Caphalor was sunk in thought. "Perhaps Sinthoras is partly right, perhaps it's our own fault that the mere sight of an älf is no longer enough to put an enemy to flight. Have we lost our ability to terrify our enemies?"

Aïsolon did not answer.

It was already dusk when they passed Dsôn Faïmon's frontier. They left the beech forest and crossed the two-mile cleared strip of land that took them to the defense moat, and closer to Radial Arm Shiimal, where they both lived.

The moat was, in reality, a broad, fast-flowing river nearly fifty paces wide. Artificial islands had been placed at regular intervals along it and well-armed fortresses stood on each of them. Weapons had been specially designed for the forts so that only small teams were needed to operate the catapults in case of attack, though the most powerful catapults were driven by waterpower and could reach targets well into the middle of the cleared strip of land—that was if any beasts, barbarians or other enemies even dared to draw near their borders. Access to the forts could only be gained by long drawbridges which, when closed, pointed up toward the sky.

The two älfar approached the bridgehead.

Aïsolon gave the bugle signal and the drawbridge began to rattle downward in response.

"Be on your guard with Sinthoras," he said suddenly.

Caphalor looked at his friend. "Why do you say that?"

"The Inextinguishables have awarded you the Honor-Blessing he craves, and that'll be reason enough for him to hate you. But you also represent everything he despises, and he knows that many of the other warriors will follow you blindly, whatever you ask of them. If you are not on his side, you must, in his eyes, be his enemy"

"A bleak prospect, Aïsolon."

"I told you he tried to win me over. When I sent him off he warned me that in battle I could not count on his coming to my aid. He hinted at arrows going astray."

Caphalor was about to respond, but the drawbridge was settling into its place on the riverbank and the hefty chains were making a great deal of noise as they reached full tension, making conversation impossible.

When the earsplitting screech of the metal chains had died away, Aïsolon stepped onto the drawbridge and turned to Caphalor. "Be on your guard," he repeated as he set off. "I can't say more than that."

Despite realizing his friend did not want to talk about the subject any longer, Caphalor joked, "It's him who should be on his guard—he's the one who ruined my surprise for my daughter!" But he was suddenly aware of a greater danger for Dsôn Faïmon than any posed by a neighboring state, however aggressive: a schism within their own land—the turmoil of warring factions. *Comets opposing Constellations—active expansion versus defense.*

The Inextinguishable Ones would soon have to put a stop to the smoldering conflict, one way or the other.

CHAPTER II

The Inextinguishable Ones prayed to the Creating Spirit to give them a sign.
And the Creating Spirit wept when she saw what had befallen her children.
Where, like flaming stars, her black tears fell, blessed craters were formed.
* The rulers of the älfar recognized the signs and in the first of the craters they*
founded Dsôn Faïmon. That is how it came to be hallowed and kept safe, this
cradle of our kind.

Epocrypha of the Creating Spirit,

1st Book,

Chapter 1, 8–11

Ishím Voróo (The Outer Lands), älfar realm
Dsôn Faïmon, Dsôn (Star-Eye),
4370th division of unendingness (5198th solar cycle),
summer.

Sinthoras raised the heavy granite door-knocker and let it fall against the stonewood. A single heavy blow sounded.

He took five slow paces backward in order to get a better look at Demenion's luxurious house, a blackwood construction. The improvements on the façade were now complete: interlocking carved shapes, small decorative pillars, and polished silver disks attracted the gaze of the passer-by.

Envy gnawed at his soul.

At the start of each division of unendingness, Demenion would treat himself to a new façade for his six-sided residence on the south side of the popular Tâm Square. No other älf could put such a breathtaking a collection of silver and bronzed tionium figures together—especially as Demenion worked with the most important artists in Dsôn, creating some of the most unique art in existence.

A magnificent battle scene four paces high portrayed Demenion himself at its center. At his feet lay slaughtered óarcos, trolls, and barbarians—their bodies fashioned from metal, the original faces of the dead preserved under varnish. Preserving these faces involved an extremely complicated and time-consuming procedure that demanded utmost skill and precision from the artist. The flesh was so unstable and perishable that few would attempt this delicate task: to create the best art, the skin could not lose its color or become wrinkled and could not dry out in sunlight or, worse still, start to putrefy—something that might have conveyed a fascinating insight into unstoppable decay, but was not the desired effect on the façade of a house.

Sinthoras took a closer look at the dead: their faces displayed pain, torture, and fear, and where they had been injured you could see open wounds and fractures. In the metal rendering of the bodies you could see detail right down to tumbled intestines and broken bones jutting from flesh. Spectacular, without a doubt—and extravagant in the extreme, even boastful.

However, if you lived in the Star-Eye—especially so if your house was on Tâm Square—you showed what you had. You only got to live there if you were a hero, an influential älf or a celebrated artist and each site cost a fortune. There was no shortage of älfar ready to expend all their savings and assets in an effort to keep up, but many were forced to admit defeat: expensive multi-storied buildings sometimes changed hands so quickly that people had not even met their neighbor before he moved out to make way for a more prosperous älf.

Sinthoras' lips had become a thin line. He belonged here, and soon he would possess one of these Star-Eye houses. He had chosen a triangular tower on this very same square. It was a wonderful building, playful in its architecture and made of sigurdacia wood; the walls were inlaid with metal that shone brighter at night than any of the runes and signs on the surrounding houses. He deserved it. His promotion would be coming soon—a promise given by the highest source he carried in his pocket—then Demenion would learn what envy was.

The door was being opened for him now. A human slave, about ten divisions of unendingness in age, stood there in a light blue robe, bowing and moving aside to usher him in.

He strode past the slave with neither greeting nor glance: the ugly human was not worthy of being acknowledged.

Sinthoras was affronted to note that Demenion let his slaves work unveiled. At least Raleeha was pretty and her appearance could be appreciated if you understood simple pleasures. But *this* one? With those broad cheekbones and those fat lips? It looked more like a donkey.

He soon reached the assembly gardens and the courtyard with its protective sunshade. Here there was a lawn of rare bone-white grass and Demenion had planted night narcissi, black roses and soft baby's breath, while pale red ivy grew over gray stones at the edges. It was as if most of nature's color had been omitted: Demenion had a sense for plants pleasing to the eye.

Sinthoras could see his host and four other älfar sitting at a dark brown table. They had goblets in front of them and were talking quietly amongst themselves: Comets, one and all. He was the only one in armor—the others had all chosen light clothing in subdued tones. In Sinthoras' view this showed the difference between them and himself: the others were occasional warriors whereas he lived and breathed the fighting life. The only time he put aside his armor was at his easel; when he painted he became a different person.

A slave alerted the gathering.

Demenion rose and approached with outstretched arms. The gesture of welcome was careful, full of grace and a degree of softness. It was too soft for a real warrior, though it suited a politician.

"Sinthoras! We have been longing for you to arrive," said the master of the house with a wink. "We were beginning to worry that your newest painting might have taken precedence over our cause."

"I had to go and get some more paint," he answered quickly, and held out his hand to Demenion to avoid being embraced, he had a horror of most physical contact—especially the unwanted type. Sitting down at the table he surveyed the faces: the leaders of a new military strategy for the Star State—Dsôn Faïmon.

Khlotòn raised his eyebrows. "Something special, I assume?"

"Yes, pirogand yellow." He was annoyed with himself for even mentioning it. Now he would have to admit that Caphalor had pulled one over on him. He gave an abridged version of events. "And so I could not finish the picture," he said. "I threw it on the fire."

"Caphalor, eh?" Khlotòn looked over at Demenion. "Isn't it strange that it was you two who ended up eyeball to eyeball?"

"Samusin seems to enjoy watching powerful opposites clash," agreed Sinthoras. "But enough about that coward—what news from our spies in Ishím Voróo? Anything we can present to the Inextinguishables to convince them of our cause?"

Demenion nodded and pointed at Rashànras, who, as usual, stood up to speak. Sinthoras considered him a boaster, but he was unfortunately a boaster with an excellent network of spies. And most of them were currently watching the east of Ishím Voróo.

"There are signs that Farron Lotor is winning out against the other barbarian tribes. I am quite surprised, I must admit. They have already eliminated their first opponents and assimilated their armies—so the Lotor family is now in command of around 30,000 barbarians, and at least half of these are óarco-riders." Rashànras made a sour face. "Of course, their mounts are nothing like our night-mares, but this does mean they are in a position to conduct a 15,000-strong lightning strike on an enemy. Give the miserable band half a division of unendingness and I see Farron subjugating the entire barbarian region."

"That would make how many in total?" interjected Sinthoras.

"If Farron were to conquer all the kingdoms and control their armies, it'd give him a fighting force of 100,000-strong," was the growled response.

Khlotòn took a sip from his wine cup. "Send an assassin to deal with him, then the possible successors will destroy each other. That's what always happens," he said condescendingly.

Sinthoras raised his hand to register his objection. "We shouldn't do anything yet. Let Farron try to make himself ruler—that would give us a reason to go to war against such a 'threat,' and what could be a better excuse for expansion than that?"

"Do you think so? I beg to differ," countered Rashànras. "If we wait too long, they'll have time to prepare for an attack and we might end up with greater losses. We should not risk spilling our precious blood unnecessarily. Besides that, I'm not sure we can rely on our vassals' loyalty: they were barbarians originally and are still óarco-riders in their hearts, who knows which way they'd go on the battlefield? Blood is thicker than water."

"And is better for painting," added Demenion, a comment met with laughter.

Sinthoras inhaled sharply and glared at Rashànras, then he reached into his pocket and took out a parchment, spreading it out in front of them. He relished the surprise and envy on the faces of the Comets when they saw the seal of the Inextinguishables. "I am to meet with the Sibling Rulers tomorrow. They wish to speak to me."

"Inàste is with you!" Demenion could not tear his eyes from the invitation. "They will Honor you, Sinthoras!" There was respect and awe in his voice. "You will get their Blessing, what a privilege!"

"An important development for our cause," Khlotòn chipped in enthusiastically, his voice betraying none of the usual animosity he spoke to Sinthoras with.

Sinthoras was aware of Khlotòn's pretense: the älf wanted the notice of the Inextinguishables as much as he did, and as such, would grovel to anyone whom they showed favor. All the same, Sinthoras was enjoying the attention the parchment generated, and he wondered how long it would take to put together an enticing argument for war. Could he weave all the information from this meeting into a convincing enough web of words to persuade his rulers to expand?

If necessary, he would go without sleep until after his audience.

*Ishím Voróo (The Outer Lands), älfar realm Dsôn
Faïmon, tip of the Radial Arm Shiimal,
4370th division of unendingness (5198th solar cycle),
summer.*

"Is she still furious?" Caphalor ran his fingers through his companion Enoïla's long black hair, carefully smoothing the four yellow strands that ran its full length: permanent marks of honor she had attained for having given life to four children.

Every älf-woman was accorded such decoration if she gave birth to a child that survived its transition to the world. If all of her sons and daughters had survived, Enoïla would now sport seventeen of these strands, but infant mortality among the älfar was distressingly high. Some women of her acquaintance had never even had the chance to rejoice in a pregnancy, let alone a birth: not every älf-woman was as fertile as Enoïla, she was an exception in many respects. She bent her head and kissed the palm of his hand, smiling. "She will forgive you once she is over her disappointment."

He sighed. "You were right. It would have been better if I hadn't said anything at all about the baro." He returned her smile and stroked her cheek, then turned to the balcony door, walking out into the morning air.

Caphalor loved the view that met him there; he could see all the way past the defense moat and over to the black foliage of the groves in Ishím Voróo. A large flock of birds circled the tops of those far trees, flying toward the island fort in the middle of the river. He took a deep breath of the cool, pure air: he could detect no scent of incense or perfume and nothing artificial, just pure morning.

He felt Enoïla's slender hand on his shoulder, and her warmth. "You will find another baro to bring home for our daughter," she consoled him.

"I was not thinking of that." He took her hand and walked further along the balcony that ringed their house, gently pulling her with him.

They lived at the end of a small road, the last nonmilitary building of the radial arm. Caphalor and Enoïla had planned it themselves: a five-sided building with four stories, painted in a light black color, with many little bay windows and turrets and a roof of silver thatch.

The bottom floor contained the stables and servants' quarters, then the living area and the family rooms; above came the bedchambers, other large rooms and the ceremonial hall. At the very top he had designed a large-windowed studio—providing plenty of light for himself and his wife: here they could paint, sculpt or compose melodies on their lutes.

The further Caphalor walked along the balcony, the more he could see of Dsôn Faïmon. His house was at the very tip of the radial arm, so the topmost two stories were higher than the plain surrounding the crater arms, and because the radial arms were set on a decline toward the Star-Eye, he and Enoïla could see out over all the other buildings and slave-farmed fields stretching outward. You could even see the Inextinguishables' Tower of Bones in the distance.

Caphalor pointed toward Dsôn. "*That's* what I've been thinking about." He gripped the railings with both hands.

"You've been thinking about the future of our empire?" Enoïla leaned over, resting on her forearms on the railing and letting her gaze run over the horizon. "Did the meeting with Sinthoras have such an effect on you?"

Caphalor took another deep breath. This time the wind brought him the fragrance of smoldering pajoori herbs; someone was making a sacrifice to the Inextinguishables.

He gave a nod of his head and a slight quirk of his lower lip, a gesture she knew well.

Enoïla laughed. "You're just in one of those moods when you feel particularly sorry for yourself. Am I right?"

He looked at her in surprise. "Me? Complain?"

"Yes," she giggled. "Have you got another bone to pick with Immortality, dearest companion?"

Caphalor found himself breaking into a grin. "You know me too well."

"I *understand* you. There's a difference." Enoïla's eyes shone in spite of their blackness. If there was no sunlight he could admire the bright blue of her eyes. "You also feel sorry for yourself because our eldest three have moved to Avaris and Riphâlgis."

He nodded, "That's one artist daughter and two priest sons, all wanting to have as little as possible to do with their father."

"That's not true. They like visiting us."

"There you have it: *visiting* us. It's a duty, an obligation, a bit of a bind."

"But you know they love you and admire you. Even Tarlesa," she added, teasing him.

"Except for Olíron. He's one of those that prefer to follow Sinthoras' views. My own son, a Comet! Has he learned nothing?"

"It's time I met this Sinthoras," she replied. "If my husband and my youngest son are so keen on him, perhaps I'd like him, too?"

Caphalor pulled her to him and pretended to grab her arms tight. "Stop that at once! I couldn't take it if my älf-woman left me."

Laughing, she gave him a kiss on the forehead and rested against him. "I'll stay. Eternal life with you—what could be better than that?"

He bent his head down and kissed her soft lips, enjoying the feeling of happiness that pervaded his being whenever Enoïla was with him, or when they touched, or looked into each other's eyes.

Many älfar asked soul-touchers for assistance when they wanted to open themselves up to their partners; this allowed them to attain a togetherness more intense than the purely physical. He and Enoïla had never needed such services. They found their souls in each other's eyes and when they made love their souls bonded naturally, melting into one. No experience went deeper than that. It was something lesser beings— dwarves, humans, ogres, gnomes, even elves—would never understand.

He and Enoïla had shared this harmony of souls for more than twenty divisions of unendingness now—a length of time that was unusually long for the customs of their people, but neither of them had wanted to leave.

Something kept them bound to each other. It was not dependence but a deep connection neither of them had felt before: a complete harmony of thought and emotion. Neither Enoïla nor Caphalor was willing to give that up in exchange for something less.

He gently released her lips, taking her face in his hands. "Are you sure you don't want to leave here?"

"Not that again!" She sounded annoyed. "What would I want with living in the Star-Eye? It's a den of decadence, boasting, and political intrigue. Here we're left in peace. Even Tarlesa likes it and she has plenty of animals and slaves to try her skills out on." She slipped out of his arms and gave him a swift kiss. "I've got things I must get on with. Don't forget that Móreaoo io expecting you this afternoon. He mentioned a surprise—I wonder what it is."

"I promise I won't ask you again." Caphalor bowed to her and waited till she had left, then he went to the outside staircase and hurried down.

Going into the stables, he called for his night-mare to be saddled and when it was, climbed swiftly up and rode away, taking the road to the west. The beast's hooves thundered along as they passed the fields and meadows, throwing up lightning sparks. The humans working in the fields sank down on their knees and pulled off their headgear, looking down at the ground until he had passed.

They were his property—his slaves. Caphalor possessed 200 barbarians, three half-ogres and two trolls for the really heavy work. These had either been captured on the battlefield or selected on outings to Ishím Voróo. He had built them a camp complete with tents and huts seven miles away from his fields.

He was pleased with the breeding program and the slaves' performance record: the barbarians in particular were multiplying successfully—mostly because he ensured they were well fed—so there were always enough hands for the labor. The disadvantage of these lesser races, of course, was that they kept arguing amongst themselves about who had rights to whom when it came to mating. Some of the men would throw their weight around and harass the womenfolk, whether or not they were already spoken for. Fighting had broken out in the camps on several occasions when some of these young men had caused trouble. It did not make things any easier that the barbarians were keen to breed at any time of year. One name in particular kept cropping up: Grumson, a strong, possessive fellow. Perhaps he should have a few of the most aggressive ones castrated.

His thoughts took a strange turn via the slaves and back to Dsôn.

The question he had put to Enoïla had not come out of the blue: if Tarlesa turned out to be skilled at magic, she would have to go to an academy. The best one was in Dsôn, but his daughter was too young to be allowed into the snake pit by herself. Would she accept his protection or would she hate being mollycoddled?

Caphalor prayed to Samusin—the god of the winds and of justice—
that she would prove to be a perfectly ordinary älf-girl with no outstanding qualities. His sons were said to be exceptional, why did his daughter
have to be, too? He would reduce her instruction in the älfar arts if it
proved necessary.

Toward midday he reached Herumôn—a settlement of perhaps five
thousand älfar—where he was known to every man, woman, and child.
Honored heroes would usually move to the center of the realm, to Dsôn
itself, or to the Radial Arm Wèlèron, where other warriors tended to
reside. But despite his power, riches, and fame, Caphalor had not turned
his back on the ordinary people and the villagers loved and respected
him for it. He had no airs or graces and could often be seen visiting the
market, chatting to älfar less fortunate than himself.

Herumôn was a classic älfar settlement for Radial Arm Shiimal.
Families lived there with their slaves, who in turn provided the labor for
agriculture. Unlike the slaves in Dsôn they enjoyed certain freedoms:
they were not forced to wear masks or veils and their quiet lives were
spent in service to the älfar. As a result, Shiimal had the highest birth
rate in the whole state.

However, there was one thing that stood out: the houses were built
of black basalt instead of the native timbers—sigurdacia, nightwood,
stonewood—and because of the weight of the stone, the buildings were
low and not as extravagantly decorated as elsewhere in the radial arm.
This was a legacy of the Ancestors' remedial work: they had dug into
the ground to straighten and strengthen the arms, and the resulting
rock wastage had been used to build the houses. The locals had tried
to lighten the oppressive effect of the black stone by means of refined
murals and *trompe l'oeil* additions: creating the appearance of artificial
arcades or extra windows, which meant that the whole of Herumôn
was a trick for the eyes. If you were visiting for the first time, you might
assume you were about to stride through a huge stone archway, but this,
too, would be the work of a skilled painter. Many a bumped head had
resulted from an unexpected meeting with the hard basalt.

Caphalor rode through the streets. Tiny white pellets crunched
under the night-mare's hooves—gravel that had been formed from the

ground bones of slaughtered enemies. This gave a muffled sound and a road surface that was softer on both hooves and feet. Bones of slaves and monsters could be used for the same purpose. If you looked closely at the colors and textures you might even be able to tell the age and race of the victim.

He reached the marketplace.

The people's greetings were returned with a friendly nod and one of the merchants handed him a rare samu fruit as he rode past. He bit into it and relished the taste that was sweet, fruity, sour, and refreshing at one and the same time, his mouth tingled with it. As he rode on, he wondered what Mórcass wanted to talk to him about: he had bought corn from him in the past—perhaps he wanted to renegotiate the price for the next harvest?

Caphalor finished off the samu fruit and came to a halt. Dismounting from the night-mare, he stood in front of the large barn where Mórcass lived and ran his business. Two human slaves emerged: one of them took charge of his mount, the other bowed, inviting him with a humble gesture to follow.

Caphalor entered the property a little behind the slave and followed him through cool rooms and corridors. Eventually he came to a pair of doors that opened out on to a workshop Mórcass had never shown him before.

The merchant was standing in front of a large cube that was draped with a blanket. He wore a long leather apron, similar to the ones worn by butchers, executioners, and slave bath attendants. He smiled, enjoying his business associate's curiosity. Caphalor could hear a low snorting sound coming from under the cloth.

"Welcome, noble Caphalor, Honor-Blessed hero of Dsôn Faïmon," said Mórcass, stepping forward to greet him. As he did so, the small table behind him came into view. It was piled with an array of different tools, including pliers and saws.

Caphalor's curiosity increased. "Thank you," he said, eyeing the tall cube. "What have I done to deserve this surprise?"

Mórcass looked disappointed. "So Enoïla let on?"

"Only to say there would be a surprise waiting."

The merchant's face lit up. He called out some names and three muscular half-giants entered the barn. They were much taller than Caphalor, dressed in armor and equipped with leather helmets and tough gauntlets. A loud whinnying and the sound of metal chains rattling could be heard coming from the covered cube.

"I confess I am very curious as to what you're going to show me," Caphalor said.

Mórcass laughed. "First of all, I should like to thank you for the many divisions of unendingness we have done business together. In the hope that we shall continue to be good partners, I would like to offer a token of my esteem. I hope you will accept it."

Caphalor was aware that Mórcass was showing sound business acumen. If he accepted the gift the trader's reputation in Herumôn would grow; the more valuable the present, the greater his fame.

"It sounds like a horse."

"Better than that."

"A night-mare?" Caphalor wondered. If he had interpreted the snorting correctly, Mórcass had spent a great deal of money. Night-mares were desanctified unicorns and the best specimens were extremely expensive to buy and to keep: they needed large amounts of meat and were unpredictable if allowed to go hungry. Caphalor had been forced to kill one of his night-mares when the beast had attacked him, and before that it had devoured two slaves in a frenzy and four other slaves had been badly injured. He had no longer been able to trust it.

"No, not a night-mare," Mórcass replied, grinning.

With a dramatic gesture he removed the cloth, revealing white, strained flanks and wide staring eyes. Caphalor caught his breath: a unicorn.

It snorted and whinnied, and after catching sight of the älfar and the half-giants, it tried to break out of the cage, but it was tethered fast to iron rings at hooves and neck. It stopped straining and stared at the warrior, snorting. Mórcass indicated the unicorn. "Here you are. This is my gift to you."

Caphalor gave the animal a suspicious look. "It is said that they are dangerous; that they hate our kind so much they attack on sight. Even my daughter might not be able to tame it."

"That is probably true, but this unicorn won't exist for much longer."

Now Caphalor had no idea what was going on.

Mórcass gave some orders to the half giants. They took the ends of the chains and pulled them tight, forcing the unicorn forward. The merchant opened a small door in the cage so the creature's head and spiral horn could pass through, and one of the slaves moved the little table of tools nearer.

Caphalor understood. "You want to turn it into a night-mare?"

"One worthy of you: a thoroughbred, genuine night-mare—not one of the degenerate new interbred versions." Mórcass selected a fine-toothed saw. "Collect some of your blood, we need it to effect the transformation and ensure the animal is bound to you." The unicorn tossed its head, the tip of the horn narrowly missing the merchant's right shoulder. "Wait, you white demon. Soon you will take to us," he panted.

Caphalor made a cut in his forearm and his black-red blood ran over his light skin, dripped down and filled a shallow dish one of the slaves was holding out. He covered up the wound with a bandage the slave handed him; the slight pain did not bother him.

"How long will it take to change?" asked Caphalor. He knew it must have cost Mórcass a fortune: unicorns were very rare indeed and they were difficult to capture alive. If word got around that Caphalor had accepted such a grand gift, the merchant would soon be able to move to the center—to Dsôn itself if he should so choose.

"There are differing theories in various books, not much is remembered," Mórcass answered. "Sometimes it is said that the transformation is quick, a few heartbeats only, and sometimes that it might take a whole division of unendingness."

Caphalor stood next to Mórcass. "Let me help."

The merchant gave a sign to the half-giants and the chains were tightened again. The unicorn's head was forced mercilessly against the lower edge of the cage opening; if it had to stay in that position for long it would suffocate. "I've got to cut the horn off and then you pour your blood on the stump."

"No special formula? No ritual?"

"It seems not, your blood and the älfar power it holds should be enough." Mórcass applied the saw. "But I won't hide the fact that it might not survive the procedure. I read that, too."

The fine serrations of the saw made quick work of the horn as the creature tried desperately to escape mutilation. The muscles swelled under its coat and the half-giants renewed their stances, pulling harder on the ends of the chains and grunting with the effort. Even so, their rough shoes started to slip and dust clouds rose. Caphalor admired the creature's enormous power.

"Hold it fast, damn you!" Mórcass yelled, speeding up his work with the saw. The white splinters fell thick and fast; he was nearly halfway through. Caphalor held the dish ready.

The unicorn went wild: bright red blood shot out of the horn, drenching the saw and Mórcass in its flow. One of the half-giants lost hold of the chain and it kicked its hind leg free, meeting the iron bars of the cage with an almighty crash. Then it bucked and hurled itself around violently, forcing the rest of the half-giants to let go.

"Catch it!" Mórcass commanded, looking at his hand where the skin burned from contact with the unicorn blood. He put the saw down and took up a big hammer, intending to snap the horn off.

He flailed for a moment as the animal bucked, but then the half-giants had control again, and as Mórcass hit out once more there was a loud crack and the horn splintered. More blood sprayed out and the unicorn screamed, a sound of pure agony; it pained Caphalor in his mind and in his soul to hear it.

"Get ready," said Mórcass, bringing the hammer down again. The animal pulled its head away and stabbed the merchant in the chest with the remains of its horn. When it pulled its head back the splintering ends of the horn got stuck in the älf's ribs and he was shaken to and fro, then hurled against the iron bars with tremendous force. The horn snapped off; the merchant älf collapsed in front of the cage and did not move. A wide pool of blood formed under him.

With great presence of mind, Caphalor tipped the contents of the dish over the stump. The unicorn whinnied again—a continuous, piercing sound, such that he thought he might go deaf. He bent to the merchant's body, turning him over onto his back.

There was nothing to be done, the horn was deep inside the gaping wound and the bones were shattered and bent, the lungs destroyed. The dying heart continued to pump blood out through torn arteries until it slowed and then finally stopped.

The light went out of Mórcass' eyes: the älf's soul had been freed to join the unendingness—and this well before his time. Mórcass had not been old by älf standards.

Caphalor looked at the unicorn collapsed against the sides of the cage. It kicked out desperately and gasped, its tongue lolling out. Bright red blood flowed out of its gullet and its teeth came loose and rolled over the workshop floor: sharp fangs took their place, erupting like blades through the gums. Its transformation had begun surprisingly rapidly.

Caphalor got the slaves to carry the dead body of their master into the main house and told them to send for a healer. Even though this was a useless move now, he did not want to have to tell the merchant's companion her partner was dead. Instead, he sat down by the cage and observed the changes the unicorn went through.

The blood from the stump stopped flowing and the animal's coat became dull, turning first gray and then black, its tail, mane, and the long hairs round its fetlocks all following: the magic in his älfar blood had destroyed the purity of the unicorn. Caphalor wished Enoïla could be there to sketch the process, she was better than he was at drawing and would have been able to capture the excitement of the transformation.

Toward evening, the stallion fought its way back onto its feet. The first whinny was deeper and fuller than it had been previously. To any creature other than an älf, it would be a horrendous sound. Its eyes shimmered a glowing red as it turned its gaze on Caphalor; its snorting breath sent the message: *set me free.*

And he would.

Caphalor stood up and raised the cage door, then took several steps backward and waited to see what the night-mare he had created would do. His heart beat wildly; he felt no fear, but had not experienced such excitement since breaking his sword in battle against far superior numbers—and still going on to win.

The stallion left its prison carefully; white sparks played around its hooves and it hissed loudly. Its nostrils flared and it sniffed the air surrounding the half-giants, then stretched out its neck and turned its head to Caphalor. Walking over to the älf, it snorted and bared its fangs.

The broad, bloodied head came nearer and nearer until the nightmare bowed to its new master.

Caphalor stroked the stallion's cheeks, patted the neck and ran his fingers through the mane. "What a magnificent gift, Mórcass," he said, voicing his gratitude to the dead merchant. "I will treat it with honor. Let the name be Sardaî."

He went to the stables behind the building to find Mórcass' companion and express his sympathy. It had been a senseless death for the sake of an unnecessary gift.

The stallion followed Caphalor as if it were the most natural thing to do, head high and red eyes watchful. None of the half-giants dared to stand in its way or to attempt to put on a halter.

"Mind my night-mares, especially the new one," he ordered as he passed two human slaves. "If anything happens to them the same thing shall be done to you."

Sardaî waited beside Caphalor's mount while the älf entered the building to express his sympathy and assure Mórcass' partner that he would continue to do business with their house.

Longin was so terrified by the älf's command that he started to sweat under his hood.

How on earth was he to look after this red-eyed beast? If he approached and tried to put a halter on it he'd lose an arm, for sure. He had watched the death of his master from the doorway and did not wish for the same fate.

Mórcass had not been a considerate owner: he'd had a foul temper, treated the slaves badly and would often fly off the handle. Longin did not regret his passing, but he hoped the mistress would keep him on—he would rather carry sacks of grain and push carts of corn round the place than be gathering in the harvest, cutting his hands to shreds on the dried, thorny stalks.

"Kuschnar," he called to one of the half-giants in the barn. "Come here."

The creature ambled over, avoiding the night-mare, and looked down at the man. As a human, Longin had the authority to give the half-giant simple orders and he was about to make use of that.

"Watch the night-mares," he said, pointing to the beasts.

Kuschnar, still in his armor and gauntlets, lifted his visor and tapped the side of his head.

"You can't refuse you great lump, or I'll tell the mistress! And Caphalor will cut you into little strips before he kills you."

The half-giant made a face and put his visor down. The newly created beast gave a low warning snort and snapped at the other night-mare, which just managed to avoid the teeth aiming for its neck.

"Get on with it!" Longin shouted, kicking Kuschnar. "Separate them!" He was sweating even more now. This was going to be a disaster.

Kuschnar moved carefully over to the night-mares. The old night-mare was tied up and could only protect itself with its hooves—its younger rival, on the other hand, was running free, dancing around then surging forward, snapping its teeth at the other.

Kuschnar stopped dead; he did not dare to get any closer to the fighting animals.

"No!" Longin clapped his hands to his mouth in despair as the younger night-mare lunged again, grabbing the back of the older night-mare's neck and biting down hard, shaking and tearing like a wild cat. He shouted for the other half-giants, but they too kept well back: no one was following his orders. With a scream the older night-mare collapsed, its flailing hooves knocking over one of the half-giants. Desperately, Longin grabbed a bucket of water and hurled the contents over the beasts, but it didn't have the slightest effect.

More slaves hovered in the doorways, watching. The younger night-mare had bitten through the other's neck and blood was bubbling out of a severed artery and onto the courtyard floor.

The winning night-mare had not suffered the slightest injury. It stood over the corpse of its rival, sniffed the blood and put its tongue to the growing puddle. The stallion gave a snort and then drank the defeated creature's life-juice.

The door of the main building flew open and Caphalor stormed out. Longin nearly fainted with fear, he knew it would be useless to run, the älf would just take it out on his family. Caphalor slowed his steps and came to a halt in front of Longin.

"Master, forgive me. I—" Longin stammered, throwing himself at Caphalor's feet. "We couldn't get them apart. We didn't dare get near..."

"Because you were afraid for your own worthless life," the älf finished the sentence, his voice cold as the north wind.

"Please, master! They were going berserk!"

The älf did not look at him as he took out a long dagger. "I gave you the order to look after both. One of them is dead, do you remember what I said would happen?"

"That I would suffer the same fate," he whispered.

"Exactly, but I've changed my mind." The älf turned the dagger round. "A hundred of your kind are worth one night-mare. I hope you have a large family."

"Master!" Longin cried out in despair. "Take my life but let the others live!"

"How would it be if I took their lives first and you had to watch?" the älf said angrily. "I'll line them up, you tell me their names and then I'll kill them—you can watch, just as I have had to watch my old nightmare die." Longin did not see the movement, but he felt hot pain in his shoulder and blood poured out of the cut. He moaned. "Humans can take three hundred wounds like that before they die. Did you know that?" The älf laughed darkly. "You will see for yourself. I'll start with your youngest child."

"No!" Longin's helplessness turned into aggression and he tried to attack Caphalor, but before he'd even reached the älf, the dagger blade had flashed down and cut through his heart. He sank to the ground, dying.

"You shall soon meet your family again, slave," Longin heard the älf say in the far distance. Despair sent tears into his eyes at the thought of all his loved ones sharing his fate.

*　*　*

Caphalor wiped the dagger on the man's clothing. The punishment had been too mild, but he had not been in the mood to do more. At least the wretch had died with needless despair in his heart—Caphalor could not slaughter his family, these slaves were not his property. He owed Mórcass' companion a replacement for this one death as it was. It was good that his slave-breeding scheme was flourishing: he would give her a better-quality worker than the one he had just struck down.

He gazed at the butchered remains of the old night-mare with regret. The blood of the defeated animal still dripped from Sardaî's mouth.

Caphalor had believed the slaves' terror, because he had witnessed the stallion's display of strength himself, but it was still the case that the dead slave had not carried out the task he had been given, and he therefore deserved such punishment.

"Take the saddle off, clean the bridle and reins and bring them to me," he ordered one of the half-giants. "Send the cadaver to my estate." He would be able to make something from the night-mare's bones, he was sure, even if it were only a bone flute.

The new night-mare bent his head again and continued to drink the blood of the dead beast. The älf observed the animal, fascinated. Sardaî's recent transformation was obviously not causing the creature any problems.

"I'm told you are Caphalor," the voice came from behind him.

Caphalor turned round. He had been lost in thought and had not heard the rider approach. He nodded in surprise.

The mantle of the fully armored älf he now looked up at displayed the arms of the Inextinguishables. Bending down from the saddle, he handed Caphalor a sealed parchment.

Ishím Voróo (The Outer Lands), älfar realm
Dsôn Faïmon, Dsôn (Star-Eye),
4370th division of unendingness (5198th solar cycle),
summer.

Sinthoras checked that his armor was sitting correctly, arranged his cloak, and brought his face closer to the reflective surface of the mirror to look for any flaws in his complexion. He was immaculate and sufficiently pale, and had rubbed a touch of soot on his eyelids to enhance the appearance of the eyes—yes, he was fit for his audience with the Sibling Rulers.

He mentally ran through the points he wanted to put to the Inextinguishables. He would win their approval for his scheme as soon as they had given him the Honor-Blessing. They were sure to agree to his plans.

He was not expecting them to promote him to supreme commander for the entire campaign, but they would certainly give him responsibility for one of the fronts. He wanted the east, where the enemy had little chance of digging themselves in: he could drive them back to the mountains and slaughter them on the slopes.

Sinthoras stretched and smiled at his reflection, confident in the coming victory and his appearance: this was how he would confront his brothers in arms once he had been awarded the Honor—then they would learn what it was like to be snubbed. He would go down in älfar legends as one of the greatest military leaders. A sweet sense of conviction pervaded his mind.

Eventually, after victory in battle, he would search for one of the craters that Inàste's tears had hollowed out of the earth. There he would found his own city, and in honor of the Inextinguishables, he would call it Dsôn Inàste.

Sinthoras was not one to leave his future to the vagaries of fate: eternal life was no use if you wasted it in indecision.

He turned as he was approached by a blinded älf whose empty eye sockets absorbed the light; white symbols had been tattooed into the surrounding skin, emphasizing the darkness. He was wearing a wraparound garment of green and black material and had a dagger hanging at his side. The embroidery at the neckline announced he was one of the Inextinguishables' privy counselors—one of the privileged älfar allowed into their immediate presence on a frequent basis. He had sacrificed his eyesight in order to protect his sanity—for to look too long on the countenances of Nagsor and Nagsar Inàste meant madness. Their appearance was too refined even for their own people to bear. Enhanced perfection. Essence of the divine.

Even blinded, Sinthoras knew this älf would be a fearsome warrior. He could not say how old he was, or how many divisions of unendingness it had been since he had been blinded, but he had heard of älfar who were trained to wield their weapons in complete darkness, perhaps this älf was skilled in the same way.

As if to prove the point, he approached Sinthoras as confidently and without hesitation.

"Follow me," said the älf, eschewing the need for greeting or politeness.

With every step that Sinthoras took through the Tower of Bones his joy and anticipation increased: he was in the very center of their realm, about to meet the most important personages in the land!

They crossed an empty hall with basalt walls and entered a tower that was at least forty paces in diameter. Five sets of interwoven stairs spiraled upward and various shades of green, gray, blue, and yellow light fell through stained glass windows, giving the place an unreal atmosphere. Birds fluttered above their heads; lost feathers floated down to the polished bone floor, changing color as they passed through the rays of colored light.

The blind älf started upward and Sinthoras followed him, climbing steps made from the shields and bones of conquered enemies. The five flights of stairs interconnected on their relentless, twisting ascent until they merged into one broad staircase.

Sinthoras looked down—the bright white of the polished floor shimmered in the distance far below them.

"The Steps of Subjugation. One thousand paces from here to the ground," said the älf, taking the final step.

Sinthoras found he was breathing faster than usual, not from the physical exertion, but due to his growing sense of excitement.

"Where are we going?" he finally dared to ask, after the älf guide had actually spoken to him. "Where will the Inextinguishables be receiving me?"

Turning right along the gallery, the älf stopped at a set of tionium doors showing the star-shaped outline of the älfar realm in relief. Runes warned visitors to lower their eyes or risk being overwhelmed by the sight of the Sibling Rulers and made insane or blind.

The älf guide waited by the door, gripping the handle firmly. "Ready?"

"Yes." Sinthoras lowered his gaze. It occurred to him that this was how Raleeha must have felt when she approached him. But not anymore— since he had punished her there was nothing for her to see, she only had her memories. He congratulated himself for making her suffer twice over.

The entrance door swung open quietly. Deep red light issued forth, falling on the leather of his boots, the hue of which turned the light black. Sinthoras kept his eyes focused on the hem of the servant's robe and followed him, occasionally glancing to either side.

Artworks hung on the walls of the large hall, pictures that could never be reproduced; they had been created using woven hair from creatures now extinct. Sinthoras was so fascinated that he unconsciously slowed down to admire them, studying attractive abstract patterns full of a dramatic radiance, yet strangely somber in appearance. Had they been produced by the Inextinguishables themselves?

He nearly collided with his guide, who had halted at the foot of a dais. "I bring you Sinthoras, whom you have summoned to your presence," he announced, stepping four paces to the side.

Sinthoras caught sight of slim-fitting pointed boots patterned in silver. At thigh level, he could see purple material decorated with gold leaf, strips of vraccasium, and diagonal inlays of tionium: clothes worth an emperor's ransom indeed.

The air was filled with incense and precious perfumes distilled from ingredients supplied by the bodies of vanquished enemies. When the älfar defeated a foe they always made a work of art out of the remains— whether that be a sculpture, relief or perfume. His people even possessed the secret of refining rotting intestines to produce a fragrant substance humans found irresistible.

"So, here we have Sinthoras." The high, clear voice belonged to an älf-woman. It held such purity, he immediately knew he would leap from the top of the Steps of Subjugation were she to demand it.

He prostrated himself at the foot of the dais that bore the double throne. "I pledge my life to you, Nagsar Inàste and Nagsor Inàste," he cried from the heart, feeling a surge of pride. He was alone in their presence, and *so* close to them.

"May your life be eternal, for we are need of an älf such as you," the male voice said. This sound, too, intoxicated him. He could hardly believe they were really speaking to him. What further grace could he be shown? What words to express how humble he felt before them?

He heard two pairs of footsteps behind him. One was an älf guide— and who else? Jealousy flared up inside him.

The footsteps came closer to the throne and a voice said, "I bring you Caphalor, whom you have summoned to attend."

A horrified *No!* was on his lips, ready to fly out in the form of a shriek, but at the last moment Sinthoras quelled the impulse.

CHAPTER III

Round the outside of the crater six deep cracks had formed, similar to the crown of the falling Star of Tears.

There, too, our ancestors settled and they named the rays of the star Avaris, Wèlèron, Ocizùr, Riphâlgis, Shiimal, Kashagòn, and the heart they called Dsôn. The ancestors smoothed and straightened the sides of the cracks.

United in the Star State, Dsôn Faïmon, our people grew stronger and from its very foundation the Star State has never been conquered.

The defeated peoples became our vassals, servants or rightless serfs.

Epocrypha of the Creating Spirit,
1st Book,
Chapter 1, 12–17

Ishím Voróo (The Outer Lands), älfar realm Dsôn Faïmon,
Radial Arm Avaris,
4370th division of unendingness (5198th solar cycle),
summer.

Raleeha felt for the beaker containing Kaila's pain-killing potion. The wounds had healed over without infection, but the sockets still throbbed, burned, and itched horribly. Even so, it was a miracle how quickly she had recovered from the devastating injuries. If she had relied on the medicines known to her own kind she might have died.

But if you had stayed with your own kind you would never have had your eyes put out, said a small rebellious voice in Raleeha's head. *With your own kind you would not have been a slave, but a princess.*

Now and then this voice spoke up and there was nothing Raleeha could do about it. Today she did not resent it at all.

She found the beaker and lifted it to her lips, emptying it in one draft. She was in the servants' hall next to the kitchens and could smell the food. Apart from Kaila and her, there were ten human slaves in the house, and they were currently teaching four young älfar how to serve: it was a valuable training opportunity for the youths. There were always new ones arriving, and as such Raleeha had never bothered to learn their names, choosing to address them all as "young sir."

She could hear the slaves talking—she could tell their voices apart now—then there was a clattering of plates and the crackle of the fire being raked with a poker. She could imagine where they were all sitting and what was happening: the young älfar trainees were preparing the food for Sinthoras, while Kaila cooked separately for the slaves. The scents of gourmet food wafted from one side and mixed with the simpler smell of broth from the other. She imagined Kaila busy at her pots and pans, the women trimming vegetables, and one of the men putting a new log on the fire.

She remembered how Kaila and the others had treated her when she had first arrived, unable to understand why she had become a slave of her own accord. It had been purely because she so admired the älfar; she was keen to study their art and wanted nothing more than to live near them—near one älf in particular.

But Raleeha would never see any of that ever again. Not even her master's face.

The returning thought saddened her, but she tried not to cry because that would make her wounds sting and the tears would wash out the healing ointment.

Raleeha felt a draft, then heard a rustle and a chair scraping along the floor. "Have you heard about your family? They're getting to be the most powerful in the north of Ishím Voróo." It was Wirian, full of gossip as usual. A smell of cooking fat accompanied the young slave girl and Raleeha was surprised how strong her sense of smell had become since losing her sight. "They are saying Farron has just won another victory against some other barbarians."

"Who is saying that?"

"Esmintaïn's slave told me at the market this morning. His master is one of the älfar who meet up regularly to discuss the current situation in Dsôn Faïmon." Raleeha felt a touch on her shoulder.

"Aren't you glad?"

Raleeha did not answer. Wirian was implying that if her brother became powerful enough, she would be able to shrug off her slave bonds whenever she wanted. She *had* recently been paying more attention to her rebellious inner voice, but in her heart she knew that she would not leave, even if her family were in a position to enforce the liberation of all the Ishmanti hostages and prisoners.

Wirian moved her hand from Raleeha's shoulder. "What is it?"

"Nothing," Raleeha lied, as she sifted through her store of memories, pictures, and impressions, starting from her first encounter with Sinthoras at his easel, then the day she first saw the city he lived in.

She had learned so much about their culture and had come to understand why the älfar were so different: älfar thought was conducted at spiritual levels never attained by the imperfect human mind, her master's grace toward her allowed her to belong to a world superior to Ishím Voróo, something she had always wished for.

How could she ever adapt again to the primitive huts, drafty castles and nomad tents of her family's lands? In the winter you froze, in the autumn your clothes were always damp, in spring there were clouds of midges and in summer you had to spend all the daylight hours helping in the fields or with the sheep-shearing. In the evenings she had been expected to sing and dance for her brother's drunken companions instead of being able to paint. Even as the sister of a prince her life had been hard and unrewarding. It was unrefined and she had no access to the art that meant so much to her.

Here, on the other hand, she was surrounded by luxury, culture, and beauty. Raleeha would forgive her master for what he had done, *I knew the rules and I did not obey them,* she told her inner voice of protest. She would die rather than leave Sinthoras. She would find some way to express her artistic talent, with or without her sight. Perhaps this would enable her to reach entirely different heights, as the älfar themselves did?

Raleeha touched her hair. She wore it in long braids draped with a night-colored veil embroidered with stars. She knew her master liked it, even though he hardly ever looked at her.

Sometimes she imagined Sinthoras selecting her as his private playmate . . .

She liked to imagine him spending time with her until he had found his ideal älf-partner. This was about as likely, of course, as her getting two brand-new eyes: älfar did not commune with other races, and certainly not with slaves and servants, whether they had volunteered of their own free will or not. She sighed.

"Have you any other news?" she asked Wirian. Raleeha could hear the other woman moving around the room, busying herself with some task.

"An älf-woman has sent a messenger to request a further meeting with the master," Wirian went on. "She's been here quite a few times. I think her name is—"

"Yantarai," Raleeha quickly supplied. Yantarai was relatively old, even if älfar tended not to show their age. She had given birth to seven children—seven girls—which made her an esteemed celebrity in Dsôn. As the givers of life, älf-girls counted for more than älf-boys. If she were seriously interested in Sinthoras there might soon be a mistress in the house to serve, not because Sinthoras would fall prey to her charms, but because she could enhance his social status. Raleeha knew her master's ambitions on this score; she knew how he longed to receive the Honor-Blessing from the Inextinguishable Siblings and how he dreamed of playing an important part in the state. That was why he had not so far cared to select a partner, even if älf-women were lining up at his door. Raleeha clenched her fists. "The master is not at home."

"That's why she has left a note for him." Wirian giggled. "They're flirting with each other, aren't they?"

Raleeha uttered a groan of disappointment. If Wirian queried her reaction she knew she could put it down to the pain of her injuries.

When Wirian started to enthuse about being allowed to attend an älfar wedding, Raleeha found it intolerable.

"I've got something I must do," she said, interrupting the flow of Wirian's fancy. She stood up and made for where she supposed the doorway was, locating the exit only after walking into the corner of the dresser. She wandered without knowing where she was going, one hand trailing on the wall. Abruptly, she felt ornately carved wood underneath her fingers. She drew in a sharp breath. She knew these doors, they led to her master's rooms.

Raleeha paused for a moment and then, against all the rules, entered his bedchamber. She walked to the bed and bent over it, breathing in the incense-laden fragrance from his pillow and stroking the fabric as if it were his face. The thought of Yantarai lying next to Sinthoras, sharing his bed, made jealousy flare up. What right had that älf-woman to set her sights on Sinthoras?

Raleeha stood up. She knew she was being ridiculous, Yantarai had many more rights than she did: as a simple slave she had no influence over her master's decisions and under älfar law she had no rights at all. There was no question of social advancement for her.

The first days in Dsôn had been hard for her: Sinthoras had told her nothing about the way things were done, or about the laws of the älfar state. She had picked up the information from the other slaves and her own observations—taking notes and making sketches as she went.

Leaving the bedchamber, Raleeha walked back into the corridor and into the restroom, which she was allowed to enter—she opened the tall windows on the east wall. Children's voices could be heard outside, just like back home, and there was a fresh smell in the air: the smell of the east wind and inspiration. The signs were favorable, she would get to grips with her old tasks under these new circumstances.

She left the restroom and went upstairs to her master's studio. She had never dared to show him any of her own drawings because she would have felt like a child bringing an adult its little scribbles—and as long as he was angry with her there was no point.

Balancing on the studio ladder she practiced locating the pots, jars, and brushes on the high shelves. Her sense of smell helped her identify the various pigments and varnishes, and she could always get one of the other slaves to verify her guesses. At first she had thought it impossible, but slowly, she began to see how to get by.

She gained confidence as she went, spending the whole day relearning which shelves things were kept on, asking for help from the other slaves, until she was shaking with exhaustion and could hardly grip the rungs of the cell ladder. Her eye sockets smarted and she was hungry and thirsty.

She returned to the communal kitchens where her supper—the remains of the soup—and the others awaited her.

"Here she is," was Kaila's greeting. "We've got a new boy, just arrived," she said, then her voice moved away slightly, toward the boy. "Here, introduce yourself."

"Good day." The young male voice did not sound confident. "I'm Quanlot. My family are the Sratins." He shook hands with her carefully.

Kaila laughed, then turned back to Raleeha, "Quanlot is twelve human years old and very skinny."

"Thin as a rake," called Wirian. "A broomstick with hair." The slaves laughed and some of them banged the table with their spoons. Raleeha was embarrassed by their behavior.

"Sinthoras bought him for sweeping the chimneys and cleaning the air ducts," Kaila explained, turning back to the boy, "I'm sorry, but you'll only have half portions at the table—master's decision—if you put on weight you'll be sold, or worse."

Raleeha felt her way back to her seat. All she knew about the Sratin family was that they excelled in lying and cheating. "Did you want me for something?" she asked Wirian.

"Yes," she replied. "Can you tell him how the black-eyes like things done?"

"Does he even want to be told?" she objected.

"Yes, I do," said Quanlot. "The more I learn about them the longer I'll stay alive—and the sooner I'll escape."

This defiant answer left the other humans speechless with shock. Nobody moved, then there was the sound of a slap and a grunt from Quanlot.

"Never say that again," warned Kaila.

"B—But—" the boy stammered.

"The mention of escape carries the death penalty," Raleeha said, starting to eat. "And it wouldn't be a quick death," she added. "It would be punishment, not relief."

"You sound just like one of them yourself," Kaila said, disapprovingly.

Raleeha swallowed a few mouthfuls of the thick and tasteless broth—how she would love to partake of her master's food. "If you want to learn then listen, Quanlot Sratin, we begin now.

"The älfar state is governed by the Inextinguishables—two sibling rulers who make all their decisions together. They are a couple—the älfar are not bothered at all about their being brother and sister—and unlike our barbarian homeland, the älfar don't have a class society, älf-men and älf-women are mostly equal in status and so are the various professions and trades. The warriors, of course, are responsible for protecting the state." She had some more soup. "Did you get all that?"

"Yes," murmured Quanlot.

"Show particular respect to älf-women who have produced many children," she warned him. "You'll recognize them from the strands of color in their hair. Infant mortality rates are very high here, so they are revered."

"The infant mortality rates are made up for with their immortality," Wirian chipped in. "Only fair."

"If they're immortal, do they always stay with the same life-partner?" the boy wanted to know.

"Älfar do occasionally marry, but tend not to so as not to be bound to the same person for eternity. On average, they change partners every twenty divisions of unendingness." Raleeha's thoughts had drifted back to Sinthoras, how she would love to lie by his side.

Quanlot's curiosity was in full swing. "What are the young älfar doing here? They're not slaves like us, are they?"

"Of course not, these are young masters in training," she explained. "Älfar children mature fast and their education goes in seven-year stages: they start their apprenticeship at fourteen and stick with it until they reach twenty-one divisions of unendingness, after that they go to a master to complete their training." Raleeha pushed her plate away and felt for the bread with her hands. "Children are always brought up by the mother, with the father having little say, but he might teach them craft skills, for example." She smiled in what she thought was his direction and broke off a piece of bread. "That's all quite different where you come from, isn't it?" She was growing very tired now. "Have you noted everything I've been telling you, Quanlot?"

"Yes," he said.

"Good. More tomorrow." She got up to go to the slaves' quarters and Wirian followed. The two women got ready for bed. One by one the other slaves joined them in the room, and as Raleeha listened to them talking about their day she nodded off, sitting up against the wall. In her imagination the wall she leaned her head against was her master's shoulder.

Raleeha smiled as she drifted off to sleep.

Ishím Voróo (The Outer Lands), älfar realm
Dsôn Faïmon, Dsôn (Star-Eye)
4370th division of unendingness (5198th solar cycle),
summer.

Caphalor saw Sinthoras lying prostrate before the Inextinguishable Siblings' double throne. Immediately after being introduced, Caphalor respectfully followed suit and lay down at the foot of the dais, glancing sideways to look at Sinthoras.

His features showed total rejection and Caphalor noted black lines of fury creeping across his face. The other älf must have been really angry to see him here.

Caphalor gave Sinthoras a spiteful grin and the fine black lines abruptly increased in number.

Caphalor had no idea why his rulers had summoned him; finding Sinthoras there was also a puzzle, the two of them had nothing in common.

"Caphalor," said their sovereign lord, his tones refined. "It pleases my heart to see you here."

Caphalor made a slight movement with his arms to acknowledge this gracious welcome.

"You may both stand." The command came from the two rulers simultaneously.

Servants brought a screen three paces high and placed it between subjects and sovereigns, thus protecting the warriors from exposure to their rulers' incredible beauty.

"Sinthoras," their lady said. "Tell us what you and your friends have learned about Ishím Voróo."

Caphalor saw Sinthoras' shock at these words and his curiosity grew.

"O, Inextinguishable Ones," Sinthoras began hesitantly. "I come to inform you about the campaigns of the barbarian tribes in the north: Farron Lotor, head of the Ishmanti barbarians, subjugates one barbarian leader after another, vanquishing them in battle or converting them to his cause. The army's numbers may swell to several thousand if he gains total power; according to my calculations it could be as much as 100,000." He was watching the silhouettes on the paper screen intently, as if standing face to face with his sovereigns. "As well as this, the trolls have been carrying out organized attacks on the Tandruu barbarians, and they obviously mean business: each of the troll units has around seventy mounted fighters, and so far ten units have been deployed. They have been trying out new tactics against the Tandruu, it's as if they were practicing for something—but I do not know what. I am also concerned to learn that the botoicans—feared by the other nations because of their magic—are attempting to invade fflecx territory from the west." He held himself erect and raised his arms for emphasis. "The poison-blenders haven't been attacked for hundreds of divisions of unendingness, if the botoicans aren't daunted by them, what will their next objective be?"

Caphalor had heard these rumors, but the barbarian numbers Sinthoras was citing were far greater than the estimations in the marketplace.

Sinthoras and his friends must have a good network of observers and spies on the ground feeding information back to the capital. Caphalor had to admit a certain admiration for the älf.

"On the other side of our borders everything is in flux: armies are assembling and this morning Samusin sent us his west wind, a harbinger of war—it won't be long before battle determines the victors among the barbarians and beasts, and I am convinced they won't stop until they've formed an alliance against our own Star State. What I say is: let us preempt any attack, we should be motivated not by fear but by foresight. In order to protect our own kind it is vital we wage war on Ishím Voróo. Victory will be ours and the ensuing peace can then be enjoyed: the peace won by the greatest triumph ever to be celebrated in the Legends of the Älfar."

After a moment's reflection, Nagsor Inàste thanked Sinthoras for the information he and his colleagues had collected and turned to ask Caphalor's opinion, his voice soft as velvet.

"As your graces have summoned both of us, I assume you are interested in hearing two opposing views on how best to protect our homeland," Caphalor began slowly, glancing over at Sinthoras, who made an impatient gesture. "My view is that we should reinforce our borders and turn Dsôn Faïmon into a veritable fortress. We could construct a high wall immediately on the far side of the defense moat and—"

"Nonsense!" cried Sinthoras furiously. "The more land we have the safer we shall be."

"We do not have enough soldiers to control the regions we already govern, let alone mount an attack." Caphalor faced his opponent and saw that Sinthoras was about to lose his temper: that would be good—it would show Sinthoras up and his plans for a belligerent multi-fronted campaign would die a death. Caphalor's tone was assertive and challenging. "And I wouldn't like to rely on the loyalty of the slaves and serfs we've forced into servitude for our defense: if we sent them out to the battlefield, we wouldn't be able to guarantee that they would fight for us." He folded his arms. "And there's a further danger: we would have to deploy every single warrior we have, the vassal nations might take advantage of the situation and destroy Dsôn Faïmon from within."

Sinthoras glared at him. "I've worked everything out to the last detail. We only need half of—"

Caphalor's smile was false as he interrupted the other älf. "Admittedly we are exceptionally skilled warriors experienced in dealing with superior numbers, but the unexpected can always occur. You know the fflecx and their poisons. What if they supplied our enemies with a substance that could kill off hundreds of our soldiers so that the entire front collapsed? Reserve troops would take too long to organize and we would not be able to repel an attack. Dsôn Faïmon would be in dire straits. I don't think you and your Comet friends have properly weighed up the risks." Then he grinned maliciously. "Comets fly across the sky and burn themselves out, that's why I favor the Constellations; they shine for all eternity."

"Hold your peace!" Sinthoras shouted, his arms half-raised, the black fury lines issuing from his right temple crisscrossing wildly. "You are a coward, a prevaricator: you live in the past, I live in the present and look to the future; my plan will make our state safe, your policy will land us in a never-ending battle on the banks of the river-moat until we run out of food and soldiers and Dsôn Faïmon falls." He turned back to the Inextinguishables. "I beseech your graces, do not heed his words, they will bring total devastation. A waiting game would mean the destruction of our empire, we must make a preemptive strike and eradicate everything that threatens our existence."

Silence reigned.

The siblings made no move.

"There is something important missing," said Nagsar Inàste finally, with a faint rebuke for Sinthoras in her voice that pleased Caphalor. "Something missing from your intelligence on Ishím Voróo. In the northwest, beyond the territory of the fflecx, a new being has taken up residence. It is said to have the appearance of a cloud of stardust."

"And it is reported to have extraordinary arts at its disposal; making it an excellent potential ally for us." The brother had taken over so smoothly that there was no pause between the words of the two siblings. "We have many plans for the coming division of unendingness and to put it all into place we shall need to learn more about this creature. You have both shown courage in battle, intelligence and skill. You represent the extreme contrasts that destabilize Dsôn Faïmon."

"We are aware," his partner went on, "that our subjects are sharply divided, and this is the reason we have chosen to entrust both of you with the task of traveling to the northwest to make contact with this being. We want you to negotiate with it and win it for our cause."

"So we are preparing an offensive?" Sinthoras asked, unable to contain his excitement.

"Not in the way you mean," said Nagsor Inàste.

"Not in a way you could have imagined," murmured the sovereign lady. "We plan to bring about the end of the elves."

Caphalor grew hot, to march on Tark Draan, the refuge of the elves, was an age-old dream of the älfar people. But the Stone Gateway—the entrance to the dwarf realm—had always stood in their way. Did this now mean the älfar had found a way around it? And, ultimately, did it mean that the Inextinguishables were giving up Dsôn Faïmon? He did not dare to ask his question.

Sinthoras' countenance had regained its normal color, with joy taking the place of anger. "You make me your happiest subject with this decision," he cried passionately, sinking down on one knee and inclining his head. "I shall do all in my power to win this creature as an ally for our cause."

"And I shall do no less," vowed Caphalor. "Will your graces tell us what special powers this creature has that make it so useful in war?"

Nagsar Inàste sat up straight on her throne. "Only one: it has the ability to break the spell that protects the Gateway." She raised her right arm and snapped her gloved fingers. Four servants stepped out of the shadows at the back of the hall. "You will be given whatever you need for the journey, but do not take a retinue. Make sure you travel alone. The way to the northwest is fraught with dangers you must go around rather than confront: your true mission must remain secret."

"Return successful or not at all," her brother-partner told them, his voice ice-cold. "We don't have to stress what responsibility you bear, or how heavy a weight lies on your shoulders." He indicated the door. "Go with our good wishes."

The servants approached and made it clear that they were to be escorted out.

Caphalor could see that Sinthoras was hesitating. He knew what the other älf was waiting for: he wanted Nagsor or Nagsar Inàste to award him the Honor-Blessing.

The servants turned toward the door and strode off, taking Sinthoras and Caphalor in the middle: there was no mistaking the obligation to leave immediately if one did not want to risk gross impropriety.

Caphalor gave a cool smile. Sinthoras would be accorded promotion only on completion of the mission; his traveling companion thus remained lower in status.

This provided an excellent opportunity for Caphalor to score over his rival: he must be the one to persuade this mist-demon to enter an alliance. A few steps later, Caphalor's idea had become a firm intention, not because he felt the same burning ambition as the obsessive Sinthoras, but because he wanted to prevent the warmongering Comet faction getting a shining icon for their warrior-leader.

They left the hall in silence and went down the stairs of the Tower of Bones, at the base of which the four blind servants dismissed them.

"A pity they did not give you the Honor-Blessing," Caphalor began, innocently. "It is such a wonderful feeling to be touched by the Inextinguishables . . ."

Sinthoras' head snapped round, lines of anger marking his face. "Try to provoke me, it won't work. Dsôn Faïmon will soon have three times, even four times as much land and neither you, nor anyone else, can stop that happening."

Caphalor turned and looked up at the Tower of Bones. "Oh yes? Are you the missing triplet for the Inextinguishable Siblings? The way you talk they'll have to have a third throne made. Will you be sitting to the left or the right of Nagsar Inàste?"

"Your way of thinking is very small-minded. Empires are not created by defending one's borders," Sinthoras replied haughtily.

"We already *have* an empire," Caphalor contradicted him. "You are just out for personal gain: win a few big battles, then come back home and advance a few rungs higher on the ladder." He came closer. "You and your friends are forgetting one thing. We obey the Inextinguishable Ones, theirs are the laws we follow, not those of the Comets or the Constellations."

"Absolutely, but the rulers listened to *my* views before they give their orders," a hostile Sinthoras replied. "Älfar like you deserve to be hounded out, Caphalor." He grinned like a wild animal. "And that is exactly what I shall do, as soon as we get back."

"Now you are showing your true colors." Caphalor wanted to say more, but one of the court servants came over and handed each of them a leather bag before turning and reentering the tower, leaving the two warriors to stand alone in the light of the setting sun.

Caphalor remained silent and opened the catch to look inside the bag: it contained maps of the various regions in Ishím Voróo with their route clearly marked.

He was particularly concerned about the journey through the territory of the fflecx: a gnomoid, dark-skinned race known for their skills in concocting poisons. They had a tailor-made toxin that killed instantly for every tribe and nation in Ishím Voróo. The alchemancers, as they called themselves, were experts in a wide range of substances and their kingdom was the only one besides Dsôn Faïmon that had never been conquered.

"We shall be on this journey for a long time," he murmured, turning to Sinthoras, but the älf had disappeared.

Caphalor saw him fifty paces further down the steps that led to the base of the hill. "We ride in four days, at dawn," Caphalor called out. "I'll meet you on the fourth island at Welèron."

Sinthoras gave no sign that he had heard.

Caphalor began the descent. There were 4,000 steps down to the plateau where his night-mare was waiting. He surveyed the landscape as he walked.

In the north of Dsôn, set on an incline, there were many domed buildings, like countless eyes staring up at the sky from the crater floor. Only a few were brightly colored; most were black, white, silver or metallic. Some of the houses had been designed to glow at night, leaving the impression of smoldering coals. Between the Tower of Bones and these houses, there were slender towers that leaned against each other like reeds. In Dsôn itself it was so difficult to acquire land that people would build on a site the size of a handkerchief: the smaller the area, the more extravagant the tower.

It occurred to Caphalor suddenly that it looked like a pincushion.

The largest, most elaborate, buildings were clustered around the hill he stood on; further away they were more conservative, getting more impressive again toward the edge of the crater.

Caphalor was fascinated by some of the techniques used by Dsôn's architects, and walking through the Star-Eye, he picked up a couple of ideas he thought he might try out on his own property, but to him, the capital city merely represented a nice change from the rural setting he lived in. He'd never want to live there.

I'd end up having Sinthoras as a neighbor, he thought, grinning in spite of himself. Then the grin gave way to a frown: he had to obstruct his rival wherever he could. Sinthoras had declared war on him—so why should he show any restraint? From now on he would have to show the harder side of his nature, especially in regards to this mission.

He had arrived at the platform where his night-mare stood.

The animal was dancing about, wild still, as he attempted to get into the saddle, but he had never had a better mount. This night-mare of his was the genuine article, quite incomparable: Sardaî never tired and utterly relished a prolonged, hard gallop. His long black mane would stream out in the wind, and the only sign of exertion the beast would show was slightly heavier breathing. Caphalor looked forward to seeing the envy in Sinthoras' eyes when he saw the animal in action: elegant, powerful, and fiery.

On his way home, he wondered how he was going to break the news to Enoïla that he was going to have to leave. He would not be able to give her the slightest hint of his real mission.

But one thing had to be tackled first: he did not want to leave a mess for his wife to cope with, so he would have to instruct the slaves to obey her during his absence. It was good that he had asked Tarlesa to meet him at the slave camp.

*   *   *

It was dark before Caphalor reached the encampment. He could see from the shadows at the windows of the community house that the slaves were at supper, but there was no sign of his daughter.

Caphalor dismounted and entered the house.

"It is the master!" the overseer called, gesturing to the slaves to kneel.

Men, women, and children all humbly showed respect, but it did not escape Caphalor's attention that Grumson was taking his time about it: the look in his eyes told of suppressed rebelliousness. Caphalor's visit was timely, he needed to remind the slaves whose grace they depended on.

"Good evening, Father," said Tarlesa behind him. "I'm sorry I'm late, I had to finish preparing some enali stems. I'm going to do a blood exchange on one of the slaves tomorrow."

"I've only just arrived myself. Is the slave worth all that trouble?"

Tarlesa nodded. "He's the best thresher and smith we have, and the others can learn a great deal from him. He was injured and the wound became infected, so we're going to drain his blood and give him some from his brother instead." When she smiled, she looked like her mother's younger sister. Her features were a little sharper—he thought that was his own contribution—and she had his eyes, too. Today she was wearing a heavy leather apron over her light robe and thin gloves. A rolled bag lay on the rough floorboards beside her. She smoothed down her apron and picked up the bag. "This way I get plenty of practice. Dealing with the hollow enali stems is not easy. Now, which one is it that I'm to cure of his rebellion?"

Caphalor pointed to Grumson and summoned him over.

The barbarian stood up, barefoot, and walked slowly over. A prime example, indeed: tall, strongly built, with a simple face like most humans, no spark in the eyes. Many älfar did not believe the barbarians had souls, and he couldn't blame them.

"I'd like to try something different," Tarlesa told Caphalor, using the Dark Language so the slaves would not understand.

"Why?"

"Castration robs them of their virility and they can put on a lot of weight, so I have devised another procedure."

His daughter ordered the man to lie down on the only table in the room. Food and drink were hastily pushed aside as he complied, looking apprehensive.

"Hold him down," Caphalor commanded. "Anyone who lets go will be killed." Some of the slaves took hold of Grumson's arms and legs and braced themselves. "Try anything you like," he said to his daughter.

"Thank you," she beamed, unrolling the bag to reveal a set of surgical instruments: pliers, knives, blades, and metal prongs. A murmur went round the room.

Tarlesa took the medallion from round her neck and swung it slowly to and fro in front of Grumson's eyes, intoning as she did so a repetitive älfar chant.

Caphalor watched his daughter with interest and pride. He saw the barbarian's anger recede and his face relax and become expressionless, indifferent: she had paralyzed his mind.

She put the amulet back round her neck. "I don't know if this is going to work," she warned her father, as she picked up a thin steel implement with a blade at the end. "I've got it wrong a few times, but I always learn from my mistakes."

"You never told me you'd practiced," he said, surprised.

Tarlesa smiled. "I wanted it to be a surprise. Mother knows, she bought the examples for me to practice on."

"How many?"

"Eight so far, nothing of high value: the dealer was going to sell them to an artist to make wind chimes and storm flutes out of." She held the barbarian's eyelids open with her free hand before inserting the needle past the side of the eyeball and into his head. "I've reached the arch that separates the eye socket from the brain," she said, explaining why she had paused. She selected a small hammer from the instrument roll. "It only takes a little tap and we're through the thin layer of bone."

Tarlesa hit the end of the needle with the right degree of force and heard the light *tock* over the metal clink. There was a sharp intake of breath from the watching slaves.

"Now I can manipulate the needle directly into the main part of the brain. It only needs to go in to the depth of about five fingertips.

That was one of my mistakes: I kept pushing it too far in. I was able to observe that when I opened up the skull later on." She introduced a second long needle through the other eye socket. Then she took hold of the ends of both needles and moved them gently from side to side.

The watching humans groaned out loud, they did not know what the älf-woman was up to, but Caphalor was fascinated by the level of precision his daughter used. At the same time he listened to the noises made by the barbarians—should any of them decide to move against his express orders he would kill them on the spot, he could not let them get away with anything.

"What I'm doing here is destroying the part of his mind that wants to rebel," she explained. "According to my observations so far, this will cut the connection between perceptions and emotions: our barbarian will be a peaceful, friendly fellow when I wake him up."

"How on earth did you work all that out?" he asked.

"I had been reading reports about the results of arrow wounds to the head: the victims' personalities changed after their injuries, that's what roused my curiosity." Tarlesa drew the two needles out slowly, then she spoke three älfar words and clapped her hands. "You can let go now," she told the other slaves holding the man down.

Releasing the man's limbs, they stood back, muttering to each other, wondering what the mistress had done to him.

Grumson's eyelids fluttered and he sat up, rubbing his temples and moaning a little.

Caphalor heard the spectators sighing with relief. A glance at Grumson showed that he had kept his indifferent expression and his eyes remained dull.

"Perfect!" Caphalor exclaimed. "Tarlesa, you have excelled yourself! I'm delighted." He smiled at her. "What a clever daughter I have." He sketched a bow in her direction and she blushed in response.

Then he addressed the slaves: "Wildness does not pay. We have destroyed his soul and the same will happen to any of you if my wife or I hear of any fighting. If you want to keep your souls, serve us well." Then he put his arm round Tarlesa's shoulders while she put her instruments away and took off her apron. "Wait—would you like to try it on another one so they see we mean business? Take one of their young."

Tarlesa smiled happily.

Ishím Voróo (The Outer Lands), älfar realm
Dsôn Faïmon, Radial Arm Wèlèron,
4370th division of unendingness (5198th solar cycle),
summer.

The morning might have been made by Samusin for a propitious start to a journey. The air was chill and there was a slight fog hanging low over the defense moat that the sun was slowly burning off, making the island fort look as if it were floating on clouds. Under the mist, Caphalor's excellent hearing registered the sounds of the river.

He was enveloped in a gentle melancholy that he found as enjoyable as slight intoxication or a light kiss. He was sure he would be the one to set up the deal with the mist-demon; he'd trump Sinthoras in the eyes of the Inextinguishables. The thought brought a smile to his lips. He observed his surroundings and breathed the fresh air in.

After a moment a frown creased his brow, why was there no sign of Sinthoras? It was not like the ambitious älf to be late for the departure. *Unless . . .*

Caphalor sounded his bugle for the drawbridge to be lowered, stopping to question the guard.

"Am I the first to cross today?"

"Yes," came the answer.

Caphalor's mind was not put at rest. "When did the last älf cross to Ishím Voróo?"

"Yesterday," he heard. "His name was Sinthoras."

Anger boiled up in Caphalor. Obviously his unwished-for travel companion had decided to get to the mist-demon first and secure the alliance for himself. Then he would be the one to receive the praise . . . and enjoy the increased standing this would mean.

With a curse, Caphalor urged Sardaî over the bridge. His rage transferred itself to the stallion, which covered the ground in huge strides, snorting furiously. They neared the end of the bridge—not yet fully lowered—and the night-mare leaped easily over the gap between water and land.

Caphalor pulled sharply on the reins to bring Sardaî back under control, noting that his night-mare only settled when he did. "I see you are attuned to my state of mind," he said, stroking its broad black neck. "You are astonishing."

The stallion snickered, enjoying his rider's attentions.

After gauging his location from the height of the sun and the information on the map, the warrior älf urged Sardaî on, storming over cleared land and into the steppes where the grasses stood a good two paces high.

The first part of the journey was through neutral open country that did not belong to anyone. On the one hand that was a good thing, because there were no patrols or guards he might have to kill; on the other hand, it meant he might come across a troop of óarcos, a band of trolls or a small army of barbarians on the lookout for prey and easy booty. He also had to think of the obboona, the flesh-stealers who hunted älfar and flayed their skin, cutting off their ears, noses, and other items in order to attach them to their own bodies in an effort to be like the älfar, whom they so admired, thinking them demigods. They were thought to be as good as eradicated after the Inextinguishables' many campaigns against them—but you could never be too careful.

It was the same situation with the cnutar—symbiotic creatures made up of three component parts that could separate and merge again at will. The form that took precedence was fairly random: it might be an animal, a particular race, or even an object, but the components of one creature could not remain separate for longer than sixty heartbeats at a time or they would die. If a cnutar remained whole, it measured three paces in height and was as heavy as an ox; it would not be an easy opponent.

In Ishím Voróo, anything he encountered would be an enemy, that was why he kept his bow to hand: the long arrows he carried would stop them dead at first shot with no need for prolonged fighting, which was perfect—Caphalor had no time to waste in fighting, he had to catch Sinthoras up. The fact that he had been duped before their journey had even begun was eating away at him. It was also seriously affecting the beauty of his personal appearance: cold hatred and the thought of revenge transformed his features into a terrifying aspect.

Sardaî kept up the punishing gallop across the steppe.

At midday, Caphalor granted the beast a short rest on the banks of a slow-flowing river. It was intriguing to see Sardaî greedily grabbing the best fish from a passing shoal, water alone not being enough to keep the stallion going—it needed flesh and blood.

For himself, Caphalor took out a small tin which contained a special nutritious paste composed of every food group a warrior needed on campaign: herbs, meat, and fat. He used the tip of his dagger to scoop some out and then licked it directly from the blade. The sweet, sharp flavors slowly dissolved on his tongue.

He swallowed it down with some water, stowed the tin and pulled out the map, then calculated how much ground he had covered and where he could hope to be by nightfall. The night-mare had made excellent progress—at this rate he might even be able to overtake Sinthoras before they reached fflecx territory.

With a snort Sardaî raised his head; red-stained water splashed down from his muzzle. His ruby red gaze was fixed on the reeds to their right.

Caphalor noticed the tall reeds swaying with the gentle movement of the water, but the rustling sound he could hear did not correlate with what he could see.

Dropping the map, he picked up his bow and arrows and with half-closed eyes concentrated on the direction the sound was coming from. When he was quite sure he had pinpointed its source, he drew the bow and let the arrow fly.

There was a high-pitched scream and a splash.

Caphalor's mouth twitched. The scream sounded like a barbarian woman's.

The water between him and the reeds was turning red. He got the next arrow ready and waited patiently for her to show herself.

He heard more rustling and splashing sounds and then a black-haired woman crawled out through the reed bed, his arrow lodged in her thigh, though the fletching had prevented it going all the way through. A closer look brought something else to his attention: she had an älfar slave collar round her neck. That was a surprise. How had she managed to escape from Dsôn Faïmon? Why would she still be wearing that badge of slavery if she were on the run?

"Don't kill me, noble älf," she begged, sobbing. As she lifted her face he saw she was extremely attractive—for a human. Her eyes were covered with a black band, decorated with lace, and she was wearing a dark gray dress with a black bodice; a silver dagger dangled at her belt.

"How do you know I am an älf?"

"The arrow, I can feel the fletching." She gave a moan. "Älfar arrows are unique." She dragged herself along until she reached the pebbles of the shore.

Catching a whiff of her blood, the night-mare snorted. It was hungry still.

Caphalor waited. "And what are you doing here? Are you trying to get back to your family?"

"Never!" she cried. "I was following my master, who . . ." The girl blushed and fell silent.

". . . who is called Sinthoras," Caphalor completed. It was obvious—how many other älfar were traveling on this path to the north west of Ishím Voróo?

She nodded. "My name is Raleeha Lotor, noble lord."

"Have you been blind long?"

"No. It was my master's punishment for me, I had been negligent," she said, her tone contradicting her words. "I am following him to show that I would give my life to save his, to make up for my mistake."

"And indeed you nearly did give it."

Her name meant something to Caphalor. There had been talk of a human from the Lotor family voluntarily entering into service with Sinthoras. She must have fallen in love with him. It happened a lot: humans were attracted by the beauty of the älfar, or else fascinated by their art. There was no way of knowing which had been the case for this barbarian.

He had nearly killed his rival's slave.

Caphalor paused for a moment. Wasn't it the Lotor family that was said to be amassing a huge empire in the barbarian lands? Caphalor put down his weapon and went over to her. Under different circumstances he would have enjoyed letting his anger toward Sinthoras have full rein; he could have let Sardaî eat her. But he would let her live: she would be able to tell him more about his rival, and she was a Lotor. One way or the other, she would prove of use.

"Prove yourself," he said, cutting through the arrow shaft close to the skin of her thigh.

"Noble lord, what shall I—?"

"Pull the arrow out," he told her gruffly. "I want to see which is stronger, your fear of pain, or your will to survive."

Raleeha grabbed hold of the arrow with both hands, grimacing. She took a deep breath and then pulled; the arrowhead caught fast in the ground. She cried out with the pain, then released the tip of the arrow, adjusted her hold and tried again.

Caphalor watched her face as she struggled: pain, defiance, and anger chased each other across her visage and her lips were bloodied where she bit down on them. He was entranced by the sight of her. With another cry of pain she yanked the arrow out of her thigh.

"You did better than expected, but you still made too much noise," he said, cutting a strip of cloth from her dress to use as a bandage. "How did you get away?" He took great care to ensure her blood did not sully his person.

"I came out with a cart taking soldiers to the island fortress," she explained. "I swam the defense-moat and followed the tracks of my master's night-mare as far as I could. I could feel the scorch marks where its hooves had been. But after a while I lost my way."

"So I have saved your life." Caphalor was enjoying himself. "You are in my debt."

She hesitated and then bowed her head. "I will do anything you ask, noble älf."

Caphalor knew she was pretending, but he admired the strength of her will. For a barbarian she was extraordinary. He laughed and restrained Sardaî when the beast tried to snap at her. "We'll find something for you to do."

Chapter IV

The älfar who settled in Avaris were wealthy and of high standing. No älf could make his dwelling here without the assent of all other residents.

Wèlèron was the area set aside for the warrior class and priests and those with talent in the magic arts. However, the älfar had very few powerful wizards. The magic in their blood did not allow this to happen.

But their understanding of the workings of the body flourished.

Soon their healers had learned how to open up the skull without killing the patient, and how to cure the sick from tumors. Festering flesh could be replaced with healthy tissue, diseased blood exchanged for fresh and organs be removed or modified. Älfar were practically immune from death through injury or disease.

Epocrypha of the Creative Spirit,
1st Book,
Footnote

Ishím Voróo (The Outer Lands), älfar realm
Dsôn Faïmon, Dsôn (Star-Eye),
4370th division of unendingness (5198th solar cycle),
summer.

Nagsar Inàste stared out of the open windows looking over northern Dsôn.

"We have sent fire and water out together on that journey," said Nagsor Inàste, striding through the spacious room toward his älf-partner.

Turning, she revealed the immaculate features that only he could look upon. Nagsor remembered how one älf, while receiving the Honor-Blessing, had mistakenly raised his eyes and looked on her directly. He had watched the älf gradually lose his mind: at first he had smiled, enchanted, then his smile had become horribly exaggerated and black tears had spilled down his face. His eyes had grown brighter and brighter, before losing their color. The älf had become blind and had lost the power of speech, and from then on was no more than a shell. They had had him killed so as not to prolong his unworthy life for all eternity. Just as no one could stare at the daystar without damage, no one could survive her startling beauty with impunity.

Nagsor soaked up the sight of her with intense pleasure. The window glass was tinted red, so half of her face was blood-painted, the other half white, illuminated by the daystar. One eye shone black in the light, while the other, in shadow, shimmered with a color that defied description.

She was clothed in a transparent black nothingness of a dress that showed every detail of her perfect body. Nagsor shivered with delight at the sight of her. Only he was allowed to touch her, to share her bed, no one else.

"Was that not our intention, brother?" she answered. "Whichever is the stronger of the two will return to us, bringing our new ally. There will be an end to the discord amongst our people." She closed the window and the transparent shimmer of her dress faded. She came over to him, put her arm gracefully around his neck and kissed him passionately.

He touched her slender waist and slid his fingers up her back, stroking her gently until their kiss was ended.

Nagsar Inàste looked him in the eyes. "We have done the right thing."

"I just wonder what might happen if *both* of them returned having completed the mission successfully? What if fire and water were to combine to make steam? Steam under pressure is incredibly powerful."

"We are the Inextinguishable Ones, no älf presents a threat to us." The älf-woman removed her arm from his shoulders and moved over to a tall door; he followed her.

"Did you hear that a slave has escaped?" he asked.

"Yes, I was told she belonged to Sinthoras."

"Her family are the Lotor, do you think she ran back to them?"

As Nagsar opened the door, golden light illuminated her features. The room behind was lined with gold leaf and great amber lanterns hung from the ceiling suspended on long ropes of pearls, emitting a warm glow.

In the center of the room was a miniature version of their empire and the adjoining lands. Nagsar had constructed the model; she had painted the outlines of the territories on the floor and had used soil and sand for the landscape, and water for the rivers, lakes and seas. In the middle there was a representation of the Tower of Bones—their center of power.

They walked up the spiral staircase to the glass floor above, where they had a bird's eye view of the model. A clever treatment had rendered the glass invisible, with not even a reflection to obscure the view.

"I thought Sinthoras had good control over her. It's said she followed him of her own accord. I am surprised to learn she has run away, unless she were here as a spy for the Lotor."

Nagsor laughed. "The barbarians would never dream of attacking us."

Nagsar did not look amused. "I had the slaves and servants in their household questioned: Raleeha is known to have made sketches of practically all the main buildings in Dsôn. She has been here for one-third of a division of unendingness—time enough to sketch all the important roads. And now Sinthoras has blinded her, perhaps she feels she can do no more here."

Nagsor Inàste lost his gaiety. "Even if I don't believe Lotor would have anything like that planned, I'll put extra guards on watch down at the moat."

"Farron's army is growing with each daystar-rise. In losing Raleeha, we have lost a valuable pawn and allowed our security to be compromised," she hissed, stamping down over the top of the Ishmanti territories, as if she were grinding them out with her foot. "Curses on him! We can't be doing with rebellious humans at this stage in our enterprise."

"Then let's send out a few assassins," suggested Nagsor, a malicious smile on his lips. "Or I can go in disguise and kill him myself. I think I'd enjoy that—it's a long time since I slaughtered any barbarians."

"There is no need to send out an assassin yet, but let us keep a *very* close eye on them." She moved forward gracefully, until she stood over the supposed abode of the mist-demon.

Nagsor Inàste was still studying the area Lotor held. "What reason could there be for an escaped slave not to run back to her family?"

His sister-mistress laughed. "Perhaps she is like a dog following its master and is merely following Sinthoras out of misplaced devotion."

"But if she has been blinded? She would never get . . ." He fell silent. She had, after all, managed to trick the border patrol. It was important not to underestimate her. "I'll have a few slaves executed," he decided. "That will serve as a deterrent; we don't want any of the others following her lead."

"Keep their blood for me," she instructed. "And get them to purify it and take the color out: I only need the clear fluid, it's perfect for mixing with pigments."

Nagsor nodded. "And we can show one of the corpses and say it's Raleeha; officially she will have been captured and executed."

"A good plan." With her left foot, Nagsar circled the assumed position of the mist-demon. "I wonder what he will be like and what his conditions for joining us will be."

"We will have to be ready to accept almost any demands to get him to support our campaign," he reminded her. "We need him to go to Tark Draan. As far away as possible."

"He's bound to like it with the lesser races," she said to calm him. "And I'm so sure that Sinthoras and Caphalor will talk him round that I would bet my own immortality on it. The two of them are so keen to get our approval: ambition is always a strong motivator—ambition and enmity."

"What about love?" he responded with a smile. "I don't hate you, and I don't want you as an enemy and I don't feel the urge to be better at anything than you, my shining star."

The älf-woman laughed enticingly and held out her right hand. He strode over to her, clasped her fingers in his and pulled her to him. Together they gazed down on the mist-demon's land. "Yes, I'd nearly forgotten about love, because it only exists between the two of us in its purest form," she murmured, stroking the smooth skin of his cheek. "The love between brother and sister." She turned his face toward her and kissed him passionately.

He returned her caresses. Intoxicated by her nearness, he asked, "When will you give me a child? A Sìntoìt?"

She hung her head sadly. "That is not up to me to decide, my love. I have tried all the tinctures and potions. We must be patient and wait."

Nagsor kissed her on the forehead, stroked her hair and closed his eyes. Waiting. What torture.

Ishím Voróo (The Outer Lands), Lar Too (no man's land), near the border of the fflecx kingdom, 4370th division of unendingness (5198th solar cycle), summer.

Sinthoras headed for the nearest hill. About a mile away from where he stood, he could see a brightly colored wooden palisade fence. It was a strange sight in the midst of all the dry, pale grass that surrounded it. Those absurd colors on the tall timber posts might lead a wanderer to think they marked the territory of a friendly race: all it needed was lollipops on ribbons and candied fruit the way the barbarians liked them.

The appearance was deceptive.

The land behind the palisades belonged to the fflecx: the black gnomes known as alchemancers, whose skill in concocting poisons was only surpassed by their duplicity and malice.

All along the length of the fence he could see trapdoor openings, through which he assumed defenders could send out missiles. The main gate was painted in a shrieking shade of green. Sinthoras studied the inscription on it using his telescope.

"Say *friend* or *foe* and walk in—we're not fussy, we kill both," he read under his breath. This was the black humor the fflecx were known for. They followed the motto on their gates to the letter, but they were known to reward wit and imagination.

"Well then," he said to his nervous night-mare. The animal fixed its bloodred eyes on the palisade, its ears twitched. "Let's see if we can do business with them." He pressed his heels lightly against the stallion's flanks and moved swiftly off.

Sinthoras was supremely confident. Everything so far had gone according to plan, and he had left the rather naïve Caphalor waiting in Dsôn, so he had a head start. This way he could reach the mist-demon well before his arrogant rival and he could conduct negotiations on his own account. Then the campaign against the elves could be launched.

He had been prepared for almost anything to be asked of him, but not for the Inextinguishable Ones to express a desire to attack Tark Draan, not at this point: the opportunity had to be seized.

There had been plenty of attempts in the past to get round the dwarves' mountain barrier, but his people had always fallen foul of the rocks, with the mountain ridges claiming many deaths. The gods wanted to protect the mine maggots. Wherever the älfar tried constructing tunnels they collapsed, were filled up with molten rock or got flooded, or else their slaves and machines would be swept away in storms. The only option they were left with was tackling the Stone Gateway.

The land on the other side was another matter. Sinthoras had often captured and questioned merchants from Tark Draan. They were an effeminate people—the sort that would appeal to the elves who sat around all day playing on their harps, besotted with trees. Sinthoras had never been able to understand how these qualities led them to be admired all the more. They should be an easy people to conquer.

In his mind's eye he saw the new territories in Tark Draan his people would win; he saw the elf kingdoms vanquished and harps made out of the bones of their dead, their hair used for the strings.

"Cowards," he exclaimed in disgust. The elves had crawled under the skirts of those dwarf mine maggots—simple folk and arrogant wizards—because they were so terrified of his people. Soon, though, they would be eliminated.

At his ease, Sinthoras rode up to the colorful obstruction.

He had observed that some of the small trap doors were slightly ajar. He could hear shrill giggles: the fflecx were probably looking forward to seeing him ride through the main gate.

The entrance creaked open invitingly. Behind it was a straight road leading deeper into their kingdom. None of the gnomoids were visible, but he could hear them whispering together behind the fence. He found their squeaky voices contemptible.

Sinthoras brought his night-mare to a halt.

"Hear this," he called out in the language of the fflecx, "namely, that I say neither *friend* nor *foe*. And I'm not *walk*ing in, I'm *riding*." That should have got round their trick. He urged the stallion on.

The beast's hooves hit the earth with loud thuds, lightning flashes issuing where it trod. The night-mare snorted aggressively at the invisible danger. Step by step, they approached the opening until Sinthoras was level with the gate hinges and the stallion crossed the threshold.

There were still no fflecx to be seen; the gate was open wide and hid them from view.

"Halt!" came the command from the invisible guard.

Sinthoras reined in his night-mare. "Yes?"

"You did say friend and foe, after all." This sharp retort came from behind the gate on the right.

"And you may be riding, but your night-mare is walking in by the gate," this from an unseen know-it-all on the left.

"What do you want, black-eyes? It's been moonflights since we've seen one of your kind here," someone higher up the fence wanted to know.

"I want to ride through your kingdom and see what jokes I can collect from you," he responded. "The fflecx are famous for their jokes."

"Are you a writer?" one of them screeched.

"A liar, more like," yelled another over the laughter of his comrades. "You are a warrior, black-eyes, you won't be carrying that spear round with you just to toast your supper over the fire. You won't be boiling yourself up a fine little soup in that poncey armor of yours, and then slurping your broth out of your fancy helmet."

Sinthoras heard a few metallic clicks and the gates started to swing closed, narrowly missing his night-mare's tail as they slammed shut.

Midget fflecx were grinning at him all round the parapet walk. If he were standing, they wouldn't reach higher than his kneecap. They wore bright-colored leather armor, and their helmets had holes for their long, pointed ears to stick out. Their skin was black and covered in warts, making a contrast to the smooth armor. Their cunning eyes were set far forward on their ugly faces, which were slightly more refined than an óarco's; they were whistling and grinning at him, showing stumpy teeth.

"We respect your clever attempt to get round our motto," one of them called out, crossing his thin arms proudly over his chest. He carried a metal blowpipe at his belt, as did most of the others. A leather strap over his chest secured the darts that went with the blowpipe; the arrow tips were treated with poison and protected with glass caps to stop them drying out. "So we're not going to kill you." The yelling became unbearably loud. He raised his arm for silence. "But perhaps our wuzack will do it for us." An animal roar could be heard in the distance. The fflecx scuttled up to the top parapet walk. "Wuzack! Wuzack!" he began to chant, and his companions all joined in.

Sinthoras cursed inwardly—here was proof enough of how little these gnomoids were to be trusted. Unfortunately, the only road to his destination ran through their territory. He held tight to his spear and watched the woods on either side of the path.

Something massive was approaching. The trees shook as it came, sending their leaves fluttering to the ground.

A creature two paces tall and twice as broad as Sinthoras burst through the trees. In its right hand it held a thick branch, which it thrashed around. It looked like a huge naked fflecx and its claws and teeth dripped with a bright yellow substance.

"A wuzack," one of the fflecx called out, "is our king's invention. You are honored to be able to measure your strength against it. Its claws and teeth are poisoned; that should work on a black-eye like you." This announcement was greeted with more raucous laughter from the throng.

Sinthoras did not doubt that he would emerge the victor. He swore silently that he would kill each and every one of these fflecx afterward. He would have to do it quickly, however, if he were not to waste too much time. Caphalor would be pushing his night-mare to make up ground and get to the mist-demon ahead of him.

The wuzack ran at Sinthoras, swinging the improvised club wildly at his night-mare's neck.

Sinthoras pulled the stallion out of harm's way, stabbing at the monster as he did so.

The wuzack avoided the blow and its fist connected with Sinthoras' spear, jarring his arm and nearly dislodging it from his grip. Using the impetus from the clash he rolled backward off his night-mare and sprang to the ground, commanding the stallion to kick out at the wuzack.

The wuzack again swerved out of the way of the bucking night-mare and aimed a mighty swipe at its front legs with the branch.

Screaming with pain, the stallion reared up and snapped at the wuzack, sinking its teeth into the bony shoulder, crushing the joint.

The distraction won Sinthoras time to attack again and he lunged upward, both hands on the spear shaft: it pierced the creature's throat. The wuzack gurgled horribly and hit out once more.

Sinthoras launched himself into the air, activating the mechanism that split his weapon in two. The front end stayed in the creature's neck while the second section revealed a sharp, elongated blade. As Sinthoras came back down, he rammed it into the creature's eye so powerfully that the tip went straight through the skull and came out the other side.

The wuzack stood for a moment, then swayed and collapsed to one side on top of the injured night-mare.

When Sinthoras saw his wounded mount, hatred began to course through him. His trick had worked, but he would never have wished for the loyal and valuable animal to have such an end. Having pulled the two spear halves out of the wuzack, he turned slowly round to face the fflecx, his weapons dripping with the wuzack's life-juice. "I have passed the test," he whispered darkly. "Who will compensate me for my night-mare?"

The fflecx who had been speaking to him from the high walkway gave a contemptuous retort. "You should compensate us for the loss of the wuzack: the king trained it himself." Taking his blowpipe from his belt, he casually selected one of the long feathered darts. "The king will decide the compensation you owe." With that he inserted the dart into the pipe.

Sinthoras hurled a spear at the smug gnomoid; his blade pierced its ribcage, and the fflecx tipped forward with a screech, plunging from the walkway, forcing the spear completely through his torso as his body landed.

"Now take me to your ki—"

He was not able to finish the sentence. Tiny darts whizzed through the air from all sides. Most broke on his armor, but others sought out its narrow gaps and hit where he wore no protection.

Suddenly, he was very hot and his fingers and toes burned. His legs went numb and he staggered, losing his sense of balance. The world around him grew bright, the colors on the fflecx helmets and fences so strident now that it burned his eyes, and the single daystar had become ten dozen burning spheres falling, laughing, from the sky to dance around him.

Sinthoras tried to catch one of them. He picked up a blue one but it exploded in his hand, throwing him into the air.

Sinthoras flew and flew and flew . . .

Ishím Voróo (The Outer Lands), Lar Too (No man's land) near the frontier to the kingdom of the fflecx, 4370th division of unendingness (5198th solar cycle), summer.

Caphalor and Raleeha made camp for the night in a ravine, under an overhanging rock.

Caphalor studied the map and looked up at the path lying before them. In the distance, he could see the brightly colored fence that marked the fflecx frontier. He had also found hoofprints from Sinthoras' night-mare on the path. They had been fresh; he could only be half a day away, if that.

Raleeha was sitting by the fire that he'd made earlier. He'd hidden it in a niche in the rock so that the firelight would not betray them; in Lar Too, beasts were attracted by fire and Caphalor was largely relying on his instincts, his night-mare and his skill with weapons.

The girl was having trouble drinking the water he'd provided. He'd poured it in a hollow in a stone—her slave lips would not touch his drinking pouch—but he had not loosened the throttling slave collar at her throat. He considered for a moment, he knew that it was important she kept up her strength if he wanted her to be useful.

He stood up, went over and undid all three buckles, then threw down some rations. "Eat that," he ordered.

He sat down opposite Raleeha and waited until she had stilled her hunger. She did not resemble any of the unsophisticated barbarian women who worked his fields. Her hands were elegant and soft and her complexion as white as marble. He concluded she must be from a high social position in the Lotor family. Even now, with her robe torn and her hair untidy, she kept her upright posture.

"What can you tell me about your master?" he asked her. It was the first full sentence he had spoken to her since they had left the river.

The girl inclined her head. "I do not understand your question, noble lord."

"What does he like and what doesn't he like? I want to learn more about him."

She hesitated. "Are you pursuing him for some crime, noble lord?"

Caphalor shook his head, realizing too late that she would not be able to see that. "No," he said. It occurred to him to scold her for her uncalled-for question, but he thought better of it, it might be wiser to appear friendly; that way he would learn more. Anyway, she was not his property. "We were to travel together but he left without waiting for me. I'm trying to find out why he might have done such a thing." He knew only too well why Sintho-ras had gone ahead, but he did not want to tell her everything.

"I cannot tell you that, noble lord, for he does not take me into his confidence. Only when it is a question of painting, only then do I—" She broke off. "That is, I used to be allowed . . . until recently. Until the matter of the yellow."

"Yellow? You mean pirogand yellow?"

"Yes," she said, surprised.

"Then it is down to you that I was not able to bring my daughter a living baro—your master killed it for the yellow!"

Raleeha started to tremble. "Forgive me, noble lord," she whispered. "My negligence has caused distress on many counts." She shifted away from him.

Caphalor had stretched out his hand for a leather strap to chastise her with. He restrained himself again. "Samusin has a strange way of ensuring justice: I save a slave's life, and then learn she deserves death at my hands. You now carry a double debt of obligation to me," he said, barely restraining the anger in his voice. "Tell me about yourself: what is your importance to the Lotor family?"

"I am Farron Lotor's sister," she said reluctantly.

Caphalor drank some water. "So the beauty of an älf robbed you of your senses and made you give up your fine life as a princess."

"It was not such a fine life, noble lord," she answered. "I cannot tell you the reason I came under his spell: his appearance, the painting I saw him do, the realization that I was in the wrong place, the urge to be an artist myself, these all might have had something to do with it." She spoke with sudden fervor. "Whatever the reason was—I do not mind. I am happy with what I do, noble lord."

The älf raised his eyebrows. She could never be an artist, not measured against älfar standards, and only a human girl could be stupid enough to leave everything she had known to try. But he was not going to let her feel his surprise and the contempt it implied—he must find out more about his rival. "Who did Sinthoras meet with?"

"I don't understand—"

"His friends in Dsôn," he interrupted roughly. This was all taking far too long, he had never had to talk to any barbarian in this way to get the information he needed. "Did he ever mention names? Did you ever overhear conversations?"

"No."

"I can tell when I am being lied to, and I punish it with death as a rule. Do you want to die before we find your master?" he whispered coldly. Caphalor concentrated on his innate power. One of the älfar talents was their ability to heighten fear and now he could feel this power pulling inside him. He felt a sudden heat as it shot up his spine, sending out black streams of dread that spread like ink in a glass of water. They rolled forward languidly and soon reached Raleeha, entering her mouth and her ears, creeping in under her blindfold and seeping in through the pores of her skin, causing gooseflesh and making her shiver.

"Fear can kill, slave," he whispered ominously. "Fear obeys my will." He increased the power feeding the fear and she moaned, pressing her hand to her heart in pain. "Who are his friends?"

Names Caphalor knew well came tumbling out of Raleeha's mouth. It was good to know who was not on his side. "Describe your master to me," he demanded. "Tell me his strengths, his weaknesses." He withdrew the fear a little to encourage her.

She curled up, shivering with fright. "He is a good warrior and fights better with the spear than . . ." This was followed by praise of Sinthoras' fighting prowess. Caphalor did not interrupt the flow, but let his own thoughts range.

He wasn't fooled; Raleeha might well be able to hold information back, even though she was frightened to death. She would die for her master, right now if need be—anything other than betray him.

In spite of himself he registered respect for her steadfast nature. This had nothing to do with the obedience of a slave, it was to do with that deeper feeling that he and Enoïla shared: love—as simple as it was indestructible.

It surprised him to learn that humans were capable of it, particularly when it was an impossible love that would never be reciprocated. Caphalor could not think of a single älf who had ever had a dalliance with a human, and Sinthoras would be the very last one to contemplate touching a barbarian woman—except to punish her. Now he was curious. He interrupted her. "What do you think of Dsôn Faïmon? What do the barbarians say about us?" Caphalor removed the fear from her mind.

She stopped to think, breathed deeply and took her hand away from her chest. "My opinion of Dsôn Faïmon will be worth little. For me there could be no more beautiful or more fascinating place, noble lord. There are so many things that are unique to the älfar that would be impossible to achieve elsewhere if we applied human standards to it." She felt around for her rucksack, and finding it, took out a folder and notebook. "Here, I made lots of drawings before I lost my sight. Perhaps you would like to look at them, noble lord?" She passed him the folder.

Caphalor took the notebook from her. The slave girl had recorded her observations in charcoal and ink within its pages. The pictures were impressive: not as perfect as älfar sketches would have been, but perhaps noteworthy and far from primitive. "If you are a spy, these pictures would be invaluable for our enemies," he said quietly. "I would have to burn them."

Raleeha shot her hand out protectively, but then stopped. "If you must, noble lord. They are of no further use to me. I would never forgive myself if I were doing your enemies a favor."

Caphalor was about to cast the first of the pages into the flames—but found himself unable to complete the action. Instead he stowed the sketchbook in his saddlebags. "I'll keep them. I may need them."

She nodded in his direction, her expression reflecting her gratitude. "Noble lord, how old are you?"

Caphalor laughed out loud. "Remember your station, slave. It is not your place to ask questions."

"Forgive me, I . . . I find it fascinating how old some creatures can be without it being apparent," she explained. "Your voice, if I may say so, is melodious. I would have liked to see the features of the one who saved my life." He noted her sincere regret in the tone of her voice.

"That won't be possible," he said sharply, getting to his feet. She was getting above herself, and he had probably encouraged her. He tightened the buckles on the slave collar so that she might realize that the friendly interlude was over. "Lie down, we meet the fflecx in the morning."

Raleeha sank down next to the warmth of the campfire, covering herself with the horse blanket Caphalor had given her. "There's something I must tell you, noble lord, about Sinthoras."

"What is it?"

Caphalor turned to Sardaî, who was settled and still. The night-mare would warn them if anyone approached, but something about the stallion's stillness worried him. He watched the night mare, standing immobile with closed eyes, a perfect model for a statue. "Sardaî?"

The stallion did not move.

There was a rustle behind him. He whipped round to see the slave girl slump forward, a tiny arrow piercing her temple.

Fflecx! Caphalor jumped up, grabbed his bow and quiver, and ducked down behind a rock. He sent out black waves of magic to extinguish the flames.

The darkness enveloped him. He listened intently, letting his eyes were grow accustomed to the starlight.

He heard a low giggle, then a screech of laughter. Something clinked against the rock next to his ear and liquid sprayed against his neck. A dart had narrowly missed his neck.

Caphalor put an arrow to his bow and drew it. When he saw a silhouette the size of a child, he loosed two arrows in quick succession. The attacker was felled and loud shouts of dismay rang out from his companions. This enabled the älf to work out where the other fflecx were located and he dispatched a second as quickly as he had done the first.

This is all due to Sinthoras, he's set them on to me—why else would they leave their territory?

Caphalor reckoned he had about thirty fflecx to contend with. He would have to change his position—he'd be trapped if he remained behind this rock.

He reversed his journey and crept along past his night-mare. He heard a swift patter of footsteps coming from the bushes: a fflecx was trying to outrun him.

Caphalor's ability to move silently was his greatest advantage in the dark. Unobserved, he slipped into the thicket behind the fflecx and delivered a kick to the back of his neck. There was a crack and the gno-moid lay still. He had not even been able to shout a warning.

The älf followed tracks leading straight to a group of three fflecx hidden behind a rock; they had their blowpipes at the ready. Luckily for him they were aiming in the wrong direction.

Loosing a long arrow, he transfixed the ugly skulls of all three at once and they tumbled to the ground in a heap, anchored together. He grinned. How had they thought they could defeat him?

A sound so slight that only his älf ears could hear it warned him of an attacker approaching him from behind.

Caphalor spun and hurled a dagger. He heard his blade enter the fflecx and saw the small body fall. Swift as lightning, he had his second dagger in his hand and had turned up to the left, where more rustling had caught his attention. Another fflecx was staring down at him from a tree, his cheeks puffed out to send a dart.

The dagger hit home . . .

. . . and Caphalor felt a prick in the back of his right hand. He went numb all over; it was like being drenched in the icy water of a mountain waterfall. Even his thoughts began to freeze as a milky glaze covered his eyes.

Ishím Voróo (The Outer Lands), territory of the fflecx,
4370th division of unendingness (5198th solar cycle),
summer.

Sinthoras came to his senses but kept his eyes shut. He wanted to listen to what was happening around him.

He was lying on his back and the floor beneath him was cold. In the distance he could hear a rushing sound and the echoing voices of a large number of the fflecx. There was a draft playing round his face carrying the smell of damp, moss and iron.

What was that he could hear? Stringed instruments, strange melodies; it sounded odd and foreign to his ears, plonky and foolish, like children making a deliberate hash of their music practice.

He tried to work out what had happened to his body. Nothing felt particularly unusual. There were no pins and needles or anything indicating paralysis. He opened his eyes and looked around.

The floor was a brightly colored mosaic, which had been laid chaotically and contained mirrored stones. Some fflecx in full armor stood to one side, watching him with grins on their faces. The wall behind them was as bright as the floor.

The rushing sound came from artificial waterfalls cascading down from the ceiling and splashing into a wide moat that surrounded the mosaic floor.

When he turned his head in the other direction he saw Raleeha next to him, and next to her was Caphalor, sitting up and watching him. The look in his eyes promised death. He sat up, then realized their weapons and armor had been taken away.

"So, the black-eyes have awakened," said one of the fflecx in a mocking tone, to be met with delighted and raucous laughter from the rest of them.

Five paces in front of them sat a fflecx wearing a robe that would have suited a barbarian court jester: it displayed a wild mix of colors and patterns. On his black hair he wore a crown of yellow gold with little silver bells attached. His face was chubby and he had a clownish beard on his chin. The contrast between his bright clothing and his black skin was so strong that the clothes overwhelmed him.

He was sitting on a throne that had been fashioned in the shape of a hand, with the thumb and little finger forming the armrests and the other fingers standing upright to make the back. He was flanked by two ugly, scantily clad fflecx females, their buxom breasts nearly bursting out of the thin dress material. *This must be their king.* Sinthoras' disgust showed in his face.

"You are lucky," Caphalor said. "I thought at first it was your fault I'd been captured, but I can see you're no better off yourself."

"What is Raleeha doing here?" Sinthoras retorted. "Who gave you permission to take my slave?"

"You discourteous oafs," hissed the female on the left, spitting at them. "Hold your tongues and listen to what the great Munumon has to say."

The king crowed with laughter. "You tell 'em, Jufula. These black-eyes have no manners. First one kills my wonderful wuzack, then the other one shoots a bunch of my soldiers."

Sinthoras was keen to say more to Caphalor, but their mission for the Inextinguishables had priority: they had to get safely out of this interrogation and back on the northwest road. "They set the creature on me. I acted in self-defense, great Munumon," he responded, standing up. Caphalor also got to his feet.

"Who said you had to kill him? Have you any idea how long it takes to make a wuzack?" shrieked the king in a high voice. "Seven moon-courses. *Seven!* And that's not even counting the time you need for the serum."

Caphalor kept his counsel and waited; he glanced swiftly at Raleeha who was still lying on the floor. He was relieved to note she was still alive. He might have a use for Farron Lotor's sister.

Sinthoras understood what the fflecx king had been driving at. He gritted his teeth, "What recompense do you demand, great Munumon?"

His large eyes narrowed. "It's strange to find two black-eyes and a human wanting entry to my kingdom. Are you here to spy? What do your Incest Siblings have planned?" The other fflecx round the throne started to giggle. "The truth, now!"

"We are to bring you their greetings and ask about new poisons." Sinthoras could lie extremely convincingly. "Your reputation as alchemancers is well known, and—" He fell silent as Munumon raised his little arm.

"We haven't supplied the Incest Siblings and their breed since we stopped trading with them: nobody else gets to use our poisons and that's final," he announced, to applause from his two female companions. "If that's what you want you've had a wasted journey. Now, you've caused damage here—I therefore command the three of you to travel to the northeastern frontier, where you will find a gâlran zhadar sky fortress. They got my favorite crown and an important parchment from me with trickery, *you* will bring it back."

Sinthoras was struggling to stay calm; to be forced to be the fflecx king's henchman was intolerable, but he had no choice for the present. "How will I know these items?"

"For that," Munumon giggled, "you will have to ask the gâlran zhadar who rules the fortress. One more thing; when he has given you both those items you are to cut his head off and bring it back." He jumped up and struck an attitude, the little bells on his crown jingling away. "I want his head by the toe of my boot. If you bring me these three things, I will forgive you for killing the wuzack and my soldiers." Munumon threw up his arms and in response his courtiers howled their approval, screaming and clapping so loudly that it echoed from the walls and drowned out the noise of the fountains.

Sinthoras did not have the slightest intention of doing this royal idiot any favors. As soon as they had left the hall, their road lay northwest. Time was not on their side.

A soft moan came from Raleeha as she tried to sit up. She said nothing, listening.

Munumon skipped down the steps toward them. He had to throw back his head to look the älfar in the face and as he did so his crown slipped; he caught it before it fell. "I know what you are thinking, black-eyes," he said, hands on hips. He gave a nod and a dart flew from nowhere, burying itself in Sinthoras' throat. Where the poisoned tip touched him there was a burning sensation.

Caphalor got the same treatment. Only Raleeha was spared as she struggled to her feet. She felt around to get her bearings, grabbing Caphalor's arm to steady herself. He brushed her off and hissed at her to keep still.

Munumon rubbed his skinny hands with glee and stamped his right foot; the little bells on his crown jingled again. "It's a slow-working toxin. You'll both be dead within the moon-course. I'm sure I don't have to tell you that I'm the only one with the antidote." Giggling, he bit his own fist with excitement and hopped back up on to his throne. "Be off with you! Get going!" He shooed them off.

Waves of hatred rose in Sinthoras and he felt a hot spasm in his temple where the black lines of anger were starting to spread. These oafish, inferior beings all deserved to die. They painted their strongholds ridiculous, childish colors and their only function was to mix these infernal poisons. Why let such useless creatures live? The älfar would not even have to run a prolonged battle campaign, sacrificing their own troops: all it needed was to burn the warty freaks' whole kingdom down. The thought calmed him and he reined in the anger that was urging him to kill Munumon on the spot.

Glancing at Caphalor, he was pleased to see the anger lines on his face, too. At least in their fury they were united.

Munumon gave a shrill laugh and pointed at them both. "Look how upset I've made them, our terrifying älfar!" he chortled. "We've got the better of them now. Defeated by Munumon, ruler of the fflecx!"

His court fell about laughing, a further humiliation for Sinthoras. He was worried that Caphalor would not be able to keep his temper. "Do nothing," he whispered in the Dark Language. "I've a plan for making them pay for this as soon as we've completed our mission."

A piece of purple fruit came flying over and hit Raleeha on the breast. She cried out in shock. This was the overture to a veritable hail of leftovers raining down on the three of them.

Sinthoras took off his belt and fastened it around Raleeha's neck to lead her to the door. Caphalor strode at his side, trying to keep his dignity in the face of such insult. Even he was powerless against both the poison *and* an enemy outnumbering them a hundred to one.

As they left the hall, their armor and weapons were flung at their feet by two of the fflecx guards. "Here you are, black-eyes, here's your stuff," one of them scoffed. "Off you go, to the northeast. You'll have no problem finding what the gâlran zhadar has built."

While the älfar picked up their gear in silence, a dozen extra soldiers approached to march them out, the poisoned tips of their spears held threateningly in their direction.

When they had left the confines of the building, Sinthoras could see that it had been built into a stone hillock hewn roughly into the shape of a fflecx head. Its eyes stared toward the east, and the rock had been painted black and covered in green, blue, yellow and white fflecx signs. Wonky huts of various sizes plastered in loud, clashing colors encircled the hillock.

"This place is a nightmare," Caphalor muttered, moving over to a fountain to remove the dirt from his clothing. He scooped up some water and poured it over his head. He stayed like that for a short while. "Thank you," he said to Sinthoras.

"It was vital to stop you," Sinthoras said, washing his hands. Raleeha waited behind them, until they gave her permission to use the water. "We'd never have got out of there alive otherwise. Our mission is paramount."

"Our mission," Caphalor repeated with emphasis as he wiped the water from his refined features.

"You are angry because I left Dsôn before we had arranged. Let me explain." Sinthoras stepped away from the fountain and allowed Raleeha to wash. "It was a mistake."

"A *mistake?*"

"I think I must have misheard you when you told me the meeting time. I was at the rendezvous and there was no sign of you, so I set off; I thought you must have been trying to trick me." He smiled, hoping to appease the other älf. "Until I remembered what you had actually said."

Caphalor snorted. "Obviously you had no opportunity to stop and wait, or even to turn round and ride to meet me?"

"It was too much of a risk." Sinthoras examined his spear—the thin blades had bent slightly out of their true lines, but they had not broken off. The dwarves thought their weapons high quality, but älfar weapons were vastly superior to the kind of trash those mine maggots produced. "We might have missed each other." He ordered Raleeha to clean his armor. "Samusin has brought us together, but I still do not understand why you ran off with my slave girl."

"That's such a bad excuse that I'm embarrassed to know how stupid you must think me: you wanted to find the mist-demon before me," Caphalor retorted. "I am neither a thief nor a kidnapper. I found your slave girl following your tracks. She set out after you in secret—she wanted to put things right after her mistake with the pirogand yellow. She had lost her way and I took her with me."

"Is that right?" he asked the woman, astonished at what he had heard.

"Yes, master." She stopped drying her hands on her dress and bowed her head. "If your life had been in danger, I would have given mine instantly to save you."

It amused him to hear what she gone through to be near him. He was aware she was besotted with him; she thought of it as love rather than admiration or infatuation. He would never have thought her capable of completing such a dangerous long journey on foot. The girl had stamina, indeed.

"Will you look at that, Caphalor? My slave follows me into the wildest regions, far from home. And blind, at that!"

"And she'd have drowned in the marshes if it had not been for me," his rival added, savoring his victory. "You would have lost a brave and loyal slave if I hadn't saved her."

Raleeha thanked him with a bow in his direction.

"So awfully gracious of you," Sinthoras said, looking ahead now. "It would not have been any real loss. Did you enjoy her? Was she suitably grateful?" He leaned back taking his weight on his spear, keen to see how his traveling companion would react.

"She is a human and nothing but a slave. Moreover, she is *your* slave: two insuperable barriers to my ever being tempted to touch her, let alone take her to my bed."

Sinthoras gave a mild smile. "I know some of your Constellation friends are not above taking up with their slaves . . ."

"This discussion has nothing to do with our mission, Sinthoras," came the reprimand.

The provocation continued: "I understood it was the Constellations' custom to consort with inferiors—probably because they are too weak to get themselves an älf-woman."

Caphalor was not prepared to give a response, thereby giving Sinthoras satisfaction. Instead he asked, "What did you mean about making Munumon pay?"

"You'll see, as soon as we are on our way back." Sinthoras saw two fflecx leading a night-mare along the road. They were guiding it using two long, hooked poles attached to its harness, keeping a safe distance from the stallion's vicious teeth. "What a fine creature," he said. "I've never seen such a splendid specimen, no wonder you were able to catch me up so quickly! Where did you get it?"

"A friend of mine, now dead. It was a gift." Caphalor did not go into detail, but he was relieved to see it again, having secretly feared the fflecx would have killed the animal. "Where is yours?"

"Killed when I fought the wuzack." Sinthoras assembled his spear, fixing the two halves firmly together.

"Then you'll have to walk," Caphalor decided, a certain satisfaction audible in his tone. "Sardaî would never accept an extra älf rider."

The fflecx released the animal, which trotted up to its master whinnying with joy.

Caphalor held the muzzle and stroked the stallion's powerful neck, where he could see several bloodied abrasions. The fflecx must have had their work cut out controlling it.

"Hey, you lot!" Sinthoras shouted at the fflecx. "Get me a horse, Munumon's orders." He pointed to the night-mare. "As big as this, if you've get anything that size in your kingdom."

The fflecx gave him a startled look and hurried off.

"Is that a yes or a no?" wondered Caphalor aloud, adjusting saddle bags, bow and arrows, before swinging himself up onto the night-mare's back.

Raleeha handed Sinthoras his clean, but still damp, armor. "I expect they'll give me a horse so I can get to the gâlran zhadar quicker than I would walking. That little swine on the throne won't want us dying from the poison before we get there."

Caphalor ran his fingers over the place where the arrow poisoned with the lethal scrum had hit him, aware now that his own immortality had been set limits. But he was not prepared to dwell on that. Indicating Raleeha, he asked, "Will she know what a gâlran zhadar is?"

"She doesn't have to—she won't be able to see him, will she?" Sinthoras put the armor over his head and tugged the straps to ensure it fitted snugly. Then he checked his own bags. The fflecx seemed to have given them both everything they would need for the trip.

To his surprise, Caphalor began to explain the gâlran zhadar to Raleeha. "They look like groundlings," Caphalor told Raleeha, "but they are very different. The groundlings grub about under the earth, whereas a gâlran zhadar will build his stronghold at giddy heights. They are good at magic and are excellent fighters with a tendency to take things that don't belong to them: they call it 'collecting.' Not much other than that is really known about them. There's only said to be a handful of them in Ishím Voróo and I've never encountered one."

"Thank you, noble lord," she said, her head bowed.

"They keep slaves like we do," Sinthoras added, getting to his feet, "and they collect just about everything that takes their fancy. Perhaps this one will take a liking to you, Raleeha."

"Or to you," snapped Caphalor from the saddle. He pointed down the road. "Here comes your mount."

Sinthoras turned and saw what they were bringing him: a beast that was an eccentric mix of donkey and bull. Four pitiful horns stood out at odd angles and its light-brown coat sported isolated clumps of hair. The back was long enough to take both him and Raleeha. "I will never ride that thing," he whispered, shaking with anger, seeing himself made fun of again.

Caphalor sat upright in his saddle, one hand on his hip, and intoned smugly, "But for the sake of our mission . . ."

Chapter V

Ocizür was home to the craftsmen; they shared their knowledge with each other harmoniously. They founded schools and universities to enable them to perfect their skills.

Riphâlgis was the area where the artists lived, they too merged their various forms of creativity and invented a new one. Death was their main fascination and so they chose, where possible, to work with materials provided by the end of life.

Epocrypha of the Creating Spirit,
1st Book,
Footnote

*Ishím Voróo (The Outer Lands), the kingdom of the fflecx,
4370th division of unendingness (5198th solar cycle),
summer.*

They sat in a cave protected by a grove of thick-trunked targo trees, forced to rest during a period of inclement weather. Caphalor watched Raleeha trying, despite her blindness, to make notes for herself. She was doing this quite cleverly—scraping marks onto paper with a pointed stone and checking with her fingertips to see if she could read the words she had formed.

Sinthoras was on guard at the mouth of the cave, eating some of his provisions; he had left his mount out in the rain, while Sardaî munched on a rabbit toward the back of the shelter. It was obvious from the splintering and cracking that the night-mare was enjoying devouring the creature. The cold air of the cave carried the smell of blood.

"You have found a way to manage, then?" Caphalor observed.

"I lost my eyesight. I didn't lose my mind, noble sir," she said crisply. She blushed, realizing how arrogant that had sounded, and stammered an apology.

The more Caphalor learned about Raleeha, the more she fascinated him. She did not sit lamenting her fate or complaining to her master, who had said she was surplus to requirements. She had an open and intelligent mind and a pleasing nature for a barbarian—and she was wasted on an älf like Sinthoras. A slave like that was very valuable, particularly coming from the Lotor family. It was true, blinding her *had* reduced her value to some extent, but she was still worth more than any other human slave. Then there were her feelings for her master: she loved him to the point of self-sacrifice. It was unconditional love.

Caphalor decided to try to win her trust: loyalty was more important than obedience and this situation demanded strategic thinking. It was quite possible that Raleeha might suddenly find herself in line for the barbarian throne and at the head of a 100,000-strong army: a force of that size would come in extremely useful. He wanted her to remember him later, and in a good way.

"Perhaps you should try drawing like that."

Raleeha kept on practicing her letters. "It won't be aesthetically pleasing: any drawings I made would be ugly distortions, and I don't want that. I'll stick to words, noble lord."

Caphalor was deep in thought. He was still assuming that they would complete their missions successfully: the errand set by Munumon *and* the main assignment for the Inextinguishables, but what if they were to die from the poison before they completed their tasks? "Tell me, Raleeha. What would you do for your master?"

"Anything, noble lord," was the swift response.

"Would you be prepared, for example, to take on an obligation to help save the lives of thousands of älfar?"

Raleeha raised her head as if she could see him. He could read the surprise on her features. "I am waiting, noble lord."

He was not sure how far he should go. "The moment has not yet come," he said, after a little more thought. "But if it looked as if Sinthoras and I were not going to be able to return to Dsôn Faïmon alive, it may be up to you to complete our mission."

She stood up and made a deep bow. "That would be the greatest honor I could think of, noble lord. I am glad that you place your trust—"

"In a blind woman?" Sinthoras, called out in disbelief from the cave entrance. "Caphalor, get yourself a slave of your own if you want to hatch plans. Leave mine alone, understand? It's stopped raining. We should get underway."

Raleeha jerked back in shock, as if she'd been caught doing something wrong.

"Unlike you, I am trying to think about how we could save our mission if we fail," Caphalor retorted, unmoved by the other's harsh criticism.

"We are not going to fail," said Sinthoras in a superior tone. "Or rather, I shan't fail. Giving any guarantee for you would be like putting a hand into an óarco's mouth and hoping it wouldn't bite." He chewed slowly on a strip of dried meat. "She is only a slave, and she's blind. She could never take on our mission. If it weren't for us she'd be dead in a ditch or chopped up and fed to the óarcos as stew. Don't go putting some idea into her head that she could ever prove useful."

For once, Caphalor was pleased that Sinthoras was behaving so arrogantly: it would make him appear nicer in comparison. Even if his rival were not wrong in principle, they could not discount anything on this mission; the fflecx poison could have killed them instantly if that had been Munumon's intention. "I see it differently," he replied roughly.

"The only reason she is still alive," countered Sinthoras, "is that she is a Lotor and her brother is gathering the barbarians into a large army. Otherwise I'd have had her head off her shoulders in a flash after what she's done. Think about it—her running away from Dsôn, any other slave would be put to death for even mentioning the idea."

Caphalor saw Raleeha pale in dismay.

"What's with your great plan for destroying the fflecx kingdom?" he asked sarcastically. He felt like provoking his arrogant rival. "What part do I play?"

"None at all," came the contemptuous reply. "I don't need your help. My plan will remain a secret, or you might try to take the credit."

Caphalor gave a pitying laugh.

Sinthoras suddenly whirled round and grabbed his spear; then he stepped further back into the cave and laid a finger on his lips. "Keep quiet," he whispered.

Caphalor tightened his bowstring and hurried over to Sinthoras, quiver in hand.

He could hear and smell what was approaching: trolls, a whole band of them marching through the woods. There must've been a good dozen of them; the forest floor was shaking under their weight and the targo tree branches were swaying wildly. What these hirsute beasts lacked in intelligence they made up for in size and brute strength.

Caphalor grasped what they were saying because they spoke in short phrases. They were incapable of complex sentence structures.

"Gold," roared one of them. "Want gold."

"Meat better," called another. "But not tough. Want tender meat again. Naked girl meat."

"Right. Girl flesh. Hope he has naked girl," shouted the first one excitedly.

Naked girls were barbarians. That was what the trolls called them because, compared with themselves, barbarians had so little hair. Caphalor could not place their dialect. They certainly were not eastern Ishím Voróo trolls, and they were too far away to see.

"It be fine," yelled another of the trolls. "We get in strong castle. She say we do."

"Yes," shouted someone rowdily. "Yes, we go. Nobody do this. Only us. We break him open. We pull arms and legs off. Like beetle. We eat him."

General merriment ensued. "Break fortress," they screamed. "All silly turrets. All fall down." This caught the attention of the two älfar.

Sinthoras was the first to set off after them.

"Wait here in the cave for us," Caphalor told Raleeha. "Never fear, they are too big to get through the entrance." With that, he left in pursuit of Sinthoras.

He was already out of sight, employing his gift of silent movement as he made his way through the undergrowth to creep up on the trolls. Only the slight swaying of the foliage as he passed would have given him away.

Caphalor chose to move through the forest at treetop level.

He swiftly fastened the strap of his bow round him and climbed the nearest tree to leap to the next one, alighting for a second before launching himself into the air once more. In this way he was able to cover a great distance surprisingly swiftly. The trick was to make sure his bow did not snag on a branch; a fall would be dangerous and would make him look ridiculous, even if no one were watching.

Caphalor soon caught sight of a troll's white-furred back. This one was wearing a loin guard studded with protective iron plates and his legs were wound round with rope, presumably to guard against knife slashes. His weapon was a coarsely fashioned long-handled club, stuck with seven lengthy spikes at the business end.

Caphalor was surprised by the troll's size; not more than four paces tall, but much more muscular than trolls he had seen, fought and defeated in the past. These must have originated elsewhere in Lar Too. Perhaps they were on a scouting expedition? Or a ritual journey?

"Hey! Slow down!" one troll shouted angrily. "Can't do so fast."

He received a stone thrown at his head in answer.

"Shut up." The command sounded suddenly from between the trees. "Gålran zhadar not deaf."

"Good. Got it," the white-furred troll called back.

Caphalor could only shake his head. Stupidity and ugliness everywhere you looked—that was Ishím Voróo all over.

He darted above the troll's head without being noticed and overtook a heavily laden gang of younger trolls trotting through the woods, giving no thought to military discipline, relying solely on their strength.

Caphalor settled himself on a branch ahead of them to watch their approach.

They were huge, ragged-coated creatures that Caphalor supposed would scare any normal opponent away. They had weird yellow eyes and repulsive gaping muzzles set into vulgar faces. Their broad cheekbones, thick lips and long, prominent teeth were obscured with thick beards, filthy with bits of food and twigs.

The smell of them turned Caphalor's stomach.

The troll at the front of the gang was their leader and, unlike the others, he was wearing full armor; it was rusty and looked as if it had been cobbled together from various different suits—perhaps those of defeated enemies. Of course, there was no hint of any armor that might have belonged to an älf.

Caphalor heard a whistle coming from the right. Sinthoras had hidden amongst the ferns and was alerting him to his presence. He did not have to be afraid of being noticed, as the lesser beings like óarcos and similar were not able to register such high tones.

"Fujock," the leader called out, and up trotted a troll, panting. Caphalor noticed a harness on the other troll's back, attached to something square covered by dirty blanket. It looked heavy.

"Put heavy on floor. Run to end of forest. Say me where tower."

The troll groaned as he slid the straps of the harness off his shoulders. There was a crash as the object landed on the ground. The cover slipped off and Caphalor saw the metal bars of a cage.

"Stinking idiot face!" the leader swore at him. "Not bang. You break! Need Thing to get in tower. Tell you before."

"Stinking idiot face," echoed another of the gang, picking up a branch and chucking it at the clumsy troll.

The unpopular one complained under his breath while the others put down their baggage and gathered round their leader. Quietly—at least it was quiet for a bunch of trolls—they chatted about how best to approach the tower.

"Idiots, all of you!" The leader took over. "Easy get in to tower. Thing tell us where door is. Big secret door. Nobody know we come."

Caphalor could not imagine a secret entrance large enough for a gang of grown trolls, nor could he imagine why this "Thing" should want to tell them how to get round the gâlran zhadar defenses—unless it was a trap for the trolls.

One way or the other, he did not like the sound of what they were up to. The tower forces would certainly notice a rampaging horde of trolls and would be on high alert, making their own mission much more difficult to execute. The trolls had to be stopped, he and Sinthoras could find out what the Thing was after that. He climbed up to the top of the tree, peered toward the northeast—and saw the sky fortress.

It was a cloud-eater of a construction. There were six towers each with a diameter of at least fifty paces. They rose steeply skywards, tapering toward the top. An arrow shot vertically would never reach as high. The tops of the two towers on the left were veiled in cloud, so it was unclear exactly how tall they were, perhaps even higher than the visible ones.

Connecting staircases and intricate tubes ran between the towers in the topmost third of the fortress's height. At first sight it looked chaotic, but a moment's reflection showed Caphalor it was merely an aesthetic that he was not used to. He could see the attraction: it was almost as if the gods had planted these towers in the earth. He had never seen anything like it, no matter how wonderful the buildings created by Dsôn's best architects. He was eager to view it from closer up.

How do they manage to construct something like that? He thought, *and how long would it take to build?*

A high whistle interrupted his examination of the fortress: Sinthoras was calling him.

He climbed back down onto his branch, arriving back on his observation perch just as the scouting troll returned to make his report. Caphalor whistled a signal to his hidden colleague that he should prepare for an attack. He notched an arrow to his bow.

Aiming for the leader's right eye he let fly, already grabbing and shooting the next arrow even as the first was underway. No more than three heartbeats lay between the two shots; he knew that no other älf would be able to outshoot him in speed and in accuracy, and certainly not a human.

The first arrow pierced the leader's eye; the second hit its fellow through the pupil. At such a short distance the missiles lost none of their momentum and they passed through the entire skull. The leader collapsed, falling against two other trolls, his right leg jerking uncontrollably.

The gang of trolls roared in unison and jumped to arm themselves, ducking down and looking around frantically for the assassin.

You are too stupid to notice that you are already dead. Before his hiding place could be located, Caphalor shot the next troll twice through the throat; then another fell to a shot in the back of the neck, while a fourth staggered and collapsed with two arrows through the heart. He put number five out of action with an arrow straight into its gaping mouth.

The brutes still had no idea what was happening.

Caphalor was looking forward to finishing off the whole gang at his ease from his elevated position. It was a shame he would not be able to use their blood or collect the skeletons to take home: he could have made a wonderful instrument from all these bones, perhaps he could take a shinbone back as a souvenir for Tarlesa's collection.

But he had not reckoned with Sinthoras' reaction. Caphalor didn't know whether it was his attention-seeking nature, envy or his need to fight—at any rate, Sinthoras darted from his hiding place to attack the remaining five trolls with his spear.

Sinthoras slit a troll's throat while still in midleap; the brute was too late to ward off his attack. It fell coughing and choking, spraying light gray blood from the gaping wound.

Two of the last four trolls were facing away from him and therefore still harmless, so he dealt with the two charging toward him, their teeth bared.

Sliding between the open legs of the nearest troll, Sinthoras jammed his spear into the ground to trip his victim up and then pivoted round, using his own weapon as a fulcrum, avoiding the angry blows of the next assailant. The impact of the trolls' clubs left a deep indentation in the ground, throwing up soil and dirt all over him.

This was how he liked it! Why should Caphalor have all the fun? Anyway, he was keen to find out what was in the cage before Caphalor did.

"You want pain? Try this!" he called. He pulled out a long, thin blade and pushed it under one of the trolls' leather aprons, slicing from right to left. The troll let out a shrill, high scream, dropped its weapon and grabbed its genitals in both hands; blood came pouring down its thighs as it collapsed to the ground.

On his feet again now, Sinthoras sprang onto the back of the troll he had just felled, plunging his knife into the broad neck. The brute's massive body slackened. Sinthoras dragged his knife out of the troll's neck, waving it round above his head to produce a whirring sound, then he grabbed the end of the spear, activated the blade contained within, and thrust it violently forward to stab through the neck of another assailant.

Sinthoras vaulted off the troll's back and flipped the spear closed again, so he had a short spear in his hand by the time he landed. One supremely agile turn later and he was facing his final foe: the troll that had been carrying the cage—the one they had called Idiot Face.

Yellow eyes swiveled right and left, taking in the sight of the dead bodies, then the troll gave a strangled moan. It took a step back and brandished its weapon in the älf's direction, hoping to hold him off.

Sinthoras' laugh was full of malice. He used his native talent to intensify the troll's fear. Black webs shot out toward the frightened troll who breathed them in, making its face grow pale.

"Is our poor ugly troll all by his little self all of a sudden?" Sinthoras mocked sweetly, feinting with his short spear. "Come and try to get me, Idiot Face. That's what they called you, wasn't it?"

The creature turned and ran off. Sinthoras was setting out in hot pursuit when an arrow whizzed past, hitting the troll centrally in the back of its head. A second shot entered his neck and a third, going through the back, pierced the brute's heart. Gasping for air, it staggered into the thicket and lay motionless.

* * *

Caphalor jumped down and approached the cage. Nothing moved inside it. *Perhaps the prisoner is waiting to see the outcome?* He thought: an enemy of the trolls was not necessarily the prisoner's friend.

With considerable effort, Sinthoras wrenched the front section of his spear out of his last victim's flesh, wiped it clean on the creature's fur and put the weapon back together. "You stole my last one," he said reproachfully.

"It didn't look as if you wanted to kill him, I thought you were just racing to get to the cage before I did."

"Is that what you thought?" Sinthoras moved the cage cover with the tip of his spear, cursing loudly at what he saw. There was a similar expression of disgust on Caphalor's features; he placed an arrow to his bowstring, ready to shoot.

They were looking down at a very slender young female, her clothes in shreds. Pointed ears, cut to shape and not the girl's own, stood up through the short brown hair. Her face—thin and with scars on the cheekbones—was an unnatural, crooked shape.

Caphalor knew what it was they had found: an obboona.

The scars were from a brutal procedure she would have undergone in order to make her face narrower: her flesh would have been cut into, the cheekbones fractured and some of the broken splinters of bone removed.

The obboona's big eyes stared at them both. She had tried to dye her eyeballs black, but the pupils were still visible; the disguise was not perfect. However clever her people were in this, they had never managed to copy älfar eyes.

"Samusin has sent us a flesh-stealer," Sinthoras spat. "I say let's show her what it's like to be flayed alive."

"I say let her live." Caphalor lowered his bow. "She knows how to get into the sky fortress."

"That's only what the trolls said. Who knows if it's true?"

"You want to go to the sky fortress?" The obboona slid to the front of her cage. "It will be an honor to show two demigods the way in."

Her voice did not sound natural, either. Caphalor saw a scar on her throat and a slight lump below it. Something had been inserted to press on the vocal chords, changing the way she spoke with the intention of making it more älf-like. But no one could ever really attain the wonderful tonal range—melodious yet dangerous—that Inàste had given his people.

"Your voice is an insult for our ears," he yelled at her.

"Forgive me," she responded humbly, cowering down.

"Who says we need her knowledge at all?" objected Sinthoras. "She'll just be a burden." He raised his spear to jab at her.

"I used to be in service with the gålran zhadar who owns the tower," she said quickly. "I know all the towers, every corridor, and the secret gate I used when I escaped—and then I ran straight into these trolls." She smiled, showing immaculate, brilliant-white teeth. "What have you come for? Do you want his life or his treasures? His hoard is so big that he's having to get a new tower built."

Caphalor gestured to Sinthoras to come over and they turned away from the cage. "We should ask her to show us."

Sinthoras shook his head, blond hair swinging. "Too risky. She could be leading us into a trap, she'll want to kill us and take our skin."

"I've seen the sky fortress, Sinthoras, we won't ever get in without her knowledge of it."

"When did you see it?"

"Just now, from the top of that tree."

Sinthoras was thoughtful. "How far away is it?"

"A couple of miles . . ."

"So from two miles off you can tell we don't have a chance on our own? Wish I had your eyes, älf. But I wouldn't wish for your faint heart." Sinthoras raised his eyebrows contemptuously. "I'll take a closer look at this sky fortress and then decide what to do with the flesh-stealer woman." As far as he was concerned the matter was closed. He left Caphalor and went over to the cage, rattling his spear tip along the bars before heading into the undergrowth.

Caphalor turned to watch him. "I should kill him now," he murmured. "It would be better than having to fight him every inch of the way." He followed, sighing, and put the cover back on the cage, ignoring the obboona's cries. If he had not overheard the trolls talking, he would certainly have avenged her people's vicious mutilations of his own kind. As it was, she might yet prove useful.

Caphalor entered the cave, finding Sinthoras already sitting beside the fire: his friendly way of indicating that he did not want to do guard duty. Caphalor stayed by the entrance, leaning against the rock wall, keeping his eyes on the surrounding area.

Raleeha approached him, bringing the drinking flask he had left behind. "Could you tell me what happened, noble lord?" she asked.

"Did your master not say?"

She shook her head.

He quickly summed up the events.

"Flesh-stealers," repeated Raleeha with a shudder. "That sounds horrible. Why are the obboona given that name?"

"They have only one aim in life—to be like the älfar," he explained, after taking a long draft from his flask. "They were once a vassal folk of ours and they worshipped us as demigods. They started mutilating their own bodies to make them more like ours, but this obsession led them to act in ways that made them our sworn enemies forever: they started to hunt älfar down. They conducted disgusting surgical experiments, taking the captured älfar's body parts, or cutting off whole limbs in order to transplant them onto their own bodies."

Raleeha's jaw dropped open and she shuddered with revulsion. "By Samusin!"

"Others would take facial features, dry them out and then stick them on themselves," Caphalor went on. "They would fix our ears on top of their own, or drape älfar hair over their scalps. The Inextinguishables waged a short, sharp war against them, driving the obboonas north—I would never have thought I would come across one here."

"These . . . limb and organ transfers," she asked, "did they actually work?"

"No. That's what makes this revolting practice even more horrific. They were killing their idols, their demigods, for no reason: they knew perfectly well they could never make themselves like us, not even in part." In fact, Caphalor had no idea whether those experiments had ever been successful, but he was not prepared to tell the Raleeha this. "Now return to your master."

"Of course, noble lord." Raleeha bowed and walked slowly over to Sinthoras, who had been watching her.

But, shortly before she reached him, Sinthoras jumped up, grabbed the girl by the collar and dragged her back out of the cave, flinging her down at Caphalor's feet.

"Here!" he fumed. "Take her, if you like her so much."

"Master!" she breathed in dismay. Sinthoras kicked her in the ribs.

"Keep your mouth shut! As I said, Caphalor, she's yours now." He glared at his rival.

"Why would I want her?" Caphalor said, taken by surprise.

Sinthoras pulled out his dagger, grasping her hair with his other hand. "Then it's best if I kill her, then she can't betray us . . ."

"All right." Caphalor gave a nod. "I'll take her before you kill a slave belonging to the Lotor family. She may well prove useful to us."

"Useful? Nonsense! We don't need any help to defeat barbarians in battle!" Addressing Raleeha, he said, "Serve him better than you have served me. You've already lost your eyes, don't risk losing anything else." Sinthoras cut his symbol out of the leather collar and scratched Caphalor's mark in the bare skin underneath. The slave girl inhaled sharply as the blade drew down her neck, but only put up her hand to stem the blood when he had finished. As he moved back to the fireside, he sneered: "You belong to him now."

Raleeha knelt at Caphalor's feet, sobbing quietly. He knew it was not the pain that was making her cry, but the loss of her master—the älf whose slave she had volunteered to be, and for whom she had gone into voluntary exile from her homeland.

"Get up," he said gently, much too gently for an order to a slave. He repeated the command roughly. "Up with you!" Raleeha obeyed.

It was fascinating to observe her tears oozing out from under the black lace blindfold. She had an älf-like look about her in the warm light of the flames. She was undeniably attractive, but it was the mixture of pain and melancholy in her face that was really capturing his attention.

Caphalor drank in the sight of her distress, wanting to hold the moment fast as he did not have the requisite talent to capture it in paint: his main gift was for carving in bone. "Lie down. You can take Sardaî's blanket if you are cold."

She bent her head. "Of course, noble ... I mean, master." Raleeha was turning aside when his hand came forward to undo the three buckles on her collar. She stood still in surprise.

"Don't forget to eat," he said firmly. "Make sure you eat and drink. Tomorrow you will wait here for us while Sinthoras and I take the obboona to investigate the sky fortress."

"That's if the obboona is still alive by then," was the comment from Sinthoras, his back turned. "The carrion-eaters will be finishing off the troll cadavers tonight. The obboona's cage had better be sturdy."

As if prompted by his words they heard a shrill cry of terror from the prisoner, then the roar of an animal, and the squawks of a flock of vultures. The obboona was not going to have a restful night. Caphalor had not an ounce of pity for her.

Ishím Voróo (The Outer Lands), the kingdom of the fflecx,
4370th division of unendingness (5198th solar cycle),
summer.

Dawn arrived swathed in mist, allowing the älfar to get up close to the sky fortress without being seen.

They ran from tower to tower, examining the masonry. Sinthoras saw that stone block fitted neatly into stone block with almost invisible joins and no use of mortar. The whole structure derived its stability from the sheer weight of the enormous edifice.

Using the hilts of their daggers, they tapped carefully against the base here and there, hoping for a different tone denoting a hollow area. But in vain. Caphalor even dug away at the grass at the foot of one of the towers to see how far down the foundations went, but had to give up— the stone blocks had to go ten paces or more.

The sun rose higher in the sky as the älfar investigated, melting away the morning fog. Sinthoras looked up to the tops of the cloud-hung towers and noted huge metal rings fixed to the walls at the height of the connecting corridors and stairways. Steel cables as thick as an arm were attached to the rings.

He assumed this must be to prevent the towers from swaying in a strong wind and he could not help admiring the engineering expertise. "It's amazing," he said. If only he could put up a building like this—only smaller, of course—in Dsôn! Caphalor would never be able to afford anything like that.

"Perhaps we should take this gâlran zhadar prisoner rather than chopping his head off," Caphalor mocked sarcastically. "I'm sure he'd be able to run you up a pretty little house like this in Dsôn."

"Why not? We could use a building genius like him. Why should he die for the sake of an old crown and a bit of parchment? I'm sure I can persuade those fflecxy freaks to let me have him as long as I bring them enough fancy sparkly stuff from his treasure chests."

"There's one thing you're forgetting, Sinthoras." Caphalor laid a hand against the wall. "How are we going to get inside without the help of the obboona? Do we climb up a vertical wall hundreds of paces high with no toe- or handholds to be seen? I could manage twenty paces perhaps, but this? Not my thing."

Sinthoras looked at the blank walls. He hated admitting that he too could see no way in, but there were not even any windows in the towers.

"I wonder what's so special about that crown for this gâlran zhadar to have bothered to steal it in the first place," Caphalor muttered. "And what's in the parchment?"

"Who cares?" retorted Sinthoras. "Munumon could have demanded a pink pony and a harp with the strings missing."

"I don't think it's as simple as that," objected Caphalor.

"He's got us between a rock and a hard place. Or do you hold the antidote to the toxin that's in our blood?"

"If the parchment and the crown, for example, held the key to successful invasion of Dsôn, and we were able to discover this before we took the items to Munumon—would you still say that?"

Sinthoras sighed with irritation. "You're not making any logical sense."

"But I'd like to know the significance of the crown and the parchment."

"Then I suggest we ask this gålran zhadar. That should set your mind at rest—and you can stop pestering me with your stupid questions," Sinthoras snapped. He was being careful not to lose his temper entirely, or risk giving them away, but his anger at Caphalor was always there in the background. He despised Caphalor for his weak Constellation beliefs that were typical of the whole Constellation faction. Cowards, the lot of them. Honestly, who hid in a tree to shoot their enemies instead of fighting properly, toe to toe?

It was Caphalor's fault that he had given Raleeha away. He had been infuriated that she was asking the älf so many questions and it had been stupid of him, but he could not take her back now without losing face. On the other hand, Caphalor was not going to make it back to Dsôn alive, so it was not worth worrying about; he really ought to stop dwelling on it.

"Yes, let's ask the gålran zhadar," agreed Caphalor, sounding for all the world as if he were serious.

Sinthoras found him exasperating. Why could he not have had one of his own Comets with him on this mission? They would have reached the mist-demon and negotiated an alliance by now.

Suddenly, they heard a deep throbbing hum as if something heavy were starting to move. The tone slowly grew higher and higher.

As he placed a hand on the wall of the tower, Sinthoras noticed a vibration; *something must be in motion inside the building.* "Is there a winch in there?" he asked. He took a careful look around and sniffed the air, but could not detect any unusual smell that might indicate the use of fuel.

"Look! Up there!" Caphalor had moved a few paces to the side and was squinting upward, shielding his eyes.

One of the pieces of tubing had loosened itself from the network and was being lowered to the ground on five cables. At one end there was a wooden gate—had they been spotted? Was the gålran zhadar sending down warriors to intercept them?

The tube came closer through the swirling mist.

"We need to get out of here," said Sinthoras, turning. Then he stopped. "Or do you think that might be how we get in to the castle? We could climb on top of the tubing and get pulled up with it. Then we wouldn't need to use the obboona."

"No," replied Caphalor. Now the tube section had come down lower they could see there were spyholes in the side of it, and faces at each of them. There was no chance for them to stowaway.

The tube settled onto the ground and the gate opened, letting a wagon with ten armed men roll out and move north.

The älfar watched from a safe distance as the gate was closed and the tube was hauled up again.

Sinthoras ground his teeth. It was clear they would have to employ the services of the flesh-stealer after all, instead of going ahead and killing her. He had been looking forward to torturing her.

He knew what he would do: he would hang her up by the heels, hooking into the tendons. Then he would make a cut and peel off her skin like a garment she had no right to wear. Then he would beat her raw flesh with a switch and destroy the blood vessels, letting her bleed to death in agony. The life-juices would clot instead of being used on a canvas. All of her blood would seep away, decay, disappear completely.

Sinthoras gave a satisfied smile. Yes, that was exactly what the flesh-stealer deserved. As soon as she had served her purpose.

Chapter VI

Shiimal was the region attracting älfar who specialized in agriculture and animal husbandry. Farms of enormous proportions were started up, producing meat and grain for the entire realm in the one radial arm.

    Kashagòn is the home of the true warriors! Älf-men and älf-women dedicated to the art of battle came here and founded academies where the hardiest soldiers, the best and most deadly combatants of all were trained.

Epocrypha of the Creating Spirit

1st book

Footnote

Ishím Voróo (The Outer Lands), the kingdom of the fflecx, 4370th division of unendingness (5198th solar cycle), summer.

Caphalor ran behind Sinthoras, still trying to assess their chances of getting into the sky fortress. There was no quick way of taking such a stronghold and there would certainly be hefty defense equipment in place to deal with any attempt to storm the towers. It was a supreme work of construction from both the aesthetic and military points of view.

He thought about the simpleminded beasts they had slaughtered in the forest. "And the trolls really thought they could break in and steal the treasure," he said.

"Does that surprise you? However stupid the obboona is, she must've had a field day with those trolls." Sinthoras' voice was redolent with barely contained fury.

Caphalor knew why, but however much it went against the grain to leave the flesh-stealer alive, there was no alternative. "We will have to assess what she knows. This morning's mist will have concealed us while we examined the tower, but we can't rely on the gods protecting us all the time. Especially not if we climb up the walls."

"Don't go on about our needing that *thing*," replied Sinthoras angrily. "I want to . . ." He clenched his jaw and gave a snort of frustration. "She deserves to die. She has earned death a hundred times over."

"And she shall have it—after serving our purposes," said Caphalor, sharing the disgust the other felt. "Do you think I'm enjoying the prospect of using her help?"

"I wish she were dead, then we would not have the option."

They walked through the place where they had found the obboona. Overnight the troll corpses had gone, but pools of blood and drag marks on the ground could clearly be seen: the carrion-eaters had taken what they wanted.

She was crouched down in the middle in the cage watched greedily by four, drooling wolf-like creatures. The obboona had cuts and scratches on her arms and legs, evidence of her attackers' attempts to get to her.

One of the animals leaped up and snapped at her, its long jaws closing a hair's breadth from her face. She punched it on the nose and it fell back with a yelp. The others sat and waited.

"Look! Those animals can't be very bright: the obboona is still alive. There should have been deeper bites by now." Sinthoras laughed cruelly.

Caphalor took his bow from his shoulder and reached for an arrow. So far there had been two arrows he had not been able to retrieve, so he still had forty-eight, either in the quiver or packed in his saddle roll on the night-mare. He had also brought thirty replacement tips in case he needed to make his own arrows. "I—" He was about to tell his traveling companion he was going to shoot the animals when Sinthoras stepped out through the trees, spear in hand. Caphalor left the cover of the trees with a sigh and a shake of his head. Sinthoras' craving for attention was incredible. *You finish them off, then, if that's what you need to do.*

"Watch me," said Sinthoras, looking back over his shoulder. "This is how to do it."

"Sure." Caphalor observed the animals that were now focusing on them. They abandoned their lethargy, eyes bright with hunger and bloodlust. The obboona prostrated herself on the floor of her cage, calling out something about honor and thanks and demigods. The rest of what she said was drowned out by the barking and growls of the predators.

"You don't believe me?" Sinthoras bent down to pick up a leaf from the clearing. He held it in his outstretched hand. "Before this touches the ground I'll be done." He let it fall.

One of the beasts sprang and Sinthoras avoided it by turning his upper body, whirling his spear and ramming the point into the animal's flank. The first of the attackers fell to the ground, but the second was aiming a bite at his calf.

Sinthoras pulled his leg out of the way and delivered a downward kick to the animal's skull, then launched himself off the other foot to leap onto the top of the cage. He jabbed the sharp blade of the spear into the gullet of the third beast.

Caphalor watched the leaf's slow descent. "Time's nearly up," he announced, smiling.

The last of the wild things was eyeing Sinthoras, who jumped down nimbly, turning the spear. The animal slunk away.

A handy breeze lifted the leaf again momentarily. The sharpened point of Sinthoras' spear flew into the last of the animals, piercing throat and back, until it collapsed—exactly the second the leaf settled on the floor.

The obboona clapped like an excited child and praised the skill of her demigod.

"I was taking my time," Sinthoras claimed, beaming. "I enjoy the anticipation of any triumph, however small."

"The leaf landed at exactly the moment the animal died." Caphalor's grin was just as broad. "You claimed you would kill them all before it fell." He did not need to say anything else, Sinthoras' face had fallen; he would be gutted by his failure.

The obboona slid forward, stopping an arm's length from the bars at the side of the cage, watching Caphalor. Her dark eyes sparkled and he could see they had once been green: the intensity of the black color on the eyeball was fading.

"You will be needing me, worshipful one?" she breathed, humility and cunning in her tone. "You did not find a way in to the fortress? That is no dishonor, not even for demigods."

Caphalor had to muster all his self-restraint not to strike her dead on the spot. "We are giving you your life, flesh-stealer," he spoke darkly. He sent her black, oily skeins of fear through the intervening space, enveloping her in a mantle of pure threat. He wanted her to writhe on the ground and learn what it meant to confront an älf. "In exchange you take us into the castle."

"Of course," she said, looking longingly at him. Taking a deep breath, she inhaled the black wisps of fear as if they were a fragrance. Caphalor could detect no trace of fear in her. He watched her, reading the madness in her eyes.

Sinthoras scraped aside the leaves in front of the cage with his spear. "Draw us a sketch of what's kept where in the castle," he commanded, making no attempt to hide his disgust. "Which tower does he keep his treasure in? Where are his rooms?"

She smiled, transported with ecstasy. "My name is Karjuna," she announced solemnly, as if it were something holy.

The blunt end of the spear banged her between the eyes. She fell backward with a cry, blood shooting out of her nostrils to cover mouth and chin. Sinthoras had lost his temper. "You are an obboona, nothing more!" he shouted at her. "Low life forms have no right to names—do what you were told!"

Karjuna threw herself to her knees. "Forgive me," she whimpered, distraught. Crawling over to the bars she reached between them, took a twig in her filthy fingers and sketched the layout. "Around 600 men and women live in the fortress, all servants and slaves," she said hesitantly. "Each tower is a village, with its own stores and its own soldiers. The lord of the castle lives in whichever of the towers he feels like, but always at the very top—up there he is closest to the gods."

Caphalor nodded. "And how do we get inside?"

Karjuna gave a cheeky grin, but as soon as she realized what she was doing she cast a look of dismay toward Sinthoras, discovering to her relief that he had not been watching. "It's the fourth tower," she said hurriedly. "There are chains running in the castle supports, connected to counterweights under the earth. That's how they let the cell sections down. There is a hatch I discovered by chance."

"A hatch wide enough for a horde of young trolls to go through?" asked Sinthoras suspiciously, without taking his eyes off the drawing.

"No, indeed they would not have fitted through the hatch, demigod," she hastened to explain. "But I had to lie to them to save my own life. I don't know all the defense schemes the gålran zhadar has built into the towers, but the ones I'm aware of were certainly up to dealing with a few trolls."

"Telling lies so that you might live," Caphalor repeated, pointedly, his hatred for her growing more intense by the heartbeat.

Karjuna took a moment to understand what he was implying. "No! No, by Samusin, Inàste, and by Tion, my demigod!" she cried out in dismay. "I would never dare to deceive you!"

"Why not? You obboonas kill our kind whenever you get the chance!" he retorted. In his imagination, he saw her kneeling over an ambushed älf, stripping him of ears, nose, and skin to attach to her own face. He could no longer tolerate her presence: the wish to see her die became urgent, almost painful. His right hand was already on the grip of his dagger.

"I could never lie to you," she repeated stubbornly, not responding to his objection.

And Caphalor was certain that she was lying to him at that very moment, and there was nothing he could do about it, except . . . with the knife.

"Control yourself," he heard Sinthoras say in their älfish, speaking too fast for the obboona to understand. "We can hurt her, but we must

not kill her. Anyway, I insist we share the pleasure of her slow and painful death."

Caphalor nodded. He remembered the poison running in his veins.
The antidote was waiting for him, but he could not get it without
her help.

The obboona looked at each of them in turn. She knew her life hung
by a thread.

"I believe you," Caphalor said finally, bending to open the lock of her
cage with a fine hook. "What is the best time for us to try to enter the
castle?"

"At night: most of the slaves and the others will be asleep, there won't
be more than a few dozen awake." At a sign from him she left her cage,
crawling to their feet in the dust, trying to kiss their boots.

Sinthoras kicked out at once, hitting her right shoulder. "Don't you
dare!" he whispered hoarsely. "Pray to your degenerate gods that I don't
kill you before we get there!"

"My demigod," Karjuna implored Caphalor. "I beseech you!"

Caphalor could not help himself. He kicked her, too, striking her in
the face. The skin on her cheek tore open revealing the bone plate that
had been inserted to change the shape of her face. "Remember who you
are, flesh-stealer," he warned her quietly as he turned away. "Follow Sinthoras. You are to observe the fortress from the edge of the wood and
wait there for nightfall," he ordered. "It's possible the guards spotted us
just now."

Sinthoras did not move. "Who do you think you are, Caphalor, to
issue orders to me?" he asked. "And what are you up to? You want some
time to be alone with Raleeha?"

The acid sarcasm tested Caphalor's patience to the limit, but he was
able to fight back with the same weapon. "I'm the one who has been
awarded the Honor-Blessing," he said with a smile. "Being honored by
the Inextinguishable Ones is an exquisite feeling—like being given a
splinter of divinity. Knowing you, it's unlikely you'll ever experience it:
what could you do to deserve it?"

Gray lines flitted over Sinthoras' countenance but disappeared at
once. He turned away and headed for the forest undergrowth. "Come

with me and keep quiet," he hissed at the obboona. "If you don't, I'll make you sorry."

She hurried after him, throwing a hasty glance at Caphalor. Was that desire in her eyes?

Vowing to himself that he would throw the obboona from the very top of the sky fortress, he went back to the cave. He wanted to let Raleeha know what had been happening: it was important to have her on his side; if he were kind to her and could get her to trust him, this potentially valuable barbarian girl might transfer her affections to him.

He pulled up short on entering the darkness of the cave: Raleeha had gone. The night-mare snickered happily to see him. "Oh, it's you, master," he heard her voice coming from somewhere above his head. He stepped further in and saw she had climbed onto a narrow rock shelf over the entrance where she was perched with one of his long war arrows in her hand, ready to strike.

"Did it go well?" she asked, bowing her head.

Caphalor was impressed: for someone who had recently lost her sight it could not have been easy to climb up to that shelf, let alone find a place to hide. She could not have heard his footsteps. "Was it Sardaî that betrayed me?"

"He would not have greeted any but his master like that." The slave girl stood up and adjusted her position, tilting her head slightly, listening. "You are alone, master? Has something terrible happened?"

Caphalor realized the fear in her voice was for Sinthoras. He recapped the day's events and told her that they wanted to get in to the fortress with the obboona's help. "We will be back soon."

"Do you trust the flesh-stealer, master?"

"No. We'll get her to show us the way in. Then she will die," he said, going to the cave entrance. "Be ready. When we leave here, we'll be leaving very quickly, I expect."

"No one will spot you, master. You are älfar, after all."

It did not help us with the fflecx, though.

"Yes, we are älfar," he said after a pause, before leaving the cave without further words to her. He set off to follow the tracks of the obboona, which led directly to where Sinthoras was concealed.

The obboona was startled to find him at her shoulder. Sinthoras did not even look up, but kept his eyes on the daystar-lit towers ahead of him.

"Anything special?" asked Caphalor.

"No."

Caphalor climbed up to the highest fork in the tree and settled down for a nap. He would need all his strength for the night mission. "I'll take over in a bit," he told Sinthoras, closing his eyes.

"I shall watch over you both, my demigods," Karjuna called up to him. The next moment she yelped.

Caphalor smiled with satisfaction. He did not have to look to see what had happened: Sinthoras would have punished her for her arrogance. As soon as he had slept a little he would climb down and discipline her himself. He hoped she would make lots of mistakes.

Under cover of night they made their way quickly toward the towers.

Caphalor was struck by how quiet it was: the forest had been alive with sound, but as soon as they were on the plain silence had fallen; there were no insects, no animals. The sky fortress was not sending out good vibrations.

Karjuna was in front and heading straight for the fourth tower, making as little noise as possible. She was nowhere near as silent as the älfar, of course, but still quieter than any other creature would have been.

Caphalor cursed the fflecx. *Wretched gnome folk. Nothing in their brains at all and then stupid enough to get robbed by a gâlran zhadar.* He was not yet noticing any ill effects from Munumon's poison.

"Here," said Karjuna, stopping at the base of one of the mighty support columns. "It was here." She ran both hands over the surface of the wall.

Caphalor watched her while Sinthoras observed their surroundings. The obboona's movements were smooth and flowing, but much too coarse to be anything like those of the älfar she so admired. She might have been able to fool one of the lower monsters, but any creature with half a brain would catch her out immediately, seeing her as a miserable imitation of true perfection.

Karjuna had finished testing the wall's surface and had found a small hatch the size of her palm with a large metal ring fixed to it. She pulled the ring and there was a loud click as a trap door swung open, only large enough for an älf or a slim human to crawl through: a perfect trap.

But the obboona was not put off by any thought of treachery and she disappeared through it into the darkness. She called the two of them to follow her.

"You first," said Sinthoras with a smile, bowing to Caphalor. "The Inextinguishables' Honor-Blessing will protect you from any ambush."

"Their award makes me more valuable as a prisoner," he countered. "If this is a trap the obboona is leading us into, nothing must happen to me."

"So you're saying the Blessing is not worth having?" Sinthoras feigned a friendly tone. "The Inextinguishable Ones will be sad to hear that."

Caphalor paid him no further heed, stowing his bow and arrow so that he could follow Karjuna.

He plunged into the blackness. It smelled of cold and of stone, of iron and oil. He looked about him as he forced his way carefully through the narrow opening—he had to make sure he did not get caught on anything. He found himself in a vertical tube, his foot hovering over an abyss; warm air streamed up toward him, blowing his hair about his face. He stopped and listened.

"Be careful!" came Karjuna's voice above him. Her warning was not as prompt as it could have been. "There are chains in front of you. They're for the counterweights. Stretch out your hand and hold them. Take care—they are oily and slippery."

Caphalor did as she said. The links were huge, each one half as tall as him, and they ran deep into the ground until they reached the weights that had enabled the tower's corridor sections to be lowered. He wondered what forge had produced such things: this gålran zhadar must be ingenious indeed, and have the skills of incredible master craftsmen at his disposal.

The ascent began. He climbed determinedly upward, but after a time his arms and legs grew tired. He began to concentrate on each individual movement, ignoring the pain in his tortured muscles: one hundred, two hundred, three hundred times he completed the same sequence of steps and holds on the enormous chain, pushing himself onwards. The tips of his fingers were tingling—this was new—perhaps an effect of the toxins in his blood. This augured badly for the future. As he climbed, he grew more and more furious that they had ever fallen into the hands of the fflecx.

The obboona stopped. "We've arrived." There was another click and a faint blue light appeared from a new opening in the wall. Karjuna pulled herself up and went through.

"What if she closes the hatch now and raises the alarm?" said Sinthoras, close behind him.

"She could have done that earlier."

"Are you saying that to allay your own fears, or have you been off your guard?" Sinthoras mocked. "Perhaps there's an army waiting for us up there, and the Honor-Blessed älf will be heading straight into their arms . . ."

Karjuna's face appeared, looking down at them. "Demigods! Where have you got to? Hurry up!"

Caphalor would have loved to kick his rival back down the tube, but he could see Sinthoras had anticipated that and was staying out of boot-reach. "Let's get on."

They covered the remaining distance and emerged to stand in a corridor next to the obboona. The bluish light came from a luminous living moss placed behind glass at intervals. Caphalor had seen this before in the Inàste temple. This lighting technique produced no soot or fumes and the air remained fresh.

He looked down and noticed his clothing was oil-smeared from the climb. He would have to be careful not to leave any tracks that might give them away.

The doorway gave on to a large, low-ceilinged room where the chain ran over a pulley and then off to the right, disappearing through the wall. Caphalor assumed that it was fixed to one of the movable sections.

"You first," he said to Sinthoras, pointing to stairs going up. "If I slip on all this oil I wouldn't want to drag you down with me."

"Don't worry about that. I shall move out of the way quickly enough to watch you break your leg," his rival responded. "After you, O Honor-Blessed älf."

They swiftly climbed the steps, stepped through a doorway and found themselves bathed in warm light.

A high, wide corridor veered off to the right and another led to the left. The stairs carried on, ending at a door ten steps up. This part of the fourth tower was illuminated by enormous petroleum lamps hanging from long ropes, the light magnified by the use of mirrors. The lamps swayed gently, hypnotically, as if to lull any intruder.

Caphalor could hear nothing except the sound of Karjuna's breathing. They were alone here and safe from discovery. "Let's find out where this gâlran zhadar is," he suggested and Sinthoras nodded in agreement. "Where will we find a slave?" he asked the obboona. "We can ask one of them—I doubt they owe much loyalty to him."

The obboona inclined her head and then selected the right-hand corridor. Her shoes left the same dirty marks as their own, being able to move silently was not going to keep them from discovery for long.

Caphalor urged her to speed up: the tower's soldiers would soon realize there were intruders on site.

He was still surprised they had encountered no traps in that shaft. It had all been far too easy. The gâlran zhadar must surely have reckoned with one of his slaves absconding and perhaps betraying the secrets of the sky fortress: something was not right.

He and Sinthoras both picked up the sound of a melodious humming and a rhythmical clinking approaching from ahead of them.

Caphalor pushed the flesh-stealer into a niche in the wall before going to investigate, leaving Sinthoras to guard her.

He sought the protection of the shadows, increasing their hold on the corridor with his magic. Silently, he drew his dagger.

A human came toward them, humming a tune. He was wearing a hooded linen jerkin and had a bunch of keys at his belt, jangling against his thigh with each stride. He was not carrying any weapons.

The man slowed his pace and stared at the dark footprints on the floor. He looked up at the petroleum lamps with a puzzled air.

Caphalor's magic doused the wicks still further, sending shadows sweeping past the man on both sides and plunging him, terrified, into darkness.

Only then did the älf slip out from his cover and stalk up to the man. "Greetings from death, human," he whispered. "It is up to you whether death walks on by or takes you now. Do you understand?"

Wide-eyed with fear, the man nodded.

"We seek your master, the gålran zhadar. We want to present ourselves to him. Where will we find him?" Caphalor held his dagger pointing at the man's eye. "I am going to permit you to speak. If it were to occur to you to shout for help it would be the last thing you ever did." Then he withdrew some of the black fear overwhelming the man.

The man stared at him, still rooted to the spot with fright, but then his expression changed as he saw Sinthoras and the obboona standing behind Caphalor. Fear turned to hatred.

"You traitor!" he hissed. His teeth were rotten and his stinking breath blew toward the älf like a cloud of pestilence.

Karjuna grinned and folded her arms. "I told you I'd be back to take my revenge."

Sinthoras punched her in the face so that she fell to her knees.

At this the man laughed with pleasure. "It doesn't look like these people are your friends, Karjuna. Where's that army of yours you were going to bring back?"

Caphalor immediately let him taste terror again. The tip of his knife traveled the man's face, leaving four painful shallow cuts round his eyes. "Watch yourself," he threatened in a low voice. "If I don't get an answer to my question your greasy skin will soon be hanging in strips from your ugly mug. And after that I'll let the obboona strangle you. Is that the kind of death you had in mind?"

The man writhed, abject with fear. "The gålran zhadar is resting. But you'll never get near him. His guards—"

"Where is the treasure?" Sinthoras interrupted him, earning a sharp look from Caphalor. "We seek a parchment and the crown he stole from the fflecx."

At this their captive looked extremely worried. "You are in the service of the alchemancers?"

Sinthoras lowered his head and sent out webs of fear, not finely calculated as Caphalor's had been, but like a wave crashing against a cliff.

The effect on the human was remarkable: he pressed one hand against his forehead, the other against his chest, then sank to his knees gasping for air and whimpering.

Caphalor guessed the barbarian would not be holding out for long. "So you know what we want and where we will find it," Sinthoras murmured softly, sounding more dangerous than if he had shouted wildly. "I hold your cowardly heart and your feeble mind in the palm of my hand. Remember: one thought from me and you are dead."

"Round to the left!" cried the terrified man. "Tower number six!"

Caphalor had been about to reprimand his fellow älf, but the ploy had been brilliant. Now they had their hands on a barbarian who could take them straight to where they needed to be. He looked at Karjuna and beckoned her over. "Mind he's not tricking us."

The obboona bowed her head and he saw that she was disappointed. She was hurt that they did not trust her to lead them. He, on the other hand, found it incredible the creature expected them to.

They hurried through the corridors and tubes and hallways of the sky fortress. Their captive led them at a fast pace and Karjuna nodded that he was going the right way. Occasionally they had to take a detour to avoid colliding with others.

Caphalor suddenly asked, "You called her *traitor*. Wasn't she one of the gålran zhadar's slaves? Or did she have a more important position?"

The man spat. "She was the supervisor of all the slaves until she robbed the master. She was due to be executed but she escaped. We thought she had jumped off the tower to avoid torture."

"Why didn't you look for the body?" said Caphalor. *Barbarians can be so stupid!*

Their captive didn't answer—he pointed to a branch of the corridor and a narrower tube. "Down there. It leads to a chamber where the most important things are kept."

Sinthoras pushed him into the corridor tube, then nodded to the obboona. "Caphalor will go first. I'll keep my eyes on the two of them." He grinned. "The Honor-Blessed älf will bring us luck by going first."

Caphalor complied, holding his bow and arrows at the ready as he went down the corridor. As he passed the lamps he dimmed them so that he could move along in a mantle of shadow.

After he had gone twenty-eight paces the corridor bent round and he heard the low voices of perhaps eight or nine creature of various kinds.

He did not douse the lights completely, but peered cautiously around the corner.

His acute hearing had not let him down: there were four humans, one gnome, and four óarco half-breeds. They were standing in a triangle formation in front of an iron door, with the gnome at the front. His face was green with yellow marbling; either this was a whim of the gods or he was a horribly deformed fflecx.

They wore helmets, studded leather armor, chainmail gauntlets, and protective plates covering forearms and legs. Their weapons were swords, battleaxes, and two morningstars. They were talking quietly among themselves; the topic was the construction of a seventh tower. He assumed they were all there to guard the treasure store.

Would he be able to tackle them on his own? They were standing diagonally behind each other, ideal for an archer: he could take out three or four at a time. But they would be bound to move, thus presenting multiple targets, and they were all at different heights.

Common sense told him to go and get Sinthoras, but his pride told him to try to manage on his own. He wanted to show his arrogant companion that he was not the only one who knew how to fight. After all, he was the one who had received the Honor-Blessing, and deservedly so. If he was quick enough he could get into the chamber and grab the items they had come for, completing the task on his own: a further humiliation for his rival.

Caphalor adjusted the quiver and drew out three arrows. He nocked one and held the other two in his mouth. This meant he would only be able to draw the bowstring back the length of the bow arm, but at this distance the shot would be powerful enough. And firing them would be quicker.

He stepped around the corner, loosed the first arrow, took the second one out of his mouth and pulled back the string, noting with satisfaction that the four men on his left had all fallen to the ground, mortally wounded. The third arrow let him dispense with the two monsters in front, but then the remaining three guards woke out of their frozen state.

The gnome grabbed a whistle and the two last óarco half-breeds rushed at him, brandishing raised axes.

They could not have chosen to do anything more stupid.

It gave Caphalor the chance to fire the next arrow into the gnome before he could utter a sound: he had just put the whistle to his lips and was drawing breath when the missile hit him. The tip of the arrow went straight through the tin whistle, crashed through his teeth and disappeared down his throat. Gurgling, he fell backward.

Seconds before the half-breeds reached him, Caphalor sent out waves of darkness and killed the lamp, ducking out of the way of his attackers.

He felt the draft as the axes whizzed past him, meeting air rather than flesh.

Dropping his bow, Caphalor drew out an arrow and listened for his adversaries' movements: he did not need to be able to see them. He leaped upward and stabbed down rapidly several times, meeting soft tissue; the resulting gurgling noise was proof that he had hit them in the throat. Warm liquid splashed against him and the first one collapsed heavily. The remaining half-breed slashed around wildly with his ax, hitting his own partner in the belly. The älf stabbed sharply with his knife and heard his victim groan as the blade clanged on his helmet.

The sound guided Caphalor as he dealt a sweeping blow that sliced through enemy flesh. He followed through—jabbing right and left through the leather armor, tripping the beast up at the same time.

As it fell, the half-breed tried to grab hold of his arm, but he was not that easy to catch. Caphalor nimbly avoided the hold with a shoulder turn and the clumsy fingers lost their purchase. He jammed his dagger through the guard's neck.

A dull thud. And then silence.

Taking a deep breath and releasing it slowly, Caphalor allowed the lamps to flare up again. Tendrils of black fear dissolved into nothing. The shadows retreated. "I knew it." It was Sinthoras coming round the bend in the corridor. "The doused lamps told me what you were up to. So our Honor-Blessed älf could not resist a fight."

He did not bother to answer, annoyed that his plan of entering the treasure store on his own had been foiled. He took the amazement on the faces of the obboona and their prisoner as praise enough for his feat, even if their admiration meant little to him. "Open the door," he ordered the man, lifting a blood-smeared dagger to his face. "One of those keys of yours should fit. Let's hope so, for your sake."

Their captive blanched. "No. They won't fit. The master holds the only key." He licked his dry lips and squinted over to Caphalor. "Please! I'm sure I can be helpful in other ways."

Sinthoras shook his head. "You tell us that now? You deceived us on purpose, to save your own skin."

The barbarian fell to his knees. "Mercy!"

"Mercy you shall have." Sinthoras spat the words, contempt written on his features. Caphalor could see what was coming. The slender blade of the spear pierced the man's neck quick as a bolt of lightning and was pulled back. "You die with little pain."

The man fell forward to the floor without a sound. Caphalor turned him onto his back.

Fascinated, he and Sinthoras watched the barbarian's eyes change as life ebbed away and a milky sheen took over. This was the veil that death brought.

Caphalor had heard many theories about why this phenomenon was to be observed in higher and lower creatures alike. It could not be taken— as humans believed—to signify the departure of the soul, because óarcos and other monsters did not possess a soul. Was death really the great equalizer? He wondered if his own pupils would one day dim like this.

Sinthoras turned to Karjuna, his spear pointing at her belly. "You knew about the lock mechanism, flesh-stealer. You shan't trick us again!"

She threw herself at his feet. "I know how to open the door, demi-gods," she cried out devotedly.

Caphalor wiped the blood off on the dead barbarian's clothing. He was finding the necessity of the obboona's presence increasingly infuriating. "Get on with it," he barked. "There's no time to waste."

She went over to the door and the älfar followed her a few paces behind.

As Karjuna manipulated patterns and jewels set in the door, a series of clicks could be heard. Her hand movements did not seem to follow any particular pattern, but suddenly the door started to open. Caphalor reckoned the steel was three hand spans thick.

Her purpose now served, Sinthoras raised his spear to strike her down.

"Wait," said Caphalor softly. "Who knows what we might still need her for?"

"After you, demigods," Karjuna announced, bowing low and gesturing them to enter.

"Go first," Sinthoras growled to her, elbowing his rival aside and leaving him to bring up the rear. "You can cover our backs with your fabled archery skills, O Blessed One," he said sarcastically. The room was lined with shelves carrying chests, boxes, and small trunks, each bearing a label in strange runes. It smelled of leather and wood, like a tack room.

"He keeps exact records of everything," Karjuna told them as she turned to face them, eyes sparkling. The black in her eyes had completely faded now. "Unfortunately I can't read his language. But this one"—she pointed to a chest in the corner—"wasn't here last time I looked."

Caphalor was sure she had tried to steal treasure from this hoard. He warned himself not to underestimate her, not until her death: the death he and Sinthoras were itching to bring her.

They went over to the chest and told Karjuna to open it.

Inside was a crown about the size of a gnome's head. It was made of gold and varnished clumsily with thick paint; engraved silver balls topped each of the seven points and looked as if they had been stuck on as an afterthought.

Caphalor noted the mysterious radiance. He was not able to work magic as the Inextinguishable Ones and the botoicans could, but most of the älfar were able to detect its presence. There would be a slight tingling, as if a thunderstorm were in the air, and the nearer one got, the stronger the sensation. Next to the crown he saw a rolled parchment with a broken wax seal.

Sinthoras unrolled it. "Just some ludicrous gnome scribble," he said after a short scan of the contents. "Probably a recipe, but it makes no sense at all."

"Coded, maybe." Caphalor watched the entrance. He reached out and took the scroll.

Sinthoras bestowed a smile on Karjuna that was velvety soft and full of menace. "It's time we expressed our thanks for your cooperation, flesh-stealer. The reward may not be in the form you might have wished, but I promise you it will be extraordinary." The tip of his weapon hovered at the level of her heart. She took a step back, the horror on her face rendering her uglier than ever.

"Look at this," said Capahlor, pointing out the ink that had run on the bottom of the parchment: the writing had become illegible, but it looked to have been done on purpose.

Sinthoras tutted impatiently. It was obvious he was savoring the prospect of killing Karjuna. "What's that to us? Munumon wants the parchment. He never said what condition it had to be in."

"We need the antidote, don't we? He won't give it to us if the parchment's damaged, he'll think we did it." This gave his companion cause for thought.

Karjuna spoke up, pointing to the smudged writing. "I can read it."

"You?" Caphalor laughed at her. "You'd say anything to save your skin."

"No, my demigod!" As always when she addressed him directly, her voice took on a timbre implying begging, desiring, longing. "I can see the indentations made by the quill. It's the medication I take to make my eyes look like yours. It sharpens the vision. I beseech you: let me live!"

Sinthoras let out his breath in exasperation. "I say get rid of her."

"No, it won't hurt to test her." Caphalor looked at Karjuna. He would have loved to kill her, but perhaps his own life and the key to their whole mission was in her hands.

Sinthoras stared at him, then said, "We'll regret it. I feel it in my bones." He looked around for something to stow the crown and the parchment in and located a leather bag.

A small silver-topped vial the size of a finger caught his attention in one of the open boxes. A whitish substance was within, swishing gently against the sides of the tiny flask. The writing on the label was damaged, but he knew that one of the runes stood for "demon." He was aware of a strong magic force emanating from it.

Sinthoras glanced at his companion then quietly slipped the vial into a fold in his clothes. Perhaps it would come in useful, it would be his secret.

"Let's go." Caphalor took the lead and headed for the entrance. "Now all we need is—"

A creature that looked remarkably like a groundling sauntered in, hands behind his back. He was wearing a splendid suit of palladium armor on his muscular body and under the metal he wore a padded black tunic. Round his head there was a broad, worked band of the same metal as the armor, set with diamonds and rubies, sparkling in the light. His hair was dark black and cut short but his sideburn hair had been allowed to grow long, reaching down to his chest. The expression on his furrowed features was almost friendly, and certainly carried an air of polite inquiry as he entered the room and looked the intruders up and down.

"Gålran zhadar," mouthed Karjuna, stepping back to hide behind some shelves.

Sinthoras raised his spear. "Very decent of him. We don't even have to go looking for him to collect his head—don't you dare—"

In an instant Caphalor had his bow up and two arrows fired at the newcomer. He did not care if Sinthoras was keen to measure himself in combat against the lord of the sky fortress. The openness with which the gålran zhadar was confronting them did not augur well.

Their new adversary brought his arms forward. In each hand he held a short-handled war hammer, on the heads of which decorative silver, gold, and jewels refracted the light. He held the broad sides of the hammerheads crossed to protect his face. He did take a step backward when the arrows hit and shattered, but he was unhurt.

"That's a bit slow," he remarked mockingly in a deep voice. "For an älf." The door behind him clanged shut.

Caphalor nocked the next arrow but Sinthoras stepped into his sightline. "You've had your chance, Honor-Blessed laggard. Now it's mine!" He advanced on the waiting gålran zhadar, who was holding the hammers crossed on his chest.

Caphalor was surprised. Either the gålran zhadar knew nothing about älfar fighting skills, or he considered his own to be superior. "Obboona! Open the door," he ordered, sending an arrow skimming past his companion's hip. This one too was repelled. "Samusin!" he cursed, stowing his useless bow and drawing his short sword and his dagger.

Karjuna slinked through the shadows and stood up against a shelf by the door, but then stopped, too frightened of the gålran zhadar to pass him directly.

Sinthoras attacked with rapid stabs and struck the gålran zhadar with the blunt end of his spear. He evaded them nimbly, or parried with a growl. He was obviously concentrating hard and having to make an effort, but Caphalor could see he was enjoying himself.

"Let's see how you deal with this!" Sinthoras increased the pressure, adding kicks and elbow jabs to the spear blows. The palladium armor saved the gålran zhadar's life on three occasions as the blade slipped on the engraved surface, unable to penetrate the metal.

"Not as easy as you thought, eh, shortlegs?" scoffed the älf. Caphalor moved to help but Sinthoras shoved him aside. "Out of the way! He's mine!"

At that moment one of the war hammers hit Sinthoras on the left thigh. The jewels glowed and a pale red sphere flared, enclosing the hammerhead and then flashing round the room like a burst from the daystar.

Sinthoras was hurled backward and his leg armor bore a long black scorch mark.

The gålran zhadar roared with deep-voiced laughter. "Where are you off to, black-eyes? I've only just begun." He threw the hammer up to rotate twice, then caught it and circled his arm in the air. "Karjuna! Where have you got to? You've brought some friends this time to rob me? I thought you were brighter than that." He winked at Caphalor. "The same goes for you two."

Without warning, he attacked.

Chapter VII

Dsôn!

Pulsating with life, this is the heart of the Star Realm, and the chosen stage for statesmen, whose alliances, enmities, and conspiracies are followed by the select few. Academies and universities stand side by side; they, too, are surrounded in webs of intrigue and cutthroat competition. There is always a war being waged in secret in Dsôn.

And over all the Inextinguishable siblings reign supreme.

Epocrypha of the Creating Spirit
1st Book
Footnote

Ishím Voróo (The Outer Lands), the Kingdom of the fflecx, 4370th division of unendingness (5198th solar cycle), summer.

Raleeha lay on the high rock shelf just inside the cave entrance, listening to the sounds from outside and the snorts of the night-mare. The leaves rustled quietly, making her sleepy.

But she told herself she must not drift off. As long as her present and former masters were on this mission, she must keep watch. She was not sure whether she was protecting the night-mare or whether it was the other way about, or whether or not it would eat her, given half a chance.

She turned, inadvertently knocking against something that rolled down onto the cave floor. Feeling along the rock shelf, she worked out that it had been her drinking flask.

How she longed to have her sight back. To see the stallion, to see the sky fortress, even the obboona—and, of course, to see Sinthoras' enchanting features. She did not take it amiss that he had given her away like some useless possession. She was well acquainted with his moods and she knew he would be regretting this action.

The tension between Caphalor and himself prevented her former master from simply asking for her return. As long as she was able to be somewhere near Sinthoras, it did not matter to her whose orders she was under.

Her thoughts wandered. Her family would never be able to understand why, of her own volition, she was still following the älf who had slashed her eyes. She sometimes found it hard to understand herself.

For as far back as she could remember, she had taken pleasure in serving others, no matter that she was the sister of a prince. And because of her own creative streak she was attracted to the art of the älfar and had loved the stories she heard about them as a child. To her the tales were thrilling rather than morbid or terrifying.

Her fascination was aesthetic. Where other humans felt only revulsion at their art, Raleeha admired the älfar concept of it: works executed in blood, wonderful sculptures in bone and metal, magnificent towers and opulent dwellings. She had always fantasized about their achievements and had longed for an opportunity to study an älfar city and behold the evidence of their preeminent skills with her own eyes.

She remembered how she had been a better artist than anyone in her hometown: the works she produced had a vibrant but mysteriously somber quality to them that no one else could replicate. People called her conceited and resented her prowess. Her best piece, exhibited in the town hall, was slashed and defaced by some envious soul who had scribbled a crude caricature of her on the door.

The more she enthused about the älfar, the more people distrusted her and she had been forced to hide her passionate obsession. She wanted to avoid repercussions that might damage her brother's reputation. However warm his feelings toward her, even Farron had never understood his sister's opinions.

As a member of the Ishmanti tribe she had lived a nomadic life for many years. Then the extended family had settled and founded a small town relatively near the älfar frontier. One day she had seen Sinthoras as he sat painting.

Despite her brother's pleas she had gone after him, wanting nothing more than to travel widely throughout the älfar regions, even if she had to do it as a slave. Obsessed by the beauty she saw, she had sketched and painted. The architecture, the philosophy of the älfar and even their military skills far surpassed anything she had experienced before. She admired their whole way of life—in death and in art.

Raleeha was distraught about never being able to see any of it again. However, her punishment had been merited, so she suppressed the voice inside her that tried to complain about her treatment, while she reveled in her memories of älfar art.

The rebellious voice told her that a beating would have been sufficient punishment, her mistake had not been so significant as to deserve the loss of her eyesight. Without Caphalor's help she would have drowned out in the marshes, or might have been ravished by óarcos or even eaten . . .

She must stop accusing Sinthoras. *I brought it upon myself.*

She steeled herself to climb down from the ledge for the drinking flask.

That same internal voice repeatedly urged her to return to her brother's people and to abandon her existence as a slave, but she hesitated. She was proud of her brother, the renowned warrior prince, and was loath to be a burden to him if she went back home. The rumors would persist and she would be suspected of being a spy for the älfar. Nobody escaped alive from their captivity, so how could a blind girl do it? *Farron's reputation must remain spotless.*

She had heard that the Ishmantis were planning a campaign against the Star Realm and that would be a further reason for seeking her brother out: to try to dissuade him. He would be going to certain death and taking tens of thousands with him.

No one back home had any idea how strong the älfar military were. She knew, though. Sinthoras had once taken her with him on maneuvers—there had only been a thousand soldiers on the exercise, but they were more lethal than ten thousand of her kind. The defenses they constructed would have claimed thousands of lives before a human ever set foot in Dsôn Faïmon.

She was torn between concern for her own people and the arguments that held her back. She was amazed at the ideas that had come when she lost her sight; the beauty of the älfar cities had shut down any critical faculties for thought, they were too confusing.

Raleeha had reached the ground now and crouched down to feel around for her flask. She found the strap and tugged.

At that point she registered that the night-mare was no longer snorting.

To her right she heard a hoof meet stone. She could imagine the sparks playing round the creature's fetlocks and she could feel the static on her face. She jerked upright with a cry and tried to move away, but the stallion had stepped on the hem of her dress. The night-mare was set on having her as his next meal and had just been waiting for her to come down from her sanctuary.

"No!" she cried, trying to pull herself free. She lifted an arm in defense and encountered the creature's soft nostrils.

Raleeha plucked up the courage to stroke his muzzle.

The stallion moved its hoof aside and she was free. She could hardly believe her luck.

"Good boy, Sardaî."

Without moving her hand away she got slowly to her feet, talking calmly all the time. The animal allowed her to stroke the blaze with her other hand. Until, that is, she touched the place its horn had been.

The night-mare screamed and it pawed the ground.

Jumping back, Raleeha narrowly avoided the snapping jaws.

"Off with you!" she shouted, yanking an arrow out of her belt and turning at the same time to the wall. Climbing swiftly, she tried to reach safety. A blow on her back thrust her upward. If the creature had still had its horn she would have been pierced through.

Dropping the arrow, Raleeha climbed further and pulled herself up.

The night-mare sank its teeth in the heel of her right boot, tearing it off. Before it could attack her again she reached the ledge. She was sobbing and coughing at the same time; she ran her fingers over her back to check whether she was bleeding. The stallion stormed around the cave, its noise echoing from the walls. She implored it to stop, tears streaming down her cheeks. "You'll have our enemies on us like that. Be quiet, can't you?"

Her voice made the animal wilder still.

Raleeha covered her ears and wept. At that moment she would have given anything to be back with her brother and her family.

Ishím Voróo (The Outer Lands), Kingdom of the fflecx, 4370th division of unendingness (5198th solar cycle), summer.

Sinthoras had not realized that the gålran zhadar had such strong magic. The power had cut right through his body and everything around turned red and hot as a furnace. His leg was throbbing and felt numb and swollen under the metal greaves. Maybe he would lose it completely. The botoicans' strongest sorcery was child's play compared to this.

Biting his lips against the pain, he cut the leather greave straps on his armor and sprang vertically upward to avoid his adversary who was storming toward him. His plan was to thrust his spear down into the back of his neck as he passed underneath.

But the gålran zhadar had anticipated the move. One of his hammers crashed against the spear with such violence that the shaft bent in the middle; the second hammer—aimed at Sinthoras' lower leg—only narrowly missed.

Robbed of his support, Sinthoras lost his balance and collapsed in front of his waiting opponent who raised his hammers expectantly and stood grinning. The hammerheads were beginning to glow again.

Sinthoras released a web of darkness to extinguish the lamps. The power of fear flew toward the gålran zhadar, confusing him enough to make his next blows go astray.

The light dimmed in response, but the effect was nowhere as strong as it usually was. The gålran zhadar remained unimpressed, though he was unsettled enough to withdraw three paces.

"Stupid little games!" he shouted furiously. "Instead of an honest fight you hide behind such tricks!" He lifted his hammers and leaned forward. Crackling flashes of lightning shot out of the handles. "I'll show you what I can do! You stand no chance!"

"Hey!" Caphalor was standing by some shelves holding a burning lamp over one of the open chests; there was a smell of petroleum. "There's a lot of paper in there. I bet it'll burn really well if I drop the lamp in."

The gålran zhadar lowered his arms.

Sinthoras growled; he was certainly not going to be thanking his companion for barging in like that.

"You want my treasure," said the gålran zhadar, assessing the älfar. "And I won't let you take it." He raised his right hammer and spoke to Caphalor. "What have you stolen? Put it back and you can go if you leave the traitor here."

Sinthoras laughed maliciously. "Of course. Your word is good enough for us," he said sarcastically.

"I'm not giving you more than my word."

"Then we'll kill you and leave the same way we came in," Caphalor answered.

"Do you think you would have got in if I hadn't wanted you to?" The castle overlord regarded them disdainfully. "I left the way open for Karjuna to return so that I could punish her. I did not expect her to be bringing reinforcements." Still holding fast to the hammers, his body tense, he went on, "I've given you my offer. Take it or you will lose your immortality sooner than you want to, and all because of a worthless obboona." He narrowed his eyes. "How did she manage to persuade two älfar like you to go out on the rob?" His gaze wandered along the shelves. "You've chosen something very valuable."

"Only valuable for a gnome," Sinthoras replied. He had checked out his spear and thought it could still be used, though the mechanism had been damaged, so he would not be able to separate it into two pieces.

The gålran zhadar laughed with disbelief. "They sent you to retrieve their crown and the parchment? Munumon is more of a coward than I thought—wouldn't try it himself, or bring his own army." He raised his arms, relaxing the muscles. "You'd never have got this far without the obboona."

"Believe me: we would have killed Munumon if we'd had the chance. We had no choice. We've got to take the things back that he needs." Caphalor held the lamp dangerously close to the papers. "Let us go free."

"What else did you need?"

Sinthoras hurled his spear at the gålran zhadar and rushed forward, drawing his sword. "Your head," he called, laughing, getting ready to strike.

His opponent only escaped the full force of the blow because the spear was bent out of true and wavered in flight. Otherwise, the point would have got him in the middle of his forehead. As it was, it landed on one of the hammers and the blade tip shattered on impact.

Sinthoras had calculated for this: using the distraction, he struck again as he ran, aiming for the throat this time.

The gålran zhadar raised his second weapon, deflecting the älf's blade and pushing it aside; then he attacked with the first.

Sinthoras cursed and delivered a high kick to the other's wrist. The gålran zhadar's grip on his weapon faltered and Sinthoras caught the hammer elegantly as it fell. He used the momentum, twisting on his own axis and swinging the heavy implement.

Hammer clanged against hammer. The gålran zhadar had parried the blow.

Now great swathes of magic were released, hurling Sinthoras off his feet—it felt like being swept away by a mountain torrent—and the breath was driven out of his body. Forced to drop the weapon, he crashed into the shelving and slid to the floor. Through a red veil he saw the gålran zhadar lying on the other side of the room, a pool of blood round his head.

Caphalor leaped in and grabbed Sinthoras by the arms, pulling him upward and shouting, "Up!"

To Sinthoras the voice was slow and faint, as if Caphalor were yawning while he spoke.

"The obboona has opened the door. His men are on their way."

"Kill them," said Sinthoras, wondering why his own voice sounded so strange. The words were clear enough in his head, but they came out wrong. When Caphalor let go of him he had to grab hold of the shelves for support. Arms, legs—everything was feeble, as if his bones were melting. He had spots before his eyes, but now they were turning to fog. He had to admit he was in no state to do any more fighting.

He staggered unwillingly after Caphalor, bumping into obstacles, grabbing something off a shelf that looked like a spear. He had lost his own, useless now anyway.

His senses tricked him, turning the flesh-stealer into a real älf. "I slipped out before the door had quite closed and opened it again from the outside," she said, her voice tinkling like a bell, as full of promise as the warm smile she bestowed on him: he could do anything he wanted to with her. "When we are free I'll complete the parchment for you, demigods. Not before."

Sinthoras shook himself, tripped over his own feet and fell. The others had to haul him up and help him along.

He had no idea which way they were going. His legs barely functioned and he felt so odd. There was shouting. Caphalor stopped every so often to shoot some arrows and then Sinthoras had to crawl through an opening after him. He was seeing double: he did not know which of the hands were really his, so his fingers failed to grasp the metal links.

"Pull yourself together!" Caphalor yelled at him angrily. "Do you hear? Pull yourself together and climb down the chain. If you fall, you've had it. Think of our mission and pull yourself together! What will our rulers say? Do you want to bring shame on yourself?"

No, he certainly did not want that! He brushed away the fog in front of his eyes and made his way down as best he could. However he hurried, the others were a long way ahead of him now. He put the spear in his belt and tried to catch them up.

After what seemed an age he reached the side shaft and tumbled out of the hatchway. They ran through the night, heading for the protection of the forest.

Sinthoras turned his head.

All the lights were blazing in the sky fortress, the windows were lit up and there were fires on the tops of all six towers. An impressive sight indeed. They heard a loud clanging and a metallic screech, repeated ten, twenty times over.

"Run!" shrieked Karjuna, scared to death now. "Don't stop, run for your lives!"

Sinthoras could not help himself. He simply had to wait to see what would happen.

The towers were moving!

Then he realized his eyes were deceiving him. Parts of the external walls were rumbling aside, exposing hatchways and large openings. The fortress was growing flaming eyes and incandescent mouths. He wanted to stop and make a painting of it—with the black night as a background, the castle was of another world entirely.

Deep-throated brass sounded the alarm and shrill pipes sent out urgent signals.

The first of the connecting sections were being let down on long chains. The fortress was not going to let robbers and murderers get away scot-free.

Sinthoras stared, wide-eyed in amazement. The darkness had gone and the whole plain was filled with light: a hundred stars rose to the skies from the walls of the castle, shooting up to illuminate the clouds, making their way up to their celestial siblings. Their comet tails formed sparkling patterns, painting the firmament in glowing hues, overtaking each other, competing to go higher, highest. No, he would never be able to capture this magnificent scene on canvas.

"By Inàste," he whispered in awe. "What beauty!" Near tears, Sinthoras swallowed hard.

But the distances were too great, it seemed, for these piteous new stars.

Their flights ended, they described great arcs in the sky and turned toward the earth, about to burst and shatter on the ground.

"No!" he cried, stretching out his arms as if to catch and save each of them. "See how they fall, the stars! They—"

"You fool!" Caphalor shouted in his ear. "It's fire-arrows! They're shooting at us with fire arrows!"

Sinthoras felt his shoulder being grabbed and he was dragged away under a growing hail of blazing stars.

When the first missiles hissed down next to him, igniting the dry grass, he came to his senses and shook Caphalor off, running after him of his own accord.

All around them arrows came whizzing down. The first salvo had spared them, although he saw one had narrowly missed him, piercing his drinking flask.

The whooshing sounds changed, and the missiles this time became flaming leather bags, as big as a man, with great flaring tails. Black shadows hurtling through the air proved to be large stones fired in their direction. Behind them the whole plain was alight.

His mind finally became clear as his pounding heart pumped the confusion out of his head and the fresh air sobered him. "Get to the cave!" he shouted to Caphalor, who was racing ahead.

A burning arrow from above penetrated the obboona's right shoulder. Sinthoras heard the hiss as the flames were smothered on entering her flesh; she screamed out but kept running, though slower now, and she was soon overtaken by the two älfar.

Sinthoras did not waste a glance on her as he continued on his path through the forest. He realized that several had hit him in the back and were lodged in his rucksack—luck would not be on their side for long.

The älfar raced through the undergrowth between the stout tree trunks without stopping.

A huge boulder landed just in front of them and rolled over and over before coming to a standstill. Trees, leaves, and branches came crashing down and soil spurted up on all sides as the älfar ducked and weaved. The forest's wounds gave off the smell of resin and damp earth.

Sinthoras wondered what military engines the fortress had employed to send a missile of that size such a distance.

"Let's get on," he panted, swerving round an uprooted tree.

There was a sudden flash, a hissing cloud of smoke and a burning sack fell out of the treetops, bursting into flame and raining molten fire. Heat and light filled the forest.

"By Tion!" exclaimed Caphalor, bounding away out of danger and out of Sinthoras' field of vision.

Dazzled by the flames, Sinthoras ran off in the opposite direction.

He saw more and more missiles landing: the castle defenders were doing their best to cut off the intruders' retreat and were burning down their own forest, rather than see them escape with their lives.

Finally he saw the split in the rock that was the cave entrance—their safe haven.

"It's me, it's Sinthoras!" he called, so Raleeha would know who was coming. He could hear one of the huge boulders flying down at him. At the last moment he flung himself through the narrow opening ahead of the crash.

The boulder landed with an enormous thump, shaking the ground and throwing up clumps of earth. An instant later and he would have been buried under it.

He sat down, gasping for breath, and felt a further shuddering impact. Pebbles showered down on him: their shelter had been hit for a second time.

"What is happening out there?" Raleeha asked from her high perch. She had an arrow in one hand and a dagger in the other. The heel of one of her boots was lying on the ground next to her drinking flask.

"Quiet!" he snapped at her, his newly acquired spear at the ready. He could see the fire arrows he had thought to be shooting stars, but he was still having other hallucinations. He put it down to gnome poison and prayed the gods would spare him further bouts.

A shadow swept past the entrance and Caphalor pushed his way through.

A shame, that. Sinthoras could see that the other älf had only made it by the skin of his teeth. His armor and clothing showed scorch marks. He must have gone through the fire to reach the cave.

The smoke and the smell of burning were getting stronger; the wind carried sparks into the cave and the crackling of the fire was growing louder.

"We can't stay here," Caphalor coughed. "There's only a narrow section of the forest that's not burning yet. If we don't go now—"

Another missile hit their shelter. This time the night-mare whinnied loudly and pawed the ground in terror, its tail whipping from side to side. Caphalor was attempting to calm the beast when another boulder slammed down outside.

Parts of the roof started to cave in and a cloud of bluish gray dust rose up over Caphalor and the stallion, preventing Sinthoras from seeing them. *Let's hope that one got him,* he prayed to Samusin.

"It's me, demigods," Karjuna called, climbing carefully in through the entrance.

A petroleum bomb slammed into the rock wall above her head and a waterfall of fire engulfed her.

Giving a scream unlike any sound Sinthoras had ever heard, the obboona ran through into the cave, hurling herself onto the floor and rolling in the dust, scattering burning drops of petroleum and scraps of charred material. This extinguished the flames. She shrieked with pain, then fell still and remained motionless. The stink of burning flesh was in the air.

Sinthoras glanced over to the entrance where the fire was still raging. A thin finger of fire made its way harmlessly through, running down the floor of the cavern. Outside the entire forest was aflame. Hot wind invaded their shelter, making it difficult to breathe.

Stepping round the obboona, he took a look outside.

Flames shot up wildly, interlinked and overlapping, thirty or forty paces high on all sides, lighting up the whole sky. The crackling of the fire was terrifyingly loud and the flames were a sea of bright yellow and dark red: a sight he would never forget, if he lived through it.

Smoke and heat forced him to turn his face away.

"We must block up the entrance with the debris," came Caphalor's voice next to him. "Otherwise the draft will bring the fire in here and we'll be baked like loaves of bread in an oven." His face showed new grazes and cuts and he was covered in dirt and dust—but he was still alive.

Sinthoras saw a dust-covered Raleeha cowering in the corner, trembling all over, coughing and trying to hold her sleeve over her face. The obboona was still lying on the ground. The night-mare did not fancy trying her flesh.

It seems that Inàste has put a charm on your life. Sinthoras nodded and helped Caphalor block up the entrance. *But that will all change soon.*

They worked swiftly to prevent the air from getting even worse. The narrow burning line of petroleum on the floor provided light for them to work by. When they had finished they sat down and listened to what was happening outside, taking it in turns to drink from Caphalor's flask. Boulders were still being shot at the forest, but no longer landing in the immediate vicinity.

As it grew hotter and more stifling in the cave, Sinthoras began to sweat. The stallion snorted constantly and Caphalor was unable to calm the animal, whatever he tried. Raleeha did not dare to speak.

Sinthoras seized the chance to check over his rucksack. The crown was undamaged and the parchment had a hole in it, but it had not been burned. A pain in his right hand made him catch his breath. His fingers tingled and then went numb: the gnome poison at work again.

"All in order," he reported. "Have you got the gålran zhadar's head?"

"No."

"What?" Sinthoras sprang to his feet, holding out the rucksack in reproof. "We were supposed to bring Munumon his head!"

"There wasn't time."

"That was the third requirement for us getting the antidote!"

"We had to escape from the castle. I could do nothing against those numbers all on my own," Caphalor answered sharply. "You were no help."

"Are you reproaching me, after I felled the zhadar?" he snapped in reply. "It's your fault we haven't got the head."

"Only because I was having to look after you. We'll be able to talk Munumon round, I'm sure." Caphalor's tone was confident.

"The gålran zhadar was lying in the corner! How could you not—"

"Stop!" Caphalor threw him an icy look. "There was no other way to get us out of there. Not least because of the state you were in, an instant more would have been our undoing!"

"Just because you are always escaping death doesn't mean your luck will hold," Sinthoras retorted, tossing the sack onto the ground. He was not going to take the blame for this. "What do we do if Munumon is not satisfied with what we have to offer him?"

"He will be satisfied with it."

"I'm not counting on it." It did not take him long to decide on his best course of action. "You take the rucksack and crawl on your belly to the ugly gnome. I'll get on my way to the mist-demon." The smoke was making him cough.

Caphalor stared at him. "Has the magic affected your sanity? Your body carries a poison that will finish you off before you're halfway there."

"It's not certain the poison is lethal," Sinthoras contradicted stubbornly, trying to convince himself. "Perhaps Munumon was lying to us, and anyway, he might just kill us when we've handed over what we've got: the parchment—damaged—and the crown, but not the head. You won't be able to fight off one hundred gnomes, however Honor Blessed you are. You haven't got enough arrows, for a start. You stand no chance." He placed the spear over his knee. "As soon as the inferno has died down and the ground has cooled I'm heading for the northwest."

"Then our ways part here," said Caphalor calmly. He did not try to dissuade Sinthoras. "Your decision will cost you your life, but I shall bury your body when I pass it."

The obboona gave a sudden moan and started to push herself up from the floor. She groaned, staring at her scorched hands, then yelped when she felt her face: the false ears came away in her fingers, turning to ashes. Croaking, she got up and staggered round the cave, begging for water.

"Oh, look! If the gods are with you, Caphalor, you can get our flesh-stealer to complete the parchment. That's if she can still hold a pen." He mocked Karjuna: "The cleansing fire has returned your own skin to you." He pushed her away with the blunt end of his spear before she could touch him. She fell on Raleeha's drinking flask and poured the water down her throat, tears of pain coursing down her face.

Sinthoras would have loved to ram his borrowed spear right through her heart and then shove her outside for the flames to finish off.

He began to examine the spear more closely. Running his fingers down the shaft of the new spear he discovered a little opening—if he put his finger over it a hissing sound came from the spear tip, where a tiny hole was visible, as small as the eye of a needle.

He immediately grasped the significance: if he stabbed an enemy with this spear and then pressed on that valve, a rush of air would destroy the victim's guts. No one would survive that.

He was forced to admire the gålran zhadar's inventiveness. The gnome had probably stolen the idea from someone else, of course. Who cared? This unique weapon was now his.

They heard a splash.

The sound of falling drops was repeated, the intervals getting shorter all the time until it sounded like a fine spray of water.

"You know what that means?" Sinthoras ran to the blocked exit and chucked some of the stones aside, letting clouds of steam into the cave. There was a strong smell of smoke—it was pouring with rain and the downpour was slowly putting out the fire.

This was his best chance of getting away—if the gålran zhadar's soldiers did not find their bodies they would be after them in hot pursuit. He enlarged the opening until he could crawl through.

"My thanks, Samusin!" he cried, bowing his head. "The god of justice is with me."

"You're really going?" Caphalor stepped up to him, his concerned expression concealed by the steam vapor. "Think—"

"I hope when you and your two women get there you find Munumon is having one of his good days." Sinthoras shouldered his spear. "I shall get to the mist-demon first, Caphalor, and I promise we will meet again—alive. Then you will serve me in my army when I lead it against Tark Draan. Don't imagine your Honor-Blessing will help. They'll forget about you. The älfar will be praising *me* soon." Then he left, giving Caphalor no opportunity to reply. It was such a good speech, he did not want it spoiled.

He hurried away through the swirling mists of hot steam.

Chapter VIII

Phondrasôn.

Discovered by the Inextinguishable Ones. Kept hidden and made secure by the Inextinguishable Ones.

It is Unspeakableness, living under the earth, and not a world that may be stepped into. Here there be horrors, monsters and nameless creatures, and its extent defies measurement. Criminals are consigned to its deepest regions, warriors come to face their ultimate challenges, but nothing that possesses the power of reason can reside in this region.

And if any were to attempt it, their reason would be forfeit.

Epocrypha of the Creating Spirit
1st Book
Footnote

Ishím Voróo (The Outer Lands), the kingdom of the fflecx, 4370th division of unendingness (5198th solar cycle), summer.

Standing at a safe distance, Caphalor surveyed the devastation on the empty plain in front of the fortress.

The torrential downpour had put out the flames and turned the ground into a steaming black morass. About a hundred of the gâlran zhadar's soldiers were combing through the area, leaving no fallen tree unturned in their search through the ravaged zone. They were searching the ground methodically in groups of ten—eight warriors and two archers—looking for the burned remains of the älfar.

One of these units had a pack of white hounds on long leashes and they plowed straight through the debris toward the cave where they had sheltered.

Caphalor, Raleeha, and the obboona had set off immediately after Sinthoras had left. Caphalor had no wish to get involved in any more fighting, not when Munumon and the antidote were waiting. Hardly had his thoughts turned to the poison in his blood than his eyes dimmed and his vision blurred. His hands were turning numb. He shook his fingers and rubbed his eyes. Everything was normal again. "They won't catch us up now," Caphalor muttered. He turned the night-mare's head and told it to walk on, leading Raleeha behind him tied to a long rope. He feared despair might make her try to follow her Sinthoras and she was still too valuable to risk losing in Ishím Voróo. She had grazes on her arms and shoulders from the rocks that had fallen in the cave and was coughing a great deal from smoke inhalation.

The flesh-stealer limped along, bringing up the rear. The ugly mount Sinthoras had been given by the fflecx had not survived the fire.

Interminable rain fell from gray skies. It washed the burned skin from Karjuna's shoulders and cooled the wounds she had incurred. Caphalor could not kill her yet, however much he wanted to. First he had to get her to complete the inscription on the parchment.

He was worrying about what to say to the gnome when they met: they had not carried out their task in full, but the king was getting his stolen property back. That should be worth the antidote.

He felt pangs in his side again and there was pressure in his chest that made him fear he was suffocating. He coughed and was able to breathe once more: the poison was making itself felt more and more frequently. Ignoring the protests of the two women, he urged Sardaî on.

He wondered what he could do if Munumon were not in a conciliatory mood. Surely he could tempt the king with some other offer? The obboona might serve as a hostage he could exchange? Or he could fashion a musical instrument for him: a bone and skull flute made from the obboona's skeleton? One would not normally use fresh bones for an instrument, but it would be good enough for the gnome king.

He was sure the fflecx, being gnomoids, could easily be charmed by any small thing that aroused their curiosity. Caphalor thought he could invent some silly story to go with the flute and perhaps Munumon would be so intrigued he would hand over the remedy.

It annoyed him to know that he could not simply kill the fflecx, though he was loath to dismiss the possibility entirely—it would be a magnificent feeling to have Munumon and his entire court dead at his feet, as long as he had secured the antidote first, of course.

Caphalor wiped the rain out of his eyes. His thoughts strayed to Sinthoras and how he had once more shown his true nature by charging off on his own: inconsiderate and selfish. He did not believe for a single moment that the älf had set out alone from any sense of altruism: it was his own skin he had been concerned with when he made off from the cave—and with any luck he would wander directly into the arms of his own mortality.

Looking back, he saw the two women would not be able to keep up the pace for much longer. They were nearly exhausted from struggling through the mud, but they were not going fast enough.

When they came across a fflecx driving two ponies and a cart, Caphalor forced him to cooperate with a good dose of terror and let the women ride on the cart while he rode next to them on Sardaî.

They had to stop when evening fell, as even Caphalor was feeling tired. They pulled off the road and used a tarpaulin from the cart as a tent for shelter. They built a fire while the gnome saw to the ponies.

Karjuna used this rest period to examine and rework the parchment.

Caphalor noticed she was leaving several gaps in the text and asked her why.

She attempted a smile on her ruined face. "My demigod, I admire you and will do anything you ask, but forgive me if I build in some security for myself." Her cracked lips split as she spoke and blood ran down her skin. "As soon as we reach the palace I'll fill in the gaps and, as my reward, you will let me go free."

He stared at her and then burst out laughing. "Of course, obboona," he said, amused. "Today, you decide what I do." His manner became deadly serious and menacing. He picked up the loose end of a rope that was securing the tarpaulin and he whipped it across her torn face. The skin ripped open and more blood coursed down.

"If you dare to speak to me like that ever again," he threatened, "I shall kill you. Finish the parchment, *now!* And if I see even one drop of your filthy blood on it, I'll open your veins and let you bleed to death."

She nodded hastily and wiped the blood away with her arm.

Caphalor noticed that Raleeha's expression had grown somber. She was trying to keep her distance from the flesh-stealer, but it was not easy under the tarpaulin shelter. "What's the matter?"

"Pardon me, master," she answered, facing him. Her black hair hung in wet strands across her face. She was soaked through. "I don't want to touch the obboona. She is the most hateful creature imaginable."

Karjuna snorted with derisive laughter.

"I'm almost glad to be blind," Raleeha exclaimed, "so as not to have to behold your face. Your deeds against the älfar are truly horrendous and you all deserve death a hundred times over. If I could see I would take a weapon and kill you myself!"

This passionate tirade made the obboona laugh even louder, causing the skin on her face to split open further. Raleeha clenched her fists in anger.

Caphalor found it strange that a human would defend his kind so fervently: she must really want to be with Sinthoras, but she was obeying the demands he had made of her when he had given her away. It was älfar law.

"Silence!" he commanded, leaving it open to debate as to which of the women he was addressing.

The sight of Raleeha gave Caphalor an idea. He walked up to the obboona, who flinched and cowered over her parchment task, hoping she had not dripped any blood on it.

"My demigod, it isn't easy to complete the runes," she stammered in her own defense.

Without a word he took the parchment from her and handed it to Raleeha. Then he crouched down at her side. "Touch the parchment and try to feel what has been written. Can you detect the scratches made by the pen?"

"No, demigod," screeched the obboona. "Of course she can't! She's only a stupid little slave girl. It's only me that can read it and save your life. I . . ."

Caphalor ignored her and watched Raleeha pass her fingers carefully over the writing with a smile that might have graced the countenance of an älfar girl.

"Yes, I can feel the marks," she announced. "It's not easy, but I can feel the indentations with my fingertips."

An object flew past Caphalor's face; he had already stretched out a hand to catch it before it could hit Raleeha. It was a hammer from the toolbox on the cart. He cast an icy look over his shoulder.

The obboona had stood up. "No! Don't let her! She must die!" she hissed. "I want to save you; she can't! You are my demigod. You have to be in my debt and then you will belong to me!" Wide-eyed, she stared at him. "I want you to be mine!"

In answer Caphalor hurled the hammer back at her, catching her full on the breast. She fell backward with a groan.

"Master?" called Raleeha in concern.

"The flesh-stealer and I both realized at the same time that she is no longer needed." He got up and approached Karjuna, but she crawled quickly off into the undergrowth. "I wish it had occurred to me earlier." Caphalor sprang onto Sardaî's back and pursued the fleeing obboona through the pouring rain.

The night-mare only had to go a few paces before dancing round, snorting heavily. Sardaî had caught his rider's anger. Sharp lightning flashes shot out of the hooves as it jumped over the obboona, kicking her.

Moaning, she rolled into a ball, covering herself with mud.

"Please, my demigod," she whimpered. "I only did it because . . ."

Caphalor looked down at her, overcome with fury and disgust. He got Sardaî to place his left front hoof on her back. This time the lightning flashes lasted longer; she shrieked like a wild animal as the shape of the iron shoe buried its way into the charred skin of her back. "You shall die, obboona, but it won't be me or my stallion killing you, that would be too much of a privilege—the fflecx scum will execute you in whatever fashion they want." Sardaî withdrew his hoof and neighed loudly, his ears pricking up in alarm. Something was making the night-mare uneasy.

Caphalor took his bow out of its carrying sheath and opened the saddle quiver to select an arrow. He had let himself become distracted by the thought of killing the obboona.

Caphalor saw their camp not three paces away, with the gnome carter standing by the vehicle looking at him questioningly. Raleeha stood in silence, waiting. The obboona lay still, the burn mark on her back smoldering slowly.

Then they heard branches and twigs breaking underfoot and there was a thump of something heavy in motion. A thick branch came hurtling out of the thicket, heading straight for Caphalor.

The älf needed only to apply the lightest pressure of his thighs to make the night-mare swerve out of the way; the wary stallion had already sensed the danger. The missile struck the gnome instead, crushing his chest and his head, then continuing to destroy the side of the cart.

Caphalor loosed a shot into the thicket. One heartbeat later a pale gray troll lumbered out of the undergrowth, clothed only in filthy, soaking bearskins and brandishing uprooted saplings as makeshift clubs. The arrow had caught him in the shoulder, but this was only increasing his rage. He bared his yellow teeth and opened his throat to emit a terrible roar. He looked hungry.

Remaining calm, the älf called up the fear and concentrated on the next shot. He would not get another chance—the troll was too close. Struck through the right eye by the second arrow, the creature slowed, staggered and fell into the mud with a groan.

Loud roars issued from the thicket. The troll had not been alone.

The ponies bolted with their cart, whinnying in terror. One of the ropes had caught round Raleeha's ankle and she was jerked off her feet and dragged behind the fleeing vehicle. The ropes snapped and the tarpaulin ripped through.

Hunger-crazed trolls charged out of the undergrowth on all sides, and in the confusion Caphalor could not work out how many there were. The hunger made them more aggressive and unpredictable than ever. He had a dangerous fight on his hands. Warm magic spread up his spine—but then stopped. He saw black stars circling before his eyes, taking over his field of vision. His bow arm failed him: the poison was at work again.

Three trolls ran to Caphalor as if they could sense his sudden weakness.

He turned the night-mare against the first of the three and urged the animal to bite. The knife-sharp teeth ripped out a chunk from the troll's belly, causing gray blood to pour from the severed arteries. The monster fell screaming to the ground, hands clutching the open wound.

Caphalor concentrated hard and made the stars recede; his arm regained its strength. He shot the next troll through the mouth, killing it on the spot. The third foe executed an unexpected leap forward, thrashing about him with a long, heavy chain.

The älf ducked under the flying black links, but the chain hit the stallion, so that it lost its footing on the soft mud.

Caphalor tossed his bow away and launched himself out of the saddle to avoid being crushed under his own animal. He somersaulted back on to his feet and vaulted to the side.

Drawing his serrated short swords, the älf took a run at the monster that was wielding its chain like a whip. The troll's attempts to catch him with the flying links failed and Caphalor prepared to leap at his attacker and slit the unprotected throat.

The undergrowth disgorged yet another foe: not a troll, but something bigger than a wild bear; it was more muscled, too, and with a longer snout and smoother coat. It was up on its hind legs, its front paws ready to strike. The muzzle was wide open showing teeth as transparent as glass.

Caphalor knew what this new enemy was: a srink. He was surprised to find one here; the territory of the fflecx was thought to be free of these marauding beasts. The alchemancers had used their poisons to exterminate everything they did not like, except for the gålran zhadar.

In battle its fangs and claws would lose their steely strength and break off in a wound, splintering like glass and making it almost impossible to remove the splinters from the flesh. Often their attempted removal would cause more damage than the original injury. The srink would simply grow new claws and teeth.

The srink sank its teeth into the troll's flank and Caphalor heard snapping noises, then the srink sprang back with a bark. The troll screamed pitifully and scrabbled around in the gash in its side, trying to remove the teeth, but the fragments sliced through the troll's fingertips and were pressed further into its flesh. Its cries grew louder and it collapsed to the ground, forgetting both älf and srink.

Caphalor whirled round when he heard Raleeha call for help.

The cart had been stopped by five trolls: two of them had already torn the ponies to pieces and were devouring the hot flesh greedily, another was chomping on the remains of the gnome carter and another had grabbed Raleeha and was stripping her muddy clothing off, preparing to eat her. The fifth troll was waiting for his friend to finish.

The srink had also heard Raleeha's cry. It put its head back and uttered a loud roar.

Samusin, where are you? I need your help! Caphalor implored.

Caphalor sped past the srink, took out his long-distance bow and raced over to Raleeha, firing as he went.

The rain had softened the bowstring, reducing the effectiveness of his shots, and he was only able to kill three of the trolls, the other two were only injured. One of these whirled round and charged the älf, who abandoned the bow and took up his short swords again.

"Samusin!" he shouted into the skies. "Give me the strength I need to overcome the scum!" He launched himself at the foe.

It was easy for Caphalor to avoid the reckless assault and turn on the troll, slashing its thigh with repeated rapid strokes. The beast thudded to the ground with a yelp of pain and Caphalor dealt with the last enemy, who was still holding Raleeha in its grasp, not letting her feet touch the ground.

"Watch out, demigod," Karjuna shouted suddenly, throwing herself at the troll's broad back. In her hand she held the gnome-carter's sword, aiming for the neck.

Hearing her, the troll cast Raleeha to the floor and whirled round to catch the obboona in full flight. He hurled her down into the mud at his feet.

That exploit won't save your life, flesh-stealer. Caphalor had used the diversion to get behind the troll. *The beast first, then you.* He slashed through the leg tendons at the back of the knee and then stabbed it in the kidneys as it fell. The troll arched its back and roared but then collapsed. Caphalor stepped nimbly aside and jumped onto the corpse to get a better view.

"Master?" Raleeha called out, helplessly trying to get her bearings. Her dress hung in rags, but she did not look like she cared about being half-naked. She was covered in dirt.

"Shhh," he said, turning round to see if there were other threats. "Keep quiet, Raleeha. There might be . . ."

Five more srinks stormed out of the forest, furry ears upright and alert. They circled round Caphalor, Raleeha, and Karjuna, who stood up groaning, a short sword in her hand. She spat out a mouthful of mud and swept the glade with her eyes.

"I can hear wolves," Raleeha whispered fearfully.

There were more sounds from the forest: other srinks were approaching at speed, while these stood watching them closely.

"Not wolves—srinks," he told her. In Dsôn srinks were said to be reasonably intelligent—he knew of two Dsôn älfar, at least, who kept srinks to guard their slaves because they were cleverer and quicker than dogs. They gathered in packs of about thirty or forty at a time, roaming in forest areas where the cover was good. "I can't understand why they're here: since the gnomes tried to wipe them out, they avoid the region altogether . . . supposedly."

One of the srink, a solidly built specimen, had a red scarf with runes on tied round its belly: the leader! It might be enough if he put this one out of action.

For a terrifying moment Caphalor's knees went weak again. These were not the best conditions for facing another crowd of opponents in battle.

Raleeha slid over to the troll cadaver where Caphalor was perched. "Master, give me a weapon so I may defend myself."

"Be quiet," he said. He could see the obboona backing slowly toward his vantage point. Caphalor would be forced to accept the flesh-stealer as an ally in the coming fight. "I shall forgive you. You have one more chance to win my trust," he lied convincingly. "Come up here, obboona," he commanded. "Stand here next to me."

"Gladly, demigod," she exclaimed in delight, clambering up onto the troll corpse. With her badly burned skin she was a horrific sight; a thick liquid mixed with blood was oozing out of the cracks in her flesh.

"What's with these srinks? They are different." Caphalor pointed at the red embroidered scarf and surveyed the area swiftly, calculating: there must have been about seventy of the creatures surrounding them. They all had breast plates, protective headgear and a range of weaponry. The original six had only their own fur. "It looks as if they are attempting to imitate the runes my own people use."

The obboona was about to reply when the srink with the red scarf gave a barked command. His troops all sank down on one knee, bowing their heads to the älf. "At last we have found you, demigod," the srink croaked, head held high.

Caphalor mastered his growing relief and his initial surprise that they were versed in the Dark Language. Älfar were apparently worshipped by these srinks.

He caught a swift movement out of the corner of his eye, but was too late to avoid the clenched fist crashing into his chin.

Wheels of fire swirled in front of his eyes and a black curtain descended. His limbs were heavy as lead. Still staggering from the blow, he was kicked in the stomach, all breath driven from his body. He dodged the next kick, but the one after that found its target. He collapsed in front of the obboona's boots and was on the point of losing consciousness.

Caphalor saw Karjuna approach, smiling and apologetic. He could not catch her words. Miles away Raleeha was calling him and he wondered how, after all his warnings, she still dared to use his name. He was her master! The obboona merged into the darkness swamping him. His last act was to stab her when she tried to get closer. He heard her scream and then passed out.

Caphalor shot up, startled, and reached for his sword—his fingers closing on empty air.

He saw by the dim light of the smoking lamp that he was naked. Raleeha cowered under a blanket at his side. He saw that lines had been marked on his toned and muscular body. Cutting lines—it looked as if the obboona was preparing to use his skin.

He did not understand what had happened.

"Master!" Raleeha exclaimed in relief. "You are awake at last."

"What—" He broke off. She would not be able to tell him what had happened.

"They dragged us off through the forest," she began. "I don't need to see to be able to see to know what's happening. You were carried. The obboona and the srink were talking in a language I don't understand, but I can assure you, master, that they already knew each other. It sounded as if she were issuing the orders."

Caphalor studied the stone walls. They must have been let down from the opening above their heads. It was the only way in to this prison. "Where are we?"

"It was a long march before we reached shelter," she told him, taking care not to omit anything. "Unless my ears deceived me, I would say the srink captured a farmhouse to use as their camp. They put us in what I think was a barn, and then lowered us down here on ropes through a hole."

Caphalor studied the walls. He tapped the stone, not really thinking he would find a hollow place behind. The masonry was cold and solid. "Did the flesh-stealer say what she intended?"

"She said I should tell you that she regrets having attacked you but that it was the only way to save your life." Raleeha's voice revealed her disgust. "She will come to visit you soon and you should think about ways to thank her."

"To *thank* her?"

"For letting you live, master."

Caphalor laughed outright. "I am so grateful to her that in return I plan to release her from her scummy existence." In his mind's eye he saw the obboona before him; in his present state, he would even have undergone the indignity of strangling her with his bare hands. "Do you know what happened to my night-mare?"

"Either he was killed in the fight or else he took flight," she replied with a sigh. "I despair, master. What can we do?"

This was the very question Caphalor had put to himself not five heartbeats earlier, having to admit that the answer was: nothing. "We'll have to wait. I can't see any way out of here." He checked the floor of their prison to see if there was anything that would serve as a weapon. All he found was a sharp flint, but that would be enough to slash skin and rip open an artery. That meant he would not be forced to throttle the Obboona but could catch her unawares and kill her as soon as there was an opportunity.

He toyed with the fragment of stone. "She must be their leader. Perhaps she was planning to storm the sky fortress with the srinks and that was why she had entered the zhadar's service in the first place," he mused. "When she escaped, maybe she was on her way back to her troops and fell into the hands of the trolls. We freed her and she kept up the pretense, knowing that, sooner or later, her people would find her."

"May I speak, master?"

He remembered his plan to put up a show of courtesy in order to win her trust. Purely as a stratagem. He still believed he could make it back home. With her. "Yes. Tell me your views on this."

"It makes sense, what you say." Raleeha shuddered. "I would guess there were at least a hundred of these creatures. I mostly know about srinks from hearsay, but I did once see one, in Dsôn. He was quite different. More like a dog. Did I hear correctly: are they wearing armor and carrying weapons, master?"

"They are." Caphalor studied the girl. She was in despair, without question, but she had not lost her capacity to use her intelligence and her logical mind.

Despite himself, his eyes wandered down from her face. Her flesh, though dirt-streaked, was in itself flawless and her limbs were straight and true. Perhaps he could make something exceptional from her after her death, if she were not needed for anything else. The skin would make a fine canvas, her hair could be used as yarn for tatting. His wife was good with her hands like that. The long bones would have a special place; he imagined an artwork with a series of figures. Or perhaps an abstract piece, a sculpture to stand in his garden.

He realized he had been staring at her for some time. Longer than he would usually need when getting inspiration for his art. He stopped to ask himself whether his interest in her was more than the purely artistic.

Caphalor had to laugh. *Utterly ludicrous, the very thought.* She was a human, pretty perhaps, and graceful, and her features were similar to those of an älf, it was true, but a long, long way from their own standard of beauty. She could not hold a candle to his own wife, for example. Not at all.

"Master, why do you laugh?"

"Just a ridiculous thought." What else could it be? How else could she ever be of interest to him other than as material for a work of art? There was absolutely no question of him stooping to that level. Caphalor decided it must be the alchemancers' poison warping his mind. Yet another cause for worry.

"There must be different types of srink, then, master: those that have attained a higher level of thought, and those that have not. Why are they following the obboona?" Raleeha seemed to be enjoying puzzling this out. "You know, they can forge metal," she said suddenly, as if it had just occurred to her.

"What do you mean, *forge*?" He let her speak. There was no reason she should not put her mind to work, though he doubted it would help them. On the other hand, she was not like other barbarian slaves.

"I mean, they've made their own weapons, master. Their swords have a different sound from the ones I know—from back when I lived in the castle with my brother. A sword makes a special sound when it's being worked."

Caphalor was certain she was imagining this, but did not say so. He could see the sense of it. After all, they were hiding out in the territory of the deadly fflecx. *Are they courageous? Or stupid?* They had to avoid discovery at all costs because there was no defense against the poisons the fflecx used in battle and their armor would not protect them: they wore nothing that would stop the passage of a blowpipe dart. However odd the idea sounded, they would need to kill any creature they came across, and for that they needed weapons.

That train of thought was an unpleasant reminder of the poison in his own veins, rendering him mortal. It was his own fault for listening to the slave girl.

"Get some rest," he told her, putting a stop to her talk as civilly as he could.

There was a noise from above and light fell on them as the cover was shifted. A large basket came down on a rope and there was no mistaking the sense of the grunted command to get into it.

Caphalor decided to comply. "Come up after me," he said to Raleeha. He was pulled up.

He found himself in a barn just as the slave girl had assumed, surrounded by perhaps twenty well-armed srinks. It did not bother him that he was naked, after all, his body was perfect. These ugly beasts should look their fill and be envious of his splendid proportions. Raleeha was hauled up and both of them were taken across to the main building. They passed a heap of gnome-sized broken bones. There was no doubt as to how the srinks had been feeding themselves.

Karjuna was seated in the main room on a leather chair. She had washed and her face was bandaged. She wore a flowing black robe and on her right breast she had the same rune the srink leader had displayed. Ten tall, dangerous-looking creatures protected her right and left. A warming fire crackled in the grate and there was an enticing smell of fresh bread and meat stew.

When Caphalor—still completely naked—stepped into the room, she stood up and bowed. "My demigod," she said humbly, her voice heavy with regret. The madness in her eyes had not receded, on the contrary—perhaps she did not have to keep up any pretense now that she was surrounded by her own soldiers. "I am—"

Caphalor demonstrated why älfar were so feared. His native powers did not let him down; waves of dread streamed out of him, dousing the fire in the grate and spreading terror in the air like an acrid, stifling smell. The light dimmed, making the shadows menacing and alive. His black eyes spewed fiery anger. The tugging at the skin of his face told him the black lines of fury were at work. "You are *nothing,* obboona!" His voice was deep and resounding.

The srinks murmured among themselves and stepped aside, but they looked strangely—could it be?—delighted.

Karjuna got to her feet in spite of the darkness and the terror waves. "You enchant us with your powers," she enthused. "My subjects and I have never had a chance to experience this before! Thank you, my demigod."

Caphalor was at a loss. Why had the srink had not reacted with pandemonium? He clenched his fists, feeling the flint in his left hand. He would wait. He withdrew his magic.

"Let me tell you what you have found here, demigod." She sat down. "It was always my plan to attack the gålran zhadar in his own fortress. He has killed too many of my subjects and must be made to pay. I entered his service in order to spy out the lie of the castle and on my escape I was captured by the trolls." It was exactly as he had assumed. "I had to play a role until my people found me." She beamed in her mindless but obsessive way. "Forgive me for having hit your sacred person, demigod. I could not permit you to kill any of my subjects; they would have reacted with such anger that they would have murdered you." She gestured to her soldiers. "A select unit from my army. The arrogant gålran zhadar would have stood no chance against my loyal troops."

"Give me the parchment and let me and the slave girl leave," he demanded. "You and I have no business to discuss."

"Then what will you do, demigod?" she asked. "What will happen when you have taken Munumon the things he asked for? I heard something about a mission—it is more than just your life at stake. Perhaps I can help?"

"The parchment," he repeated. "At once, flesh-stealer!" He cast a disdainful look at her soldiers. "They won't be able to stop me." He put on a confident and menacing air.

Karjuna's eyes glowed greedily as she studied the älf's naked groin. "Did you notice the lines I've drawn on your sacred skin? They show what I could do, demigod," she said, with obvious enjoyment. She hugged herself. I could step into your skin and would be eternally connected with you," she breathed. "But I expect you would be dead without your skin. I want you at my side. All day—and especially all through the night," she burst out, her voice full of desire.

Caphalor laughed in her face.

"I mean it!" she shouted, getting quickly to her feet. "My demigod, you have the choice: stay at my side to conquer the fflecx and any other foe you care to name. If you wish it, I will subjugate the Inextinguishables and seize their Tower," she enthused, as if there were any chance at all of her army of srinks ever reaching the Star Realm's defense-moat. "Or you refuse and you will have lost your chance of getting the parchment, the antidote and your liberty: then I'll flay your corpse and turn myself into a perfect älf in your skin." She sat down and glared at him.

Of course! Caphalor realized the only reason the srinks obeyed her was because they took her for an älf. The burns she had received meant she was bandaged up and the srinks could not see her true appearance. If she had a genuine älf as her consort the srinks would be more abject in their worship of her. He was convinced now that Karjuna would carry out her threat. The pressure in his chest was a constant reminder of the poison in his veins. His right arm was feeling numb. He had to lie to get himself out of this trap.

Caphalor pretended his anger had dissipated. "You would put me in power in place of the Inextinguishables?" he asked, as if intrigued and eager. It was quite an effort to make the anger lines fade away.

"Yes, I would," she responded at once.

"You would be making me into a god," he told her, sounding awed by the prospect. "But the river-moat and the defenses and the army—how would you overcome these hurdles?"

"My love for you will guide me and send me inspiration, demigod," she answered ecstatically. "There is nothing I would not do for you."

"Then I shall make you this promise," he said majestically, to remove any doubt from her mind, "that after completing my mission I shall return to you as your partner. I swear this by all that is holy to me. Many of my friends will support us. Our realm shall be mighty indeed."

"Yes," breathed Karjuna. "Yes, it will." Her compulsive infatuation led her to believe every word he said.

"And we shall stand at the top of the Tower and show our children what will one day belong to them."

"Children," she repeated, smiling.

"Think of it: how wonderful they will be. Flawlessly beautiful. And they will live forever." His voice grew soft and tender, like that of a lover.

The obboona gazed at him, hanging on his words, longing to hear more. "I can see them," she sighed. "And will you love me?"

"I swear it." He had planted the idea of a glorious shared future and had won her over. Now he had to take further precautions to ensure he would be able to come and go freely. "But you must see that I can't take you and the srinks with me on my secret mission. Munumon would see us coming and I would die of his poison. We shall have to employ cunning, not an army, in this instance."

There was a sharp intake of breath from Raleeha, but she said nothing.

The obboona made a face, sat down again and leaned back in her chair to ponder. She was obviously of two minds. She would not be able to achieve unambiguous victory—namely his immediate unconditional agreement, but on the other hand, he had not turned down her fervently desired proposal, merely postponed it. In her mind there would still be the nights of passion she so longed for. "I understand. But your word, my demigod—what is your word worth?"

"It is the word of a demigod!" Raleeha hurled the indignant retort at her. "You should honor him, not treat him like a creature lower than yourself!"

Caphalor ordered her to be silent.

Karjuna nodded at her. "Brave little slave girl, protecting her master. How sweet." She laughed contemptuously and then turned deadly serious.

"But you are right, slave. It was blasphemy of me to doubt him." She got to her feet. "You have given your word and your oath, my demigod, and so I will let you go. Come back to me quickly and I shall lay the heads of the Inextinguishable Ones at your feet. But understand that I shall find you wherever you are, should you fail to find your way back to me—for whatever reason." She gestured toward him with her right hand. "And if you deceive me, my revenge will be cruel. Even a demigod will not be spared."

"Let it be so," he agreed, relieved. "I shall return when my mission is completed."

She clapped her hands and a srink stepped forward, holding the dry clothes, armor and weapons Caphalor needed. A second srink brought simple attire for Raleeha.

Karjuna went over to the fireplace and buried the tip of the poker deep in the coals. "There's one more thing I want to give you for your journey, my demigod. We shall rule over our lands as equal partners: equal in our beauty and equal in our wounds." She pulled the red-hot metal out of the fire and came up to Caphalor. The älf's arms were grabbed by the srink soldiers. "You got your night-mare to brand me and I am returning the gesture. Let this be a reminder of your vow." She burned her signature rune into his skin.

He bit his teeth together to withstand the pain. The smell of charred flesh rose in his nostrils.

She regarded her work with satisfaction. "Now, my demigod, you may dress and depart. May Samusin, Inàste, and Tion protect you and guide your arrows to your target."

Caphalor felt the flint shard in the palm of his hand. Part of him—his pride—demanded that he launch himself at the obboona and cut her throat. She had marked him as one brands one's cattle, as one marks a slave, as one marks a criminal! That nonsense she spouted about his being a demigod was meaningless. It was all about her and her ludicrous ideas. He would certainly return to her when it was time to let her die slowly and painfully. At long last.

Your death bears the name Caphalor. He swore this on his own soul!

He began to get dressed. In full view of Karjuna and the srinks, he girded himself and put on his armor. In the meantime she had the parchment brought to her and completed her work on it. "What happened to my night-mare?" he asked.

Karjuna was staring at his sex, now covered by leather and steel, and was dreaming of passionate nights, knowing now what awaited her. "The night-mare will be roaming around in the forest somewhere looking for you, my demigod. I shall arrange for horses to be provided. The srinks are not good riders, they are better on their own feet." She bowed to him and a srink handed him the parchment. "I bless the day you return to me."

Caphalor turned away, placed the slave collar that had been provided round Raleeha's neck and strode out of the room.

His hatred of the obboona was so great that the anger lines spread over his face again. A number of miles later, they were still there.

Ishím Voróo (The Outer Lands), the kingdom of the fflecx,
4370th division of unendingness (5198th solar cycle),
summer.

Caphalor looked at Raleeha: she was examining the dress with her fingers. It was clearly too tight and too short for her: a gnome garment. She looked like a child that had outgrown its clothes. She feared the colors would be vivid and brash, making her look like a fool, but when she asked him, Caphalor gave her a quick "No" as answer.

Sardaî had quickly located his master, greeted the älf with a prolonged whinny of joy and then devoured the inferior horse Caphalor had been supplied with.

Caphalor and Raleeha had ridden in silence since leaving the farmstead: fury had rendered him speechless. He felt deeply humiliated, had lost any support that Sinthoras might have provided and was now at the mercy of the gnome ruler. He was not in the mood for working out a cunning stratagem, but would have to keep doing just that if he were to remain alive.

He could only guess why Raleeha was silent. One guess might have been that she was trying to come to terms with his promise to the obboona. He could see it in her expression. Raleeha was no warrior—she was an artist.

The barbarians were not able to combine the two callings in the way the älfar could.

"Well," he said suddenly. "We've managed to get away from the gâlran zhadar's soldiers. With Samusin's help they may come across the srinks and finish off the obnoxious obboona so that we never have to deal with her again. Even if I'd rather kill her myself."

"Yes, master," she said, breathing a sigh of relief. His words obviously reassured her. "I'm sure Munumon can be talked round."

"May the gods listen to your words," he replied. "If that fat toad thinks I would be afraid to kill him, despite the hundred guards he surrounds himself with, he's got another think coming."

"You'd attack him, master?"

"If he won't give me the antidote. If I die, let it be a warrior's death." He smiled, noticing how afraid she was of death. "You will be all right. You can return through the path I am cutting. Go back to Dsôn and wait for Sinthoras. On my death ownership falls back to him." He knew that his choice of words allowed her the opportunity of escaping to her own people if he should be killed.

"Master, that is generous," she said. "May I ask something?"

"What greater favor can I grant you than giving you your life?" he asked, condescendingly.

"You could issue me a free pass. I fear your border guards would kill me otherwise," she requested. "To them I would be nothing more than a runaway slave." Raleeha bowed her head. "They won't know my real reasons for leaving."

Caphalor admitted that he had not thought about that particular circumstance. "Of course." He guided Sardaî from the path and dismounted. "It won't be long now before we reach the fat toad's court." He took out a paper, ink, and pen and sat down in the grass to write out a few lines addressed to the bridge watch of the defense island.

When he had finished writing, he looked up. Raleeha was tying her long black hair back, accentuating her very unbarbarian features. She was really pretty.

Taken by surprise at this realization, he forced himself to concentrate on ways of utilizing her skull for aesthetic purposes: it could be covered in silver leaf and sprinkled with a pattern of diamond dust, set with jewels. A graceful barbarian such as this one deserved a life after death.

Caphalor stood up and handed her the folded paper. "Look after this. Your life may depend on it."

As he gave it to her, their hands touched briefly. He would not have been able to say whether this happened on purpose or by accident. Her skin was warm and soft. No different from that of his own wife. He halted, looked at her and then got back into the saddle.

Raleeha pretended she had not noticed, and as he had said nothing, it was as if it had not occurred.

They soon reached the ruler's court, built in the rough shape of an ugly fflecx head, embedded in the hilly landscape.

Tinny fanfares announced their arrival. Gnomes skipped out of the colorful gate and hurried up, waving their halberds like toys.

"Our black-eyes has come back," one of them cried.

"Ha ha! The black-eyes and the no-eyes," giggled another. "Quick, get off your nags and hop along. Munumon, the great ruler, is waiting for you!"

Caphalor was pleased to see they were nervous of Sardaî and were keeping their distance. He dismounted slowly, firstly to show the fflecx that he was supremely indifferent to the fact their king was waiting, and secondly because his knee felt weak. Between the thigh and the lower leg the whole area was cold and numb, a disturbing element, instead of the smoothly operating, flexible joint he could normally rely on.

Raleeha was being yanked out of the saddle by small hands. High voices shrieked and laughed as the fflecx pulled at her clothes. They had seen what she was wearing. Raleeha sighed.

"Look at her!" One of the fflecx grasped her breast. "That's a nice handful! She's hoping the king will bed her." Raleeha tried to strike out, but her assailant moved aside and grabbed her bottom. "Oh, yes, that's the way he likes them. Plump as pumpkins."

Caphalor gave Sardaî an order and the night-mare kicked the gnome in the head. There was a flash when the hoof met the skull and the small fflecx head burst open. The gnome fell dead to the floor, his blood spraying out over his companions.

The fflecx jumped away from the slave girl, screaming. They yelled at Caphalor, threatening him and his night-mare with their halberds.

"Thank you, master," said Raleeha in relief.

"She is my property, you scum," he yelled, instead of responding to her; he attempted to loose his black waves of terror at the gnomes. He was aware of the warmth in his spine, but his power only produced a few black threads this time. Caphalor jerked her slave collar, then noted with relief that his knee had begun functioning normally again.

The fflecx led them through several lofty chambers until they had reached the doors to the throne room.

Fflecx were sitting and standing all around the room wearing armor or their typical clashing garments, some were bareheaded and some sported headgear even a barbarian's jester would have been ashamed of. There was a sickly sweet smell, like sugar icing, honey, and the heavy perfume of lilies. Caphalor could hardly breathe.

The repulsive, squat little king was seated on the throne at his ease, his eyes glittering with malice, his shockingly hideous female playmates at his side. Caphalor wanted to close his eyes to avoid having to see him. The assembled fflecx were surprisingly quiet, keen to find out what was coming.

"You are to say nothing," he told Raleeha.

He had decided to try a nonchalant arrogance, perhaps the king would swallow that. "We are back, Munumon." He tossed the rucksack down and it slid, with a clink and a clatter, over to the foot of the throne. "Here are the items you wanted."

Two gnomes took the bag and held it up to the king before pulling out the contents. "The crown!" Munumon giggled. "And the parchment!" He unrolled it, studied it briefly and sniffed at it. Then he put out his tongue to lick the crown, scratching at the metal with his long nails. He was obviously checking to see if the booty was genuine. He raised his podgy face and announced smugly that he was satisfied.

The courtiers broke out in enthusiastic applause.

Caphalor looked at the king. "So where is my antidote?" he asked, raising his voice over the excited hum of the crowd.

Munumon held up his arms to show his subjects the two precious items that had been returned, demanding their attention. "And where is the head of the gålran zhadar, black-eyes? It was part of the bargain," he croaked. "Were you so keen on losing your life? Or has your horrid warrior friend got the skull?"

"No. We killed the gålran zhadar, but we didn't have time to hack off his head," Caphalor answered truthfully. "It's the same result, whether you've got the head or not: the gålran zhadar is dead and you wouldn't enjoy looking at his ugly mug anyway."

"Oh? I always enjoy seeing dead enemies. And I like trophies." Demanding wine, he waved over a fflecx woman whose breasts dangled down to her middle.

"It would only have been an eighth of a trophy."

"But I love little things!" cried the king, clapping his hands. "You should have brought it." All the gnomes laughed.

"Let me explain, king. His skull was badly damaged in the fighting. It got crushed between two huge chain links traveling in opposite directions and it was grated, like cheese." Caphalor forced a smile.

"Grated? What fun! I could have strewn it on the flower beds as fertilizer." Munumon was shrieking with laughter. His courtiers joined in.

"It would not have made good manure and it would not have been a pretty sight." Caphalor tried to turn the conversation. "Even his creator would not have recognized him," he went on, lying in the same calm voice that he had used when he was telling the truth. "There wasn't enough of it left to bother you with." The king's laughter showed he did not care two hoots about what Caphalor was telling him. For this reason Caphalor did not warn the king about Karjuna and her srinks or the zhadar's soldiers. Let them come wipe out the gnome court.

He glanced at Raleeha. Her expression showed that she was worried he would leap forward, kill the gnome king and be overwhelmed by the crowd.

"That's enough," grunted Munumon, shaking with laughter. "To hear a black-eyes try to save his own skin is quite enough entertainment for me. I shan't take your life, nor that of the little no-eyes, either."

"My thanks, King Munumon," said Caphalor. "So I can have the antidote—"

"No," guffawed the king, holding his sides. "No, black-eyes. You shan't have the antidote," he chortled. He poured wine down his gullet and swallowed loudly. "That's the punishment for failure. I'll let you go, but I shouldn't think you've got more than seven sun courses before the poison makes your blood so thick that you will die." He sniggered and pointed at Caphalor. "Look at him! Look! His face is coming to pieces!"

Fury lines were breaking out all over his visage and he was tensing his body, ready to lash out.

The little bells on the king's crown tinkled when Munumon got to his feet, while the rest of the court continued to laugh. "There are forty crossbows aimed at you, black-eyes. If you so much as move a muscle you will forfeit your grace period before you die." The king pranced down from his throne and went over to the cascades. "Get out of here! You and your slave, out! I'm going to have my bath." He handed the parchment and the crown to a servant and called his women over.

The fflecx guards advanced on Caphalor, their halberds lowered toward him. He racked his brain as to what to do. Attack? And die immediately and not even have those extra days? He decided otherwise. "Let's go," he said to Raleeha, who could not believe that he was simply giving in to Munumon and beating a retreat. They left, to the loud amusement of the court. They were out in the rain once more.

"Master, what happens now?" Raleeha could bear it no longer and had to break her silence.

Caphalor did not answer. He watched her. She did not even know if he were standing near her. She could hear nothing and there was no tug on her collar. He was trying to work out which of his hundred ideas was the most sensible.

"Master, speak to me."

"We are going to Dsôn Faïmon."

"*What?*"

"You heard what I said," he snapped, jerking angrily at her collar. She could hardly breathe. "The mission has failed. It is impossible to get where I am supposed to go within these seven sun courses."

"So you wish to die where your family is, master?"

"No. I shan't cross the border. I gave the Inextinguishables my word of honor that I should only return to present myself to them and the älfar folk if I were successful," he said bitterly. "But you must live, Raleeha."

"Me? I am only a slave—"

"From the Lotor family. Your continued existence must be ensured at all costs. Who knows what benefit this may prove to have for the rulers? I am not doing this out of pity. You are too valuable a hostage to die a miserable death in Ishím Voróo."

"You mean you would not cross the defense moat?"

"Exactly. I will deliver you to the guards and give them orders to take you to my wife. She will receive a letter from me explaining your special status. You will be well cared for in her household." Caphalor spoke clearly and firmly. His decision had been made and it had nothing to do with the fact that he found Raleeha thoroughly fascinating. It was purely her unusual bones that interested him, he told himself.

"You will confront the flesh-stealer, master?"

"The obboona shall die at my hands, as I vowed. Munumon, too, will have seen his last dawn. So it will be." He went over toward their mounts. "Mount up. I don't have any time to waste."

Raleeha nodded. "Yes, master." She felt her way to the horse and climbed up clumsily, holding onto the mane as Caphalor instructed her. He tied the reins to the saddle of the night-mare and they rode off wildly through the rain. The slave girl needed all her skill not to fall off.

Caphalor had watched her carefully when he announced his decision. He had seen the regret in her face. Regret and admiration—for him! But at the same time he had seen relief—she was probably grateful to know she would be regaining the safety of Dsôn Faïmon, where she could await the return of Sinthoras.

Chapter IX

*For the defense of their state the Inextinguishable Ones had a deep moat dug,
surrounding the whole of Dsôn Faïmon.*

*An army of slaves excavated a circular defense ditch to encompass the radial
arms. Thousands died in the construction and were buried at the deepest part
of the moat.*

*Platforms were erected in the middle of the moat, and strongholds built.
Catapults were installed, able to fire faster and further than any weapon then
in existence. These defense islands were connected to the Star State on the one
hand and Ishím Voróo on the other by means of drawbridges.*

Epocrypha of the Creating Spirit,
1st book,
Chapter 2, 1–5

Ishím Voróo (The Outer Lands),
4370th division of unendingness (5198th solar cycle),
summer.

The weather changed as soon as Sinthoras passed the border of the alchemancers' land. From now on he would be riding not through rain, but snow.

The badly made road taking him northwest twisted continually upward: it rose through hills, small mountains and then high ranges. The rocks at the roadside were dark brown, shot through with black veins.

However much he concentrated on maintaining his pace, sparing neither himself nor his mount, he always took the trouble to observe the landscape. The watchful eye of a warrior combined neatly with the appreciative eye of the artist. There was so much he wanted to paint.

It was totally different here from Dsôn Faïmon. Through countless ages, wind, ice, and water had carved bizarre shapes in the stone, giving soft contours to what had once been sharp edges.

New vistas met his gaze at every turn of the road: rock formations might rear up from the valley floor like a cluster of needles, or bright green torrents of water might gush from clefts in the cliff to crash into the chasm below. One thing was certain: the place had been abandoned by all living creatures, as Sinthoras had been pleased to discover. He did not have time to waste in combat, but it was strange that there was no one at all on this broad road. *Perhaps the gods created the whole place just for themselves—and for artists, of course.*

Sinthoras saw neither towns nor villages, nor even a ruined farmstead or a nomad's tent where he might have sought shelter. He soon left the needle-like rock formations behind him and by evening he was riding along a narrow, dried-up riverbed. It felt as if he were traveling along the veins of some giant creature. The rock walls enclosed him at times; at others the path lay open to the sky. Underfoot the ground had been washed smooth.

He could not resist removing his glove to touch the marble floor that was making the going extremely difficult for his horse. Every time it slipped or took a false step he smacked it over the nostrils with the reins. After a dozen or so sharp reprimands the animal had learned its lesson, but Sinthoras was still not satisfied. "Stupid creature! What wouldn't I give for a night-mare instead!"

He wished he could take more time to rest—or time to sit and paint. He had never seen such picturesque settings anywhere in his own country, but he must reach the mist-demon before the poison engulfed him. He was convinced there would be time later on to come back and admire the scenery. *I don't give up as quickly as Caphalor.* After he left the riverbed, the path wound up more steeply. Snowfields stretched to the right and to the left; a clump of trees in a narrow ravine plaintively held out leafless arms.

Still no sign of other life. He rode in perfect solitude.

There must have been a reason living creatures had shunned the mountain range, but he was not eager to investigate—time was so precious. He always found opportunities to fight scum or barbarians; he relished the combat before letting an enemy die, swiftly or slowly. The speed with which their death arrived, carrying his name, depended on his mood at the time. But defeating whatever had emptied this whole stretch of countryside would certainly not be done quickly.

His experience with the gålran zhadar had made Sinthoras more cautious. Sorcerers and any beings with a talent for magic had to be killed swiftly. He was almost prepared to wager that it had been a magic source that had driven life away here, even if he were not able to detect it himself.

The rhythm of his horse's hooves was disrupted, its energy flagging.

"If you fall, you will die," he threatened. He led his mount over to an outcrop of rock where he gave it some moss from the stones and some lichen scratched from a tree trunk. He lay down under his blanket. The horse snorted and sniffed at the offerings, but refused to touch anything, trembling with fear, the sweat turning to ice on its coat.

Sinthoras could not sleep. He was terribly cold and the wind whistled round the tops of the mountains, driving the snow into every crevice. However much he tried to curl up to keep warm, flakes of snow found him. His inner energy was no help. *If I don't get out of this ice-hole soon and find somewhere warmer I'm going to freeze to death.*

The horse gave a cry of pain and collapsed. The merciless ride had demanded too much of it.

That saves me having to kill you. Sinthoras stood up and called to Samusin and Tion, his arms outstretched to the sky, "Send me a sign. Something to give me hope that I may fulfill my mission!"

The gods were silent.

Looking at the blind, dead eyes of the horse, he noticed the crystal coating on the horse's back. It really did look more attractive like that.

He supposed the same fate would soon be his. The thought of being preserved forever in ice was a reassuring one: if he was going to have to sacrifice his immortality, this was a good way to go.

"Ye gods!" he cried from the depths of his soul. "Do you want the realm of the älfar to sink without trace? Then let me die. But we are the children of Inàste, we are their descendants and share their divinity, my mission must succeed!"

The wind turned and brought the smell of burning to his nostrils.

"Inàste, you shall be proud of me," he said, grabbing up his weapons and following the scent of fire. His boots left no marks in the snow and made no noise as he crept out of his makeshift shelter and slipped away through the night.

The moon still rode high in the sky and the snow-covered slopes reflected the silvery light, illuminating the landscape.

Sinthoras permitted himself to enjoy the sight for a while, to listen to the silence and to watch his own breath curling white in the air in front of his eyes. *I shall succeed*. He was mortified at having doubted himself in that moment of weakness. He would complete his mission.

The path he followed now took a sharp bend to the right and revealed a new vista. A thousand paces below him a wide valley floor hosted innumerable black tents and huts of all sizes. There were several campfires burning.

On the opposite side of the valley, at the edge of a ravine, there was an impressive stronghold, and the road to the northwest that Sinthoras would have to follow to reach the mist-demon led straight through the camp and up to the vast door of the castle.

Sinthoras cursed: it looked as if an army were settled in for a prolonged siege. He had no way of knowing how long they had been encamped.

What amateurs. Where are their battering rams and siege towers? He surveyed the slopes—the rocks at each side of the road would be nigh on impossible to scale, and the fresh snow was soft: there could easily be an avalanche. Apart from all that it would cost him too much energy to find an alternative route.

Straight through the middle of the camp, then. Should he make his way through unobserved by the soldiers or should he create a diversion? Fire would be good, particularly with all those tents. He could kill off the officers, or frighten their animals into a stampede. Anything that caused confusion would serve, and it would be fun.

Smiling, he made his way down easily to the valley floor. Necessity would be the mother of invention and he would make himself some fine entertainment on the way.

He crept through the camp, keeping to the shadows. He quickly realized the besieging army were barbarians: humans with coarse faces and thick beards, wearing simple jackets of fleece over rudimentary armor. Sinthoras shook his head. *Strutting around on their bandy little legs, so full of themselves, convinced they could slay a pack of giants.*

There was another thing about barbarians: they always took their women and children with them.

It would never have occurred to a warrior like Sinthoras to do that. The wars the älfar waged were quick and hard; they never undertook sieges. Where humans needed battering rams, the älfar used magic and trickery, their families had no place at the front.

Sinthoras was pleased. It made the humans more vulnerable. As soon as you attacked one of their women, barbarians would abandon any caution and charge straight in, regardless.

Some of the huts showed weather damage. This made him think the camp—probably 5000 strong—had been in place for some time. His lip curled in contempt: they didn't have eternal life and yet they wasted time deciding whether or not to have a battle.

Using his inner powers, Sinthoras increased the length of the concealing shadows, enabling him to flit through the open spaces. Stopping behind a tent to listen, he picked up snatches of conversation through the tent walls: they were talking about a retreat and negotiations, but he was moving too quickly to catch everything. He made his way through the encampment, past incompetent guards without being spotted and set off for the gate on the opposite side. *I did not even need to create a diversion.* A part of him was disappointed at that.

The fortress defenses would have presented a challenge for any conventional siege.

He calculated the walls were at least double the length of an arrow flight. They showed signs of bombardment: where the catapults had hit home, the defenders had breached the gaps with new stonework, scaling ladders and spent arrows lay abandoned at the foot of the walls among the debris—evidence of bitter and prolonged assault. The gate was the breadth of the road.

Sinthoras noted fire baskets up on the ramparts where sentries were patrolling and two roofed towers, which had catapults built out on platforms.

Excellent. The älf smiled. With all the damage it had undergone the wall offered plenty of footholds, and he was not discouraged by the handful of guards. He would not even have to kill them to get past. That would save time.

He strapped his spear to his back and began the ascent. The odd fragment of stone came away as he climbed, but the noise was minimal and did not alert the sentries.

He pulled himself up over the ramparts and looked both ways.

Complete martial simpletons, he thought. *Incredible.* The guards were patrolling in opposite directions, facing away from each other. That was something that älfar guards would never do: it was an open invitation to slip through.

Sinthoras studied the break in the cliff behind the fortress. The road to the northwest went through this ravine, which was crossed by rope bridges at different levels. As there were no buildings behind the gate, he presumed the defenders had taken refuge higher up. Four broad, suspended wooden bridges connected ramparts and mountain.

Sinthoras was wary because he could not see round the curve of the gorge. *The ravine could be twenty paces long or it could be a hundred or even a thousand.* It could easily turn into a trap, however skillfully he moved.

He was considering how best to get through when he noticed a dark shape cross the ground on the far side of the wall.

Dogs? Sinthoras drew in his breath quickly, staring at the vague outline. *Child's play. They won't be able to withstand my power.*

When he looked more closely it turned out to be a three-legged creature the size of a foal, with a scaly body and arms like tongs. The neck
was short, sticking out in front, with tiny lidless eyes over the nostril
slits. The mouth was made up of two simple chewing jaws: a crude mixture of other monsters.

These creatures were new to Sinthoras. He looked up and noticed
makeshift shelters further up. *Are these creatures the reason the fortress
defenders have retreated to the mountain?* But perhaps they had been
deployed as supplementary guards. Those skinny legs, which ended in
spikes rather than proper feet, would make climbing difficult.

After espying one of these creatures, he kept catching sight of more
of them lying on the ground with their legs tucked up beneath them,
immobile and rock-like. He screwed up his eyes. *Can I get past them and
reach the bridge? Will they be easy to fool?*

He watched the sentries marching back toward each other. He
crouched down and concentrated on using his power to stretch the
shadows, making them darker and denser—impenetrable. They swallowed every speck of light. *These two sad sacks will never notice me.*

The guards registered subconsciously that the shadows had changed,
and turned to patrol where they wouldn't have to walk through the dark
sections. Now Sinthoras could see their faces.

They were bony and crab-like, similar to the creatures on the valley
floor, but their bodies resembled very slim humans. Under long, woolen
mantles they wore armor of a significantly better quality than that of the
barbarians. Sinthoras guessed why only two of them were needed: their
multiple black button eyes could scan more of the surroundings.

Let's see what the little fellows down there do if they get thrown a surprise.
When the patrolling guards had passed each other, Sinthoras took his spear
and made the shadow grow so they would both have to walk through it.

One guard now came within touching distance of Sinthoras, concealed in the shadow. Sinthoras gave a deft shove with the blunt end of
the spear, knocking the guard off balance and down into the yard far
below. *This was going to be interesting.*

While the guard was still in midflight, the pack of creatures rushed
over as one, leaping up and snapping their tongs. The body had scarcely

hit the ground before they descended, ripping it apart with their powerful forelimbs.

The remaining guard pulled a whistle from his belt and placed it between his lips to blow an urgent, squeaky alarm tone.

Down below, the butchery was in full swing. Pieces of armor clattered to the ground or were hurled through the air. The insect-like outer skin burst to reveal blue-white flesh; ribs snapped and bright blue blood spurted in all directions. In their feeding frenzy the creatures developed incredible strength and speed; pulling off a limb, they would fight off all comers until the prize was safely stuffed into their maw.

Ugly, but effective. Quick and deadly. The älf was disappointed to realize that his only option to get away would be via the ropes or bridges. Two of the creatures fixed their black eyes on the ramparts as they flexed and snapped their tongs.

On the mountain, lights were starting to appear in the shelters.

His experiment with the sentries had had an effect greater than he had bargained for. He would have to abandon his plan to get through their defenses unnoticed.

I'll have to take things up a notch. He jumped over the battlements onto the walkway, landing at the feet of the startled guard who dropped his whistle and grabbed his weapons, but before his fingers closed round the grip he had been speared through the middle. Bright blue blood came gushing out of the wound.

"You don't mind if I take you with me, bug-eyes?" Sinthoras asked with malicious courtesy, tossing his victim over the other side toward the encampment before climbing swiftly down.

At the foot of the wall he picked up and shouldered the dead body. Even though it was not particularly heavy, it weighed Sinthoras down, making his feet sink into the snow. This time there would be footprints to follow.

Exactly as he intended.

"Tell him I haven't the faintest what he's on about," Hasban Strength-of-Seven, Prince of the Sons of the Wind, stared at the interpreter. Naked to the waist, the prince was sitting at table, with the smelly

remains of his evening meal still strewn before him. An earthen-
ware mug had been knocked over and there was beer swilling around
amongst the plates.

He scratched his head, making his short black hair stand up in spikes
at all angles. He had not even had time to do up his breeches properly—
and he did not care.

Four armored beetle-heads stood facing him—that was what he
liked to call the jeembina—and they were all glaring at him indignantly,
each with the ten button eyes on stalks, as they chattered insistently at
the interpreter. It sounded like high-pitched squeaks and clicks to him.
Given the choice, he would have squashed them flat.

"Tell them I'm not in the mood." Hasban peered into the jug and
took a gulp of the beer. That would revive him. "They've dragged me
away from my women in the middle of the night, to accuse me of sending them a spy and a murderer." He suppressed a belch and studied the
late-night intruders. The beetle-heads were very upset, it was obvious
from the way their eye stalks were jerking.

Hasban really did have no earthly idea what the jeembina meant. He
could not imagine that any of his soldiers would have chanced a solo
mission. What for? The negotiations with the gate guards had been
going well and a treaty with Uoilik, the jeembina prince, was near being
agreed. His own army was eager for a successful outcome of the talks.
Gaining the right to pass through jeembina territory would mean the
end of a war that had lasted for years. Before this war, it had long been
their tradition to use the road when hunting and was a vital trade route
for rali salt—an essential dietary requirement.

He gestured to the jeembina, jug in hand. "Tell them I find the noc-
turnal escapade they speak of inexplicable and senseless." He wanted to
be back in bed with his two women, continuing where he had left off
after they were so rudely interrupted by the jeembinas' arrival.

"Uoilik says he would like to believe you, because he is also at a loss
to see any reason for an attack. But it has occurred," the jeembina interpreter relayed. His voice sounded like a child's and his eyes on their
stalks waved like pondweed in a stream. "And the assailant's footprints
lead back here to your camp."

Hasban realized that words alone would not placate the jeembina. "I'll come out and take a look at these tracks," he said, emptying the jug and getting to his feet.

Half naked, Hasban's blond bedmate came in to put a fur over his shoulders, and his red-haired girl brought out his weapons belt. Blond and redhead together then carried his mighty sword over to him. It was heavy, as befitted a true Son of the Wind, and would be able to crack open the armor and carapaces of all these beetle-heads at a single swipe.

Belching slightly, the prince pulled on his fur boots and followed the delegation out.

Thirty armed soldiers had gathered outside the hut that had served as his palace now for long years. Some were holding burning torches or lamps, others had weapons in their hands. His subjects had noticed the unexpected visitors' arrival and feared the worst.

"Calm down, everyone," he called. "Put your blades away. There's been a misunderstanding, that's all." He explained to them briefly why the beetle-heads were there. "If I find out one of you is involved in any way, he'll be executed on the spot," he added. "I've been living here by the ravine for eleven years, growing from child to manhood, I have fathered children who know their own country only from stories told to them." His piercing eyes fixed each in turn. "Do I have to remind you of the bloody battles and the sieges we have endured? I started talks with the jeembina and have finally found a sensible negotiating partner." He clenched his fist and shook it in the air. "Four years of talks—is it all to have been in vain? Because some idiot wanted a bit of glory or was after drunken revenge? I'm not having our return to our homeland jeopardized like this. Our people are longing for us to come home." With these words he stomped off to follow the jeembina through the camp to where the tracks were, taking twenty of his men as bodyguard. He recalled the occasion of his accepting the crown from his father, four years previously. Hasban remembered how the Sons of the Wind had been returning from a hunt eleven years ago with a large supply of salt, to find themselves standing before a barred gateway: the jeembina had not let them pass.

Originally the fortress had belonged to people of the Gramal Dunai, but there had been a battle that the humans had lost and the jeembina did not understand why the Sons of the Wind should be allowed to return. He begged the elements every dawn that their people on the other side of the ravine might still be alive.

Hasban promised a terrible death to anyone who had put the fledgling peace at risk: he would grow icicles through him, killing him slowly, first pulling out his fingernails and all of his teeth to increase the suffering, and smash his fingers with a hammer and . . . The sight of the footprint track pulled him up short. The track did indeed lead from the other side of the valley right into their camp—you could not miss it, and the sprinkle of bright blue jeembina blood left no room for doubt.

Hasban felt sick with anger. *The idiot was stupid enough to bring home a trophy from his exploit!*

"Let's follow it," he said, drawing his sword. "Tell Uoilik, whoever it proves to be, man or woman, I shall kill them on the spot with my own hands." He strode off through the snow, following the tracks, all the way through the camp to one of the huts. He saw drops of blood, blue blood, on the wooden veranda. His men began to murmur.

Hasban's lips tightened in a grimace. This was where Fandati lived. She had once been his lover—an excellent warrior, too. They had parted in anger. Could this be her way of taking her revenge? Destroying his achievements?

The prince stormed in. "Where are you, Fandati?" he bellowed through the darkened room. The jeembina followed him into the hut and three men with lamps took up the rear.

They found Fandati slumped at the table, head on her arms; on the floor was the torso of a jeembina with her sword thrust through it. Bright blue blood from the gash was soaking the floorboards.

"Fandati!" yelled the outraged Hasban. "What have you done?" He took a step forward and kicked at the table, pushing her back.

The woman hurtled backward from the impact, hitting her head against the wall. Her eyes were open and glassy, crimson life-juice seeped from her breast.

Hasban stopped short and looked at the jeembina. *Had it killed her? Or had she killed herself?*

"Uoilik says it is obvious what has happened. You, Prince Hasban, must now regard all peace agreements as null and void," the interpreter said mournfully. "Because one of the prerequisites was that the killing should cease. As we both see, this has not been honored."

It was almost the worst thing for Hasban that he would never be able to take Fandati to task over this atrocity, but then his reason told him to question the evidence of his own eyes.

He turned to the jeembina, sword in hand. "Ask Uoilik where the weapon is that killed Fandati. Where is the jeembina soldier's head? Why are there tracks leading to the hut but no footsteps leading away?" He studied the beetle-heads while these questions were being put to them. It was hard to see any reaction on faces such as theirs; only their stalk-eyes betrayed their feelings, jerking from side to side, almost knotting themselves into a tangle.

The jeembina conferred amongst themselves for a long time.

Hasban took the opportunity to give instructions to his men. "Send out guards to search the entire camp! They are to bring me anyone with blue bloodstains on them: beetle-head, man, or woman."

The soldiers nodded and left, replaced by other guards. The prince should not be left alone with the jeembina.

"We don't know," said the interpreter at last. "Now you point it out, it is just as strange to us. It's also odd that the kimiin did not let us know a human was approaching the ravine. Though not particularly trained, they are our watchdogs, so to speak."

"So it was neither a jeembina, nor a Son of the Wind that committed the murder," Hasban concluded.

"That must indeed be so."

"But"—said Hasban, lowering his sword to indicate he had no intention of hurting any of the delegation—"who could possibly have anything to gain by this?"

"Obviously someone is trying to get us at each other's throats again," the jeembina interpreted.

"We'll find him," replied the prince, scratching his broad chest. "I've told my men—"

The lamps went out.

The door crashed shut and a heavy plank was placed across it. At that moment the first death scream was heard. A Son of the Wind had been killed.

"To arms!" shouted Hasban as he raised his sword and backed up against the wall. He held the weapon out in front of him and swept it from side to side to catch any enemy lurking in the dark. "We're being attacked!"

Blades clashed and more screams were heard. Weapons clattered and bodies slumped to the ground amid confused and despairing cries from the jeembina. The interpreter's high-pitched tones sounded like a child being brutally slaughtered. The air smelled of blood, blood, and more blood, while the screams dropped away.

Hasban had the terrible feeling that the blackness was finding its way into his very veins and was traveling up to his heart, making it race and grow hot. He had never felt such fear as was overwhelming him now. No foe, no wild animal had ever had this effect on him. He broke out in a sweat and slashed out blindly with his sword. Everyone except for him had been visited by the mysterious assailants. His friends were dying right and left, but there was nothing he could do.

With the wall protecting him at his back, Hasban hoped desperately that the men stationed outside would force their way in and come to his aid. Blows crashed against the door and rained on locked shutters. Help would come soon.

Hairs on the back of his neck stood up in terror and he sensed something approaching him. Something lethal. Silently he prayed to the elements.

"Your death bears the name Sinthoras," whispered a male voice in his ear. It sounded velvety smooth and deadly dangerous. "I shall take your life, but take comfort Hasban, prince of the Sons of the Wind, in knowing you forfeit it to serve a higher purpose. Just as your people have forfeited theirs."

Hasban yelled out and laid about him wildly, meeting metal. The pressure was returned and he scraped along the wall, tripping over something.

He fell onto a corpse. The smell of blood was all-pervading. A warm substance was wet on his face. "What are you?" he shouted, hitting out.

"As far as your people are concerned, I will have been a jeembina, Prince," the soft voice answered. "I shall cut off your head and run through the camp holding it high, churning up the hatred that had almost died. Your barbarians will avenge your death and launch an attack on the fortress, bringing the jeembina to their knees. You can be proud of them, Hasban."

Something hard hit Hasban between the eyes. He sank down in a daze, dropping his sword. "No," he stammered, gasping for air with the pain in his chest. His heart was racing fit to burst.

"And then I can continue on my journey," said the invisible antagonist with a quiet laugh. "Who would have thought it? You barbarians have your uses, after all."

Hasban frantically gathered the last of his strength, drew his dagger and leaped toward where the voice had last been. He sailed right past his attacker. His heart was glowing red hot with fear. His energy ebbed completely away.

"Your sword will serve to decapitate its own master," said the unknown figure, and then there came a soft *swish*.

Hasban knew the sound well. Countless beetle-heads had heard it before they died. A few rebellious soldiers had heard it before they received the final punishment.

But it was the first time Hasban had heard it when the stroke was aimed at him. The blade's sound in motion was unique: unmistakable, deadly, and powerful.

Strangely enough, the thought that flashed through his mind was that he would not be able to deliver the salt. A searing pain touched his throat, as the mighty sword sliced through neck and spinal column. The weapon exited and crashed into the wooden bench behind, lodging fast.

For the prince of the Sons of the Wind the waiting was over. The return to his homeland would never take place.

Barbarians! Sinthoras withdrew his magic, allowing the lamps to flare again.

The door shuddered under a hail of ax blows, it would not be long before the wood split and gave way.

Taking up the severed head of the prince, he checked with the other hand that his mask sat properly—he had cut the face from his jeembina victim to get it. The eye-stalks he had propped up with bits of wood. This, together with the cloak over one shoulder, would serve well enough to convince these simpletons that it was a jeembina at work here. What else could he possibly be?

He stuck the head onto the tip of his lance, stringing a lantern high, so the prince's face would be clearly visible, and surveyed the room, satisfied with the scene.

The corpses of jeembina and humans lay scattered; their weapons were placed carefully to give the undeniable impression that the strangers had attacked the prince. *If I play my cards right, the humans will all rush off to storm the fortress, then I can continue northwest on my mission.*

Sinthoras cut off Uoilik's head and concealed it in a cloak taken from one of the corpses. He took up position and waited for the door to burst open. He stabbed the first two barbarians to surge through the door, slipping out past them, then dodged the other soldiers' swirling blades. Fingers grabbed for him in vain.

Waving the lance with the prince's head, he imitated jeembina sounds and raced from one tent to the next. To move adeptly and nimbly enough to avoid all his pursuers took energy and concentration. He did not want to kill them; he needed them to want to kill him. He was surrounded by sleeping foes and with each shout from a barbarian throat more of the humans were up on their feet to confront him. The danger was growing by the second. Wherever he had the opportunity, he torched the tents with burning logs dragged from the campfires.

Sinthoras was pleased to see the flames shining on the bearded faces of the horror-struck humans. *Come and get me! I've killed your ridiculous prince!*

In the middle of this high bravado, his right knee suddenly gave way.

At first he thought it must be an arrow but there was no injury to be seen: *the poison!* The realization shot through him. He immediately lost the cocksure attitude that had protected him and fell against the side of a tent.

"We'll have him!" roared one of the barbarians.

Sinthoras saw the first of the archers release their arrows. *Idiots! How can you miss me at this range?*

He sliced his way through the canvas he had tumbled against and dived through the tent, relieved to find his leg functioning normally again. Going through the tent lines like this was offering good protection from the arrows. As he plunged through he stabbed at sleeping occupants and set fire to whatever he could.

The night was full of alarm drums, bugles, and angry shouting. The humans were out to destroy any jeembina they could lay their hands on. After the initial shock, Sinthoras found there was a smile back on his lips. He was certain they would follow him.

Time to bring this mayhem to a head. Sinthoras hurried to where the horses were, stole one and rode to the fortress on the snorting, nervous beast.

Halfway there, he reined the horse in and turned to see what the barbarians were doing.

In the light of the burning camp he saw around 200 men pursuing him. Behind them came a random rag-tag army, leaderless and driven by lust for vengeance. It would result only in heavy losses on their side.

"Come on," Sinthoras murmured impatiently. "You're much too slow to look like a surprise attack." Over at the fortress fires were being lit on the battlements: the jeembina had sounded the alarm.

Now came the critical bit.

He dug his heels into the horse's flanks, urging it to a gallop, and let the reins go slack; he needed both hands for this.

Ripping off the mask, he took out the severed jeembina head and brought his arm back in preparation for a mighty throw. As soon as he had reached the walls he hurled Uoilik's head into the air, aiming for the high walkway where a crowd of helmets and lance tips could be seen. "We shall destroy you!" he yelled, imitating a barbarian voice.

The response was a hail of spears.

Sinthoras sprang down from his mount and used his power to intensify the shadows at the gate. He took the lantern and Hasban's head off his spear and chucked them aside, plunging them into the pool of darkness he had created, then following them in. The darkness protected him better than any shield. He was completely invisible to the castle's defenders and he could keep close to the wall, staying still until they had passed. His light steps had left no tracks—the illusion was perfect.

The impromptu army of the Sons of the Wind thundered nearer, blind with fury. They had trundled storm ladders with them on carts, and were approaching on a broad front, thinking themselves invulnerable.

Sinthoras raised his head to watch the defense forces. *I wonder what they've got to offer.*

With a loud crash, ten steep ramps were let down from the walls, stopping three paces above the ground. Simultaneously, a shrill whistle piped up, then huge iron-riveted spinning tops shot down the ramps—metal blades flew out as they rotated at tremendous speed. These spinning tops had an upper diameter of about four paces and they had been skillfully crafted to a high standard.

These unusual killing machines bounced over, heading for the barbarian troops, whirling the snow up as they went. A second wave followed, then a third and fourth, filling the air with noise. The ramps swiveled round, shooting the spinning tops off in various directions.

Sinthoras had to admit the jeembina were ingenious. He had always thought of spinning tops as toys. *Children can teach us a lot.* The first of the machines plowed into the human ranks, sweeping through like a metal tornado, blades slicing through the soldiers. As the cutting edges were not rigid, they snapped shut after an impact to emerge again without affecting the speed of the spinning top. The trajectories were unpredictable: sometimes zigzag, sometimes curved, sometimes straight.

They did not run out of momentum for a considerable distance and, even as they fell, they were capable of crushing the enemy to death beneath their weight.

The Sons of the Wind did not falter in their march, but their anger was more vociferous than ever.

Sinthoras smiled, pleased with the outcome. *I'll soon be able to clamber over a mountain of dead bodies and get through the ravine without hindrance. Maybe I won't even have to wait.* Instinctively, he set off for one of the overhanging ramps under cover of the snow cloud the spinning tops had caused. With a vertical bound he caught hold of the sides of the ramp and pulled himself up, working his way up, unseen, past the battlements and along to the left-hand tower, where the spinning tops were issuing from.

I want to know more about this. Sinthoras slipped through the opening and into the tower. Thirty-six jeembina were working the controls of a chain-driven bank of machines. Platforms brought the equipment up from the depths. The spinning tops had long ropes coiled around them; the reserves were anchored upright by a chain.

One end of the rope was made fast, a throw of a lever wound the rope up at enormous speed, starting the rotation. As the chain was released, the platform was tilted, allowing the spinning top to skip onto the ramp to speed on its way.

An excellent idea. Sinthoras made a mental note of the techniques employed, intending to present them to the Inextinguishable Ones on his return. It was a brilliant form of defense. *You could fill them with petroleum, too, and add perforations, lighting them just before they reached the end of the ramps.* A fire-spitting weapon that could cut through anything it met! In his mind's eye he saw the idea adapted for use from cell towers propelled by a slave force. This could be applied on the foreign campaigns he wanted to take on: the effect of fiery war machines on primitive enemies would be tremendous.

A new plan shot into his head. *Why not weaken the fortress defense? Otherwise the barbarians will fail in their attack instead of keeping those cursed kimiins off my back.* He crept along the tower wall until he came to a rope and hook suspended from a winch pulley.

When a new spinning top was about to be released from the preparation platform, Sinthoras swung the pulley arm, knocking the war machine off balance. Still upright, but wobbling badly, it careered through the jeembina workforce. The blades struck sparks from the stone walls and the top jumped, out of control, mowing through the troops.

Sinthoras was watching from above, having climbed the pulley rope. He was fascinated by his victims' bright blue blood spattering intriguing patterns on the wall: the blood formed splashes and rivulets on the stone; the wall was growing blue veins.

"True art," murmured the älf in awe. Just a few more of the war machines and another batch of jeembina would be enough to decorate all the tower walls . . . but no, he would have to wait until he was back in Dsôn and could try it out with some slaves. Different races would furnish a variety of colored blood. *What would be better, canvas or stone?* His forthcoming campaigns in Girdlegard would ensure a steady stream of captive slaves.

The spinning top overturned, but the next was on its way up from below.

Sinthoras fastened the end of its rope as he had seen done, but now he altered the slope of the ramp so that it would shoot out on to the courtyard immediately inside the gate, grunting as he pushed downward to tilt it up and over the wall, a feat of strength very few creatures could hope to achieve.

Shouts of alarm alerted soldiers to the presumed mistake.

Let's see the color of kimiin blood, then. He grinned as he operated the mechanism to wind up the war machine. He released the lever and hurried to the window.

The spinning top cut through a number of the guard creatures before it crashed into the gate, sending limbs, guts, and blood spraying into the air.

So kimiin blood is silver-blue! What a shame he had no suitable container with him.

The wooden gate had suffered under the onslaught, but withstood and repelled the spinning agent of destruction, which was traveling on a random high-speed course around the yard, bouncing off the walls. Then it collided with the gate a second time.

Sinthoras was pleased. *If the gate is already damaged the barbarians will get through it in no time, making things easier for me. I wonder how well they will do against the kimiin?*

He could hear voices down below. No new war machines were being sent up. The jeembina were getting suspicious.

Taking a coiled rope, the älf climbed out of the window and up onto the roof where he perched cross-legged to observe the battle raging outside the walls.

The barbarians had erected storm ladders at various places and were trying to scale the battlements. They had already been successful here and there and another unit was breaking through the main gate.

"My brave little warriors!" called Sinthoras, amused. "Don't give up!" A second later he was remonstrating with them: "Where did you leave your brains, you idiots?"

Before the barbarians could celebrate a victory, the kimiins stormed out of the fortress to attack on open ground. The jeembina were aiming down at the barbarians from the four bridges. The ramps were being adjusted to target the invaders now streaming into the courtyard.

Within a short time the barbarians had taken the high walkways. The bridges, crowded with jeembina, tumbled into the void: the invaders had cut through the cables that had anchored them—any that survived fell victim to their own deadly spinning tops. General slaughter and wholesale butchery commenced.

Now for a nice glass of red wine, thought Sinthoras from his vantage point, *and paper and pen to sketch all this.* He was inspired by the scene, reveling in the violence and the wild, uncontrolled displays of brutality. It was the fascination of the primitive that disgusted and attracted him at one and the same time. Not that he wanted to be like the barbarians, but their way of life intrigued him occasionally. Sinthoras regretted the waste of bone and carapace shells he would not be able to work with. He had to get on.

When he noticed the first flames issuing from the windows of the tower he was perched on, he got to his feet, tied his rope to a beam and used it to swing out over the heads of the fighting troops. He landed lightly on the ground exactly at the edge of the ravine.

There was only one way to go. He strode quickly into the ravine, sure that no one would see him.

He looked back to see the wholesale destruction. This brought a smile to his lips. His ruse had worked: jeembina and barbarian were exterminating each other quite satisfactorily.

They should be grateful. I've helped them to get a clear decision in the matter instead of all these feeble compromises. In a compromise both sides lost out. In a decent battle only one side would win.

The narrow ravine ended after a hundred paces, opening up into a valley. He laughed: *all that fuss over a hundred paces! The humans have been besieging the fortress for an age. They never learn. They don't have eternal life so they can't waste time repeating their mistakes.*

A forest of evergreens had taken root. Their leaves were long and pointed, and their wide branches stretched to fill the valley. They were a strange dark sight against the stark white background: the snow having hardly settled on them at all.

Hundreds of silvery threads hung from the branches like seeds or peculiar leaves, but Sinthoras knew they were the rare phaiu su.

Before he could give the matter more thought, he heard the clash of blades and the wind sent a waft of disgusting sweat his way: old, acrid sweat soaked into leather and cloth. That was how barbarian soldiers smelled.

"Here's another of them," yelled a human warrior behind him.

Sinthoras wheeled round and saw a gang of about fifty unwashed humans approaching, their rough weapons held high and their eyes burning with bloodlust.

Then his knee gave way and a sickening pang shot into his upper thigh and down to his calf. It was the alchemancers' message to him— from one heartbeat to the next he was confronted with a whole new set of difficulties. This was not proving the easiest of journeys.

CHAPTER X

Slave labor was used to clear a stretch of land two miles wide on the far side of the broad moat, making any surprise enemy attack impossible. The trees that were felled supplied the timber for the huge catapults.

But the rightless slaves complained about their work, though they had no justification for doing so.

When the circle was completed, our ancestors altered the course of the mightiest river in Dsôn Faïmon and flooded the trench, drowning the slaves who were no longer of any use.

This put an end to their rebelliousness.

Epocrypha of the Creating Spirit,
1st Book,
Chapter 2, 6–11

Ishím Voróo (The Outer Lands),
4370th division of unendingness (5198th solar cycle),
late summer.

Caphalor and Raleeha made swift progress in spite of the cold winds and constant rain.

The horse the slave girl was riding was nowhere near as fast as the night-mare, but they still ate up the miles on the journey back to the älfar realm.

Caphalor studied any tracks they came across, keen to avoid confrontation with monsters or outlaw bands.

It was an unsettling experience for him to have to fear time. Where he had previously had the certain knowledge of never dying a natural death, the poison in his bloodstream changed everything. He was like a human, now. Mortal.

Time was being stolen from him and condensed: a finite point was now set to his own immortality while those around him would live forever.

His previous mode of existence had permitted him to plant saplings and see them mature to large trees. He could make wine and leave it in his cellars to reach its optimum age, and then taste it with his wife at his leisure. If it proved disappointing, he could wait patiently for the next vintage. Caphalor had seen the landscape change, affected by the slow erosion of wind and water, heat and cold.

Of course, there were diseases that could infect an älf, but there was magic in their blood to fight off illness, and the research and insights of their healers had put an end to death caused by this. No other race had these abilities. He had never had to fear mortality, either on or off the battlefield. Not until encountering the fflecx.

Caphalor was under no delusion that he could survive the poison. The fflecx knew what they were doing and would have calculated the fatal dose exactly. *Even Raleeha will live longer than I shall!* He quickly suppressed his fury at the injustice. He did not want to take it out on her in some unguarded moment.

Caphalor did not doubt the viability of his plan to kill Munumon and the obboona. He seldom spared a thought for Sinthoras. His concern was for his life-companion and his children. *A full life, but now one that will be far too short.*

The time limit the gnome king had placed on his life was coming nearer: he had six moments of unendingness to deliver Raleeha to Dsôn, perhaps a little more if Samusin and Inàste were on his side.

Sardaî snorted, eying the edges of the wood ahead of them.

Caphalor studied the road surface. It was late afternoon and the day-star was dropping down behind dark rain clouds on the horizon. They would be entering the wood just as the light failed completely.

Normally he would have welcomed this circumstance, but he was worried by the night-mare's reaction and by the tracks that he noted on the ground. He stopped, pulling Raleeha's horse up, too. "We'll have to take a detour," he told her.

"What has happened, master?" Raleeha sat upright in the saddle, trying to pick up sounds. She had lost weight in the course of the journey and was now as slender as an älf-woman. Except for the ears and the missing refinement of her features, of course, she was becoming more and more älf-like. Once more, his inexplicable fascination with her came to the fore . . .

"The forest is full of outlaws," said Caphalor to distract himself. "I can't risk attracting their attention. They would try to get you and without a night-mare you'd be too slow." He turned Sardaî's head. "About two miles back we passed a crossroad. We can skirt the woods to the north and reach Dsôn Faïmon that way," he explained, adding with a sharper voice. "You are to stay at my side, Raleeha."

"Of course, master."

Caphalor did not sense anything suspicious in her tone. He had not issued the warning without reason: by taking the diversion they would come near Lotor's territory. The prospect of flight might seem attractive to her, especially given that she was not in the company of her original master. He would do everything to ensure he did not lose the hostage he wanted to preserve for the Inextinguishables.

They returned to the crossroads and kept riding until the daystar had gone down.

The dim light was enough for the night-mare to pick its way, but Raleeha's horse was exhausted and kept stumbling on the uneven ground. Caphalor halted at an old abandoned house and made camp in the ruins. At least they had protection from the rain. He chose not to light a fire, unwilling to give possible scouts or robbers any clue as to their presence.

He doled out their rations, pushing Raleeha's share over to her while he chewed his own. Bow and arrows were close at hand. He could see she had something on her mind. "Speak."

"This house stood until very recently, master," she said, pulling the horse blanket tighter round her shoulders. "The smell of burning is quite fresh."

"It'll be the work of the bandits hiding out in the woods," he remarked. "I saw the tracks of large horses such as the eastern barbarians ride. I expect it will be one of their scouting parties heading west to spy out the land." He collected rainwater in the palm of his hand and took a few sips. "This is how things have been in Ishím Voróo for thousands of subdivisions of unendingness. Races and tribes come and go, conquering and being conquered in their turn."

"Except for the älfar," Raleeha contradicted with pride. "Your folk, master, are constancy itself. I don't understand why the älfar have not taken over the whole of Ishím Voróo. If any one race is capable of it, then it is your own."

Caphalor watched her with sympathy. She sounded as if she thought of herself as an älf, whereas she was nothing but a barbarian with a pretty face and an eccentric passion for the wrong race.

"It's not something we have ever needed," he answered, despite not wishing to discuss it. Certainly not with her. "Why should we need an extensive empire?"

This was not the truth. The population of Dsôn Faïmon was shrinking all the time because the birth rate among the älfar was so low. Not enough girls were being born, but there was also an unfortunate lack of male progeny: in the future they would not have sufficient soldiers. The Star Realm found itself in a perilous balancing act that the surrounding nations must get no hint of. There was no acute danger at present, but unless there was a change in circumstances and Samusin helped them . . .

"You would have more vassals and more power," Raleeha went on. "You could bring order where there is chaos and you could drive the monsters off the most valuable fertile land. Ishím Voróo would no longer be a lawless desert, but become strong under älfar leadership. Any creatures with understanding would side with you and worship you out of sheer gratitude, master."

"Creatures with understanding?" Caphalor laughed "Not many of those in Ishím Voróo. Not even amongst the barbarians. You've been thinking about this for some time, haven't you, Raleeha?" he said, amused. "And I can tell you that Sinthoras is one of those älfar who think the same way and can't wait to set out on campaign."

"But not you, master?"

"No." He hesitated. "My view is that our borders are secure and we should remain within them." He was amazed at himself, talking to a slave girl about politics as if she were an equal. The poison in his blood must have affected his character, making him more patient—and making him more liable to become attracted to a slave girl. He must put a stop to it. "There is no more to say on the subject." With that, the conversation was over. His right hand was hurting. He rubbed his fingers as if he could massage the toxins out of his system.

"Master," she said after a while, without asking for permission to speak. "Are you ever prey to fear?"

"What's the meaning of asking me such a question?" he hissed, feeling himself caught out. He had indeed been contemplating his own mortality.

"I think this must be one of the key advantages of the älfar: being afraid of nothing."

Caphalor thought carefully before replying. He listened to the regular beats of the rain falling on the roof. *How many more times will I hear that?* "No, I don't think I have ever been afraid of anything. Not in the sense of being frightened to death." He swallowed hard. "But now there is something inside me that I was not prepared for," he added in a soft voice. "I carry death within me. My life always ran with the certitude that I might die through violence or accident, but that I would never become old and feeble or that my body would let me down." To his surprise it was a kind of relief to be able to talk about the burden he carried. He caught some more rain in his hands to splash over his face. He had been feeling hot. "The alchemancers have placed death in my veins. The poison inside me is seeping into every crevice of my body. It is killing me." He sighed. "I think I am afraid of that—afraid of dying. I don't even know when I shall die, or in what manner: will my heart suddenly stand still? Will my blood coagulate? Will my brain start to melt?" He closed his eyes and took several deep breaths.

"It is the uncertainty that frightens you, master," she consoled him. "This uncertainty about the time of one's own death tracks a human all through his lifespan. We know that we must die. This much is certain. One of your privileges has been taken away from you, master."

"The most important one," he added thoughtfully. He looked at her. "I thought it was as natural as a heartbeat or taking a breath." Caphalor put the next piece of food back in its wrapping. He had lost his appetite.

"Your affairs are in order, master?" she prompted tactfully.

"Yes, they are." Without wanting to, he found himself telling her about Enoïla, about his children, about their life, until he noticed that she had fallen asleep in her exhaustion. *Lucky Raleeha. Fear has taken away my sleep.*

He had been reminded of what he would lose through death. Anger at Munumon boiled up within him and he felt the heat and pressure in his face as the fury lines spread.

He could not return to his homeland because he had not successfully fulfilled the Inextinguishables' mission. "Return triumphant or do not return at all," Nagsor Inàste had told them. The shame would be unbearable. "I'll make you suffer for this, you misbegotten gnome," he swore in a whisper. "You shall suffer as you have never in your contemptible life suffered before."

Their punishing ride began at daystar-rise.

First they headed up a gentle hill with the forest on the right. The hilltop formed a ridge fifty paces wide, starkly delineating the surrounding landscape; they took it at full gallop.

The elements were showing a certain consideration and the rain now held off. The wind had lessened, making gray and black cloud pictures above their heads and forming a violent thunderstorm to their left, with lightning flashes and almost constant claps of thunder.

"I would so love to be able to see that storm, master," sighed Raleeha on hearing the first rumble.

"You've Sinthoras to thank for that," he retorted. Sardaî's behavior alarmed him. The night-mare's eyes kept going back to the forest where swirling columns of mist were rising. *What is hiding there?*

Their path revealed a magnificent view, but the bare slopes left them extremely exposed. There was no cover of any sort and they would have to keep to the ridge for some time.

Then Caphalor saw what had spooked the night-mare: riders rushed along on a narrow path below the ridge trying to catch them up. They were barbarians riding the large horses whose hoofprints Caphalor had noticed at the edge of the forest.

After a moment, he realized the soldiers were not chasing him and Raleeha, but a smaller group of riders ahead of them. *So, the barbarians are hunting each other down.*

His relief was short-lived.

The smaller of the two units veered to the left, heading up to their ridge. They would be appearing ahead of them any moment now—and at this speed their pursuers would collide with himself and Raleeha.

I have to prevent this. Caphalor reined Sardaî in and brought Raleeha's mount to a standstill. The paths crossed around three hundred paces ahead: a safe range for a skilled bowman such as himself. He prepared his weapon and selected an arrow from the quiver at his saddle. He flexed his fingers.

Raleeha heard what he was doing. "Is it an attack, master?"

"Not necessarily. I hope for their own sake that the barbarians are going to leave us in peace." He told her briefly what he had seen. Then the wind brought the low thunder of hooves and the first group appeared, with the second close behind. The drumming sound grew louder and they could make out the clattering of metal armor and weaponry. The pursuing party had closed the gap to less than four horse-lengths. So far Caphalor and Raleeha had not been noticed.

"There'll be fighting now," he told her. A tinny hunting horn sounded. "They're heading straight for each other."

"O, great Radnar!" Raleeha exclaimed. "One of the groups must belong to my brother's forces. Is there a split wolf's head on their armor? Forgive my insistence, but please tell me what you can see."

Caphalor thought for a moment before taking out his spyglass to observe the fray. The emblem she had described could be clearly seen. "The smaller group has that symbol. I'm afraid they stand no chance against the others. The other unit has three times their number, their horses are bigger and their weapons have a longer range. It won't be pretty but it will be quick."

"Master," she begged, her voice unsteady. "I swear I shall do anything that you or your wife demand of me if you can help my people now."

"You would have to obey us anyway," he reprimanded her.

"But I shall serve your family when you die. I shall carry out any task you give me!" she implored him. "I'll look after your children . . . or . . ." She sought desperately for services she might offer.

Caphalor noted in her face the distress and the fear she felt for her people's warrior band. Once again, he was surprised at himself for sympathizing with this pathetic young slave girl. *I must stop this. She is nothing but a barbarian.* But he heard himself saying, "I will tell you what you owe me when we reach Dsôn Faïmon." *I am only doing this to bind her to me in gratitude,* he told himself in justification. *No other reason at all.*

Stowing the spyglass, he pulled out the first of his long-range war arrows and guided the night-mare to one side, so that he could use the larger bow unhindered.

The black-feathered projectile found its target and the first barbarian fell dead from the saddle. The älf followed through at lightning speed. The next arrows hissed through the air like black rain to reap destruction. Before the soldiers had recovered from the surprise ambush, Caphalor had slain seven of them. The odds were now twenty-two against five Lotor men. *I shall have to go easy with the arrows in case I have to kill all of them.*

The barbarians on the larger mounts roared at him and ten of the bravest charged up, short bows at the ready as they slid down from their saddles to use the horses as cover.

A neat trick. It won't help. Caphalor knew why they had closed up: they had to compensate for the lack of range their weapons had. "Dismount and stand away from your horse to the right," he instructed Raleeha. "If it starts to run, throw yourself flat on the ground." He placed the next arrow on the string.

These barbarians obviously had no experience of fighting älfar, or they would never attempt to outshoot him. They would have fled immediately.

Fear me, barbarians. Caphalor drew the bowstring back and off flew the first of the arrows, thudding diagonally through a beast's neck and skewering the man behind, who screamed and fell, to be trampled by the hooves of his companions' horses. Älfar war arrows packed too much power to be stopped by mere flesh.

You are just target practice for me. Caphalor killed more of the barbarians and their mounts. They fell at full gallop, bringing down those behind, while arrow after arrow rained down. He had dealt with eight of them without the slightest hesitation; the remaining two soldiers turned to flee.

Caphalor's smile was icy. *You pathetic cowards, it's too late for flight.* They presented the perfect target. He got one with an arrow to the back of the head, the other he pierced through the heart, anchored to their horses by the long shafts. In their distress, the horses raced along the ridge, plunging through the melee of fighting men.

"You can get back on now," he told Raleeha, his eyes on the combat. Bow in hand, he urged Sardaî on as soon as the girl was back in the saddle.

The barbarians on the larger horses headed off, while the four remaining Lotor soldiers hung around uncertainly, aware now that only their attackers had been targeted, but still keeping their axes and round shields at the ready.

Those would not help you if I chose to kill you. "These are your people," he told Raleeha. These soldiers looked to him like any other barbarian: dirty, hairy, holding rotten weaponry, and wearing ineffectual armor and untidy clothing. Nonetheless, they seemed so proud— with not the slightest justification. "Tell them they have nothing to fear. If they get uppity and start attacking me it will be the last thing they ever do."

"Yes, my master." Raleeha called over to the soldiers in a strange dialect that he could not follow. It sounded horribly primitive.

Another sign of their inferiority: barbarians did not even possess a unified language. They had a variety of tongues and completely different areas of interest. *They would never be able to retain power in Ishím Voróo, even if it were handed them on a plate.*

One of the men replied, sounding delighted. The others waved their arms in the air and shouted, overjoyed at having escaped with their lives. They rode over to Caphalor and Raleeha to meet them halfway.

Caphalor surveyed them arrogantly. He did not even rein in his night-mare, but trotted past.

The men watched him from under heavy brows, admiration and fear in their eyes. They had obviously heard of the älfar. They could not understand why an älf would have come to their aid.

One of them was talking to Raleeha, trying to convince her of something.

"If he's trying to persuade you to escape, you know what will happen to them all," he said, matter of factly. "You are not to leave my side."

"Master, forgive him. He does not understand why I follow you of my own free will." She sounded distressed and worried. "Please excuse their ignorance."

"Tell them not to follow us. If they do, they'll be shot." He did not have many arrows left, truth be told, but the humans would not know that.

Her compatriots, riding alongside, were arguing with her, trying to get her to go with them.

Caphalor urged the night-mare and the horse into a gallop. One of the barbarians rode up and stared until the älf turned to face him. The expression in the man's moss-green eyes was serious and grateful. The he raised his ax in farewell and peeled away, followed by the other three.

"Thank you, master," he heard a relieved Raleeha say.

He did not answer. His lips had gone numb and he could not speak. The alchemancers' poison was at work.

Ishím Voróo (The Outer Lands),
4370th division of unendingness (5198th solar cycle),
late summer.

Initially, Sinthoras had contemplated taking on all of the barbarians, but fifty seemed a bit on the high side, even to him. With the advantage of surprise it would have been a different matter.

They surrounded him. Leaning on his spear, he smiled politely, the essence of calm.

The barbarians could see he was not a jeembina, but were not able to place him.

It was refreshing not to be met with craven fear simply on account of his älfar appearance. *Like big children.* It was time to teach them who they faced.

"You are no jeembina," one of the barbarians yelled. The man's speech was ugly, but at least it was intelligible.

"I am named Sinthoras and am one of the Shindimar," he lied, grinning broadly. He avoided the word älf in case they knew it. "The jeembina took me prisoner, but I was able to escape when you attacked them." He pointed to the wood. "Some of them made off that way. They were chasing one of your soldiers."

The barbarian passed the message on to his men via a translator and they drew their weapons and headed out along the path into the trees. Most were keen to storm off immediately, but some stayed put, deep suspicion on their ugly faces.

The leader, the one with the best armor, looked a bit like Hasban. Sinthoras assumed he was a relative of Hasban. He smiled at him. *Soon you shall follow him, little barbarian.*

It was this man that gave the orders to move. He even returned the smile.

"You'll be coming with us," the barbarian said.

"Gladly." They moved aside for him and he strode off in front.

"You're from over here?" the barbarian asked.

"Yes." He kept up the pretense. "The jeembina captured me when I was out hunting here in the forest." He was pleased to note that the men did not realize the danger they were in. The trees and sharp leaves were harmless, it was the pretty phaiu su that were lethal.

They went ever deeper into the woods, the snow crunching under their boots while Sinthoras walked silently and left no prints. *You won't forget this lesson, if you survive it.* With his spear held loosely in his right hand he jogged along, light on his feet, pointing right and left occasionally to make them think he had heard something. He was diverting the barbarians' attention away from the real trap.

It was not long before the leader grabbed his arm and forced him to stop. The warriors formed a double circle round them both, their shields reinforcing the ring. The interpreter said, "My lord demands to know what you are up to."

"I'm taking you to where your men are in trouble. Why have we stopped?"

"Because there are no footprints," was the sharp response. "Our soldiers can't fly and nor can the jeembina."

The leader drew his sword and held the tip against the älf's throat.

There was no mistaking the threat. "We can go back if you like," he said, raising his arms to show he represented no danger to them.

Let's begin the lesson. What none of the simple souls noticed was his spear tip touching a low-hanging branch, releasing some of the threads to waft in the breeze.

"What have you brought us here for?" the barbarian demanded to know, pressing the blade harder on to his throat. "You are on the jeembinas' side?"

"Of course not!" laughed Sinthoras, staying relaxed and showing no fear. "You know, of course, that there are ways of concealing one's tracks. I have the ability to detect where this has been done." He watched the silver filaments drift. *Exquisitely beautiful.* He paid attention neither to the leader, nor to the translator.

One of the threads landed on a soldier's helmet and slipped down over the leather neck protection. A gentle breeze lifted the loose end onto the man's naked skin.

Here we go! Sinthoras was looking forward to what would happen next.

More webs drifted down onto other soldiers who were still blithely unaware. Other threads, attracted by body warmth, were blown around until they found somewhere to land.

At times like these, Sinthoras was grateful that the älfar had a vast store of knowledge in their libraries. He had read about many Ishím Voróo secrets in the old books, and this was one such phenomenon recognized.

One silver thread wobbled over toward him. He blew it away sharply so that it touched the face of the leader, sticking to the man's skin.

The barbarian raised his hand to brush it away—then he opened his eyes wide and gave a shocked exclamation. The thread swelled up, becoming as thick as a man's finger. No matter how the man tried, the filament, no longer silver, but first purple and then dark red, could not be dislodged.

The leader's face turned pale. He dropped his sword, sinking onto his knees to tackle the pulsating rope that clung to his face.

Well, there you go. Exactly what the textbooks say. Sinthoras watched closely, without his book-learning he would have been a victim, too.

The attack on the barbarians' leader was the signal.

The filaments dropped down onto the horrified men as soon as they sensed the proximity of unguarded skin and they puffed up, gorging themselves on their victims' blood. The men slashed at them in vain.

Pointless, you ignoramuses. When they bit, the web-like creatures secreted a substance that prevented the blood from clotting. Even if you pulled them off, you bled to death. *It does not look as if any of them will survive this little lesson.*

"You knew about this!" the translator shouted, jabbing at him with his sword. "You led us—"

Sinthoras parried the attack by punching the flat side of the man's weapon. He turned his spear upright and stuck it into the ground, slamming his fist into the barbarian's windpipe. The älf seized his spear again before it had a chance to topple. The translator fell with a gurgle, gasping for air. "Do you simpletons still not realize why barbarians are never able to hang on to power?" he mocked.

All around him the soldiers were dying. More and more of the phaiu su floated down, attracted by the smell of blood.

Don't touch me, I provided all this food for you.

Sinthoras stepped to one side and sheltered under a tree that harbored none of the webs. He rubbed a couple of the filaments on his armor with gauntleted hands and they disintegrated just like spiders' webs. *Harmless.* He kept one as a souvenir, wrapping it carefully in the material of his sleeve cuff. As long as it did not touch skin it could do no harm. "Come along, little one. If Caphalor gets back alive, you shall be my gift to him. A secret gift."

The leader had managed to tear the phaiu su off his face and it had left a long open wound reaching down to his neck. It was bleeding badly. The man shouted at Sinthoras.

"Are you cursing me, little barbarian?" Sinthoras burst out laughing. "I serve gods whose blessing would be a curse on you. What should I be afraid of?" He grabbed the floating filaments from nearby branches with the tip of his spear and diverted them toward the young man, who did not move aside swiftly enough. Three of the threads clung greedily to his skin. "Follow your relative into death. I shall follow my destiny."

As he left he liberated more phaiu su from the trees.

The wind carried them to the Sons of the Wind. They would complete what he had begun.

This journey was becoming enjoyable.

Ishím Voróo (The Outer Lands), ten miles north
of the älfar realm Dsôn Faïmon,
4370th division of unendingness (5198th solar cycle),
late summer.

Caphalor's view of his surroundings was blurred and he was seeing double.

The symptoms caused by the fflecx chemistry were increasing. The more he tried to ignore them, the stronger the waves of pain. Even the tarto gathered by the roadside—and normally helpful in cases of poisoning—did not help. The alchemancers had tailor-made their toxin.

His right leg was numb and useless. His senses were playing tricks and the air had smelled like fresh bread for miles, though his tongue was plagued by the taste of metal. *Keep going,* he told himself. *Gods, let me make it to the border. Afterward, grant me the strength to defeat Munumon.* It was a wish he no longer believed would be fulfilled. The poison was affecting him too badly now. But Samusin might help, and maybe the herbs would slow his decline. "Master, what is holding us up?" asked Raleeha.

"The horse," he said. His speech was affected now and he chose to restrict his talk to essentials.

Caphalor was overcome by a terrible lethargy and his eyes kept closing.

"Rest," he ordered weakly, sliding out of the saddle. He dropped his bow and, gasping for breath, tried to retrieve it. At the third attempt he picked it up and used it as a support.

"As you command, master." Raleeha followed the sound of the bow as it fell. They were standing under a tree that was devoid of foliage and offered no shelter. "Master, is there somewhere we can get out of the rain? Why did you choose to stop here?" The slave girl pulled the blanket round her shoulders.

"Liked it." He slipped down against the trunk, and fell into slumber, his head against the damp, cooling bark. He was running a fever. Only the soft rain prevented him from burning up completely.

The fever brought dreams.

He saw his life-companion calling to him as she slipped off her clothes. As he embraced her, he saw she bore Raleeha's countenance. Yes, suddenly the slave girl had the *countenance* of an älf. The black lace over her empty eyes was strangely alluring. He bent to kiss Raleeha, feeling her desirable body under his hands, but she dissolved in smoke.

Now he was on a balcony high above Dsôn, in the Tower of Bones, the Inextinguishable Ones standing on his right and his left and the jubilant masses far below, celebrating him as the conqueror of Tark Draan.

"You are forgetting me," whispered a woman and when he turned he found the burned visage of the obboona behind him. Before he could lift his arms to defend himself she pushed hard and he plunged over the balcony, to fall, screaming, past the million bones from which the tower was made, screaming, screaming . . . until a touch on his shoulder ended his free fall still miles above the euphoric crowd. The wind played around him.

"Master!"

He tried to open his eyes but the lids were heavy as stone. Someone was shaking him.

"Master! Wake up! Please! They are looking . . ." Then Raleeha shrieked. In the distance Sardaî whinnied.

Caphalor woke from his daze and looked around.

The slave girl was being held by two masked figures; three others had hold of the night-mare and were trying to calm the beast before it could bite through the ropes with its sharp teeth.

He was nearly too late to notice the shadows. His vision was returning slowly, but he could not focus on the three blurred figures directly in front of him.

"Caphalor is your death." He sprang up, drawing his short swords, clashing their blades against each other so that they rang out. "It is an unforgivable error to lay hands on my property. No sane person would steal from an älf."

The bandits froze at a sign from their leader. Their faces were partly hidden but their eyes showed fear. Barbarians: outlawed barbarians. "We thought you were dead, älf," the leader said, putting on an ingratiating tone.

"I'll show you the difference between a live älf and a dead one." Without warning Caphalor hurled his short swords and dashed forward at the group of humans, long daggers in his hands.

The blades pierced the leader and the man on his right. Caphalor slit the throat of the third.

Something *whizzed* through the air.

The noise made Caphalor draw his head back. The feathers on the arrow shaft brushed his nose, so close did it come.

"Master, take care!" Raleeha's warning reached him. "One of them must be near you . . ."

Another vague shape confronted him, roaring and swinging a weapon over its head.

Caphalor was about to drive this one back with his power, but there was a flash inside his skull; he saw stars, smelled fresh bread and tasted metal. His arms fell useless at his sides and his legs were fragile as glass, about to shatter under his weight. He could hear them cracking. *The poison!* He expected the bones to break.

His adversary appeared as a glowing figure whose attack was suddenly halted. "What's the trouble with the black-eyes?" he asked laughing.

"Don't waste time!" someone yelled. "Hit him now before he comes round."

Again the stallion whinnied. Hooves thundered close and the outlaws shouted wildly in confusion.

When Caphalor's vision finally settled he saw the bloodstained, blind slave girl obviously searching for him several paces off. *Why is she walking free?* He could not speak. He knew what was happening: the alchemancers' poison was killing him. Perhaps the exertion of the fight had hastened the reaction.

He noticed the sudden stillness of the forest. In front of him he saw the worried face of a familiar älf. "Caphalor! I go hunting without you just the one time and..."

Aïsolon! His friend's voice was soft, but Caphalor could not think anymore.

His senses deserted him.

CHAPTER XI

Nagsar and Nagsor Inàste saw that the empire they had created was good and well formed.

But they needed a monument to exemplify their triumph over all other races and to symbolize their claim to power.

And so they caused a mountain to be constructed in the center of the crater with steps leading all the way up to their palace.

A residence built solely from the skeletons of their enemies.

Epocrypha of the Creating Spirit,
1st Book,
Chapter 2, 12–17

Ishím Voróo (The Outer Lands),
4370th division of unendingness (5198th solar cycle),
late summer.

Sinthoras galloped along an overgrown path on the stolen horse. Brambles and bushes threatened to block his progress, but he urged the sweating animal mercilessly onwards; he had been catching the smell of peat fires, but he had not seen any houses. Was he imagining it?

He thought he had noticed a hint of numbness in his fingers. This would be the legacy of Munumon's malign influence and it would surely be increasing day by day.

He had gleaned directions to the mist-demon at a nomad campfire one night, listening to their conversations from the darkness. The barbarians had called the northwest region the Land of Endless Death and avoided it. It had been said that nothing created by the gods would survive there, and that something terrible had taken all life from the place.

This all sounded satisfactorily like the work of the creature, and thus was the direction to head in.

What Sinthoras saw on his way only strengthened his suspicions: he had ridden through abandoned villages, seen ruined temples on the plains, and had passed a toppled statue originally dedicated to the god of light. The gods were being blamed for the disaster. Barbarians and gods alike had fled the area.

Soon I shall find this being, he promised himself. *Then I shall have triumphed over Caphalor and all of the Constellations. We Comets shall lead Dsôn Faïmon to its glorious future.* He preferred not to think about his own death. Sinthoras firmly believed that ignoring the poison's effects would keep him healthy longer than if he were constantly watching out for new symptoms. He was totally convinced he would make it back to Dsôn alive. He wanted his triumph, he wanted to receive the Inextinguishables' Honor-Blessing, he wanted to be part of the campaign against Tark Draan and to have his military success elevate him to leadership. His name *must* feature in the legends of his race. *The strength of my will shall protect me,* he told himself. *I shall prevail and live, and Caphalor will die.*

His mount plunged through a wall of foliage and Sinthoras saw— two paces before him—a yawning abyss.

In that same moment he realized that his horse was moving too fast to be able to stop. He did a backward somersault, released the saddlebags from their straps, and landed neatly on his feet, using his spear for balance.

The horse tried to veer away from the cliff edge at the last minute, but failed, sliding over and disappearing with a pitiful whinny of fear.

The älf stepped forward to look over the precipice, stunned at what he saw.

Before him were gently sloping mountain ranges, perhaps 800 to 1000 paces high, all interlinked, with no sheer cliffs or rock faces. They varied in tone from soft brown to shimmering green. In many places clouds of smoke rose up and whole sections glowed dark red like tobacco in a lit pipe. The hillocks and the flat land between were made of peat— and all of it was on fire.

The continuous smoldering had burned deep holes into the subsoil; craters gaped, sending up plumes of whitish steam.

Sinthoras found this scene of devastation intensely invigorating. *Overwhelming!*

He saw a forest that consisted of charcoal sticks and next to that the remains of a town, its walls collapsed, consumed by fire. The conflagration had eaten away at the foundations.

Truly this is the land of demons. In great excitement the älf started to make his way down past the broken carcass of his horse. It was about midday when he approached the ruined town.

Walking ankle-deep in ashes, he could feel the heat radiating up through his boots. The sky was hardly visible through the steam and smoke; the daystar was nothing more than a dirty, glowing ball. The burned trees crackled and snapped as he passed.

At last he arrived at the shell of the town.

Sinthoras took in the holes that had opened up between the houses. In other places the ground had caved in, bringing whole buildings down. He was fascinated by the destruction, and found it aesthetically pleasing: a whole town had been turned into a work of deconstructed art, a work of decay. *I'll create the same effect in Tark Draan.* He strolled around, discovering new shapes and structures in the ruins.

He came across human remains, nothing but charred bones, all displaying the same feature: the head had been chopped off or the skull had been smashed in. This was certainly no accident.

How can I find the mist-demon? From his previous vantage point he had gained the impression that the burning mountain ranges radiated out in all directions. A creature made of mist would be difficult to locate in all this smoke and steam.

The wind was coming from the south now, enveloping Sinthoras in an acrid cloud of smoke. Coughing, he tied a cloth around his mouth and nose.

He decided to climb to the top of one of the neighboring hills and sound his horn. If the demon turned up, all well and good. If, instead, barbarians responded to the signal, he could interrogate them.

He marched across hot, dry ground, feeling the heat under his feet as he started the climb. Everything was permeated with fire.

Tiny flames danced over cracks in the soil and bursts of gas ignited without warning, presenting new dangers for Sinthoras, however carefully he watched his step.

Occasionally the earth creaked and groaned like an ice flow and sank even under his slight weight. He imagined the red-hot chasm that lay underneath the fragile crust.

What a bizarre world, he thought, catching sight of the hilltop emerging through the smoke.

He climbed cautiously to the summit, took out his bugle and put it to his lips, repeating a sequence of notes. The signal sounded over the mountains, its echoes forming a somber canon. *How the melody suits this dark landscape! If one could only include sound in a painting,* he thought as he let his gaze wander.

The light was failing and heavy drops of rain fell, splashing on the horn as he blew. Then the deluge started, drenching Sinthoras to the skin.

The earth at his feet hissed with thirsty greed as fire and water instantly created steam that covered the hills.

It became difficult to breathe. Droplets of moisture formed on his forehead, armor and hair; within a few heartbeats the cloth round his mouth was soaked. His lungs seemed to be cooking. He saw stars dancing in front of his eyes.

<Who are you?> said a voice in his head.

Sinthoras was startled. This was not a trick of his hearing. "And who are you?"

<I asked first.>

"Show yourself!" he challenged.

<You won't see me in this mist. I do not have a physical presence as you do, my body is ephemeral. And now, who are you and why are you making all that noise?>

The mist-demon! The demon had found him! "Greetings," he spluttered, coughing. "My name is Sinthoras of the mighty and invincible folk of the älfar." He pulled himself proudly to his full height, his voice velvety now, eager to please and impress. "My rulers, the Inextinguishable and Eternal Siblings, send me. I have been seeking you and have the honor of offering you an alliance." Despite his exhaustion he wanted to cry out in excited triumph. The success of his mission was now at hand! *My success, mine alone!* He thanked Inàste for her help.

<Älfar? What's that?>

The question was an insult. "A race."

<Like the humans?>

"In no way! We are far superior to any other race!"

<So why do you need to form an alliance,> the demon's voice reflected his amusement, <if you are better than everyone else?>

"My rulers are offering you sovereignty over a realm of your own on the other side of these mountains," he went on. This was not going as he had planned. He was furious to learn that the demon had never even heard of his people. *Or is this his idea of a joke? Is he trying to make a fool of me to see how I'll react?* "You will rule over humans there. The Inextinguishable Ones will support you with an army bigger than any previously seen in Ishím Voróo."

The voice inside his head merely laughed. <What makes them think I want to rule over anything?>

Sinthoras could not grasp this. "Surely everyone wants to rule? You yourself have made this place your own; you defend it and you have killed or driven out the humans who once lived here."

<It is sheer fluke that this is where I landed. I could have ended up in the south or the east. I did not plan for all this to happen. It does tend to occur, though, if I settle anywhere. Nothing I can do about it.>

Sinthoras did not get the impression that the demon was particularly interested in getting to Tark Draan. This surprised him. It surprised him a lot. He no longer thought the demon was testing him. *What is the point of a bored, indifferent ally?*

"What would you wish from us, then, in return for your support?" he put to the demon, mystified now.

The rain was easing off and a sharp wind drove the smoke away, allowing him to see the mist-demon floating a foot-length above the ground. It was disappointingly unspectacular for a demon.

<Can you sing, älf?>

"Of course, what—?"

<I quite liked that tune on the bugle, but a good song really touches me. If I like your voice, älf, it is possible that I might consider paying a visit to your Incxtinguishables. And then I might perhaps think about negotiating with them. Possibly.>

Sinthoras did not hide his amazement. He had bargained in the past with others for gold or weapons or food supplies and he had traded in works of art, but to have the fate of his homeland depend on his singing? It was lucky that he sang tolerably well. "Then lend me your ears. I shall sing the Lay of Inàste's Tears."

Sinthoras raised his voice and sang as he had never, in all his long life, sung before.

Tears, heavy with sadness,
dark and deeply troubled.
Blackness of the sky,
Tears shed for our sake,
for us,
us, the immortal ones.

They gave us courage,
brought us homeland and hope.
Divinity descended,
donated to us,
us, the immortal ones.

Elevated and highly blessed
by our mother Inàste,
they stand above all else,
as we stand above all others,
we, the immortal ones.

Tears shall no longer flow,
dark and deeply troubled.
We live eternal, praising her,
the mother, proudly.
That pride itself
was gifted us,
us, the immortal ones.

Others should now shed their tears:
the mothers of our foes.
Inàste herself will laugh with joy,
over the bones of our enemies,
slain by us,
us, the immortal ones.

The final tone echoed over the mountain ranges. Sinthoras was extremely gratified by the quality of his own performance and was sure it would have had the desired effect on the demon. He sank down on his right knee. "Now let me describe to you how we shall travel to Dsôn—"

<I took no pleasure in that, älf>

"What?" Sinthoras was certain the demon had been lost for words.

<Your performance touched me and I lost myself a little in your voice, but I did not like the song, it was too dark and disheartening.> The sparkling cloud spread in size, becoming transparent. <Look around. Do you think I need anything extra in the way of depression? Why not something jolly? That would have been more sensible.>

Sinthoras could not understand how this creature was criticizing his singing. Before he could bring himself to suggest a different song, the mist rose up and let the wind drive it back into the heart of the smoke. The rain had not been sufficient to douse the peat fires.

<Go home, älf,> Sinthoras heard, <It was nice to meet something that is not afraid of me, but I would advise you to leave my refuge at once before the curse hits you. The humans have paid a heavy price for not recognizing what danger they were in.>

"Wait!" he shouted, trying to pursue the cloud, but it melted into the smoke and disappeared. "Demon, you must not leave!" he called in desperation. "Demon? DEMON?"

He listened out for the voice in his head but heard only the hissing of the hot damp earth.

There was no word.

"By Tion!" he roared, ramming his spear into the ground. "What do I do now?" *My dreams are shattered and it was my singing that did it. I chose the wrong song.* Sinthoras uttered a sound that was pure helplessness. *I must think of something! I must!*

He whirled round on hearing footsteps.

Seven figures approached over the brow of the hill; they were in heavy armor and bore shields and swords. A hodgepodge of the usual races ranging from barbarians via an óarco to a fflecx. The cnutar they had with them was a symbiotic creation, an interesting novelty.

Sinthoras pulled his spear out of the ground, threw down his saddlebags and readied himself for the fray. *This is no chance encounter.* You would never see such a mixed group under normal circumstances, not even in Ishím Voróo. They must have been dragooned into serving together. "What do you want?"

They fanned out and the barbarian, his face mostly obscured by visor and beard, stepped forward. "Apart from your death, älf? We want the vial you stole from the castle of my master, the mighty gålran zhadar."

"I do not have it; my companion took it," Sinthoras lied. He was angry with himself for not noticing he was being followed. He had not really paid attention. He had not left tracks, of course, but his horse had, and he would pay for this oversight. As these seven adversaries had managed to avoid all the obstacles of the journey, they must be good at what they did.

"If so, the troops pursuing them will soon find out," the barbarian replied.

You think you are going to defeat me? By placing his finger to his lips and putting his head on one side, Sinthoras pretended to be thinking hard. "Wait! I think it was the obboona who took it. She knew what its importance was."

The barbarian shook his head. "I don't think so." He drew his sword. "I think you know exactly what you stole, otherwise you would not be here and we would not have found you, would we?"

Sinthoras was curious. Of course, he had studied the vial and had sensed the magic it contained, but he had no idea what it was for. From what the barbarian was saying, it sounded like it might have something to do with the mist-demon—that would tie up with the damaged inscription. "Possibly," he answered vaguely, twirling the spear in his hands.

"Then we'll start with your death and we can look for the vial ourselves." The barbarian gave the signal to attack and the other six moved in.

Sinthoras was dismayed to see the fflecx selecting a dart from his belt while the others spread out to surround him.

He did something he had previously only done once, in all his years as an älf warrior, and then only under express orders: he turned and ran, weaving this way and that to avoid the alchemancer darts. *If you are stupid enough, do what your leader says and come after me!*

His speed gave him a head start. He would seek out suitable places for a counterattack to avoid meeting them in open combat: the numbness in his fingers was spreading up his arms and it would affect his precision with weapons. He would have to set traps.

The gâlran zhadar's henchmen were forced to act; before they could take either the vial or his life they would have to catch him.

I'll kill the fflecx first. He took out the phaiu su he had kept in his cuff, and taking the silver filament in his gauntleted hand, he ran into the midst of the densest smoke, threw himself into one of the smoldering pits and held his breath.

Sinthoras sank down into the ash. A heat haze swirled round him like water. He relied on his armor and on his own stamina to be able to suppress the burning pain for long enough.

He soon heard his pursuers. When he heard the soft steps nearing he sat up and opened his hand, blowing the phaiu su off his gloved hand. *Fly and find yourself some food!*

His breath was enough to waft the strand on its journey.

At first it seemed it would land ineffectually on the plated shoulder of the óarco in front of the fflecx, but the gnomoid's playful nature sealed his fate: he reached out for the web-like thread and a light breeze waved it into his face.

The phaiu su sat fast and the fflecx screeched like an old woman. His companions rushed up and tried to help him. The barbarian, however, shouted a warning: the fflecx was a goner and they must look to their own safety.

You are so easy to trick. The general confusion helped Sinthoras. Still in his hiding place, he stuck the end of his spear into the cnutar's right leg, activating the weapon's hidden switch.

The artificial blast of air inflated the flesh, bursting it open. Blood and shreds of skin shot into the air and the leg bones were laid bare.

At once the parts of the symbiotic creature separated and took on human form. They desperately attempted to stem the bleeding of the other part, but death was too quick for them. Sixty heartbeats later the other two sections keeled over as well. There was no sign of the other pursuers. *They must be out in the mist somewhere.*

Five. Sinthoras jumped up and ran deeper into the swirling fog, leaving a trail of sparks and ash. *I can cope with five, even in my present state.*

He received a sudden blow on his back that felled him and heard an óarco mock him in a deep, throaty laugh.

"The black-eyes always used to be quicker than that," came the taunt.

Sinthoras heard a whistling sound and rolled over onto his side; the sword missed him. He could no longer feel his arms but at least they moved and obeyed him. "Quick enough to kill you," he announced arrogantly. His movements were jerky and inelegant. The óarco had no problem parrying his spear thrusts.

On his right side the barbarian loomed up out of the mist, aiming a sword thrust at this head.

Sinthoras met the opponent's blade with his spear shaft, deflecting it to strike the óarco, but the creature protected itself with its shield.

Is there nothing I can do properly? His acute hearing told Sinthoras that the ground under his feet was cracking. Without a moment's hesitation he rammed his spear into the ground and activated the mechanism again, springing backward simultaneously.

The high-pressure air-jet tore a hole in the earth's crust, swallowing up the barbarian and the óarco. A cloud of sparks erupted and a red tongue of flame shot up to the sky. Another of the barbarians, hurrying to help his friend, fell into the pit himself. The chasm had opened quickly and his heavy armor had pulled him to his death.

I can do this after all. Sinthoras landed outside the danger area and started running. *Only two . . .*

As if from nowhere the edge of a shield hit him on the chin.

Sinthoras was thrown off his feet, hanging suspended in the air for a moment before falling. The spear slipped out of his fingers and disappeared into the fumes with a clatter; he could not breathe and he was sure his jaw was broken.

He jumped up and whirled around, spitting blood and drawing his long knife.

Then he was kicked in the side so that all the air was driven out of his lungs. He heard a shout of triumph and saw the ugly face of a half-troll looking down at him. Then a shield smashed against the älf's face.

This made Sinthoras cry out in pain; blood dripped from his mouth, but there was worse to come: his arms and legs gave way and he had no resistance against the poison exerting its full effects at the worst possible time. *Samusin, be gracious or I am lost!* Any thought of his defeating his enemies was fading fast.

"Over here!" yelled the troll, kicking Sinthoras over on to his back with a steel-tipped boot. "Over here! I've got him!"

"There's only one left besides you," Sinthoras croaked indistinctly, attempting a malicious laugh. It was incredibly painful and so he stopped trying. Robbed of any strength in his limbs he could not think of anything he could do to avert the impending defeat. He had been so close. *All the fault of that indecisive demon!*

"As if I care," the half-troll mocked, above him. "The only thing that matters is that I've caught you, black-eyes." He lifted his huge foot and stamped down on the alf's stomach with his heel. "Let's see what you have had to eat," he said with an ugly laugh.

The armor took most of the murderous impact, but the half-troll increased the pressure, breaking four of the älf's ribs. Fighting for air, Sinthoras arched his back.

And heard glass breaking.

The half-troll had shattered the vial with his foot.

Ishím Voróo (The Outer Lands), älfar realm Dsôn Faïmon, tip of the Radial Arm Shiimal, 4370th division of unendingness (5198th solar cycle), late summer.

Caphalor opened his eyes.

And was amazed.

He had not reckoned with being in a position to do that ever again.

And he had certainly not reckoned on ever again seeing his own bed-room ceiling.

I'm dreaming! He turned his head to the left.

It really was his own bedchamber—and his life-companion was lying at his side. Her eyes were closed and her breathing irregular.

Caphalor wanted to call her name but his lips refused to move. He was so very tired, so very weak. His mind was sluggish, as if he had drunk too much wine.

"Father, don't try to move," came his daughter's voice.

Is this still a dream? Presumably he was lying in the mire at death's door and the alchemancers' poison was playing these tricks on his brain.

Here was Tarlesa and she was smiling at him. There were bloodstains on her simple brown clothing. Standing behind her, he saw Raleeha in her high-necked gray dress, a band of black lace over her eyes. She looked more älf-woman than barbarian. It was only the collar that told of her lowly status as a slave. She was holding a basin of water; drops of red ran down the outside of the bowl, and there were bloodied towels over Raleeha's left arm.

His vision blurred and he tried to lift an arm.

"No, Father. Don't move. You are not yet out of danger. You will need to rest for many moments of unendingness before you can get up with your powers restored," his daughter told him gently.

Caphalor swallowed. "How did I . . . ?" But his voice failed him.

"Aïsolon found you and the slave girl when he was out hunting. He killed the outlaws who attacked you and brought you back to the border. The troops brought you home," Tarlesa explained.

He groaned. This was what he had most dreaded: *shame and dishonor, from hero to laughing stock.* This would only serve to reinforce the reputation of the Constellations as cowards. He had not found the mist-demon, he had not killed Munumon, and the obboona was still alive and here he was, helpless as a kitten. The Inextinguishable Ones would revile him for returning with only failure to report.

A fate worse than death.

His daughter read his expression. "No one knows you are here in Shiimal, Father. The soldiers are sworn to secrecy. They are all Constellation supporters. And Aïsolon is the last älf who would ever betray you."

Caphalor sighed and closed his eyes. *I have failed—I, who had been granted the Honor-Blessing.*

The thought troubled him deeply. He was plagued by the thought of still being alive in these circumstances. He would have preferred the Inextinguishables and the älfar people all to presume him dead in a heroic attempt to serve his rulers. A lesser warrior could have been forgiven failure, but not one who had been Honor-Blessed.

"If I die, burn my body secretly," he whispered. "Nobody must know that I am here. It would reflect badly on all of you."

"Father, I am not going to let you die," Tarlesa replied, her tone kindly but determined. "As soon as you are restored to health, you can set off again in secret and complete your mission."

He forced himself to lift his eyelids to look at his daughter. Then he stretched out his left hand to touch her face—and saw his wrist. An enali-tube had been inserted into a blood vessel in his arm and there was dried blood on the skin nearby.

Tarlesa pressed his arm down again. "No, Father, please." There was a click and he felt her fasten his arm to the bed with a metal cuff. "If you move you might pull out the enali and then you would both bleed to death."

"What have you done?"

"Learned from my studies. These enali tendrils are hollow and very flexible. I rinse them in alcohol so that they don't cause any infection. Most healers would use boiling water, but that would cook the tubes and make them useless." She gave his shoulder an encouraging rub. "The slave told me the fflecx had administered poison, so we had to remove the diseased blood. I opened an artery in your leg and at the same time Mother and I gave you some of our own blood through the enali tube. Mother is giving you the last quota. Then she must stop or she will become too weak." Tarlesa kissed him on the forehead. "Sleep, Father. I shall ensure you can return as a hero."

Caphalor closed his eyes. He was not yet able to hope, but pride in his clever daughter left him feeling calmer.

Chapter XII

Because the Inextinguishables did not want to sacrifice their loyal slaves and their servants, they sent their warriors out against the tribes and the creatures of Ishím Voróo.

The älfar forces swept out, bringing death and destruction in all directions, exterminating civilizations and uncivilizations alike, in order to found a seat of power appropriate for the Inextinguishables.

No one could stop them in this endeavor.

Epocrypha of the Creating Spirit,
1st Book,
Chapter 2, 18–23

Ishím Voróo (The Outer Lands),
4370th division of unendingness (5198th solar cycle),
late summer.

Sinthoras lay immobile on the warm ground. There was a bright light on his chest and a silver ball was hovering above his damaged armor. *What did the brainless idiot do with that ill-advised kick?* Sparks shot out, hitting him and the half-troll, but not causing injury.

The älf felt nothing—apart from the strong magic force radiating outward.

The half-troll leaped backward, shield raised in defense and club aimed at the luminous sphere. "That won't help you, black-eyes!" he growled, baring uneven but very sharp teeth. "Your sorcery's not going to save you!"

Sinthoras had no idea what it was that had been released from the vial, but it wasn't harming him. Perhaps it could even be employed to his own advantage—he could make use of his enemy's fear.

"If you don't move away I'll have your skull burst open, beast!" he shouted. "Go back to the gålran zhadar and tell him about my magic powers!"

The silvery ball, still floating in the air, started to spin. More sparks issued, forming jagged flashes of lightning that pierced the clouds of mist and disappeared.

It seemed to Sinthoras that they were searching for something.

The half-troll was certainly impressed by the harmless spectacle; it took two giant steps back, becoming almost invisible in the fog.

"Hey!" it called out. "Help here, ho! Help! The black-eyes is doing magic stuff!"

Sinthoras racked his brains. Try as he might, he could not move his limbs. The poison had affected them badly. By the time the last of the gålran zhadar's henchmen turned up he would surely be done for— he would be hurled out of his unendingness and extinguished. Everyone would forget his name and he would not even get a mention on the hallowed Wall of the Departed.

Never! Tion, I beseech you! He stared at the whirring sphere.

An elf approached him through the swirls of mist. *An elf? Did it have to be an elf?* A so-called creature of light—arrogance personified. When those pathetic creatures fell it would be best for everyone.

The sight of the elf summoned up his last reserves of energy. He thought, full of hatred, of Tark Draan, where the scum had hidden from the älfar, crawling away to find refuge with the groundlings, barbarians and second-rate wizards. To find an elf on the loose in Ishím Voróo was strange indeed.

I must not die. And certainly not at the hand of an elf! His mood lifted when he beheld the terror on the elf's face. It was obviously not seen as a good thing that the silver sphere had been released.

"Rambarz!" The elf's ridiculously high voice rang out. Sinthoras could have slain him for that sound alone. "Get over here at once!"

The half-troll appeared out of the gloom, his shield before him and his weapon held at arm's length. "The Thing is still there," he said accusingly. "Make it go!"

The elf held two long swords in his hands and he pointed at the sphere with one of them. "This is not the work of älfar. It was contained in the vial."

Sinthoras laughed out loud. "Your clumsy troll destroyed the flask when he kicked me. Your gâlran zhadar won't be pleased; his own people have destroyed what he wanted so badly." His broken jaw was painful; it was swelling up and making his speech unclear.

"It was his property, thief! You stole it—and you took it without knowing what it was." The elf stowed one of his swords and looked around. "Keep watch," he ordered Rambarz. "If you see the cloud I told you about, break the amulet."

"Yes, Dafirmas."

Sinthoras felt an icy wave course through him, freezing his heart. *Samusin, save me! I cannot end like this. This cannot be my destiny!* For two blinks of an eye he believed his life was over; then his heart started to beat once more, struggling to pump the chilled and thickened blood. The pain from his shattered ribs and the ache in his jaw stopped him passing out.

Dafirmas knelt at his side, placing his second sword down on the ground; he formed his two hands into a semicircle, keeping two hand widths away from the silver sphere. Eyes closed, he murmured a sing-song incantation.

Sinthoras supposed the mist-demon would be interested in this sphere. *Very interested. Let's see what he says.* He started to sing at the top of his voice, as loud as his injuries permitted. He chose a jolly song to lure the demon.

Dafirmas opened his eyes and glared at the älf. "Silence!"

Grinning and coughing, Sinthoras continued his song.

"Rambarz, make him stop! Make him stop for*ever*!"

The half-troll stepped out of the fog, making a detour round the glowing sphere. He lifted his club, ready to strike.

Sinthoras bellowed out the rest of his song.

Behind Rambarz a shimmering light appeared and the älf laughed, relieved, gasping for air and spitting blood: the broken ribs had damaged his lungs.

Dafirmas looked up, recognizing the demon. "Sitalia, I beseech you!" The elf's face turned ash-gray. "Help me . . ."

The silver ball gave a final whirr and sparks shot out into the shimmering cloud, which grew brighter by the moment.

Dazzled, Sinthoras shut his eyes and felt a wave of heat wash over him, driving out the icy cold and the pain, making his limbs supple once more. *Ye gods, what game are you playing with me?* He dived for the elf's sword blindly and dealt a wild blow, opening his eyes again at the last moment.

Sensing the attack, Dafirmas tried to bring his second sword into play, but Sinthoras was too quick. He struck the elf on the shoulder and followed up with a stab to the throat. "Your death bears the name Sinthoras." He released the sword. Dafirmas died beside him, eyes filling with hatred before they dimmed.

Sinthoras grasped his spear with the other hand and managed to deflect the half-troll's plunging war club, then he stabbed the half-troll through the foot and activated the gas mechanism.

There was a hiss and the troll's boot doubled in size; blood sprayed out of the shaft. His adversary stumbled backward with a roar.

Sinthoras got to his feet, holding the spear in both hands and twirled it in the air. The effects of the fflecx's poison were hardly noticeable. *Don't be too sure,* he warned himself as he looked at the mist-demon.

A war was being waged within the writhing fog. The sphere hovered in midair, flashing out in all directions, tearing holes in the creature of mist, which darkened and intensified like a thundercloud. An aura of horror, malignancy, and fear seethed out from the mist. *Wonderful!* Sinthoras savored it.

Rambarz was not to be seen. The half-troll must have taken to his heels. *Too much magic here for the simpleminded.*

Sinthoras stopped, eyeing the mist-demon, which was now preparing to fight back. All at once it turned white as snow and a loud cry resounded in the älf's head. The sphere went dark and the humming ceased as the ball became transparent, until sparkling points of light were released from the interior, lodging in the cloud to merge with the tiny stars.

The creature's cry faded slowly into a laugh. <What a fantastic gift you have presented me with. The name was Sinthoras, wasn't it?>

The älf nodded, his excitement at a peak. The mist-demon had changed: it was speaking in a teasing whisper, but there was malicious trickery there, too—a trace of threat in each syllable. The sleepiness and boredom in his voice had vanished. "Yes, that is my name. I am delighted you liked the present."

<Why have you only just given it to me?>

"I wanted to understand you better, to get a clear impression. Pardon me for keeping you waiting." Sinthoras did not have the faintest idea what was happening, or how the pain caused by the poison had been lifted away, but it was good.

<I understand and forgive you, my friend.>

Sinthoras smiled. "In that case I am a happy älf."

<I can feel my energies increasing.> The mist-demon wafted over to Sinthoras and played round his legs, snaking upward and around them. <And I remember you had a request. There was support you had asked for, for a war in the south. You promised I would receive my own realm.>

The voice was cautious, challenging, and deadly dangerous. Sinthoras had the feeling death was closer now than before his sudden miraculous recovery.

He had imagined how he would accompany the mist-demon to his homeland, presenting him as a new ally, an ally he had won over with no help from that failure, Caphalor. He imagined being rewarded by the Inextinguishables with the longed-for Honor-Blessing.

That dream now departed, but he might at least convince the demon to join the campaign and give him directions to Dsôn Faïmon.

"My rulers will give you Tark Draan as soon as it has been conquered, I swear."

‹That sounds good. I can hardly wait!› The mist embraced him, enclosing him completely. ‹You carry death within yourself, älf. Poison. Tell me: is it your wish to die? Is this journey intended to be your last?›

"No, by Samusin! The alchemancers poisoned me to force me to do their bidding. They are supposed to give me the antidote, if—"

‹Shall I rid you of the poison?›

"Can you?" Sinthoras could not decide whether or not to take up the offer. This urgency, this greediness, made him uneasy. The silver sphere had completely transformed his new ally. Unfortunately he could not ask the elf what had been in the shattered flask.

The mist-demon gave off a luminous glow and tiny stars radiated around Sinthoras, heating him mercilessly, as if he were being baked in an oven. Sweat broke out of every pore, drenching his apparel and soaking his face. He was as wet as if he had just stepped out of a lake. Then the heat receded.

‹So, my friend, that should have helped.›

Sinthoras looked down at himself, his sweat was colored dark brown and gave off a horrible smell. "Was that the poison?"

‹Yes, with a little magic and some heat I have driven it out of you.› The mist withdrew from around the älf, twisting and swirling in front of him. ‹When are we off?›

"Off?"

‹On your campaign, älf! I want to see the land that's going to be mine. Your rulers will have been making preparations, I presume?›

"We wanted to be sure you would be on our side." Sinthoras still could not grasp the fact that he had so simply and quickly been saved from certain death. He laughed out loud. "You have saved me!"

‹After you gave me that splendid gift it was only right and proper to help.› The mist darkened. ‹Now, when do we set out?›

There was no mistaking the threat from this combination of whining child and petulant monarch. Sinthoras was aware of the burning landscape all around and he thought about the destruction and extermination that had taken place here. Suddenly he was dismayed by the thought of taking this demon back to Dsôn Faïmon. *Will the same thing happen to my homeland? And what if the demon prefers the Star Realm to the prospect of Tark Draan?*

Sinthoras decided: the demon must not be allowed access to the realm of the älfar. "I shall leave immediately and will bring the Inextinguishables the good news. Then we shall assemble the armies. When that is done I shall send a messenger for you."

The mist creature was silent. <I don't want to wait out here in the wilderness. I've spent too long watching this land die.>

Dafirmas shot up with a screech. His throat was still transfixed by the sword and his eyes were dull, yet he moved like one alive. He hissed and growled and hurled himself at Sinthoras, attacking with bare hands, his fingers curled to claws.

Sinthoras swung his spear and drove it into the elf's body, keeping him at arm's length. "Will you just lie down and be dead?" The elf writhed as if it had contracted a maddening disease. If the spear had not had arresting lugs, Dafirmas would have driven it through his own body in his efforts to reach Sinthoras.

In a flash the älf recalled the beheaded skeletons. Drawing the sword out of the elf's throat with one hand, he chopped through the neck while retaining his grip on the spear with the other. Vertebrae severed, Dafirmas collapsed to the ground.

<The other thing you can do is incinerate them,> said the mist-demon. <I used to dislike this talent of mine, but it comes in useful in battle. We could have a whole army of soldiers that never tire.>

"Excellent," said Sinthoras, jerking his spear back out of the elf cadaver. He would be very careful on the way home—all of his victims that he had not lured into fire pits would be waiting for him. He bowed to the demon. "I'll be on my way. Wait here until the message comes."

<No, don't send a messenger, just sing.>

"What did you say?"

<You are to sing, my friend. Sing that ghoulish song you sang for me the first time. Not the jolly one.>

"But I'd be hundreds of miles away," objected Sinthoras.

<I shall hear it. Go now.> The mist-demon withdrew. <I shall not wait forever, Sinthoras. If you take too long I shall regard our agreement as null and void.>

"What do you see as being too long?"

<I'll need to have heard from you by next winter. The song. Sing the song. That's best.> The cloud vanished.

Sinthoras gulped, raised his hand and watched the stinking poison drip from his fingertips. *Saved. I shall see Dsôn Faïmon once more and can report my success.* Then he realized he had no proof of the alliance he had negotiated. The Inextinguishable Ones would have to take his word for it. Would they do that? Would they put the whole machinery of war in motion, mobilize the vassal armies, call his entire people to arms— purely on his say so?

Unease coursed through Sinthoras.

He would keep quiet about his own role in transforming the demon's nature. *I won't mention the broken vial and I won't say what happened to me here.* He did, however, want to warn his rulers about the new ally. *Perhaps it is possible to march on Tark Draan without using the mist- demon.* But now the creature knew about the impending campaign and wanted to be involved. It was going to be difficult.

All the same, he was now physically fit and bursting with energy— he could make it back to Dsôn. He strode off, homeward bound.

He briefly thought about finding Rambarz, whose possession of the amulet the elf had mentioned was particularly interesting, but it was more important to get back with his report on the new alliance. He wanted the renown and the celebrations that were his due. *I have earned this.* He put an exploratory hand to his jaw, but it had completely healed, and there was no pain from his ribs when he took a breath.

His apprehension ebbed away. *I shan't need the amulet.* He was returning home after he had won the powerful demon to the älfar cause, he would be a hero.

He blanked out any second thoughts about the situation.

For himself and thus for all others.

Ishím Voróo (The Outer Lands), älfar realm Dsôn
Faïmon, tip of the Radial Arm Shiimal,
4370th division of unendingness (5198th solar cycle),
late summer.

Raleeha listened to every conversation between the father and the daughter who never left his side.

She was able to understand practically everything they said. She hoped her master would not die, that he would recover, return to Ishím Voróo, and hasten to the aid of Sinthoras.

The gods were being benevolent: Caphalor grew better as each new day dawned. The älf called Aïsolon, who had saved them both, encouraged him, telling him not to give up on himself or on the mission. Aïsolon's words and Tarlesa's wonderful healing skills were restoring Caphalor's health rapidly and giving him the confidence that things would take a turn for the better.

Raleeha was delighted at the improvement: she was frantic with worry about Sinthoras and kept telling herself that he would still be alive. He was tougher than her new master, he would be able to withstand Munumon's malice and would survive until Caphalor found him. The thought that he might be lying sick somewhere in Ishím Voróo was intolerable. She would give the last drop of her own blood to save his life.

At the same time her inner voice was calling her a fool. The two älfar were deadly enemies. *The last thing Caphalor would want to do would be to save Sinthoras.*

"Come here," Tarlesa commanded. "Take these towels to the kitchen and have them boiled."

She bowed and heard the älf-girl open the door. Raleeha had not wanted to admit that she did not yet know her way about and she often got lost—it would take her some time to locate the kitchens.

Tarlesa laughed. "How stupid of me—telling a blind woman where to go in a house she doesn't know."

"I'm sure I would have found it, mistress," Raleeha said. The basin was taken out of her hands and a name was called. "Take this away," Tarlesa told the other slave who now approached.

Raleeha was guided gently by the arm. At first she thought it was the other slave who had taken her elbow, but the fragrance she picked up told her that it was Caphalor's daughter.

"You saved my father's life and enabled him to stay amongst those who never die," Tarlesa said, her voice losing all its sharpness. "You are a slave, my father's property and so this was your duty. But far away from the eyes and ears of my people, in Ishím Voróo, on your own . . ." She cleared her throat. "I mean to say—you might have left him to die, or killed him. You could easily have run away."

"No, mistress. Such thoughts were far from my mind. I choose to serve your people. I have learned so much during my time here."

"You were happy to serve *Sinthoras,* I know . . . My father says he gave you away, and he put out your eyes, but still you did everything he asked?"

"Yes, mistress."

"There is no hatred in you?"

"No, mistress." And she knew that she spoke the truth. She did not feel hatred—a deep disappointment had displaced the initial anger.

"No pride that whispers revenge? It was only a trivial matter, I hear, for which he punished you so severely."

Raleeha did not know where this was leading. Was she being tested? Why? Uncertain, she gave no answer.

Tarlesa laughed softly. "You are the perfect slave, Raleeha: not rebellious, always ready to serve and always polite. Between ourselves, that makes you rather suspect."

"Mistress!" she objected, horrified.

"Never fear, slave. You are safe from me, but as long as you live under this roof I shall have you closely watched." Tarlesa had gone up a set of stairs with her and had crossed through two rooms. Now she stopped. There was a smell of alcohol. "Over there, lie down." Raleeha was led to a couch and she lay on it obediently. "Let me see what your previous owner has done."

Tarlesa pushed the lace band up onto her forehead and Raleeha felt the air where her eyes had been. Then expert fingers felt her face, touching the cheekbones and circling the empty sockets.

Raleeha's breathing quickened. *What is she up to?*

She heard a metallic sound at her side and then something sharp traced along the edges of the eye sockets and her eyelids were gripped and fastened back.

"Oh, yes," Tarlesa murmured, and it sounded as if she were smiling. "He stabbed through the eyeball. Very exact incisions, only going as deep as necessary. Afterward you should have been treated with a substance that was intended to dry out the tissue."

"Did that not happen, mistress?" Raleeha was terrified. Her imagination had Tarlesa standing over her wielding thin needles. If her hand slipped, the needle might go through to the brain . . . She forced herself to think of something else—something nicer.

"In the left eye, yes, but the right eye still retains some moisture." There was a sound of rattling metal—the älf-girl picking up her instruments. "Perhaps there's something I can do with the right. The other one is useless."

"What do you mean, mistress?"

"You told me you had learned much from us, so I should like to give you the opportunity of learning more—I shan't promise anything I can't guarantee, but there is a powerful distillation of herbs and essences I could use." Tarlesa said. "It can be lethal if wrongly applied," she added absently. There was another metallic sound. "This tincture can bring dead tissue back to life and stimulate regrowth."

Raleeha vaguely grasped what the älf was saying. "You mean . . ."

"Indeed. The tincture may restore your right eye and its sight."

Raleeha tried hard not to clap her hands with delight; she would be able to paint and draw again, rather than scratching remembered images onto paper. *And I can see Sinthoras again and learn from his art!* "What would I have to do?"

Tarlesa laughed. "Oh, you'd only have to agree to the procedure. I wouldn't normally ask a slave for permission for an experiment—I do whatever I want—but as you saved my father's life you must have the right to decide your own fate."

Raleeha did not hesitate. "Yes, please try it, mistress. Please."

"I'm glad to hear that." Tarlesa shook a little bottle. "But I have to warn you what could go wrong—if the tincture gets into your blood you will die. In a couple of cases it affected the brains of my barbarian subjects and they went insane; the eye might overreact and burst, or it might regrow but still not function; it might become inflamed and you—"

"Mistress," Raleeha interrupted her impatiently. "Do it! I don't mind what happens. I must at least try."

"Did I mention terrible pain?"

"I'll put up with the pain."

Tarlesa finished shaking the bottle and the cork was removed. There was the sound of liquid going into a pipette. "You are a strong barbarian, Raleeha. We shall soon see what you can tolerate."

Raleeha thought she could hear the drops coming out of the narrow end of the glass tube, she felt them landing in her right eye socket. She waited nervously.

"Well?" Tarlesa asked eagerly. "Is it working?"

"No, mistress," Raleeha said, disappointedly.

"Then I must inject it into the eye capsule." Again Raleeha heard the sound of metal instruments and then a dragging noise.

Sharp pangs of intense pain shot through her head. Acid filled her eyeball socket and she jerked her head to one side. The tincture spilled onto the bridge of her nose and seeped down.

"Curses!" Tarlesa pulled the slave collar tighter. "Keep still, can't you?"

Raleeha could not breathe. She gasped for air. But the älf-woman had fixed the buckles on the collar as tight as they would go. Her mind drifted as she fell into a faint, her limbs limp and the pain in her eye lessening.

Then the leather strap was loosened. She drew a shuddering lungful of air. With her returning consciousness the waves of pain swelled back.

"I have injected the substance into the remains of your eye," Tarlesa said impatiently. "Too much of it was wasted when you moved your head, slave. Have you any idea how much it costs? You are to be whipped for that." She called another slave. Raleeha missed her name. "Ten strokes on the naked breasts for this one," she commanded sharply, as cruel as she had sounded at their first meeting. "Get her out of here."

Raleeha was dragged to her feet and pulled roughly through the rooms and down the stairs. Suddenly she found herself outside, standing in the cold drizzle.

A jerk at her clothes bared her breasts.

Raleeha did not struggle and did not cry out until the third lash. The pain of this punishment diverted her attention from the burning of the acid in her eye. After the tenth stroke she collapsed in the mud with blood running down over her belly. Her breasts felt like torn strips of sacking.

"Come, Raleeha," said the slave kindly. "You have survived it. The mistress has given me some good ointment. It will help, there won't be any scars." Raleeha sobbed and moaned as she clasped her damaged breasts. A woman bathed her with warm water and dried her gently; after that Raleeha felt a cooling layer of ointment being applied to her hot skin. Someone led her to the shared chamber and helped her to clamber up to the topmost mattress.

Raleeha could hear people talking quietly, telling stories. She heard her own name mentioned several times.

The salve was indeed excellent: the pain had almost gone and having felt her left breast, she could tell the swelling was already going down. She wondered how many barbarians had lost their lives in experiments to perfect this formula.

Once more the voice at the back of her head condemned the älfar for their arbitrary cruelty. The voice suggested she should flee, complaining that she had once again been severely punished for a trivial offense.

Raleeha stifled the voice by imagining regaining her sight. Then she prayed for Sinthoras. *He must be in Ishím Voróo, where he must surely have survived the poison and be carrying out one heroic deed after another.* Raleeha calmed her breathing, removed the lace band from her forehead and placed it under her pillow, as was her custom at night.

She was impatient. She could not wait for the moment when her sight might return. Tarlesa had given her hope. The dream must come true.

Whatever else happened.

Ishím Voróo (The Outer Lands),
4370th division of unendingness (5198th solar cycle),
late summer.

Caphalor thundered along the plain on his heavily armored night-mare. *It was high time I was back on my mission: Tarlesa's healing skills have given me a second life and I am going to use it.*

It was nonsense, of course—however breakneck the speed—to assume he would catch up with Sinthoras, or even come across his corpse.

Knowing how badly he had been affected himself, Caphalor presumed the other älf had succumbed to the poison. *His death is certain.*

So now it was up to him to make the alliance with the mist-demon, though, the more he thought about it, the more he was convinced that waging war had not been the Inextinguishables' idea. *The Comets put this plan on the table, the rulers may have given in to political pressure and powerful lobbying, though I would never have thought that possible. Perhaps my return as a triumphant Constellation can help to influence matters for the good.*

He had left Raleeha at home: her blindness would make things difficult and any horse she rode would be much slower than Sardaî. She was living secretly at his home, carrying out menial tasks and hoping Sinthoras would return.

You know perfectly well why you left her behind. She is not good for you—perhaps you should just give her back to Sinthoras. He hated having to admit that she troubled him. He had not examined the emotions, but knew she aroused feelings he would normally only have for his life-partner.

Under different circumstances—and if she had been an älf—he might have eventually left Enoïla for her. *But for a slave girl? A barbarian, who cannot compete with my own people in grace or beauty or longevity? Never.*

And yet he had lost his heart to her. Thanks to their journey, her figure was now similar to that of an älf, *and she is beautiful* . . .

Caphalor forced his attention back to the matter in hand. *I have to give her away.* He must dismiss her from his mind if he wanted to return to Dsôn without dishonor. *She is a human and thus mediocre at best. Do not waste your time with the mediocre,* he told himself, sealing off that train of thought.

The brightly colored fflecx palisade border came into view and this time he had a surprise for the repulsive gnomoids.

Caphalor brought the night-mare to a halt and opened the container with the fire-arrows. He ignited the wick on the bow just under the grip. The glowing wick would touch the fabric wrapped round the arrow tip when he drew the string to its full extent. He had brought thirty prepared arrows, of which half had fist-size bladders attached filled with petroleum; they would burst open on impact.

"Here come my greetings." Caphalor loosed the first of the arrows against the wooden palisade. With any luck the fflecx would not notice until the flames were licking high, then it would be too late.

Coolly, he sent arrow after arrow into the air; the liquid splashed out onto the wooden staves.

After his tenth arrow a small hatch was thrust open and one of the fflecx looked out.

He must have heard something.

You don't have to run about being that ugly any longer. Caphalor felled the guard with a war arrow and sent a fire missile in its wake.

The palisade burst into crackling flame along a length of twenty paces: the paint burned like dry tinder, boosting the effect of the petroleum, and the fire spread quickly along the walkways in both directions.

A single arrow would have been sufficient. Caphalor removed the wick and threw it to the ground. He waited for the fire to do its destructive work.

The fflecx were scurrying about on the palisade wall, trying to douse the flames with sand. They opened the gate and thirty alchemancers carrying buckets rushed out to tackle the blaze from outside.

Samusin is on my side!

Sensing what was expected of him, Sardaî galloped off toward the unguarded entrance with a menacing whinny.

The fflecx only noticed the älf when he raced through the line of firefighters, trampling seven of them. The stallion dispensed lethal bites to two more as they crossed into enemy territory.

"Do you recognize me?" Caphalor laughed and rode through without injury. Things were going so much better this time.

He threw a swift glimpse over his shoulder. The fire was spreading still and the palisade fence was burning fiercely. The fflecx obsession with bright colors was sealing their fate. Whatever the alchemancers used to make their paints had the decided disadvantage of being highly flammable. He smiled. He might be able to use this knowledge on his return trip.

Ishím Voróo (The Outer Lands),
4370th division of unendingness (5198th solar cycle),
late summer.

Sinthoras did not believe that barbarians could ever be victorious in battle using horses like the one he was riding. *But if mediocre troops meet other mediocre troops in combat, no one is going to notice the quality of horse and rider.* He, on the other hand, showed his mount constantly how very inferior it was. He shouted, cursed, and whipped it mercilessly and sent out waves of fear to spur the animal on. It felt as if he were hardly making any progress.

While traveling at this frustratingly slow speed, he allowed himself to imagine his triumphant return to Dsôn: how he would revel in the celebrations honoring him! And when he received the award from the Inextinguishables . . . and when he was given overall command of operations against Tark Draan . . .

Sinthoras started assembling his fantasy armies.

In the vanguard: the inferior troops, óarcos and gnomes, as arrow fodder, the flanks protected by the taller races: trolls, half-trolls and giants, these will ensure the smaller ones do not break out when the enemy attacks. He would position the barbarian archers further back and, behind them, the älfar warriors and then the älfar archers, their range being much longer than that of the humans.

Of course, he would also deploy smaller independent units for specific tasks such as lightning strikes on enemy catapult stations, or tracing and capturing, or eliminating enemy leaders on the spot. They could even lead an expedition to set fire to an enemy camp, a strategy that had proved useful in the past. The art of warfare consisted of confronting the enemy with familiar techniques, while weakening him with methods that would take him completely unawares.

But before any campaign against the hated elves and their allies can be launched, the Stone Gateway must fall. He had secured the key to this barrier for himself.

Sinthoras involuntarily cast his mind to Caphalor. *He is sure to be dead by now. His body will have been torn to pieces by carrion-feeders and his bones will have been gnawed by wild animals.* He did not regret Caphalor's passing. With Caphalor's failure, the Comet policy of älfar expansion would be shown to be correct: only the representative of the Comets would return triumphant from the depths of Ishím Voróo.

This begged the question of how he should report Caphalor's death.

He could drag his rival's reputation through the mire by telling the truth and branding him a coward, or he could embroider the story.

Or he could let Caphalor rise to fame and glory by saying that he fell fighting vastly superior numbers of the alchemancers who defeated him with poison and other devious, underhand methods.

But why would I do that? Sinthoras could not decide. *It would be almost culpably negligent not to destroy his reputation.*

In contrast to himself, Caphalor had a family to consider, with children who would develop into first-rate älfar with a variety of important skill sets. If he rendered their father a cowardly incompetent, the disgrace would stick to them forever.

Family. Sinthoras had never wished for one, he wanted to remain on his own. He would take älf-women for pleasure, but that was as far as it went. His motto had always been no commitment, and certainly no connection if it was not going to advance him socially.

But occasionally, at certain splinters of unendingness, he would envy älfar like Caphalor: they had a base, a solid foundation that did not fluctuate with the whims of society's opinion. *In good times, in bad times, at all times.*

Sinthoras avoided asking himself what would happen if his efforts did not bring him the recognition he craved.

He had no genuine friends, only political allies and intellectual partners. There was no one he knew in his own family and his parents had fallen in battle. They had brought him up to have the same priorities that had guided their lives: fame and power.

Caphalor and his companion had remained together for much longer than was normal. *Is that love?* He had never experienced it. *I can manage very well without it.*

His quarrel was solely with Caphalor, not with his life-companion or their children. He would not discredit his rival. *I shall have him die in an honorable struggle against the odds, weakened by the fflecx poison and pierced by four arrows.*

In his report he would stress how he had tried everything to save Caphalor from the howling mob of trolls—this would reflect well on himself—but the situation had been hopeless. He would say Caphalor had insisted on Sinthoras leaving to pursue their mission. That should work. *He does not deserve more . . .*

Without warning he was down, tumbling head over heels to the ground. His horse rolled on top of him, pinning him to the ground.

Sinthoras felt the beast's sweat; he pushed the dead weight aside and squeezed out from under the animal's body. His ribs hurt and he felt giddy, but was otherwise uninjured.

For just one second he had failed to pay attention and the stupid horse had stumbled and fallen. *That never would have happened with a night-mare.*

There was nothing to be done. The horse had broken its neck. "Got anything else in store, gods?" He shouted up into the morning skies, shaking his spear. Dirt fell from his clothing. "Why shouldn't I get back to Dsôn?"

A snort and the sound of hoofbeats made him whirl round. A pair of bloodred eyes confronted him—a magnificent night-mare—on whose back was someone he really had not wanted to see: "Caphalor?"

The älf sat nonchalantly in the saddle and greeted him with a nod.

"Samusin must hate me," Sinthoras said quietly.

"I think he cares deeply for you. I have found you in extreme distress."

"Extreme distress is quite different. My horse died, that's all." He stared at Caphalor. "How is it that you're still alive?"

"I could ask you the same thing. I think I must be immune to the alchemancers' arts, or at least immune to whatever poison they cooked up for us." Caphalor smiled sympathetically. "What's your explanation?"

"It was our new ally who cured me out of pure friendship." Sinthoras was furious. *Why did I have to come across him now?* "I found the mist-demon and I've won him over—on my own."

"Was it difficult? What did you have to promise him?" Caphalor leaned forward. "Can you prove it?"

This was the weakness and Caphalor had put his finger on it straight-away. "I have his word," he retorted.

"He's not with you?"

"No."

"So you have a treaty?"

"No."

"Oh. So, no treaty." Caphalor shook with laughter. "The Inextin-guishables will be impressed when the hero returns with only fine words to show for himself."

"But it's true!" Sinthoras shouted. "While you ran away whining, I led armies against each other and had hundreds of adventures, to—"

"Of course you did. Save it to entertain our rulers when you're next in the throne room." Caphalor was dismissive. "Tell me, how will you summon your new ally?"

If Sinthoras told him that the demon would turn up in response to a song, there would be more mockery. "None of your business." He placed his foot on the dead horse. "Take me with you."

Caphalor smiled. "No."

"*No?*" Sinthoras sensed the other älf was about to name his conditions for taking him on Saudaî, but he was not going to let himself be humiliated in that way.

"You will return to the Star Realm alive if we can agree about our having found the mist-demon together. You can be the glorious hero who led the talks, if you like, but in my story we both went to the demon's land." Caphalor was as cool as ice.

Sinthoras was itching to ram a spear through him. "You want to share the glory without having done a thing?" He thought of all he had gone through at the jeembinas' camp, and how he had fought off the gâlran zhadar's henchmen. "That's not going to happen!"

"Oh, I *will* have done something: I will have brought you home safely."

Now it was Sinthoras who laughed, saying disparagingly, "Ride away on your night-mare, I'll find another horse. I don't need your help to get—" He broke off, seeing the other älf place an arrow to his bow. "You would not dare!"

"There's more at stake here than your personal ambition, Sinthoras," Caphalor declared calmly. "Politics. Constellations and Comets, it is vital that they cooperate before this war begins. Unless we are united our military skills are as naught. That is why, Sinthoras, we will be going back *together* or not at all. That much I promise you."

Sinthoras took a tighter grip on his spear. "I'll show you I'm not so easy to kill as a fflecx or an óarco. When I've buried you I'll take your night-mare and ride to Dsôn Faïmon!" He made ready.

"And if I can prevent you from ever being the hero you want to be, without killing you?" Caphalor asked smugly.

"What do you mean?"

"If I drag your name in the mire, and have you made the lowest of the low? You will be little more than a servant."

"Impossible. How do you propose to do that? My reputation is spotless." His desire to see his rival dead was overwhelming now.

"It may be at the moment, but Raleeha's cleverness could break your neck just as that fall from your horse might have done. She's fine, by the way. Apart from the eyes, of course." Caphalor half-raised the bow, the arrow tip still pointing at the ground but in the general direction of the other älf. "I have seen the drawings she did before you put her eyes out. Drawings of our homeland."

"So?"

"Let's assume her humble devotion to you was all an act and she chose you because of your pride: she dazzled you with compliments and you showed her round all the key points in the land." He grinned broadly. "As I said, I've seen the sketches she made: details of the capital, plans of all the defenses, it's all there. A priceless resource for an invader, Sinthoras."

"Ridiculous! No one will believe it." *I underestimated him. He is as devious as I am.*

"What if I had exposed her activities and tortured a confession out of her? My daughter is an expert surgeon and knows better than anyone how best to inflict pain. The confession is already signed. Then, of course, the drawings are missing, nobody knows where they are." Caphalor waited a while for a response. "Sinthoras, you could be responsible for the downfall of Dsôn Faïmon. I don't think the Inextinguishable Ones would forgive something like that—if they ever got to hear about it."

Sinthoras' face was crisscrossed with fury lines. He wanted to thrust his spear right through the middle of Caphalor's self-satisfied expression and out through the back of his skull. "Tion take you—"

"Indeed. But let's get ourselves back home first. Agreed?"

Sinthoras clenched his jaws and hissed out a "Yes." For now he would go along with it, but as soon as he had found and destroyed the confession, Caphalor would taste his revenge.

Abruptly, Caphalor raised the bow, drew back his arm and shot.

Sinthoras attempted a defensive movement, but missed the arrow, which landed between his feet.

There was a rattle and a shrill piping sound.

When he looked down he could see a rat-like animal with a long spike on its tail neatly shot through.

"Your hearing must be letting you down. You ought to have noticed," said Caphalor, loosening the bowstring. Then he leaned down, hand outstretched to help his rival up.

Sinthoras sprang up onto the night-mare's back without touching the proffered hand.

Ishím Voróo (The Outer Lands),
4370th division of unendingness (5198th solar cycle),
late summer.

Sardaî was tireless for most of the day in spite of the armor and the two älfar on his back. *The beast was unique.* Caphalor was grateful for the gift. *The night-mare was certainly worth Morcass dying.*

Hardly stopping, they galloped over the plain until the daystar disappeared, crossing fflecx territory. They wanted to get back to Dsôn as quickly as possible, but toward evening they were forced to seek shelter for the night. By now the stallion was starting to stumble, its energy failing after all those miles of punishing speed.

"We don't want to end up with broken necks," Sinthoras had complained. "Not when we are so close to our goal."

Caphalor turned his mount's head toward a small group of trees where they would find cover. "This looks fine." He felt Sinthoras dismount and followed suit. As he got down his eyes fell on the saddle. "The bags have gone!"

"Is that so?" Sinthoras stretched and gave a knowing smile. "I never noticed. You'd have thought we'd have heard them fall. But then, you did point out my hearing was letting me down. Who knows? Normally I'd have heard and could have told you." With an innocent air he added, "I hope there wasn't anything important in them?"

Caphalor uttered a resounding curse. "My provisions, and all my spare arrow tips." This meant he would have to collect all spent ones from now on.

"We can't really go back to look, though, can we? What a shame." Sinthoras' tone was heavy with sarcasm. "I'm sure we'll find something to keep body and soul together." He gave a spiteful grin and settled down under the fragrant late-flowering branches of an indini beech. "Anyway, with your archery skills you never waste your arrows, do you?" He placed his spear on his knees and crossed his arms behind his head, leaning back.

Caphalor realized what else was missing. *Raleeha's drawings of Dsôn Faïmon!* He'd taken them along to study them and decide whether or not to keep them. No need now.

He ran his fingers over the luggage straps. They had torn and there was no sign a knife had helped the saddlebags on their way. It could be coincidence. *Coincidence? With Sinthoras?* Was it not just as likely that he'd had a good look through and had discovered the incriminating sketches? Caphalor could not prove anything and the drawings were lying somewhere on the plain. *It's a good thing the fflecx aren't the type to plan invasions. Even if those freaks find the papers, they won't know what to do with them.*

But he still felt bad about the loss, for both their aesthetic value and their political significance.

Sinthoras had been watching him investigate the straps. Caphalor noted his smug expression. "The leather's torn," he said. "Annoying."

"A nuisance," Sinthoras agreed. "I'll take first watch."

When Caphalor climbed the tree to rest in the branches he saw a blow-pipe dart sticking in the back of his knee. *I didn't feel it!* He took a closer look. The effects of the previous poison attack were fresh in his mind, but there was only a slight reddening of the flesh. *No swelling. No pain.* Caphalor found no indication of a toxic reaction.

"What is it?" asked Sinthoras.

In response he held up the dart. "A present from the fflecx. No more than a flea bite." Caphalor swung his way up through the branches, put his bow and arrow to one side and closed his eyes.

One of my lies has come true: I have lost the drawings, he told Inàste in prayer. *Grant that the other lie about becoming immune to the poison also be true.*

The night brought him dreams.

He saw Raleeha. She danced for him, lithe and seductive, truly älf-like. Suddenly the Inextinguishable Ones pushed their way in front, enormous in size, with visors lowered over their faces, shouting that he should do his duty. Then Sinthoras appeared with an evil sneer, applauding and taking Raleeha's hand to draw her toward himself, planting a long kiss on her lips. The slave girl repulsed his advances and turned to Caphalor, arms outstretched, begging for help and calling his name . . .

Caphalor shot awake, gasping. It took him several breaths to work out where he was. Sinthoras had let him sleep. The horizon was growing light. It was nearly morning. He rubbed his eyes. *I must put a stop to this. Raleeha has to leave.*

He jumped down from the tree, hoping he would leave those disturbing pictures in the branches, and landed close to Sardaî, who greeted him with a joyful snicker. He stroked the animal's neck fondly. "Are you rested? Shall we go on?"

Sinthoras came out of the shadows. "Good. I was just going to wake you."

CHAPTER XIII

No one could stop them. Except for one race that alone proved to be strong. Almost too strong, even for the best of the älfar warriors.
The numbers were small, not more than four hundred, but they were sufficient to defeat an army of four thousand in open battle.
And after the fighting they devoured their dead enemies.

Epocrypha of the Creating Spirit,
1st Book,
Chapter 2, 24–26

Ishím Voróo (The Outer Lands), älfar realm
Dsôn Faïmon, Dsôn (Star-Eye),
4370th division of unendingness (5198th solar cycle),
late summer.

It is magnificent! It is fabulous! Caphalor's and Sinthoras' return had indicated their success—the rulers had let the people know of their mission as a result, and it was better than anything Sinthoras could ever have imagined.

The streets of Dsôn were lined with crowds of jubilant älfar and black, red, and white flowers rained down from the rooftops. Incense filled the air and there was an escort of riders on fifty fire-bulls and fifty night-mares to bring them to the very center of the realm: to the Tower of Bones, into the presence of the Inextinguishable Ones.

. . . and I am going to have to share all this with Caphalor, the imposter grinning at my side, enjoying the attention as if he really did help seal the pact. His ambitious pride was not being allowed full rein.

Sinthoras rode next to Caphalor; he had been given a night-mare on crossing the border to Dsôn Faïmon. *At least I don't have to share a saddle with him anymore.* His smile was forced as he concentrated on not letting his anger show in his face. There were artists up on the balconies ready to capture this historical moment on canvas and paper. How would it look if his features were marred with lines of fury?

"Anyone would think we had conquered Tark Draan," Caphalor said, visibly moved. "See how they rejoice."

"You certainly don't have anything to be proud of," Sinthoras hissed. He hated the fact that his anger was ruining the mood. The gods were playing a cruel game with him: throwing him these highs and lows, so quickly, one after another. He was definitely due a high point very soon.

Enjoy it, he told himself. *Save the bad thoughts for when you are alone. For now: enjoy it.*

The cavalcade moved smartly on to where the Tower of the Inextinguishables rose on its hill. They climbed the winding path until the point where they had to dismount and continue on foot. The guard of honor remained behind at the foot of the steps.

At the entrance they were met by the blind servants.

It made Sinthoras think of Raleeha. He missed her in the way one might miss a loyal pet one quite liked to have around, but for the trouble she had caused him with those wretched drawings of hers he would never forgive her. *She made me vulnerable.* He glanced at Caphalor. It was that älf's fault, of course, not hers. He had seen the harmless drawings in the saddlebags and it was Caphalor who was going to use them against him, torturing a trumped-up confession out of the girl. He looked again at Caphalor, *I solemnly swear that you are not long for this life.*

Arriving in the same way as on their first audience, they entered the great hall, mounted the steps, and walked along the corridor. This time Sinthoras was not inclined to stop and admire the architecture of the Tower of Bones: he wanted the praise that was owing to him and he wanted it at once.

He dashed into the throne room to fling himself, with Caphalor, at the rulers' feet—eyes fixed on their boots and the hems of their royal robes. Through the open windows came music and the sound of their names being hailed in celebration.

"Dsôn rejoices at your return," said Nagsar Inàste. Her words ran into their ears like sweet honey, sticky with flattery, to swirl around in their heads.

"You deserve the adulation," said Nagsor Inàste, admiration and respect in his voice. "Kneel up now and relate to us what happened on your journey."

"O Most High and Inextinguishable rulers," Caphalor began, much to the horror of his rival. "The renown and success are owed wholly to my companion and fellow warrior, even if he is too modest to say so himself. It was he who made the pact with the mist-demon. His should be the privilege of narrating his triumph." He bowed deeply.

Sinthoras breathed a sigh of relief. It had looked as if Caphalor had been trying to steal the limelight, but he had cleverly not only ascribed to Sinthoras the merit, but also the full responsibility. He bowed and then a torrent of words left his lips. He admitted that Caphalor had played a minor role—thus including him in any liability—but stressed that he alone had conducted the decisive negotiations. He stayed silent on the episode of the vial. "And so we bade farewell to the mist-demon," he concluded. "If it is an urgent matter to break open the bolts of the Stone Gate, I should like to warn you, Inextinguishable ones, that the creature appeared extremely greedy. That is why I—why we did not bring him back here with us. I think he might take a fancy to our Star State. We have witnessed with our own eyes what he does with any land he settles in. It is fascinating, but only when it is not happening to one's own homeland." He bowed to the red hem of the royal robes.

"These are many adventures, indeed, that you have lived through. You will be remembered in the legends of the älfar," said Nagsar Inàste slowly. "Our loyal Caphalor, do you share your companion's opinions?"

"Completely," he replied without hesitation. "My sentiments entirely."

"I notice," said Nagsor Inàste, "that you are relatively reticent—as if this all had little to do with you."

Sinthoras went bright red. *I might have known he would cause trouble.*

"You misunderstand my silence, worshipful ruler," replied Caphalor. "The merit belongs solely to Sinthoras—"

"As you said." The ruler's interruption was sharp. "However, I cannot get over the impression that you are being over-modest. My sister and I know that you are not one to push yourself forward: you execute your tasks soberly and efficiently, but a little more assertiveness would be appropriate here, given the heroic nature of these deeds."

"Thank you, Inextinguishable One." Caphalor bowed deeply again.

"And I should prefer to see some evidence of this pact with the mist-demon," the ruler continued. "I trust you both, Caphalor and Sinthoras, but this is to be the crucial element in our campaign. Without the power of the demon we shall stand outside the groundlings' gate, unable to get inside. The dwarves will fire on us and our vassal armies at their leisure, destroying us while we stand defenseless."

"The demon will arrive when the preparations are complete," Sinthoras protested. "I've only to raise my voice and he will appear."

Nagsar Inàste made a movement and the fabric of her robe rustled. "But if something were to happen to you before we have assembled all the troops—how would we summon the demon?" She was not satisfied and her tone of voice had changed from honey to acid. "We have to have precautions in place, Sinthoras. So, tell us the words to use."

Sinthoras hoped fervently that Caphalor would control himself sufficiently and not burst out laughing when he explained the secret. "It's not a special word—it is my voice that he will answer to. My voice and an älf song."

"What?" the sibling rulers chorused in astonishment. Nagsar Inàste had even jumped down off her throne—her boots landing before Sinthoras.

"Forgive me. It was not my intention to arrange things like this." His declaration sounded insubstantial even in his own ears and it was giving his rival the perfect opportunity to attack him. Caphalor could stress that he had not been involved in any of these strange procedures and could put the blame squarely on him.

And here was Caphalor's voice already. "What Sinthoras says is true."

Sinthoras was astonished. His jaw nearly dropped open. *He is supporting me?*

"The demon was impressed with his performance, in contrast to his reaction to my own offering. He is a creature of considerable cultural refinement, or at least, one with sophisticated hearing," Caphalor continued. "We tried everything. We suggested sending word with a messenger, or a carrier pigeon, but he insisted he would only turn up if Sinthoras sings."

The siblings were silent.

Time passed slowly, far too slowly for Sinthoras' taste. *What are they going to say?* He saw his longed for Honor-Blessing going up in smoke— smoke mixed with the tattered mists of what had once been his shining reputation. His merits, his influence, his friends—everything dissolved into nothingness in his mind.

"It was a mistake," Nagsar Inàste said in open rebuke.

"A very big mistake," said her companion and brother.

"A mistake you both made," she said, speaking now with neither honey nor acid. "From now on, Caphalor, you are to protect Sinthoras' life as if it were your own," the Inextinguishable one said soberly. "I shall give you ten of my best warriors to help you. They will be answerable exclusively to you and will do whatever you command. Should you fail in this, your family, your descendants, your estate, your servants and slaves will all be exterminated. Your blood will cease to be part of eternity."

"I am your obedient servant," said Caphalor immediately.

"However, your magnificent achievements are not to be overlooked," said Nagsar Inàste. "You are hereby both chosen to share the supreme command of the operation against Tark Draan. Muster your armies and march your troops to the Stone Gate. Bring us the greatest of all triumphs: the end of the elves!" A black velvet glove slipped down into Sinthoras' field of vision, handing him a rolled parchment and a tionium medal with silver inlay: the insignia of a nostàroi, the highest office in the älfar military.

Nagsar Inàste herself has handed me this decoration. Sinthoras shook with emotion, already seeing the coming victory in his mind's eye. Speechless, he made a deep bow.

His delight was spoiled when a second velvet-gloved hand hovered toward Caphalor, likewise bearing the parchment and the ribbon-hung medal of a nostàroi. The älf was receiving the same award.

Sinthoras noted the blind servants silently approaching to escort them from the audience hall. *There was no Honor-Blessing. What in Tion's name do I have to do?* Another disappointment . . . So both of them shared supreme command but Caphalor would still enjoy higher esteem because he had been Honor-Blessed. It was a matter of pride: the troops would always prefer to follow an Honor-Blessed general into battle rather than a simple hero. Lost in thought and despair, Sinthoras took no notice of his surroundings as he left, guided by the servants.

Soon they were standing outside in the evening breeze, which wafted stray petals toward them.

Dsôn's crowds had dispersed and no one was there to receive them— except for the ten armored warriors waiting on the platform midway down the flight of steps that led from the Tower of Bones. These represented the new bodyguard.

Sinthoras was relieved to be left in peace. The tension fell from his shoulders and he was overcome with tiredness and disappointment. His eyelids were heavy as lead and he longed for his own bed.

"Ah, excellent, my men are here already." Caphalor fixed the insignia to his collar. "Congratulations, nostàroi," he said. "It seems your wishes are coming true: you are already a hero. When we march against Tark Draan you will be the greatest of all."

"And I have to share it with you." Sinthoras shrugged, staring at the crater. Anything rather than look at his rival.

"I'll hold back and leave you the limelight." Caphalor was in a splendid mood. "We ride to your home now, I presume?" He strode off down the stairway with a spring in his step.

Sinthoras watched him go. There was no way he could disobey the Inextinguishables' command and refuse protection: the bodyguard was a sensible precaution, but the idea of having Caphalor constantly hovering over him was driving him crazy. Then it occurred to him: *the noble siblings threatened to destroy Caphalor if anything happens to me. Could be arranged,* he told himself. A malicious smile tugged at the corner of his mouth. *I could play dead for long enough to have him killed.* He fastened his new decoration to his tunic and pulled his gloves firmly on. He felt much better. "No. We'll spend the night in Dsôn. We'll stay with some friends I have here, unlike you, O Honor-Blessed one. Isn't that a neat contradiction: Honor-Blessed but friendless?"

"The way I heard it, no one has any friends in Dsôn," retorted Caphalor with a grin. "Only enemies who pretend to be friends."

Sinthoras laughed. "So witty all of a sudden. Today we ought to celebrate. Tomorrow we will send orders to the vassals and start assembling the troops."

"That's right." Caphalor was inspecting the bodyguards before they all continued down the steps to where the animals were tethered.

Sinthoras swung himself up onto his night-mare's saddle and Caphalor rode at his side on Sardaî, while the bodyguard flanked them. He felt immensely powerful. His rival was correct in one regard: his dreams were coming true. *But Caphalor would not share in them.*

*Ishím Voróo (The Outer Lands), älfar realm
Dsôn Faïmon, Dsôn (Star-Eye),
4370th division of unendingness (5198th solar cycle),
late summer.*

Raleeha could not see her two owners, former and current, but she could hear the enthusiastic rejoicing in the voices around her. *What a reception!* She could certainly feel the air quivering with excitement and energy.

Robbed of her eyesight, she had found that her remaining senses had become more acute. The älfar chorused the names of the returning heroes as if they were words in a sacred prayer and a variety of strange instruments played—their tonal ranges creating the mysterious harmony produced by a huge orchestra. This communal euphoria was different from anything Raleeha had experienced at human celebrations: there was no rowdiness, no loss of control, and the character of the occasion reminded her more of a religious ceremony to honor the deities. The singing affected her deeply: she found the voices at once attractive and frightening. *These hymns reflect the magic power of the älfar.*

She stood behind Caphalor's family, who had brought her with them to Dsôn. This was a unique event and it was understood that everyone would attend. This much she had gathered from listening to Tarlesa and her mother discussing arrangements. It meant enormous prestige for the entire family: no älf would willingly forgo the honor of being there to watch a family member so heralded.

Raleeha was delighted for Sinthoras. How she would have loved to behold his face, to see the pride in his eyes, and then to draw his picture. This was denied her still, but the tincture Tarlesa had used was gradually having an effect and she was starting to allow herself to hope. She would soon be serving her real master once more, Caphalor had promised her this.

The increasing sound of the crowd's reaction told her that the heroes' cavalcade was nearly level with them.

"Look, Mother, look! Father has never appeared more of a hero than today," enthused Tarlesa. "Sardaî could not have a better rider."

"Your father has become a legend in his own right. His deeds in Ishím Voróo have been remarkable," Enoïla replied.

But he won't have carried out a single one of them, Raleeha thought. The play-acting by the two älfar women would work perfectly to give the impression that Caphalor had been constantly at Sinthoras' side.

The hoofbeats passed. The music and the shouting did not die down for quite some time, but the crowd ebbed away gradually. Raleeha was pulled away by a tug on her collar.

She followed obediently, listening to Tarlesa and Enoïla talking about what they had seen while other älfar kept interrupting to offer congratulations and to leave messages for Caphalor.

This almost made Raleeha angry. *Don't be stupid*, she told herself. *He saved your life! Why begrudge him the attention, even if it is going to the wrong älf?* She was well aware that she owed him a great deal.

Finally the strangers' voices died away and the group could move more quickly.

A door opened. Warm, fragrant air met Raleeha's face and she heard the bright tones of wind chimes. Then mother and daughter greeted another älf; the three women conversed too quietly for Raleeha to hear what they were saying.

"Sit down," Tarlesa instructed her and a stool was pushed against her knees from behind. "This is the home of a good friend of my mother's, so be silent and behave well. Don't do anything. Except breathe."

Raleeha nodded.

"And before you ask—no, you won't be sent to Sinthoras."

"Mistress!" she protested.

"I told you to keep quiet!" Tarlesa jerked the slave collar tighter. "My father has told us to take you home with us again. He has decided against giving you back." Raleeha made a noise objecting and received a blow to the head from Tarlesa for her pains.

"Will you behave?" hissed the young älf-girl angrily. "You ungrateful hussy! First I do my best to get you back your sight and then you make a fuss because things don't go as you wish! I'll put you back in the dark if you carry on like this."

Raleeha was shoved against the wall, hitting her right temple. She wanted to cry out, to say she did not care about regaining her sight if it meant she was not going to be able to see Sinthoras and his wonderful creations.

Enoïla called her daughter over.

Raleeha managed not to sob, but a few tears of anger and disappointment escaped down her cheeks. The small voice at the back of her head spoke up. One älf had blinded her and the other was breaking his word. *For them you're nothing more than a barbarian, a slave. Your talent and*

your noble origins are of no interest. Bad treatment was the price she had
to pay for spending her life with her idols. *But it is not fair.*

"My husband will release you as soon as the campaign against Tark
Draan has begun," said Enoïla, who had come nearer without her noticing. "My youngest is very excited after seeing her father so celebrated. It
makes her a little over-impulsive."

Raleeha was astounded. *Did the älfar mistress just apologize to me?*

"You are an important element in a strategy whose significance you
won't understand," said Enoïla, speaking kindly, almost maternally. "You
barbarians can't see the bigger picture."

She nodded and the älf-woman laughed.

"You see? You think you understand what I'm saying. You are a Lotor
and your family is about to become extremely influential. My husband
will be negotiating with the barbarians very soon and you will be useful.
To him, not to Sinthoras."

"Yes, mistress."

"Good. When these talks have taken place you will be freed."

She did not realize that Enoïla had left her standing there alone until
she heard her mistress talking to friends on the other side of the room.
From simple slave girl to political pawn. If she were any help to Caphalor
then Sinthoras would certainly not want her back. She was further than
ever from being with him and his paintings.

Raleeha sighed as deeply as the tight collar allowed.

*Ishím Voróo (The Outer Lands), älfar realm Dsôn
Faïmon, to the north of the Radial Arm Wëlëron,
4370th division of unendingness (5198th solar cycle),
autumn.*

Caphalor rode slowly along the line of soldiers. He felt like shouting at
them. *Useless, inferior creatures, every single one of them.*

Sinthoras approached on the other side, riding his night-mare and
accompanied by his bodyguard. His darkened visage made it clear that
he too was unimpressed by the quality of the troops that he had assembled in the harvested field.

The vassal nations who lived in the regions between the six radial arms had sworn they would lay down their lives in battle if the älfar demanded their service. This was the tribute they had to provide in return for the protection they received; every barbarian above a certain age had to be ready to serve.

And they had come: an army of 40,000 creatures including barbarians, half-óarcos, gnomes.

Sinthoras and Caphalor halted.

"Do you judge them as useless as I do?" growled Sinthoras, his right hand gripping the shaft of his spear.

Caphalor guessed Sinthoras wanted to behead the lot of them. On the spot. "Well, they would be fine with the óarcos as a buffer against enemy cavalry attack, or to clear the battlefield of injured opponents after the fighting." He studied the barbarians, whose hard features betrayed their fear and concern: they were aware that their masters were dissatisfied with them. "They would be no use at all for fighting."

Sinthoras swore and clenched his left fist. "40,000 warriors, but my ten bodyguards would knock out half of them before breakfast!" he shouted furiously. "How could this happen? *How?*"

Caphalor was not surprised that his volatile rival had lost his temper. Everything was at stake for the ambitious Sinthoras, under tremendous political pressure from friends. He needed to assemble the best army ever raised in Dsôn Faïmon, or his own high hopes would be dashed. *Let Sinthoras rave if he will. Let him rave—and make mistakes.* "The vassal leaders are waiting, I summoned them to meet with us." He pointed to a tent pitched half a mile away. "We can discuss the state of their troops."

"I've seen enough. I don't want to listen to their lies and lame excuses," Sinthoras growled. "These sorry specimens couldn't hold a sword or hit a target at fifty paces." He gestured to one of his bodyguards. "You there! Go for that barbarian."

The soldier did not move, but the designated barbarian writhed, terror in his eyes.

Caphalor grinned. Another mistake: the guard was under orders from himself, not Sinthoras. "I think we can do without shedding our young barbarian's blood. We both know he would stand no chance against an älf." He directed the night-mare toward the big tent. "Let them do some training until we get back."

Sinthoras snorted and cantered off on his night-mare, bodyguard close behind.

Caphalor beckoned to Aïsolon, to whom he had given command of the älfar cavalry. He wanted to have a true friend at his side. "Sort them according to race and make a note of their strengths and weaknesses."

Aïsolon laughed. "You'd be hard pushed to find much in the way of strengths." He glanced after Sinthoras. "You humiliated him twice, there."

"I did?"

"You did not allow the guard to carry out his order and then you dressed him down within sight and hearing of the troops." Aïsolon looked his friend in the eyes. "I warned you about him before—don't provoke him."

Caphalor realized he had been in the wrong and accepted Aïsolon's criticism. "Yes, you are right. I needled him on purpose. It won't happen again. Or rather, it won't happen so often," he added with a smile.

Aïsolon laughed and slipped off his mantle to reveal his black plate armor. "I always feared the vassal forces would not be as good as Sinthoras thought."

"What made you think that?"

"Simple: they've gone soft. They've had it far too easy." He pointed at the rotund belly of one of the barbarians. "They've never had to fight. The last couple of hundred divisions of unendingness all they've had to do is plant a few fields, breed the odd cow or horse, mend a road or two." He started to call out his orders to his lieutenants, getting them to divide the army into sections. "They have forgotten how to use weapons. Look, even the óarcos are overweight."

"Then make them sweat! They must get back in form." He spurred Sardaî on. "You would make a better nostàroi, Aïsolon."

"No I wouldn't," his friend called after him.

Caphalor raced up to the tent where he could hear Sinthoras holding forth angrily. *This will be worth watching.*

As he entered, he saw barbarians, óarcos and other creatures shuffling together in one corner of the tent, confronted by Sinthoras with a dagger in his raised hand. Black fury lines covered his face and Caphalor knew he was employing his power to instill naked terror in the leaders' hearts.

He has done that efficiently enough. Caphalor took up his position and a slave hurried up with a goblet of water and blossom essences. He sipped at the drink in a leisurely way, leaned back in his seat and waited for Sinthoras to calm down. He kept his nose over the goblet, sniffing the pleasant aroma. The air in the tent was otherwise a little too heavy with the various earthy smells of the vassal leaders. Fear was bringing them out in a sweat and it was not making the atmosphere any healthier. *Washing is a word they don't understand.*

Sinthoras came over, breathing heavily, took his seat and gulped down his drink. "Excuses! They make me sick!"

"What did they say?" Caphalor concealed his amusement.

"Ask them yourself." He got his cup refilled and emptied it in one draft. The dark lines paled. He placed his long knife slowly on the tray, blade pointing in their direction.

Caphalor got to his feet and invited the leaders back to the table. They returned in dribs and drabs. "As Sinthoras has made clear," he began, speaking in more measured tones than his co-commander, "we are not satisfied with the troops you have provided. Their equipment is not good enough and they are obviously unwilling to face combat. Even the óarcos have turned into shepherds and berry-pickers." He sharpened his voice without getting louder. He looked round at the assembled leaders and each in turn averted his gaze. "It has always been part of your obligation as vassals not to neglect military training."

"We are born warriors, sire," objected Tarrlagg, the óarco leader. He had been the first to throw off the after-effects of the terror Sinthoras had put on them. He showed his fangs and flexed his muscles to appear broader. "I've trained my troops myself. They can strangle any enemy with their bare hands. We don't need weapons."

"Is that so?" Caphalor asked dubiously.

"Indeed it is, sire," replied Tarrlagg with the bravado natural to his race.

I'll cut you down to size for your bragging. Caphalor put down his short swords and leaped onto the table. "Come strangle me, then."

Tarrlagg gave a nervous laugh. "Sire, I—"

"A quick wrestling bout will demonstrate the truth of what you say." Caphalor dropped his arms. "What are you waiting for? Do you want me to fight with my eyes closed to make it easier for you?" He decided not to touch the óarco's body.

The óarco climbed onto the table and took up a fighting stance, eyes burning with the determination to win.

Caphalor immediately saw his opening: his adversary was the same height but much heavier and he had his front leg too far forward. His own left foot shot out, heel grinding into the other's instep. A sensitive area even for a coarse creature like an óarco.

Tarrlagg winced and faltered—and already Caphalor had grabbed him by the belt, turned and gone down on one knee, bringing the óarco crashing face down onto the table. Its fangs ripped open its own muzzle as it rolled to the floor.

Caphalor followed through, swift as an arrow, springing up and landing with both feet on the armor-plated chest of his challenger, who was groaning loudly. "I have won, and all without laying a finger on your skin, Tarrlagg," he said quietly. "What do you think would have happened if I'd used a weapon?" He stepped down. "Your soldiers are no good," he told the leaders. "The Inextinguishable Ones plan to invade Tark Draan. As a strong fighting force you would have had a unique opportunity to go down in history. The weaklings of Tark Draan would have whispered your names with dread. You would have been feared even as we are feared." He sat down gracefully on his chair. "But you have missed that chance and it is your own fault." *That should shake them.* He saw that Sinthoras was watching him and waiting.

The leaders lowered their eyes. Tarrlagg had picked himself up and limped over to his seat. He was grumbling to himself, rubbing his shoulder and wiping blood off with his sleeve.

The leader of the barbarians, Vittran, stood up and asked to speak. Caphalor invited him to do so. "Masters, we are the victims of the good life. We have much to thank the älfar for and now that they ask

something of us in return, we have failed them. We have disgraced ourselves." He hung his head. "Give us 200 moments of unendingness and I
swear that my soldiers at least will meet your standards."

Sinthoras laughed condescendingly. "You and your barbarians would
need to train for 2000 moments of unendingness before you satisfied
my requirements. If our realm were attacked tomorrow by a wild enemy
horde, do you think they would wait patiently on the other side of the
defense-moat because you've sent them a message saying your men aren't
quite ready yet?"

Vittran clenched his jaws.

"Samusin is on your side," Caphalor said after a short pause. "We will
grant you sixty moments to train your warriors and turn them into a
proper fighting force." He nodded to them all. "That goes for all of you.
After that, Sinthoras and I will check what you have managed to do."

"If we're not happy, heads will roll," added Sinthoras. "And then
we'll set the worst armies against each other. The victors will be
allowed to take part in our campaign." He smiled and sent his waves
of fear into their minds. "But the losers . . . well, we'll find something
we can do with their remains." He stood up and left the tent. Caphalor
nodded to the leaders. *It has worked.* He had nothing to add to these
last promises of cruelty. He followed Sinthoras out, got up into the
saddle and the two of them rode swiftly back; they did not waste a
glance on the vassal army doing weapons training under the watchful
eye of other älfar warriors.

"That's 40,000 complete incompetents," said Sinthoras, shaking his
head. "We might as well let our archers practice on them as moving
targets." He sighed. "We are fooling ourselves if we think that, in sixty
moments of unendingness, they'll be up to storming the Stone Gateway
and taking on the armies of Tark Draan." He looked at Caphalor with
an irritated expression. "Why don't you say anything?"

Caphalor smiled. "Because I guessed this would happen."

"So you're smiling because you guessed right?"

"No." Caphalor relished the wait before making his next move.
"Because back there in the tent, I was thinking things through while
you were yelling at the leaders."

Sinthoras twisted his upper body round and slowed his night-mare down. "I'm listening."

"Barbarians."

"They're not the slightest bit better than—"

"Not our vassals. I'm talking about the barbarians north of Dsôn Faïmon. The Ishmantis—Lotor. Their warriors have been fighting battle after battle, they have plenty of experience, know how to follow orders and know how to defeat their enemies. Just the sort of veterans we could do with."

"You want to win them over as allies?" Sinthoras frowned. He thought about it. "Not a bad idea. We'll set them against the groundlings and won't have to worry that they'll come knocking at our borders in the future. Not that I'm afraid of any barbarians, but they can get to be a nuisance if they've got a bee in their bonnets."

Caphalor nodded his agreement. "And, thanks to your generosity, I have a slave in my possession who is sister to their leader," he added, laughing on the inside when he saw how annoyed Sinthoras was. "We could offer Farron his sister back."

"Raleeha won't like that idea."

"She is a slave, it's not up to her." Caphalor was not seriously considering giving the barbarian girl back again, but he wanted it to sound as if he meant it. Appearances had to be kept up.

When he had returned to Dsôn as a hero, it was seeing her again that gave him most pleasure. His reaction had taken him unawares and it was not proper, but in that black lace dress and matching eye mask she had looked like a true älf. No, he must not desire her! *And certainly not now that I am a nostàroi. I would lose everything.*

He was surprised to see Sinthoras indicating approval. "An excellent thought. I think it could work."

"We'll let her brother speak to her. He'll be glad to and it will be up to him to persuade her to leave our people. Nobody here will shed a tear over her departure." Caphalor wondered if he had overdone it a little with these last words but Sinthoras was looking at him with an enthusiastic expression.

"Why should it only be the barbarians we use?" he blurted out.

"What do you mean?" asked Caphalor.

"Ishím Voróo is full of scum that know how to fight. If we collect them all up under our banner and herd them off to Tark Draan, we'll be left in peace and they'll exterminate the elves for us in the blink of an eye. We should start sending out messengers in the morning." Sinthoras laughed out loud. "By Tion! I think you have got a brilliant idea there."

Caphalor gave him a wary look. *More praise? What's he got up his sleeve?*

Sinthoras read his expression. "Aha! My words render you speechless?" he asked, amused.

"Indeed they do," admitted Caphalor.

"It was the same for me when you spoke up in support of me in the audience with Nagsor and Nagsar Inàste. It would have been so easy for you to drop me in it." Sinthoras looked him straight in the eye for the first time without a trace of malice or mistrust. "Maybe it is time for us to bury our differences, now that we share a common purpose? If either of us fails, everything is lost: the campaign, our existence, and perhaps the whole future of our homeland."

Caphalor found it hard to believe that this was the same Sinthoras who had driven him white-hot with fury on their mission. The external appearance was identical but his personality had changed. *Or is this a passing whim? Or perhaps a trick to lull me into a false sense of security before delivering a fatal blow?*

"I agree," he said, deciding to put Sinthoras to the test. "I can remove a burden from your soul: there is no confession signed by Raleeha incriminating you. I never tortured her."

"I knew that," came the ready response from the blond-haired älf.

"How so?"

Sinthoras gave a twisted grin. "You are far too soft, Caphalor. I never believed you in the first place."

He had to laugh in spite of himself. "You're wrong about my being soft, but I see I must be far too transparent."

"Then I'll tell you something, too." Sinthoras pulled his spear upright and placed the blunt end on his stirrup. "I'm going to ditch my idea to play dead for a while, so your life won't be forfeit." He winked. "It was all planned."

Caphalor's blood ran hot and cold. "You were going to fake your own death, so that the Inextinguishables would—"

"Exactly so, nostàroi," Sinthoras interrupted him, laughing. "I can see you weren't expecting that. Stupid of me: from now on you'll trust me less than ever." He still sounded as if he were joking around—as if they had suddenly become good friends.

"There can't be two älfar more different than us," Caphalor summed up. The other älf's confession about the plot had shaken him to the core and he was reminded of Aïsolon's warning. *I really have been underestimating Sinthoras.*

"That is why we will be the ones to conquer Tark Draan." Sinthoras slowed his night-mare to a trot. "If an opportunity presents itself, I should like to get to know your wife."

"I'm sure it can be arranged." Caphalor rode up next to him. "When can I meet your companion?"

Sinthoras shrugged. "I don't have a mistress."

"Perhaps a male partner, then?"

"No. I prefer älf-women."

Caphalor sensed he had touched a raw nerve. *All the better.* "It is unusual for an ambitious älf such as yourself to have no family. The älf-women must be round you in droves."

"I don't have time to go looking for a bride, or to think about children. Especially not now when we are preparing for the biggest war to be waged for hundreds of divisions of unendingness." Sinthoras pretended to be indifferent.

But Caphalor picked up the strain in his voice. "What stopped you before?"

"I have things I want to do in life."

"And you think I haven't?" countered Caphalor, seeing another chance to defeat Sinthoras on the field of personal vanity. *No one else is listening. It would only be a victory for me.* "We are about the same age."

Sinthoras had lost his good humor. "You have more children than I do, yes. Do you have more friends than I do? More influence? More possessions?" he countered disdainfully. "No, you don't," he said, answering his own question. "We live forever, Caphalor. There is always time to have children, but the foundations of my power must first be made secure. I can't see myself living in the isolation of one of the radial arms like you, running a farm with slaves. My place is in the eye of the Star State. Not just for now, but for the rest of my life."

"I understand." Caphalor was surprised by this honesty.

Sinthoras cleared his throat. "But there are still times when I envy you," he said softly, as if speaking to himself. Then he came to, and galloped off as if taking flight.

Caphalor rode up to join him, but said nothing. He was deep in thought as the breeze played on his face. Sinthoras had changed and was employing a completely new strategy: he was trying to forge a friendship out of their initial mutual dislike. *He has shown himself to have a vulnerable side.*

I shan't follow him yet along this dangerous path. Sinthoras was unscrupulous and obsessed with power, it could only be icy calculation behind this change. At least that is what Aïsolon would say.

Aïsolon would also tell him to get Raleeha out of his home for good and not hang on to her as a hostage.

Her brother will persuade her to go home. I can't send her away.

Ishím Voróo (The Outer Lands), älfar realm
Dsôn Faïmon, Dsôn (Star-Eye),
4370th division of unendingness (5198th solar cycle),
autumn.

Sinthoras—flanked by his ten-man guard—swept into Demenion's house where the Comets and their followers were meeting. He could already hear snatches of their discussion. He drew himself upright, his attitude one of confident superiority.

The servants opened the doors and gasps of respectful admiration met him.

Just how it should be. Sinthoras was aware he looked magnificent in his ceremonial armor and sheer silver cloak. The nostàroi insignia shone on his right breast, reflecting the light. He had combed his hair back and dressed it in multiple braids, applying a modest amount of tinted cosmetics to enhance his dark eyes. Combined with the dark color on his cheeks, it made his face appear narrower, resembling a skull. His gloved hands were adorned with costly rings set with blood-rubies and diamonds. The fact that he was accompanied by a heavily armed body-guard served to emphasize his importance.

Sinthoras waited on the threshold until the last of the room's occupants had turned in his direction, then he raised both arms in a triumphant gesture.

The applause was loud yet refined and restrained.

Admire me! Behold, I make our group's aspirations come true. The evening's reception was being held in his honor and Demenion now came through the rows of guests to welcome him. They clasped hands and the host even bowed his head. This publicly showed who held the higher rank.

Sinthoras knew there were always two wars to wage: one at the front and the other at home. An excellent grasp of tactics was needed for both. On the home front it was about politics, the prize being social advancement and influence among the great and the good. This was the battle he was fighting now.

Luckily, his rival preferred to eschew such events and had retired to his estate with his companion. Sinthoras estimated that Caphalor did not have more than a dozen supporters in the top ranks of älfar society, but this was counterbalanced by his enormous success with the simple folk: his modest demeanor made him a favorite. Once more, the contrast between them was obvious.

Sinthoras reveled in the attention. He noticed several älf-women smiling at him, hoping to appeal. Yantarai was there, too. He had received her at his house on frequent occasions. This prompted the thought that he must find somewhere suitable to move to. *I shall start looking for a residence in Star-Eye in the morning.* Living out in one of the radial arms would be beneath his dignity. That was more Caphalor's thing.

Demenion held up an arm to quieten the guests. "Thank you, dear friends. You have shown Sinthoras an appropriate welcome," he said with a broad smile; having such an important guest of honor in his house reflected well on his own status. "He will crush the elves under his heels, exterminating our enemy and their allies, once and for all."

There was more applause, which Sinthoras acknowledged with a gentle incline of the head. He was without doubt the most popular älf in the whole of Dsôn.

"The nostàroi honors us with his presence. He has come to get to know some new friends who want to support his work," said Demenion. "There will come a time after the victory over Tark Draan we should all prepare for: it will be a time when the powerful in Dsôn Faïmon will be those who share our views." He bowed to Sinthoras. "I share your views, Nostàroi."

More than two-thirds of the guests followed suit, while the others stood and raised their glasses to the warrior.

Good. Not too many new faces. Sinthoras set himself to remember them. There was sure to be a register of newcomers' names for him somewhere. Yantarai would be on the list. So far, when the two of them had met, politics had been far from their minds.

But there was another älf-woman who caught his eye.

She was in the fourth row and had raised her glass in a half-hearted manner as she studied him with something approaching hostility. On her slender body she wore black tionium armor that was obviously designed to attract attention, in particular because of what remained uncovered.

The metal followed the form of the älfar skeleton and exposed much of the wearer's skin. Bloodred inlays copied the lines of arteries and veins and even appeared to pulsate. She had dusted herself with powdered silver and her dress was a flowing transparent robe. Her long, dark brown hair was braided in a wreath around her head. *Extraordinary.*

At that moment the guests all got to their feet again and she disappeared in a sea of faces, towering hairstyles, and extravagant hats.

Sinthoras recalled how he and Caphalor had spoken of family. It suddenly struck him that he might meet his death in the war against Tark Draan. *Who will benefit from what I have amassed?*

He swept his gaze over the assembled älfar. For now he was still part of the unendingness and he would have to take advantage of this fact, but he must leave an heir. *Soon.*

The evening would mark the start of his search for a suitable partner to bear his children. Sinthoras had extremely high standards.

Chapter XIV

The Inextinguishable Ones realized that this strong and mighty folk, whose remains they coveted for their Tower of Bones, could only be overcome by trickery.
So they offered them a peace treaty and served delicious wine for the celebrations.
But the wine had been laced with an undetectable toxin supplied by the fflecx. The älfar themselves were immune to the poison.
And so those warriors, invulnerable in battle, died writhing on the floor in agony.

Epocrypha of the Creating Spirit,
1st Book,
Chapter 2, 27–32

Ishím Voróo (The Outer Lands), älfar realm
Dsôn Faïmon, Radial Arm Wèlèron,
4370th division of unendingness (5198th solar cycle),
autumn.

Caphalor, riding on Sardaî, looked over the cleared strip of land between the defense moat and the dense woods of Ishím Voróo with mixed feelings.

He and Sinthoras had had a tent city erected to accommodate the delegates of the various races, creatures, and tribes. He wrinkled his nose in distaste as the wind brought smells and noises reminiscent of a cattle market. Älfar soldiers on fire-bulls patrolled the camp, putting down quarrels—it was not only friends who were assembling there: the half-trolls and óarcos hated each other, while the barbarians would seize any trivial reason to attack anything nonhuman.

It will be difficult to form a united and efficient army out of these hodge-podge combatants. But he might be worrying unnecessarily—perhaps none of them would agree to join them at all and they would have to see how far they got with their own vassal armies. *That would be the worst outcome. We won't get far with only 40,000.*

"Let the bridge down," he commanded the watch. The drawbridge rattled down to form a link across the deep river, while the other section connecting the island to Dsôn Faïmon was hoisted up into the air.

A unit of fire-bull cavalry trotted over to Caphalor to serve as his escort as he rode over the drawbridge. "To the óarcos," he instructed them.

The leader nodded. They brought him to a tent shrouded in black smoke.

The óarcos' evening meal was bubbling away in large copper cauldrons suspended over campfires. It stank of old meat, rancid fat, and burned ingredients that nobody in Dsôn Faïmon would think of touching. Óarcos were stirring the pots, shouting and shoving each other.

They're really going to eat that stuff. Caphalor kept telling himself he wanted to persuade the monsters to join their campaign, but the word *scum* kept going round in his head.

The óarco guards saw the älfar group approaching and yelled for their comrades. Seven of them with their shields and pikes formed a ludicrous óarco barricade the fire-bulls could have easily swept aside.

They still have not got the message that we are not going to harm them. Caphalor ordered the unit to halt and contemplated the monsters with raised eyebrows, saying nothing, waiting patiently until their small brains had come to terms with their own foolish reaction: a useful humiliation tool.

The óarcos looked at each other sheepishly. With a loud roar the filthy canvas door-flap of the main tent was flung aside.

Out stormed a wildly gesticulating óarco in crude metal armor, a splendid specimen found only in the deepest, darkest ravines of Ishím Voróo. Its energy and fury were obvious, even if its intelligence was decidedly underdeveloped.

Why should an óarco bother to think if he is as muscular and broad as a half-troll? Caphalor was pleased with what he saw. *Our vassal armies could model themselves on this one.* This was exactly what an óarco should look like. With an iron morningstar and a broadsword hanging at his belt he would win any argument.

The right-hand side of his face had been painted blue and the left eye section was white, which made a strange contrast to the rest of his green-ish black skin. The tusks were dyed bright blue and garish yellow and his long, dark hair had been gathered in a braid.

He ran to the wall of óarcos before the tent and, pulling two logs out of the woodpile, bashed the over-enthusiastic defenders on the head with them. He cursed and chased them off, hurling bits of wood after them. After that he turned to Caphalor. "Forgive the idiot heads," he said. "They were just doing what they've been taught to. They've forgotten where they are." He nodded. "I am Toboribar."

Well, well. Brighter than I thought. Caphalor was amazed to hear the óarco speak the Dark Language fluently. "I am Nostàroi Caphalor. I've come to see if we should permit your units to join our campaign against Tark Draan."

Toboribar tilted his head to one side with a knowing grin. "Let's talk." He turned tail and headed for the main tent.

Caphalor dismounted and followed, going through what he knew about Toboribar in his mind. The älfar spy reports said that this leader of the Kraggash óarcos had challenged and killed both his elder broth-ers, and had executed 400 óarcos to secure his claim. His 20,000 war-riors had a reputation for utter brutality; it was said they had been hard to control—until Toboribar took over. The Kraggash liked to live in warm, airless caves. This made them ideally suited to fighting the groundlings.

Toboribar sat down on a solidly constructed chair. "Let's cut to the chase, Caphalor," he said, still with a grin that did nothing to make him look either pretty or kind. Any timid creature would have interpreted the smile as an aggressive baring of teeth. "You want to conquer Tark Draan, but your home-grown óarcos are a tame lot who couldn't lift a sword, let alone use one. Am I right?"

Caphalor stopped short—and had to laugh. Toboribar's grin widened. *He could take a gnome's head off with one bite.* His disarmingly entertaining and open manner made up for his lack of respect.

"Well, maybe not a sword like yours, but they can handle their own."

"Then they'll be lighter than the corn stalks they pluck for you, I'll wager." Toboribar placed his muscular forearms, twice the size of the älf's, on the table. "You have a way to break open the maggots' gateway?"

"We have."

"Good. But those dwarves are stubborn fighters, you won't find it easy in their tunnels. We, on the other hand, are used to cave warfare." Toboribar smacked his lips as if savoring a delicate morsel. "What do the Inextinguishables have to offer me if we join you?"

Caphalor's plan to present participation in the coming war as a privilege swiftly went out of the window. "Nagsor and Nagsar Inàste will grant you the right to conquer and keep any land in the south of Tark Draan. For that you will render a tithe, each division of unendingness, in coin or in kind, as we find acceptable. The area you control in the south must not exceed fifty by fifty miles and must not comprise former elf territory. Apart from that proviso you will be free to do as you wish."

"Hmm." Toboribar folded his arms theatrically to show displeasure. "And what's the south of Tark Draan like?"

Caphalor rolled his eyes. "How am I supposed to know?"

"What if the south fails to *conform to our aspirational standards*?" he said, mocking the älf's speech. "What if we . . . prefer the north?"

"You have been allocated the south," Caphalor said firmly. "I realize you are taking a certain risk here, but I think you will agree it is a good swathe of land."

"No," said the óarco, with a decisive smack of the lips.

"No?" Caphalor suddenly sympathized with Sinthoras for losing his temper in negotiations—you had to take a lot of insubordination from inferior beings an älf would normally have cut in half.

Toboribar leaned forward and tapped on the table with his forefinger. "No tithes, no telling me how much new territory I can hold, and we get unrestricted access to the northern pass as soon as we've conquered it." He stared grimly at the älf before breaking into another sudden grin. "Those are my terms. Take them . . . or leave them and march off without me and my Kraggash."

That's not the way it goes, beast. Caphalor signaled the talks were ended and stood up to leave the tent. He expected the óarco to explode.

But there was silence. Toboribar let him go because he knew full well Caphalor would have to come back. The talks had been interrupted, but they were not over.

Caphalor was upset with himself for underestimating the óarco. He would have to suppress his own arrogance toward the other races if he did not want all of the talks to end like this. *I pray to Samusin that you all die in battle in an otherwise splendid älfar victory.*

He hurried off through the swathes of cooking fumes, back to his night-mare and his escort, where he found a messenger waiting.

"Nostàroi. A delegation of barbarians has arrived and wishes to speak to you."

"Tell them I will see them tomorrow, they will be first on my list."

"Nostàroi, they say they need to see you at once or they will leave."

Caphalor realized that negotiating was not really his thing. This was politics. *Diplomacy: lies, games, everything all at once.* He was still convinced this war was a huge mistake, or at the very least, premature. Sending all the scum off permanently to Tark Draan was a comforting thought, but there were still so many imponderable factors about this campaign. *Why isn't Sinthoras here? He's much better at politics than I am, in spite of his fiery temperament.* They had agreed they would always appear together, but Sinthoras was unreliable in this respect.

Angrily he turned Sardaî and thundered off, leaving the fire-bulls struggling to keep up.

First the óarco, now the barbarians! They were getting him to dance to their tune instead of the other way around. They were dictating to him, the nostàroi, the Inextinguishables' representative! His fury grew and black lines flared across his face. *I'll show them their place!*

Caphalor raced into the barbarian camp and swept into the tent where their leaders were assembled. The night-mare crashed into the heavy table, overturning it so that the humans had to spring back out of the way, hands on weapon hilts.

"You dare to summon me?" he shouted down at them from the saddle. "It's you who are summoned here. You are privileged to take part in this campaign. Who do you think you are?" He leaped down and dismissed Sardaî. The stallion went outside. "Speak!"

The barbarians righted the table and gathered on the other side of it. They all wore different types of metal-plated leather armor. Their boots were simply made. Their crude gold trinkets were supposed to make them look dignified, but any älfar child could have produced better. Two of the men were even wearing crowns that looked as if they had been made by someone with a squint: the coronets were lopsided and the inlay work shoddy. *How can they bear to put them on?*

"I am Armon of the Herumites," said one of them, who had a black beard. There was so much hair on his head and face that he could hardly see out of his eyes. "You should know, älf, that we shall not be joining you if the Kraggash are part of your force. They have caused too much harm to our tribe."

Caphalor's breath was coming hard and fast and his heart rate was speeding up. "You and the Herumites and who else?"

All of them put up their hands.

Stay calm, he told himself. Tempt them. "That means that the barbarian tribes of Ishím Voróo are not willing to put past quarrels behind them in exchange for a huge increase in territory, resources, and slaves?"

"Quarrels?" Armon was outraged. "Infamy take you, älf, if you call it a quarrel when women and children are slaughtered and settlements burned to the ground!"

A second barbarian with hair as red as the setting daystar pushed his way to the front, his face was dark with anger. "I waded through the blood of my wife, my children, my nearest relatives!"

Not surprising there was so much blood. Caphalor recalled how barbarians were constantly at it like rabbits. Given enough women, the barbarians could quickly have made up the loss, but the älf chose not to say so.

"I swore vengeance," said the redhead, his voice breaking. "And you, älf, are negotiating with the perpetrators of these atrocities. They come forth at night on the rampage and run back to the caves after their murderous forays." He gestured to the entrance. "My oath demands that I draw my sword and kill Toboribar on the spot, to get justice for those he has slain."

"He is under the protection of the Inextinguishables for as long as he is on this strip of land. Just as you are. Do not attempt to harm him or you will forfeit your life. This was explained when we called you here," Caphalor warned him. He would never have thought that barbarians would be so sensitive.

"We have 30,000 armed troops under us," Armon stressed. "The Inextinguishables can offer us whatever they like, we will not accept if those cannibals are part of the alliance. We are united in this." He glared at Caphalor in challenge.

I must weigh the pros and cons. 30,000 barbarians instead of 20,000 óarcos. The óarcos were stronger in the field, but the barbarians would be easier to control, and he could pay them less. Fewer of them would survive, so it would be easier to get rid of them after the battle.

"So, you are united, are you?" he whispered menacingly. He had had enough! *What he would really like to do with them . . .*

There was a rustle behind him at the entrance and a barbarian half a head taller than himself stepped through. He *knew* this one!

The assembled men nodded to him respectfully, but their expressions altered.

Caphalor felt the mood change. *They were afraid of the new arrival!*

This tall black-haired barbarian wore heavy, plated cavalry armor; at his belt hung a curved sword with fabric bands wound round the grip.

Hair and beard were trimmed and the gaze of his green eyes swept the room haughtily.

"Forgive my late arrival. My horse went lame." He sketched a bow in Caphalor's direction.

"And you are?"

"Farron Lotor of the Ishmantis." As the newcomer introduced himself, he laid his right hand on the hilt of his sword and Caphalor wondered if he were seriously going to attempt to attack him. "How far have you got with the talks?"

Raleeha's brother! Now he understood the other princes' reactions. This is the one who had been defeating one tribe after another. "I am Caphalor, nostàroi to the Inextinguishables. Your friends here object to the Kraggash and they refuse to join our army, the like of which will never have been seen before." He gestured in Lotor's direction. "I know you. You are the one my arrows saved from death."

"Yes, I remember it very well," Farron answered. "You had a slave at your side."

"Your sister," Caphalor admitted unwillingly. Now Lotor would state that he would only join if she were released. *It is better like that. She must not stay.*

"Our two peoples have never been enemies," said Farron. "And you, Caphalor, saved me from a cowardly assassination attempt."

It did not escape the älf's attention that Armon's right eye twitched nervously at this point and that sweat was beading on his forehead. *A traitor?*

"I will commit my support to the Inextinguishables without hesitation," Farron announced, facing the tribal leaders. "It is only right that I should put my 40,000 warriors at their disposal. Without the actions of an älf I would be dead and my kingdom lost."

Luck is on my side. My thanks to destiny and to you, Samusin. Caphalor laughed with relief. "This is loyalty indeed, Prince Lotor."

"May I speak to my sister, Nostàroi? Our last exchange was too short for me to learn how she really fares."

His reason told him to agree immediately, but he still heard himself say, "I will consider it. Do not forget, Prince Lotor, that she is my slave as well as your sister. Her life is in my hands." This he stressed, so that his words could be taken as a threat. The barbarian set great store by her. He argued with his reason, insisting that to let Raleeha go now would be foolish. *A further advantage.* Caphalor allowed himself a victorious smile of relief. *For once a good deed has paid dividends.*

"The Jomonicans are also willing to join the Inextinguishables," said one of the barbarians out of the blue.

And now they want to change sides and promise me their backing, all because Farron Lotor had pledged his support. What had been defeat now meant a boost in his forces of thousands of men. And all without any help from Sinthoras. Armon was glaring at Farron, sweating hard.

"What about you?" Lotor turned to him. "Where does your future lie?"

"Are you so audacious as to want to spread your power in the land of Tark Draan before you have achieved dominion here?" Armon hissed. "The Lotors are filth! It would not bother you to march next to the óarcos—seeing as how your ancestors mated with them in the gutter, giving birth to ugly bastards like yourself!"

Farron's features were icy. He pulled himself up to his full height.

Armon, however, had not reached the end of his tirade. "Take a look at him! Are you all blind? It's óarco blood that makes the Lotors so tall. They're all huge and thirsty for power, just like the óarcos." He turned back to Farron. "They say your tribe sucks the brains out of your enemies and uses the skulls as drinking vessels, and I have believed it ever since seeing the state of a battlefield your soldiers left behind them. There was not a single corpse that still had its head!"

Caphalor was now the intrigued witness to a full-blown row that must have been simmering for some time. One outrageous allegation followed another and he was certainly not going to get involved. The thought that Raleeha might have even the tiniest fraction of óarco blood in her turned his stomach. *It can't be true! Not her! She looks so very like an älf!*

"Is that why you sent your assassins after me?" Farron spoke coldly. "Because you are afraid of me?"

Armon spat in disgust. "Ride with the óarcos and the älfar and the rest of the rabble they're dragging up. The Herumites will—"

Quick as the wind Farron drew his sword and hurled it, striking Armon full in the chest.

The heavy blade pierced the armor and transfixed the barbarian load er's body; blood gushed from Armon's mouth. For a few blinks of an eye he remained upright, holding out his arms for help, but the others stepped back in horror. He finally collapsed at Farron's feet.

"The Herumites," said Farron, continuing the dying man's words, "will be choosing me as their new prince because they are afraid of Toboribar."

That's a turn up for the books. Caphalor could not suppress a smile: things were going his way, but he must still go through the motions of diplomacy. "You have killed a barbarian who was under the protection of the Inextinguishable Ones. The promise of peace here in this cleared zone covers everyone." He called for his escort. Then he continued. "Armon's body will be taken secretly to the forest. A patrol will find him crushed under a fallen tree." He let his gaze pass from one leader to the next. "Anyone mentioning what has happened here will die."

Farron inclined his head, the other leaders followed suit.

Caphalor turned round and gave the guards instructions to dispose of the dead body. "Then I bid you welcome to the alliance against Tark Draan," he announced to the assembly in formal tones. "When the campaign starts you will be under the command of Nostàroi Sinthoras and myself. In return for your support you may take as much land and booty as you wish in northwest Tark Draan." He ran through the terms and conditions the barbarians had to agree to. "I'll have the treaties drawn up and brought to you for signature." He took his leave.

Samusin, my thanks! Caphalor was overjoyed. *What triumph! I have won the barbarians over for the cause of Nagsor and Nagsar Inàste! And I've done it on my own!* Sinthoras would not be able to cap that.

He mounted Sardaî and rode to the bridge with his reduced escort heading back to Dsôn. No other delegates had turned up, which meant he did not have to hold any more talks for the time being. *I will leave Toboribar to stew in his own juice until he finds out that the barbarians have joined in their thousands.* The Kraggash were unlikely to sit quietly in their tents after hearing that.

It occurred to him he could spread rumors of untold riches to be had in Tark Draan. *Then they'll all be greedy enough to volunteer.* Sinthoras could get some of his spies on to that.

His thoughts wandered to Raleeha while he waited for the draw-bridge to be lowered. *Óarco blood. Unthinkable. Not with a face like hers.* Admittedly, her brother had an ugly face, but so did all the barbarians. Apart from her.

As he guided his night-mare onto the bridge, he heard the sound of hooves on the left. A beaming Sinthoras and bodyguard were riding toward him, coming from the direction of Toboribar's camp.

Caphalor did not want to ask. It was too obvious that Sinthoras had persuaded the leader of the Kraggash to join them. Without him.

Ishím Voróo (The Outer Lands), älfar realm
Dsôn Faïmon, Dsôn (Star-Eye),
4370th division of unendingness (5198th solar cycle),
winter.

"They are mustering forces." Nagsar Inàste joined her brother on the broad upholstered couch in the simply furnished reading room. She stroked his black hair as he perused a thick book. Nagsar had selected a slim-fitting dark green dress with an embroidered silver pattern against a black border on hem, collar, and sleeves. "We did choose the very best for the task; Sinthoras and Caphalor are doing wonders."

"They are indeed," replied Nagsor, without looking up. The almanacs and reference books he had asked for were piled on the floor at his side. He was wearing a dark red robe and he had left his hair to lie loose on his shoulders.

She pressed close to him and he inhaled the scent of the fragrance she wore: a hint of peach, mint, and heavy notes of blossom. "They have per-suaded Toboribar and the barbarian tribes to join us." Her lips brushed his forehead. "A good move."

Nagsor Inàste smiled into the pages of the book. "Yes."

She felt belittled. "You would rather devote time to written words than to me?" She reached out quickly, snatching the cover, about to fling his reading matter into the corner.

But Nagsor was quicker. Holding her fast, he embraced her with his other arm and jerked her toward his body only to release the pressure the next moment and plant kisses on her mouth. Slowly he drew away. "Surely you cannot be jealous of a book?" he said reproachfully.

"I don't like it if you pay attention to other things when I am in the room," she said coolly, evading his grip. "I'm talking about our future successes and you won't even listen properly."

"I am also working on what is to come." He snapped the book shut. "You won't like it."

"Old writings. Older than we are?"

"They are from another time, but they tell of something that still exists today, as we do," Nagsor replied.

Detecting concern in his voice, she abandoned her play-acted struggle for supremacy. "What is in the book?"

"Sagas." He put the volume down on his knees and leaned back, glancing up at the myriad colored lanterns that hung above their heads. "One of the stories mentions the mist-demon Sinthoras and Caphalor have won to our cause. Some call it Demon, some Spirit, others call it Affliction, Plague, The Breath of Destruction, Wind of Eternal Pestilence." He sought her eyes. "Our friend answers to many names."

The flawless forehead of the älf-woman contracted into a frown. "But we knew that before we sent for him. That was the reason we needed him in the first place, because our magic is not sufficient against the groundlings' defenses."

He nodded, but still had a worried air. "We need him for his magic, but have we considered the possible negative consequences?"

"He'll disappear into Tark Draan," she countered. "Why should we bother worrying about him?"

Nagsor lifted his arm, stretching it out toward the lamps as he admired his fingers. "I have received news from the region where the demon lives. There's been a change."

"What do you mean *a change*?"

"Do you remember how you first heard of the mysterious being, fifty divisions of unendingness ago? We've been watching him ever since."

"The closer he got to Dsôn Faïmon, the more watchful we became," she replied thoughtfully. "He never showed any real aggression but, on the contrary, was quite reserved, as if he were ashamed of himself and of what he had done to the land around it."

"Exactly, and it was I who decided to woo the creature, because I couldn't find any way to destroy this difficult neighbor." Nagsor stroked his sister's shoulder. "He has . . . an ability."

"Yes—an ability to give immortality to mortals," she said. Her voice grew angrier. "The only ones who should be entitled to the privilege are ourselves, the älfar."

Nagsor used his magic to douse the lamps a little. "Apart from that, this demon has been increasing his sphere of influence. Up till now he had been drifting around randomly, settling wherever he was permitted to rest for a while, but now he has a taste for subjugating mile after mile of others' territory."

Nagsar waited tensely. She noted the deep concern that had etched its lines on his beautiful visage: something she had not seen for many moments of unendingness. "You are *really* worried."

"I need to be." Nagsor's tired voice was hard to hear. "If this being were to raise an army of its undead, it is not just Dsôn Faïmon but the whole of Ishím Voróo that will be plunged into distress."

"Then let's tell Sinthoras and Caphalor to speed up their preparations. The mist-demon must not start thinking about extending its territory over here."

He sat up straight. "You are right. We must not lose sight of the real reason for the campaign. We have already achieved a great deal. The nostàroi must work harder and exert pressure on other races if necessary." He kissed his sister-partner, cupping her face in his hands. They remained in that posture for some time.

The perfect couple. "I will arrange it all," she said, getting up from the couch. "Keep on reading. Maybe the books will reveal the creature's weak point." Nagsar caressed his chest and then hurried out.

Nagsor also got to his feet now, stepping carelessly on priceless ancient volumes as he paced up and down. He turned the lights lower still. He thought better in the dark.

He had still not found any clue as to what had occasioned the change in the mist-demon's conduct. Could it have been the talks that it had held with Caphalor and Sinthoras? Could they have awoken an appetite that might now fix itself on the wrong object? Whatever the reason, it was clear the mist-demon should leave Ishím Voróo as soon as possible.

"By the infamous ones and their sons!" cursed Nagsor, kicking one of the books, which flew into the darkness to crash against the far wall of bone-tile paneling.

He got himself under control again, returned to the couch and turned the lamps up. He picked up the nearest almanac of magic arts and continued researching the mist-demon.

There must be something, he thought, thumbing the pages. Until he found a magic remedy, his resources must be Sinthoras, Caphalor, and Tark Draan.

*Ishím Voróo (The Outer Lands), älfar realm
Dsôn Faïmon, Radial Arm Wèlèron,
4370th division of unendingness (5198th solar cycle),
winter.*

Raleeha was sitting at a table in an unfamiliar room. The fresh breeze from the open window brought the scent of water. Caphalor had ordered her to be brought here, to one of the island towers, without indicating what she might expect. She was wearing her dark gray dress. The choke collar with the buckles was fastened as loose as possible.

Is it time? She was secretly hoping she was about to be handed over to Sinthoras, but she only believed this with a tiny part of her mind. *Why should it be done so mysteriously?* The eye that had been treated had been slowly growing, the tissue repairing, and it had improved to the extent that she could distinguish between light and dark; she could see the window as a luminous square. Tarlesa had told her it would take a long time before her vision was restored, but Raleeha was already pleased with the progress.

She noticed the smell of smoke: something was being roasted over an open fire and had been left too near the flames to taste good. *This was not how älfar liked their meat prepared.* They preferred it cooked slowly, stewed or braised, served with subtle sauces. Grilling over an open fire was held to be a barbaric custom. The älfar would only prepare food that way in an emergency or while on a long journey. From what her nose was telling her, she concluded that foreigners must have set up camp by the border.

She heard the drawbridge creak down toward the cleared strip of land, then horses coming over the wooden planks and approaching the tower. After a while she caught the sound of a few words in älfish and then there was a knock at the door.

She said nothing and waited. As a slave it was not her place to give anyone permission to enter the room.

Another knock.

She heard an älfar voice and then in response a man's low tones that she immediately recognized. The door swung open. "Raleeha! Why don't you answer?"

"Farron?" She got to her feet, her legs shaking with excitement. "Brother!" She took two paces to the side past the table and then felt his strong arms round her. Drops of water pearled onto her face. Her big, strong brother was weeping with joy.

She started to sob as she returned his embrace. His touch awakened powerful emotions in her. Even if she had not regretted leaving her previous life, there were certain people she missed and she had been missing him in particular.

They held each other for some time and then he released her and led her to a chair. He sat down opposite and took her hands in his. "I so wanted to see you again. When we met in Ishím Voróo it was so short," he said, happy and concerned at the same time. "How are you?" he asked, placing one hand on her cheek and then trailing his fingers over the blindfold.

"I am well," she answered with a smile. "I am being given treatment and my sight should soon be restored."

"Didn't I tell you your beauty would one day seal your fate?"

"But I went to the älfar of my own accord, Farron. You know why."

"Yes — my sister, the artist nobody understands," he said, half mocking and half admiring. "But they would never have taken you if you had not been so extraordinarily pretty," he insisted stubbornly. "How much longer do you intend to put up with this?"

"As long as they ask it of me and as long as it pleases me." The joy at having her brother close to her again was fading. *I should have known he would start in with implicit reproaches*, and he would undoubtedly expect her to go with him. "I like it here."

"I don't believe you!"

"You should believe it, brother." She tried to stay calm.

"I heard they put out your eyes and humiliated you! But still you sit here," he fumed. "What potions have they made you drink to dull your mind like this?"

The rebellious little voice in her head told her he was quite right. She pressed his hand and her face was serious when she replied. "Do I seem drugged or in a trance?"

"The älfar have many arts," he retorted.

Nothing has changed. He still doesn't get it.

"If that was all you came for, Farron . . ."

Raleeha was losing her temper.

Farron sensed her anger. "No, no," he said swiftly. There was a rustle of paper. "I've brought you something mother could not resist baking for you." He handed her a small package.

She unwrapped it and recognized the scent of the delicious spices their mother always used. The taste of the confection brought back happy memories of her childhood. As she ate, Farron told her what had been happening on the other side of the water.

She listened to what he was telling her, but she was following her own train of thought. *How much can I tell him of what I have been through with Caphalor and Sinthoras?* Would she be betraying her masters or was it legitimate to inform her brother? Was it perhaps her duty to explain to Farron what sort of people they were allying themselves to? *What shall I do if he asks me what I know?*

Then she heard him say: "What can you tell me, sister?"

"I don't know what you mean." She was well aware that her acted innocence was not convincing.

Farron lowered his voice. "I may have joined the älfar cause in order to secure estates in Tark Draan for our family, but I am not so simple as to believe the älfar don't already have their sights set on the end of the campaign. If you are immortal, you have to do a lot of forward planning."

"But I'm only a slave," she said.

"You're slave to a nostàroi," he corrected her. "If anyone knows secrets it's going to be you." Farron seemed annoyed. "Who do you owe loyalty to: your family or the black-eyes?"

Raleeha swallowed the last of the biscuit crumbs. "If they were planning an attack on you and the barbarians, I would tell you." She knew straightaway she had made a mistake.

"*Barbarians?*" he repeated in hurt surprise. "Has it come to that? You describe your own people as barbarians?" He pulled his hand away.

"No, Farron," she said hastily, clutching at his hand. "The word just slipped out. I didn't mean it like that."

He took a deep breath. "Raleeha, you have changed. When I entered the room I thought I was seeing an älf-woman. Soon your own family won't recognize you if you don't watch out." He was whispering now. "Come with me! I can smuggle you out of here and get you away before the black-eyes notice you've gone."

Raleeha shook her head violently. That was the last thing she wanted. "No! I want to stay here."

"I am your brother and your prince!" he hissed. "I can order you to come with me."

"You are not my owner," she replied softly. "I belong to Caphalor. If he orders me to take my freedom or if he leaves it up to me when I leave Dsôn Faïmon, then I shall go."

There was a loud crash that frightened her. Farron must have slammed both fists down on to the table.

"I don't expect you to understand," she said with a sigh. "Please let me make my own decisions about my life. Look forward to the day when I return to you and Mother and the rest of the family." *For a visit*, she added silently, she did not want to leave Dsôn Faïmon. As soon as her sight was restored she wanted to start learning, painting, and drawing. "I want to become a master artist."

"You're a fool," he murmured, at a loss to understand her, but he took her hands in his own once more. "We are all so worried about you, that's all."

"I know, I know." Raleeha smiled at him.

Silence filled the room.

"You know what?" Farron sounded as if he were about to make a request. "I don't trust the älfar. I'm afraid they are going to trick us, even if we are allies."

"I'm sure you don't have to be afraid of that."

"You might be able to reassure me, but not my soldiers," he replied, laughing. "Tell me, sister, do the älfar have a weakness?"

She went cold. *There he goes again.* "What do you mean?"

"Is there something that makes them vulnerable?" he went on. "Is there a metal that can kill them? Where are the gaps in their defenses?" She heard him move closer. "You used to draw all the time. You drew pictures of everything you saw. Did you do the same thing here with the älfar?" Her face must have given her away. "I knew it!"

"My master has all my sketches and drawings," she declared and was glad to get round this awkward question without another lie. "He took them away because he realized they could jeopardize the security of his homeland."

Farron swore. "I can see my sister has become a half-älf, and not just in looks," he said sadly. "Please, Raleeha, let me help you escape! They can't hurt me because they need my warriors." His grip on her was painful. "You cannot ever be an älf. And you shall not be one."

"I don't want to be one," she responded. "It is enough if I can live with them and learn from them. Now let go of me, you're hurting me."

His hands released her. A chair was pushed back, heavy steps went off into the distance. "I hope you see sense, Raleeha," he said bitterly, taking his leave. "When I ask you next time to come with me and you tell me you prefer the black-eyes, I shall disown you. Until then, fare-well." The door slammed shut behind him.

Raleeha sat stunned. *Disowned. Forever! Can I bear it?* Memories of her past life, her brother's questions and threats, the taste and the smell of her mother's baking—it was all confused in her mind. Weeping, she buried her face in her hands. She did not know what else to do.

Chapter XV

But when they boned the corpses and sent the material to Dsôn, the soldiers discovered that ten of these warriors, invincible in battle, had escaped the effects of the poison. The traces left by the survivors led to Ishím Voróo's westernmost region, where the tracks disappeared.

To mark the memory of the exterminated race, the Inextinguishables referred to their race as the Sons of Tion. Their bones and skulls were given a prime position at the very top of the Tower of Bones.

Epocrypha of the Creating Spirit,
1st Book,
Chapter 2, 33–36

Ishím Voróo (The Outer Lands), älfar realm
Dsôn Faïmon, Dsôn (Star-Eye),
4371st division of unendingness (5199th solar cycle),
winter.

"Tell us more about the demon that will be fighting on our side."

Sinthoras raised the glass of sparkling wine to his lips and looked at his host; he would willingly have seen Khlotòn drop dead on the spot. *I wonder if my bodyguard would do me the favor of getting rid of him?*

Naturally, the other forty älfar at the evening reception were all eager to second their host's suggestion. They applauded quietly or tapped their plates to indicate approval. The clinking sound echoed throughout the high-ceilinged room with its decorations of spun tionium clouds. Jagged silver wire symbolized lightning flashes. Behind a line of mirrors beside the long table was a dimly lit display of skulls from a variety of races. Mortality was on the other side, far removed from the älfar. Wind chimes fashioned from long, carved, hollow bones gave a constant harmonious backing to the lyrical pieces presented by a musician on a four-voiced flute.

It could have been such a nice evening. Sinthoras lowered his glass. "Forgive me if I don't. It is a secret that only the Inextinguishables and the nostàroi may be party to," he said, seizing an escape that did not put him in a bad light—his dining companions were from the most influential circles in Dsôn and he needed their approval.

There were sounds of disappointment, but nobody pressed him. Sinthoras smiled and lifted his glass once more. *They are eating out of my hand.*

"Are you implying we cannot be trusted?" asked a female älf.

His glass had to be replaced on the table yet again. Checking to see who had heckled him, he recognized the älf-woman from the recent reception at Demenion's. Thoughts of that skeleton-armor and her naked skin on show had been bothering him ever since. After his speech she had completely vanished. Now here she was again, taking pleasure in challenging him. *What game is it that you are playing, my beauty?*

Dsôn's great and good watched him resentfully, as if they had all come to the same conclusion as the heckler.

Let's see where this is going. Sinthoras took a deep breath. "I did not catch your name," he responded. She was wearing a figure-hugging purple dress with embroidery on the seams and there were ropes of pearls on her breast. A silver band set with black gems and mother-of-pearl circled her forehead. She was making quite an impression on him. "Who did you say you were?"

She raised her head instead of bowing to him. Her black hair cascaded to her shoulders, showing off her slender neck. "Timanris."

"I don't know the name." Sinthoras looked questioningly to Khlotòn for an explanation. By applying to the host rather than asking her he was demoting her intentionally. If she wanted trouble she could have it, whether on battlefield or in banqueting hall, with weapons or with words. *I am willing to take you on.*

Her attack came swiftly. "My father is Timansor. I am his youngest daughter."

Sinthoras knew who Timansor was: a talented sculptor who worked with iron and preserved coagulated blood to produce unique, intriguing structures. Presumably the skeleton armor Timanris had recently sported was an authentic creation.

One of his sculptures would cost more than one hundred gold coins—enough to commission the building of a house. Sinthoras had once cast an eye on a piece called *Energy Loss*, which featured whisper-thin streams of frozen blood set with diamonds spraying out of a perforated breastplate. The price had only emphasized his own relative insignificance in älfar society: he did not belong to the upper echelons, not by a long shot. Not financially, at any rate.

"Oh? Khlotòn, I thought it was only your warrior class friends you were inviting." Sinthoras continued to snub her.

"My partner, Robonor, sits opposite you. He brought me along even though I told him I would find your speech boring. Unlike myself, he worships you."

Sinthoras was starting to enjoy himself. At last, a female sparring partner who did not storm off the field as soon as he launched his first arrows. Most were too subservient for his liking.

Her partner got to his feet and bowed before sitting down again, throwing an unmistakable warning look at Timanris.

"Worship, my dear Robonor, is not appropriate. I am not one of the Inextinguishables," he said, addressing the älf kindly. "But praise is due because you see before you an älf who will conquer Tark Draan, and you, Robonor, will surely be among the best of my warriors."

The guests laughed and applauded, perhaps in the hope of suppressing the unpleasant interruption that Timanris had caused.

Sinthoras turned to her. "Oh, now I remember you. I thought you were not interested in war. Last time we met you looked as if you were off to a costume ball."

Timanris raised an eyebrow. "It's obvious that warriors who affect to stand at an easel with palette in hand making pretty little pictures really have no understanding of art."

"You deride my paintings without having ever seen one."

"I don't have to see them. Your daubs and scribbles are laughed at in Dsôn." Timanris smiled. "And everyone's heard of the little episode with the pirogand yellow. It's clear which of the nostàroi is the better."

"Timanris!" shouted Robonor, whirling to face her.

Sinthoras' eyes narrowed. *You have gone too far, my beauty.*

Nobody in the hall dared move a muscle or mutter to a neighbor. The line between a little teasing and outright insult had definitely been crossed. To insult a nostàroi meant severe punishment. It was the highest office in the land and Sinthoras and Caphalor could certainly be regarded as the direct representatives of Nagsor and Nagsar Inàste.

"Have you always been so unpleasant, Timanris? Why would you take gossip for truth?" Sinthoras tore off a piece of bread and put it in his mouth. The best way to deal with this attack would be to make out that she was simpleminded. "Perhaps you've sustained a blow to your head? Or maybe as a small älf-child you used to lick the varnish your father puts on his sculptures." He waved the crust in her direction as she attempted to reply. "But no, silly of me, you *are* still a child, what other explanation could there be for your insisting on chattering about subjects you have absolutely no grasp of?"

Timanris went red. "I . . ."

Got you! "Why not stick to your calling and produce art that no one has ever heard of," he threw at her superciliously.

"But—" she began, her bright green eyes flashing with anger.

That will be the last word you speak in this room. He interrupted her using deep, resounding tones: "You have never confronted beasts in combat, Timanris. You have never in all your life lost a comrade in battle. You do not know what it is to be wounded. You have never had to shelter under a shield while poisoned arrows rain down." Sinthoras leaped to his feet and pointed at her. His voice went lower and lower, causing the glassware on the table to vibrate. "You, little älf-*girl*, have absolutely no idea what I have done for this realm; for you and for your artist father. So hold your tongue while the grown-ups talk about war!" He sat down, his fury dissipating, and began acting as though nothing had happened. "As soon as the topic of art comes up, please feel free to contribute to the conversation. Until then, why not eat and drink and look pretty." Timanris got to her feet, threw down her napkin, and made her way toward the door.

"Where are you off to?" growled Robonor. "Come back here! Timanris, you are bringing me nothing but disgrace."

When she got to the door the servants were opening for her, she stopped and tossed her response over her shoulder: "I'm off to find someone who knows about art. There's no one here worth talking to." She left the room and the doors closed behind her.

She got her last word in after all. Sinthoras smiled at Robonor. "I don't envy you there." He regretted she had left. *On reflection maybe that duel would have been worth continuing.* The fight was not over yet, that was certain. *She is beautiful and she has got guts.*

The other warrior did not know how to respond, so he murmured his thanks.

"Perhaps," suggested one of the other guests, an älf in old but well-cared-for armor, "I can say something about the demon. You, Nostàroi, only have to nod if you agree. In that way you will not have been guilty of betraying a secret."

The other guests laughed at his joke, relieved now that Timanris had left the hall.

"Try your luck," a surprised Sinthoras encouraged him, "but tell me first where you derive your knowledge of the demon from." It was good if he could learn more about the mist-demon; all the books that might have been useful in his research had disappeared from the library. This had worried him, but there had been nothing he could do about it. *I can't prevent all the other älfar from hearing it.*

The other älf smiled. "I shall reveal my secret sources to you alone, face to face."

Khlotòn leaned over to Sinthoras. "That is Jiphulor, who is, after the Inextinguishables, by far the eldest of all the älfar," he whispered. "He commands a range of spies outside Dsôn Faïmon."

"The demon is spreading his reign of terror," Jiphulor began. "I have heard that every tree, every bush, every blade of grass that comes under its influence is transformed, becoming undead—even the earth itself. Living beings, too, are afflicted in this way."

Sinthoras thought of the elf he had slain. Slain twice. "That may be so."

The guests muttered among themselves. He heard words like "fascinating," "horrifying." Some were planning excursions to the demon's land; another whispered to his neighbor that wonderful works of art would result from utilizing the bones of the undead.

"But it is not true that the mist-demon is expanding its sphere of influence," Sinthoras announced. "It awaits our call as soon as we need its help. I saw the place it lives; the land is in flames, the earth burning. How fitting if that happens to Tark Draan and the elf realms."

Restrained delight broke out amongst the diners, but Jiphulor's voice cut in sharply: "No. Not anymore. The creature has lost that particular capability, but its power is spreading out in all directions." The älf raised his wine glass and tipped the contents onto the white cloth. "Just like this."

The wine splashed down onto the linen, forming a wide stain on the fabric.

"The demon is on its way to the territory of the fflecx," Jiphulor went on. "Tell me, Nostàroi, are our preparations so far advanced that you have now summoned the mist-demon?"

Be quiet, will you! Sinthoras was feeling nervous. If he thought he was safe from attack now that Timanris had left, he was wrong; her words had been harmless compared with this simple question from a very old älf. "The mist-demon hates the elves just as we do," he answered in a vague circumlocution. "Caphalor only had to mention our arch enemies and the demon was eager to go to find them." By saying this he had directed any criticism carefully on to his rival. *Word will soon get round in Dsôn, for sure.*

"So the demon is already on its way although you have not called it yet?" Jiphulor kept digging. "I seem to remember you saying that the demon could only be summoned by you, Sinthoras, because you were the one who had led the negotiations."

A further attack. If he answered "yes" he was putting their new ally's reliability in doubt—the ally, moreover, thought of as their most powerful support in the coming campaign. It also cast doubt on his own integrity. So all he could say was, "No. That's not right. I have called it so that it can arrive in time. The negotiations progressed well. The half-trolls, giants, and ogres will be easy to convince now that the barbarians and the óarcos have declared for our side."

"In that case: here's to a prompt start to our campaign." Jiphulor got to his feet and lifted his goblet high. The whole gathering followed suit. "Here's to Sinthoras! It is an honor to be allowed to ride into battle under your leadership." He drained his cup.

You could have drunk to my health a bit earlier. Sinthoras had his glass refilled. *That was a bad move on my part.* He had got himself into a hole. How could he ever get himself out again?

He seized the first possible opportunity to absent himself from the company. The campaign, the troops, supply planning, current negotiations; one excuse followed the other. They let their nostàroi depart, now that it was clear that Tark Draan would fall.

Sinthoras hurried through the entrance hall, accompanied as ever by his bodyguard. He had to speak to Caphalor immediately and the talks would have to be speeded up. What tormented him most was the thought that he himself was responsible for the mist-demon's personality change. *Should I just ask the gâlran zhadar what it was I stole?* he wondered, in a fit of despair.

"Leaving so early, Nostàroi?"

Timanris! He checked his pace and saw her emerge from behind one of the broad pillars. She had been looking at a picture on the wall. "So you are still here? Did none of the servants feel like playing with you?" She approached him and her beautiful features bore traces of regret.

"I wanted to apologize for my words," she said. "It was unfair of me to criticize your painting without ever having seen any of your work." She smiled mischievously. "Nobody is making fun of your art—Robonor and I had been quarreling about the evening and I am afraid you—"

Sinthoras took a step toward her, took her face in his hands, and kissed her passionately on the mouth before releasing her again. He noticed that she returned his caress. Her lips had opened under his, demanding more. "Tomorrow, at midday, I shall expect you, Timanris," he said, experiencing a breathlessness that was entirely new. He felt dizzy and his surroundings whirled in a dance. "Then I can show you my paintings." He turned, leaving her standing.

He knew that she was watching him as he walked away. He ran his tongue over his lips, intoxicated. It was not the wine.

Ishím Voróo (The Outer Lands), älfar realm
Dsôn Faïmon, Radial Arm Wèlèron,
4371st division of unendingness (5199th solar cycle),
winter.

Surrounded by dark red tent walls decorated with symbols, Caphalor sat on a fur-lined chair reading the letter the Inextinguishables had sent. There was no time left for long negotiations. The army had to be made ready.

He had been told more or less the same thing by a very excited Sinthoras the previous evening. The reception with those political friends of his must not have gone quite according to plan. On top of that there had been news of the mist-demon developing unpleasant qualities. *More than unpleasant, frightening, and that is saying something.*

"Right," he told himself, throwing the letter into the brazier that was heating the tent. "Then let's finish off negotiating with the scum of Ishím Voróo and put an end to the demon."

He left his accommodation, got on Sardaî and rode to the next negotiation center with his escort. Even though there were some vacant tents nearer at hand, the newcomers had pitched up on the western-most edge of the temporary settlement: new arrivals tended to isolate themselves on the perimeter of the canvas city, as far as possible from the Tower of Bones.

No banners, no pennants. "Who is it?" he asked one of his companions as he spied a single tent. "Isn't it the Fatarcans?"

"I thought it was," said the other älf, no less surprised than his general. He ordered the fire-bull riders to keep their weapons at the ready in case anyone should be misguided enough to attack the nostàroi. A bugle call to the island towers alerted the garrison to prepare their catapults: any enemy found in the camp would disappear under a hail of arrows, spears, and stones.

Caphalor dismounted and looked around, discovering only a lone black horse tied at the entrance to the tent. The nostàroi entered the tent with four of his guards.

He was confronted by a tall female form with the dark hood of her mantle concealing her face. He could not discern her features in the shadows. "Is this some kind of a joke . . . ?" he asked, his voice friendly but firm.

The figure lifted her head. She pushed back her hood with one hand to reveal burned flesh and a familiar face. "I was waiting for you, my demigod."

The guards drew their swords and raised them threateningly in the direction of the deformed flesh-stealer, who attempted a smile, only rendering her appearance more abhorrent still.

I had completely forgotten about her! Caphalor gave a discreet sign to his soldiers to prevent them from attacking the obboona. At the sight of her, the brand she had put on his own body flared up. "Get out," he said in the Dark Language. "Think yourself lucky I don't have you killed. Killed on the spot."

The white of her eyes were all the more noticeable because of the surrounding damaged skin. "Are you going to break your word, my demigod? You swore on oath that you would return to my side as my spouse."

He laughed outright. "You really expected me to do that, flesh-stealer? I would have sworn anything to escape your clutches."

She sobbed. "You are breaking my heart, my demigod!"

Caphalor realized she was quite insane. "It will go well with your broken mind."

Karjuna giggled suddenly and then laughed like a maniac, until she cowered and collapsed. The guards were still standing by, ready to cut her to pieces. "What, my demigod, if I could promise you an army?" she wheedled in falsetto tones, blowing him kisses in the air. "Leave your wife and come to my side. I shall forgive your reluctance." She lifted her head. "Is it because I am disfigured?" she whimpered, covering her visage with her hands. "My demigod, I can wear a mask if I offend your eyes, but please"—She fell to her knees at his feet, clutching at his mantle. The guards pushed her back—"please, be mine! Warm me on these cold nights with the heat of your body—"

"Enough!" he shouted, feeling the urge—because of her voice, because of her demands, because of what she had done to him, because of her very existence—to behead her on the spot. He pulled out one of his short swords and drew his arm back for the blow.

"It is forbidden!" she shrieked, holding out her arms. "Forbidden! Killing me is forbidden! I am an intermediary!" She reached under her cloak and brought out a letter that the nostàrois' messengers had distributed all over Ishím Voróo.

"You do not have a sane thought in your head." Caphalor gestured to the guards to pin her to the floor. Having mastered his anger, he now found he wanted the flesh-stealer to suffer at length—not be killed with a single merciful stroke. "You have killed your last älf," he vowed.

Like lightning she pulled out a small whistle from under her stole and blew hard into it, but one of the guards kicked it aside before it could issue a sound. The mouthpiece had her blood on it.

"What is that?" he asked her.

The alarm gong sounded on one of the island towers, to be joined by a second, and a third. Within the space of a few heartbeats Caphalor counted five of the bastions reporting enemy action. *Who would be crazy enough* . . . He looked at the flesh-stealer.

The obboona laughed. "My demigod, my demigod! Did I promise too much?" she giggled.

"What is that whistle?" he shouted at her while a guard sliced through the canvas tent wall to let them see what was happening outside.

A dark mob emerged from the edge of the forest: figures were running wildly with no apparent discipline but at amazing speed. Caphalor heard their furious tones: barks and howls—and knew they were srinks. *There must be hundreds of them!* They were racing over the cleared strip toward the tent where he stood.

"Call them off!" he commanded Karjuna.

"Then marry me!"

"Die!"

"Then let us be united in death." She looked at him longingly. "It is forbidden to kill me. I am their leader. Their queen! Their *queen!*"

That would seem to be the case. Caphalor ordered the guards to let her go.

The srinks rolled onwards, some on all fours, some up on two legs, waving weapons and wearing armor. The howling and barking grew louder and now they were close enough for Caphalor to hear their growls and snarls.

The älf guards formed a line of first defense, even though it was clear that resistance would be useless. A further signal sounded from the islands. The catapults were ready and they were waiting for Caphalor's order before opening fire. Any of his soldiers might give the order on his own responsibility and initiative if it meant saving the life of the nostàroi.

"Call them off!" he yelled at Karjuna.

"Will you take me for your wife?"

"Yes," he said, glad the guards had their backs turned so that he would not have to witness their horrified expressions. "I will go to my companion and I will renounce her. I will be back here in a few moments of unendingness and we will celebrate." *You'll be a long time waiting.*

She looked at him suspiciously. "You have deceived me once before, my demigod."

The guards brought down the first of the srinks that had come too close to the tent. Swords swished through the air and the snarls changed to screams. Blood spurted up high to spatter over the rest of the creatures as they pressed forward. His guards were keeping the attackers at bay so as not to get within range of their vicious claws and teeth, but they were being forced back slowly. They were simply outnumbered.

"Not this time," he said in the ingratiating tone he had used to good effect in the past.

"Swear by all that is precious to you!"

Caphalor swore it on the lives of his companion and his family, without meaning what he said. He owed nothing to a flesh-stealer apart from the promise: *Your death is named Caphalor.* He handed the music pipe back to her.

She raised it to her lips and blew into it while her fingers covered the holes in quick succession.

The srink attack ebbed away at once, heading back to the forest as quickly as they had come. They even took their own dead away with them. Had they not left tracks and a large amount of blood on the ground, Caphalor would not have believed the attack had really happened. He glanced across at the other tents. All the other delegations had been prepared to defend themselves. Giants, barbarians, trolls and kraggash were all in full armor in their camps.

Without exchanging further words with her, Caphalor went outside and got on his stallion. *I cannot endure the obboona's presence any longer.* "I can offer the Inextinguishables no less than 5,000 srinks," she called after him. "They are as good as four times the number of barbarians, my demigod. We obboonas will promise not to touch another demigod, we'll only take elves now to help us look like you. Do you hear? We can live in friendship with one another. Tell the gods this."

Caphalor rode off. He did not wish to know how the obboona had got the flute and how she had learned to play it. If it were up to him and Sinthoras, she and her srinks would not be participating in the invasion force against Tark Draan. But someone was bound to report to the rulers that she had 5,000 monsters at her disposal. She had given an ample demonstration of how excellent her command of them was.

He looked at the tents belonging to the other delegations. *I must get one of them to kill the obboona without suspicion falling on me. Farron is still in my debt.*

Caphalor turned Sardaî toward the barbarian encampment.

Ishím Voróo (The Outer Lands), älfar realm
Dsôn Faïmon, Dsôn (Star-Eye)
43/1st division of unendingness (5199th solar cycle),
winter.

Timanris strolled in a leisurely fashion round the easel to admire the canvas Sinthoras was working on: various shades of white on a black background, a golden line running from right to left. She touched the damp paint and sniffed it with closed eyes. A tight-fitting white dress with black flames burning upward from the hem emphasized her perfect proportions. *Well, my beauty?* Sinthoras was standing three paces away, unnoticed. He could not believe what she was doing. He had only left the room for a short while to change—exchanging his armor for the clothes he liked to wear in his studio. He and Caphalor had spent the whole day discussing military strategy and he felt he deserved some distraction.

Because he had been so busy he had sent Timanris a message suggesting they postpone their meeting.

Either she did not receive the message or she has chosen to ignore it. Sinthoras grinned. In his opinion, she had not paid his note the slightest attention. She was curious and feisty and she was an artist like her father.

Then she took a brush out of the container and dipped it into the blue, marking a small dot in the bottom left-hand corner. He held his breath. *Perfect!* He had been wondering what the picture needed. Timanris had had the cheek to smuggle herself into his private studio and alter his painting, and she had made it perfect!

With swift and silent steps he went to stand behind her. He took her by the shoulders and turned her to face him, kissing her passionately. Holding her tight against his body he felt how, after an initial shock, she relaxed, placing her hand on the nape of his neck.

They remained like this for some time, exchanging tender caresses until he released her and pointed to the picture. "You have transformed it!" he said enthusiastically.

"Is that why you were so pleased to see me?" Timanris was still breathless from his kiss.

"Not only because of the painting," he replied, taking the brush out of her hand. He wiped the excess pigment carefully off on the side of the container and dunked it in the cleaning fluid. "It dries very quickly. The blue you used is refined from the liver of a white óarco. One ounce is worth ten chests of gold."

She is amazing! Sinthoras smiled at her, suppressing the urge to take her face in his hands and press his lips to hers again. He wanted to talk to her about art, about her views on the subject of war, about the immortality of their race, about every imaginable topic—trivial or weighty. What he was experiencing was more than the simple physical desire that he had known with other älf-women. *It is more than the purely physical.*

"It's painted on óarco skin, isn't it?" Timanris returned his admiring glances, her chest heaving. He thought he could hear her heart beating. Beating for him. "A good choice; it can absorb a large amount of paint."

"Well observed! Later I shall work on it with iron nails to scratch texture into the surface and . . ." His voice failed and he was unable to think. He stared at her, his head reeling.

She gave him a smile and touched his right cheek. "It is the same for me, Nostàroi. I have been trying not to let it show, but I wanted you from that very first evening."

"So why did you leave?"

"Robonor. I intended to stay with him for longer than a half division of unendingness because I had promised my father I would. He and Robonor's father are good friends and the two of us have known each other since we were young. Two children became two lovers." Timanris drew her hand back. "Until I saw you, Sinthoras."

"I understand." Sinthoras was lying, he had only used the phrase to avoid a silence. He was not sure what to make of her confession. *Does she mean she will leave Robonor for me?*

She sighed and flung herself into his arms, holding him tight. "What's to be done?"

Sinthoras did not want her to be sad, but there was no way he would share her with another. He gently freed himself from her embrace and pointed to an empty gnome-skin canvas. "What do you think? Shall we start a painting together?"

"It would be an honor," she said at once, wiping the tears from her eyes. Then she looked down at herself.

"Wait, I'll get you something to put over your dress." He kissed her once more, his heart pounding in his chest. The taste of her, the smell of her! They belonged together. Her eyes told him that she shared this view.

Sinthoras knew that they would make love this very night, there in his studio. It would be the beginning of a long relationship that stood as firm and fast as the Inextinguishables' Tower of Bones.

He hurried out, calling for a slave.

A moonlit night enhanced the beauty of the city of Dsôn.

Robonor was enjoying the view as he walked the streets with his patrol. The Bone Tower in the center shone out in purest white, as if the bones of the defeated races were glowing from the inside. It symbolized the superiority of the älfar, their pride and their artistic skill.

The moonlight emphasized the lines of the mosaics and sculpture, frescoes and reliefs on the façades of the grand townhouses, too. Many an artwork had its own lightshow, with lamps embedded in the surface of the piece. The subjects were death, transience, decay and destruction, but transformed into an aesthetic whole—the älfar took pleasure in the things the barbarians would find repulsive, horrific and terrifying.

Robonor had been living in Kashagòn for so long that he had forgotten how spectacularly the city shimmered at night. Even though the towns there were not to be sneered at, they could not begin to compare with Dsôn. Every step he took showed him a new delightful vista.

He could not get enough of what he was seeing. He ordered the patrol to stop several times so that he could drink in the beauty at his leisure. He had stopped to admire a group of statues on the Kòlsant Square. Since childhood he had always loved the figures that made up the sculpture.

It showed an älf-woman fighting five óarcos. The metal figures were lifesize and every detail was shown.

These statues were particularly intriguing: the muscles on the arms and legs had been formed of a special material that, unlike other substances, actually contracted in the warmth and expanded in the cold; the joints were so constructed as to permit complex movements.

Robonor could follow the figures turning as the night grew cooler: the älf-warrior lowered her sword arm and the óarcos sank down at her feet; when the daystar shone she lifted her weapon and the monsters launched their attack. The warmer the weather, the more dramatic the struggle.

Robonor nodded to the älf-woman. *You will defeat them once again.* He was grateful to the two nostàroi generals for ordering these patrols while the negotiations continued. The creatures encamped to the north of Dsôn were not allowed to enter their land, and certainly not their capital city, the center of the realm. If they did it would be a gross affront, punishable by death.

"Move on," he ordered, and the ten älfar followed him. They wore light armor and carried spears and sharp-edged, triangular shields; on their backs they had their short swords. They ran through the streets and alleyways without making a sound.

A light wind blew up, causing their surcoats to billow and sway.

Robonor could smell rain on the wind and grimaced. The relief unit would be here soon. He hoped they would arrive before the next downpour. "I don't like this weather," he told his soldiers and they all laughed quietly.

"Who does?" asked one of them.

"I don't mind it," said a second älf.

"Well, in that case," replied Robonor, "you're down for the relief. One of the other poor sods will be glad to swap a wet patrol for a cozy room." He shivered. Suddenly he felt ill at ease. He looked round. *Are we being followed?*

He raised his head and looked up past the sharp-cornered walls, ornamental stone blocks and twisting façades of the nearby buildings. He waited in vain to catch sight of any shadowy figure crossing the pale moon.

"Is something wrong?"

"No, I don't think so," he replied and looked ahead. "Let's go back to the guardroom. By the time we get there we'll be due a shift-change."

They marched back slowly to their barracks, so as not to arrive too early.

A loud, shrill cry rang out.

"Over on the right!" Robonor ran back to the narrow alley they had just emerged from, where he had had the uneasy feeling. His instincts were reliable, then. The sentries ran to his side, shields raised.

At the other end of the alley they saw two figures beating up a third. Robonor knew from their clothing that they were slaves. Slaves were always brawling, especially if they had been allowed out to one of their taverns—that was when tensions would spark arguments: some slaves might be envious of others in better households, others just enjoyed a punch-up. *Barbarians.* "A bit of excitement for us." Robonor slowed down and relaxed. As long as no älf was in danger he would let the slaves finish their quarrel. "Let them beat each other up. When they've finished we'll arrest them, give them a whipping and return them to their owners where they'll get a second dose of the same." That was the correct punishment for brawling or any other unacceptable conduct.

Robonor and his soldiers waited a few paces off.

Robonor noted their lack of badge denoting their owner with disapproval—yet another regulation they were flouting. The badges had to be visible at all times.

One man ended up on the ground. The fight was over.

"Right—" Robonor called out, about to give the order to have them all arrested.

There was a crunching sound above his head. A pebble hit his armor and with great presence of mind he sprang back.

If one of his guards had not been standing directly behind him, blocking his way, he would have neatly avoided the falling masonry.

As it was, the guard's shield stopped him and its sharp edge cut his leg badly, causing him to stagger.

Then some of the carved stones he had so recently been admiring rained down on him.

Chapter XVI

The Inextinguishables made many enemies through their campaigns to collect bone supplies.

The barbarians, lower creatures and other freaks spawned by the alien gods could not understand that art demanded sacrifice and that their own lives were worth nothing.

Nothing, to us, the älfar. Although they knew what feats our warriors were capable of, our enemies united and marched against us.

Epocrypha of the Creating Spirit,
2nd Book,
Chapter 1, 1–5

Ishím Voróo (The Outer Lands), älfar realm
Dsôn Faïmon, Radial Arm Welèron,
4371st division of unendingness (5199th solar cycle),
winter.

"We have the half-trolls, ogres, barbarian tribes, and, most importantly, Lotor on our side." Sinthoras was bent over the checking list and looked up and across. "You're not listening, are you?"

"Yes, I am," was the distracted response. Caphalor was staring through the window of the island tower across to the west, where the obboona's tent was pitched. To show that he had heard the words, he repeated the names of all the participating peoples. "Someone's missing."

"The giants." Sinthoras could see the other älf was thinking about one creature in particular. "And the srinks," he added. He waited in vain for a reaction. *He is really troubled.* "Caphalor, we don't need the srinks. Neither of us need go over to her tent to negotiate."

"There are too many of them to ignore," Caphalor answered slowly. "The flesh-stealer is right: her army can't simply be dismissed out of hand. The mere sight of the srinks would have an immensely powerful effect on an enemy. The Inextinguishables would never understand why we were placing personal considerations above the fate of the Star Realm."

Sinthoras' mood was anything but dismal. He had only one thing in his mind: Timanris.

She was incredible, quite different from any other älf-woman he had ever met. Timanris was unpredictable and not obsessed with power, fame, or reputation, and she could turn any perfectly adequate picture into a stunning work of art with the simplest of brushstrokes. *How did I ever live without her?* Her gifts as a lover blew his mind. Her reactions at the heights of ecstasy told him she was similarly enthusiastic about his own talents.

"May the obboona meet her end!" he cried brightly. "Send her back home with her confounded srinks. We've got enough warriors." He worked out the rough numbers. "100,000 barbarians from various tribes, 20,000 Kraggash, 40,000 óarcos, 4,000 gnomes, 5,000 ogres, and 7,000 half-trolls. Then about 70,000 creatures and mercenary adventurers taking a punt on riches and good fortune in Tark Draan." He underlined the final figure twice and laid the quill down, crossing his arms behind his head and rocking back and forth in his chair. "Congratulations to the both of us. That, my fellow nostàroi, is an army worthy of the name. We can overrun Tark Draan in a single moment of unendingness." He stretched out his right arm. "I can already see our victories! And the total extermination of all the elves!"

Caphalor took a seat opposite Sinthoras, swiveled the paper round and checked the calculations. "You have forgotten the demon," he said, adding the name to the list. "He is our one magic weapon. If he fails us, the whole of the rest of the army is a waste of space."

"To be honest, I'm sure we can manage without him if we have to." Sinthoras could not wipe the grin off his face. *She has promised to come to me. Soon.* That was why this discussion had to finish promptly.

"What about the giants? Do I send them home as well?"

"What's the matter with you?"

"The flesh-stealer is waiting over there. She burned a brand into my skin, humiliated me and deceived us," Caphalor said sullenly. "We swore to kill her, Sinthoras. Have you forgotten? On top of everything else, she expects me to go back and marry her, she's not going to simply vanish."

"Yes, I should prefer a long, painful death for her. However," said Sinthoras, "we must not lay a finger on her while she is on neutral ground. She is a queen, a commander-in-chief." He sat up straight. "I don't like it, either. But what can we do?" He pulled the page of numbers over toward him again. "The best thing would be to include her in the campaign and make sure she dies on the battlefield. Our archers are skilled enough."

"You don't get it! She won't put her army at our disposal unless I become her spouse!"

"Of course I get it." Sinthoras shrugged his shoulders. "What's stopping you? It's only a pretense! Who's going to find out?"

Caphalor gave him a horrified look. "I can't put myself in the clutches of—"

I've had just about enough of this righteous indignation. We are wasting precious time. Sinthoras raised his hands in the air. "Right. That's decided, then. We'll go to the Inextinguishables and we'll tell them we don't want the srinks." He shoved the list over the table impatiently. "One suggestion: I'll go to our rulers, you go and deal with the giants."

Caphalor blinked. "Now I'm confused. What's got into you?"

"What do you mean?"

"You are behaving quite differently now from a few moments of unendingness ago. You laugh. You speak of *us*, you are good-humored. Where's all that bitterness I was used to?" Caphalor took a deep breath and studied him more closely. "Anyone would think you had been swapped for a benevolent secret twin."

"Oh, nice to hear what you've been thinking about me all this time," exclaimed Sinthoras, pretending to be insulted. In reality he was well aware what had caused the transformation.

"It's not just me, it's more or less everyone who's had dealings with you." Caphalor looked him straight in the eye—and then his expression changed. "By Samusin! You're in love!"

Damn. Is it that obvious? "Nonsense! I haven't got time for that sort of thing. It's bad enough that you're always swanning off to be with your companion." Hardly had he said the words than he realized the lie must be written all over his face.

Now it was Caphalor's turn to grin. "No further questions. But we have confirmed what the whole of Dsôn is saying about you."

"Oh?" Sinthoras was curious now. "So what do the gossip-mongers say?"

"That you're having a fling with the daughter of an artist and that you don't always draw the curtains in your studio at night," he related with gusto.

The moonshine was too beautiful to shut out. "Timanris and I paint together. It's a passion we share." Sinthoras was trying his best to get out of a tricky situation.

"You paint naked, do you, Nostàroi?"

"That's evil tongues wagging, eager to ruin my reputation. Others are jealous of my success, obviously." *It's quite true.* Sinthoras pointed the quill pen in his direction. "I might have suspected you of that at one time."

"Not me. Not my kind of politics." Caphalor lowered his voice. "The same envious voices are saying that Robonor's sudden death was not quite the accident it seemed."

Damn, damn, and damn! "What are they saying?" His good mood had disappeared. "Who's been saying that? And where did you hear it?" He had to think of his good name for after this war. *If my enemies are already spreading malicious gossip about me, what's the word going to be in Dsôn while I'm off at the front?'*

Caphalor got up. "I was at the market getting something for Enoïla. I overheard a snatch of conversation in a soap merchant's. I don't know the älf, but he was well dressed. I noticed his signet ring. The symbol was a lance on a broken shield. He was saying that it was your slaves fighting in the street that night as a decoy for the watch and that another two had loosened those stones on the roof that fell and killed Robonor."

Sinthoras made a mental note of the signet ring mark. It would be easy enough to find the wearer. *Didn't Jiphulor recently have something similar on an amulet?* Fury started to boil up inside him. "So that's what he thinks, does he?"

"And he mentioned that one of the guards was in cahoots with you— the one that prevented Robonor from jumping out of the way." Caphalor picked up the quill and put a tick by the giants. "They found a bad cut on Robonor's leg that looked as if it had been made by the edge of a sharpened shield." He walked over to the door. "Take care; you have rivals who do not wish you well. You are right to a degree; for a long time I would have been of their number, but there is hope now that I might actually get to like you. As long as we lead the army together you can count on my total support." He nodded. "Right, I'm off to talk the giants round."

He opened the door and noticed a female älf in a dark blue mantle. She was carrying a large sketchbook under her arm and a container with charcoal sticks was hanging from her belt.

He stood aside and ushered her in, shooting a knowing glance at Sinthoras as he left the room, closing the door behind him.

Caphalor ordered two guards over to the spy holes and told them not to let the nostàroi out of their sight. Whatever Sinthoras did, he was under observation. The bodyguards knew how to work unobtrusively. It was thanks to them that he knew what had really happened on the night Robonor had been killed.

But that was not important. The giants must be persuaded to join the cause and afterward, as soon as the daystar went down, he would seek out the flesh-stealer and see what he could achieve with carefully selected words. *Ideally, he would manage to postpone her immediate demands and yet still organize an alliance with the srinks. If not, she had better disappear.*

Caphalor crossed the bridge on Sardaî, picking up his waiting escort in the cleared zone and hurrying to the enormous tents which housed the giants. The canvas structures were fifteen paces high and sported simple banners displaying their broken tree trunk insignia.

He found four giants in front of their tent, gambling with dice at least the size of óarco skulls. The rough animal-skin garments and their own hairy skin made him think of bears. The giants' only armor was in the leg area: shin-protectors with finger-length spikes. Even their boots were ironclad.

There's no going into battle without these guys. Caphalor imagined how they would simply carve themselves a path through enemy lines, cutting the opposition to rags.

Even when seated they were taller than an älf on a night-mare. Their size gave them all the confidence they needed. They hardly glanced at the newcomers. One of them called out.

A female giant appeared from the tent while Caphalor was dismounting; she was as hairy and as strong as the males, but the animal-skins she wore were white. Her short blond hair had been interwoven with ivy strands to form an imposing headdress.

"Why," she asked, and it sounded like a shout, "do you refuse to satisfy our demands?"

The fire-bulls of Caphalor's escort instinctively stepped back at these bass tones, but Sardaî was indifferent.

"Because we can't give you our slaves to eat," he answered. "What is your name?"

She pulled herself up to her full height and glared down at him. "I am Gattalind, sister to the king. I am his strategic planner," she announced with pride.

"Where is the agent we have been negotiating with so far?"

"We sent him home," she replied. "He wanted us to accept your offer but I think we should be paid more."

Caphalor looked up at her ugly features. "No slaves to eat. In Tark Draan you can pick up as many as you want. But not here."

"But if you can't get the gateway open there'll be nothing for us at all," she argued. "We want to fill our pantries. You've got so many vassals.

Give us some of them! Barbarians multiply quickly, so you'll soon make up the numbers."

Caphalor did his best to come up with a solution. "Would fire-bulls do? They probably taste really good and they are a unique dish, I'm sure."

"No," said Gattalind decisively.

I'll have to try a little trick. "Then let's forget the whole thing. The Inextinguishables are not dependent on the support of the giants. We've got enough soldiers now and if the srinks are in with us you aren't really necessary, are you?" He turned around and started to stroll back to his mount. "I knew we didn't need you. People exaggerate about the strength thing. Being big doesn't necessarily imply being strong, and it certainly doesn't guarantee fighting skills."

"What did you say?" The giantess' shadow shortened abruptly as she bent down to grasp him by the waist and lift him up.

Caphalor signed to his escort not to interfere. *Looks like my trick is working.*

Gattalind lifted him up through the air until he was level with her face; the other giants had stopped gambling and were standing watching. "You insult my people, black-eyes! We are the strongest of anyone here. Even the ogres are afraid of us."

"You'd win any bout of single combat?" he prodded, struggling somewhat for air.

"Any and every bout."

"Then how about a contest? Me against three of your lot. If I win, the giants march with the Inextinguishables." Further details of his suggestion were drowned in thundering laughter. The air around him was filled with the foul smell of giant breath and he thought he might go deaf from the roars his ears were subjected to. He had never heard such a sound emitted from a living being's throat. Caphalor thanked Samusin the other giants had calmed down. "If I lose," he said, "all your demands will be met or you can go home."

"Done," said Gattalind. "Against these three, but you mustn't kill them."

I seem to have been a little premature with my celebrations. Caphalor cursed his own courage. How on earth was he going to be able to defeat these three hunks without using his main weapons—and without any time to prepare? "I have to be allowed to injure them." He attempted to strike a bargain.

"Agreed. When I open my fingers, let the combat begin." She exchanged a few words in their own language with the other giants, who nodded agreement and stepped back. At that, she dropped him.

When Caphalor neared ground level, a spiked boot tip came racing toward him. As he fell, he drew his two short swords out of their sheaths, crossed the blades and tucked his feet up under him.

Sinthoras kissed Timanris on the nape of her neck and planted further kisses all the way along her naked spine. "Wonderful," he whispered and lay down at her side.

They were resting in each other's arms on the floor, with only a thin mantle under them as protection from the dust.

"What was it specifically that was so wonderful?" she asked playfully, turning over. She was displaying herself to him in all her unadorned beauty in the broad light of day. There was no shyness. Timanris was proud of her body.

"You. Making love to you. Everything," he exclaimed.

She smiled again and planted a gentle kiss on the tip of his nose. Then her face grew serious. "There's a question I have to put to you, my love," she said softly. "Rumors are abroad in Dsôn—"

A bucketful of cold water in the groin could not have worked faster. *Has the poisonous gossip reached her ears?* Uttering a curse, he sat up, arms circling his knees, as he glared at the wall. "I know. Caphalor told me what they're saying."

"Is there even the slightest grain of truth . . . ?"

"No." *That was too quick, he told himself.*

Timanris placed a hand on his shoulder. "Look me in the eyes and say that."

He got up, putting on his clothes slowly. "Does it make a difference?"

The älf-woman looked up at him from where she lay, leaning up on one arm. "Of course. I can tell if someone's lying."

"Even in daylight?" he teased, his black eyes full toward her.

"You are evading my questions, Sinthoras. That's not a sign of innocence." Timanris stood up slowly and got dressed. "I did not love Robonor. He was kind; he was usually good to me even when I was difficult. He did not deserve to die crushed under a stone like an insect just because you desired his mistress."

Sinthoras fastened his weapons belt. "What do you believe really happened, my beauty?"

"It's not a question of belief. That's always been my way: I might pray to the gods but I make sure that things work even without their help." She sat down at the table and began a rapid sketch. With only a few lines she conjured up his visage on the paper, shading half of it in black. "I only know one side of you, Sinthoras. When I get to know the other half I shall be able to trust you properly and shall be happy to accept you as my partner." Timanris smiled sadly, got to her feet and came over to him.

While she was kissing him goodbye the door swung open.

Yantarai stood on the threshold.

Not now! Sinthoras had not been expecting her at all. Although they were not doing anything forbidden, he and Timanris jumped apart. The young älf-woman bowed her head in respect to the older one, who had given seven daughters the light of immortality. Yantarai had chosen her outfit with care: a slim-fitting ankle-length black dress was complemented by a dark red embroidered stole draped over one shoulder. Her feet were shod in low-heeled black sandals decorated with red thread. She presented a striking appearance, particularly considering how many moments of unendingness she had already seen.

The first gray lines were starting to cross Yantarai's pale face. So far she had been able to suppress the true degree of her anger. "I behold a talented artist," she said, speaking deliberately. "And an artist should stay where she belongs. She has no place in the world of politics." Entering the room, she espied the mantle spread out on the floor. "And no place at all at the side of a nostàroi."

Sinthoras felt exposed. Helplessly he shifted his gaze from one female to the other. Reason on the one hand struggled with love on the other, mind versus feeling. A decision had to be made. Now. Neither of these älf-women would countenance delay. He had also shared his bed with Yantarai. She had the right to lay a claim on him.

He opened his mouth but nothing passed his lips. Not even a groan or a breath and certainly not a single word.

The crossed blades clashed against the tip of the boot.

Caphalor could not, of course, halt the giant leg on its trajectory. He had bunched up his legs and so escaped the steel spikes on the giant's metal shin armor. His arms and swords withstood the impact of the kick and the momentum catapulted him vertically into the air.

He flew up past the giant, heading for the tent top. *I must think of something.* Caphalor plunged a sword into one of the wooden poles and clung to it. He still did not know how he could overcome these brutes. *Killing them would have been easier.*

They ran over and ripped away the ropes to make the tent collapse, hoping to bring him down to their level.

It'll be me who decides when I face you. Caphalor leaped up onto the central pole and sliced through the canvas to release it. As the heavy linen fell away, his wooden support stayed upright and he kept his balance on one leg on top of the pointed tip. He was up ridiculously high.

The giants pointed up at him and laughed.

Barbarians, half-trolls, and many other creatures came streaming out of their tents to see what the älf was up to. As no alarms had sounded and the island catapults were not active, it was presumed this was not an attack, but a spectacle for their benefit.

"That won't count as victory," Gattalind shouted at Caphalor.

I'm afraid she's right. I must come up with a resounding victory. Like this. With the three giants heading for the wooden tent pole, Caphalor took off and landed with his boot heels smack in the middle of one giant's head before it had a chance to defend itself. He was no weight at all, but the impact from his leap had been enough to deal the powerful creature a substantial blow, knocking him to the ground.

Let's try that move again. Caphalor launched himself up and made a leap on top of the second giant.

His opponent ducked and lunged at the älf with his bare fist.

Caphalor stabbed. The sword drove between the enormous finger bones and the giant screamed with pain and indignation.

The älf landed on the ground and executed several somersaults to absorb the impact of the fall. Heavy iron-tipped boots were crashing into the earth round about him. The giants were kicking and stamping in an effort to get him. *Now I know what a mouse must feel like in the middle of a herd of raging fire-bulls.*

He rolled and rolled and then watched his enemies closely. *I'll have to get up high again, or I'll be crushed!* A boot stamped too close to home and Caphalor took his chance, jumping onto the foot as it was being lifted into the air. Avoiding the shin-spikes, he was swept upward.

The second giant noticed what was happening and aimed a kick at the älf.

That's what I was hoping for! Caphalor did a vertical jump and the huge boot missed him, but knocked the other giant off balance, toppling him to the ground.

Still in the air, Caphalor took off again from his opponent's belt buckle and took a new direction for his flight: onto the face of the fallen giant. Before the giant could avoid him, Caphalor had landed with a thump, both feet on the nose. "Take that!" The giant's eyes rolled up in his head and his body went limp.

The giants had stopped laughing. The spectators were admiring the nostàroi's skill and dexterity. He was certainly proving that, in combat at least, the älfar had no rivals anywhere.

Unusual type of fight, but I'm rather enjoying myself. Caphalor stood up again, giving the ghost of a smile, and pointed his short sword at the one remaining contender. He had relied on his instincts, rather than a preplanned strategy.

The giant growled deep and loud, then grabbed the tent pole and thrashed it around in the direction of the älf.

Caphalor ran toward him, leaping aside at the last moment and somersaulting out of danger. Then, taking up a smaller stick, he grabbed hold of the giant's pole and let himself be carried up into the air on it. At the very last moment he let go and flew into the giant's face.

And hit home. He jabbed the stick he was carrying into the corner of the giant's eye. *Tarlesa, you gave me that idea!*

Caphalor let go and crashed into the giant's shoulder, sliding down on his bearskin clothing and jumping down in a cloud of dust that had shot up out of the hair. *Revolting. I must get someone to clean my armor.* He looked at his stunned opponent.

The giant stood thunderstruck, long arms dangling by his sides. He was staring straight ahead with an empty expression on his face, unable to move or speak. He could not even utter a shriek.

"That would seem to be it," Caphalor said to the giantess. "I have overpowered them all without killing them."

The barbarians applauded and drummed their shields in approval. The other spectators all gradually joined in and general rejoicing broke out. They had never seen the like.

"What have you done to him, älf?" asked Gattalind, pulling the stick out of the giant's head. His behavior did not alter. He was still standing like a statue.

Seize the opportunity and impress them all. "I have used the special knowledge that only the älfar have," he answered, ensuring that all the spectators could hear what he was saying. "We can rob any creature of its brain functions without needing to apply physical force. This giant challenged me and can consider himself lucky to be alive." Caphalor gestured to a companion carrying the contracts. "I expect your signature here and then I expect your warriors, Gattalind."

He did not wait to see her reaction, but strode calmly off to his night-mare.

Only he knew that his right ankle was causing him pain and that he could hardly move his right shoulder. *I'll get a healer to take a look.* He wanted the barbarians and other creatures to think of him as invincible in combat. The älfar were a myth unto themselves and should continue to be so.

It was by exploiting exactly this älfar myth that he hoped to persuade the flesh-stealer to join their army. His victory over the giants gave him added confidence. *But if the obboona sticks to her original demands it'll be a very short discussion indeed.*

*   *   *

"I must be off. A . . . meeting." Sinthoras pushed his way past the two älf-women, aghast at his own words. *What am I? Some nervous little boy?*

Timanris and Yantarai watched him go as if he had lost his mind. Both of them wanted to follow him and demand answers.

For the first time Sinthoras was glad of his bodyguard. They stood in the älf-women's path and held them back so that he could get away, although he had no idea where he was going.

Get away. Must just get away. I can't decide. He was too confused. Feelings and logic were at loggerheads. He had fought every imaginable creature in Ishím Voróo, and had won the day on countless occasions. Was he to be put to flight by a couple of älf-women?

He halted when he reached the platform at the top of the tower and commanded the guards to leave him. Here he could sink down to the floor unobserved, his eyes turned up to the blue of the sky.

Splendid weather all around and inside me a raging storm. Sinthoras hated being ruled by his emotions. Reason dictated he should take Yantarai as his partner; his political associates would applaud his choice. But everything else, his artistic side, his vital älf nature, longed for union with Timanris. She enriched his life rather than furthering his career.

I've never known a quandary like this. Samusin must really hate him.

Sinthoras watched as small clouds gathered; it grew darker; night approached and the stars came out; the bright moon moved slowly across the firmament—and he was just sitting there, on the floor. He was thinking about his situation and coming up with one decision after another, only to reject each one immediately . . .

At last he got to his feet. The decision must fall in favor of Timanris. It must! Contrary to all his sensible, logical thought.

But first he had to keep his promise; he needed to tell the Inextinguishables the srinks would not be participating in the invasion.

It was pure chance that Raleeha was in the same fortress on the same island at the same time as her previous owner. She had been hoping, with Caphalor's permission, to have a final meeting with her brother,

Farron, but the request had been turned down. She sat there, her gifts for him piled on the table, and was waiting in vain when she suddenly heard Sinthoras' voice; he was in the next room . . .

Stay where you are. Make sure you are not noticed. It was hard not to spring to her feet, knock at his door and call him out under some excuse or other; to breathe in the smell of him, to recognize the outline of his shape and to imagine his countenance. It was almost intolerable how much she had missed him. He meant so much to her.

After a while she heard a woman's voice and a murmured conversation quickly ended.

When the talk in the next room stopped, Raleeha was overcome with intense hatred for this mysterious älf-woman. The sounds coming through the wall were unambiguous; what the älf-woman was doing with Raleeha's previous owner was exactly what she herself had always dreamed of. It would never be possible, of course, for her.

Go! Don't torture yourself, said her inner voice. But Raleeha could not tear herself away from the wall. She forced herself to listen.

The lovemaking ended after an almost interminable amount of time and then a second älf-woman arrived: Yantarai. Her voice was familiar. Then she heard Sinthoras leave the room hurriedly.

He would never choose me. I should return to my own people and stop telling myself I could be anything other than a slave here in Dsôn. She turned to leave, deciding to ask Caphalor to release her. The treaties were signed now and there was no reason to keep her here as a hostage.

On the way out she bumped into someone—it felt like an älf-woman—and the sketches she had intended for her brother scattered onto the ground. They were designs etched with a quill knife on thick parchment. She had learned to check her lines by running her fingertips over the marks. The sketches were drawn from memory: the sights of Dsôn.

"Forgive me," she said, falling to her knees both to show humility and to try to gather up all the sketches.

"I should have been more careful," said the älf-woman.

It was too much! Raleeha had recognized the älf-woman's voice and did not answer, continuing her search for the dropped pieces of parchment. *Where have they got to?*

"Remarkable!" exclaimed the älf-woman. Raleeha could hear that she was leafing through the sketches. "These are extraordinary pieces of work."

She stood up and bowed. "It is nothing, mistress." *Give them back! I don't want you touching them*!

"What is your name?"

"Raleeha, mistress."

"Oh, so you are *that* Raleeha—the slave with the strange story? My name is Timanris." The papers rustled again. "No one said you were this talented. For a human these drawings are amazing."

All this attention was too much for Raleeha, *and why doesn't she call me a barbarian?* "They are just scribbles and scratches."

"You call them scribbles?" Timanris cut in. "Child, how can you say that?" She sounded completely taken with what she was looking at. Enthusiastically she said, "I'll talk to your master. You are Caphalor's, aren't you? I must introduce you to my father. I'd like him to look at your work."

Don't do that. "Mistress, I am only a slave, I have no rights—"

"Stop, Raleeha. You are a human woman who entered service with the älfar voluntarily." She could hear a smile in Timanris' voice. "In my view you are not a slave but an artist. An undiscovered artist. I wonder how your owner failed to notice your talent."

Raleeha wanted to leave. The last thing she needed was to have her rival speak up for her—and yet she was flattered by the praise. She decided to remain silent.

"Great. That's agreed, then," Timanris exclaimed. "I'll speak to Caphalor. I'll take one of these pictures with me. I can hardly wait to show my father." Raleeha felt a touch on her shoulder and the other drawings were pressed back into her hands. "You will hear from me."

An unworthy thought crept into Raleeha's head. If she were given the opportunity to be alone with this rival, what might she do? An accident? A shove at the top of a flight of stairs? Or over a parapet? And she could be at hand immediately to comfort Sinthoras in his grief . . .

No! Even if she dies he would never take me. Raleeha hurried on, hoping to escape these whispers in her mind.

But an idea had taken root. She was now thinking like an älf.

Ishím Voróo (The Outer Lands), älfar realm
Dsôn Faïmon, Radial Arm Wèlèron,
4371st division of unendingness (5199th solar cycle),
winter.

Caphalor entered the tent where the obboona had said she would expect him.

All but one of the lamps had been doused and so far he was alone. *She is late. Perhaps it is a game to show how much power she has.* She could afford to make him wait.

He took a seat, his swords placed in his lap. The freshening breeze tugged at the canvas shrouds.

The scouts had reported that upward of 2,000 srinks were lurking in the nearby forests: troops dancing to the obboona's tune or, rather, fighting at the sound of her whistle.

Caphalor had met with the barbarian prince. He'd asked whether Lotor would assist if he needed to get rid of the flesh-stealer without suspicion falling on him. *When she dies, I must be somewhere else, otherwise we will never get the srinks to comply.* Lotor had given no answer as yet.

His thoughts wandered back to Raleeha and to his resolution to send her away. *To banish her, more like.* He would take her along to his next meeting with Lotor and remove her slave collar and warn her never to return to Dsôn Faïmon. *It is better. My place is with my life-partner, I must not carry these dreams in my head. They can come to nothing.* His conscience was clear now he had made the decision and that calmed him.

Hoofbeats approached the tent and Caphalor stood up. An älf-woman entered.

"Enoïla? What are you doing here?" he asked in surprise. He saw only the vague outline of her face, but the yellow strands in her dark hair glowed in the dim light. "You must leave at once! The flesh-stealer will be back any time now and she must not see you!"

"Why not?" she whispered.

"Why do you ask? I have to persuade her not to insist on marrying me. It'll never work if she sees you." He listened, but detected no footsteps. "Has something happened? Is that why you've come?" He went over to her and took her in his arms. "Forgive me for not asking straightaway. I am too . . ." Caphalor could not go on.

Enoïla's face was like a mask, stiff and lifeless. The color of her eyes was not right! He turned the wick up higher. The light flickered in the breeze.

There was blood round her eyes and more had been wiped away under the nose. The skin was torn in places and at her throat there were further traces of blood.

Caphalor looked at her black hair. The blond strands were placed correctly. *The fragrance is Enoïla's.* "What . . . has happened . . . ?" He tried to fend off the horrific realization that was dawning on him. He pulled slowly at one of the yellow strands in her hair and it came away in his hands. Her whole face started to slide, losing its shape, becoming a caricature of her beauty. The skin hung loose, wrinkled and ugly.

Underneath was the burned and blood-stained head of the obboona. "You swore on your partner's life," she giggled. Enoïla's blood sprayed from her lips and wet his face. "Since you were betraying me a second time, my demigod, I have taken what I am due; the things that you value above all else." She smiled and drew the skin of his daughter's face from a small bag hanging at her belt. She threw it down at his feet and stretched out her arms. "You are free of her now, my demigod. Free for me!"

Caphalor had lost the power of speech. He had lost the power of thought. He had lost the power of reason.

He dropped the flayed skin of his life-partner's face, fell to his knees, picked it up once more, held it gently, tried to smooth the hair, bent over it. Only then did he allow himself to utter a horrendous scream.

The guards stormed in to the tent.

"Don't touch me! I have not hurt him!" Karjuna shouted, laughing. "I am the queen of the srinks! I am protected by the word of the Inextinguishables!"

"Nostàroi!" One of the guard approached him. "Nostàroi, what has happened?"

"He is mourning for his companion," the obboona responded for him. "She has found her death. It was his own fault. He should not have broken his word."

More slowly than a leaf falling to earth on a windless day, Caphalor lifted his head.

Fury lines covered his countenance. He put down his life-companion's flayed skin and got to his feet. He seemed to be gathering his energies, preparing for a mighty eruption. A growl escaped from his throat, growing louder and louder, becoming a roar, full of pain and hatred. His fingers sought the hilts of his swords.

"You must not harm me, my demigod." Karjuna said uncertainly. "You swore an oath and you broke it. Are you also going to break the solemn agreement your rulers made?" She placed her whistle between her lips. She was afraid; even the guards drew back from the nostàroi.

The roar became a groan that increased again in volume to a renewed scream. Swollen veins of anger burst and dark blood flowed down in vertical lines over his pale face. His eyes were transformed into deepest black although it was nighttime.

Caphalor sprang at Karjuna, his short swords held high to stab down at her. The blades sliced into her left shoulder and her right, cutting down through the flesh, splitting the obboona all the way to her hips.

Her body collapsed to the floor.

Caphalor lifted his heel and stamped her skull into the ground with one powerful movement, driving the whistle right through her brain; he kicked her in his rage again and again.

From outside he heard the howling voices of many, many creatures.

"The srinks!" yelled out one of the sentries. "They're attacking!"

"Let them!" cried Caphalor, storming out of the tent. *Let them! They will take losses such as a single warrior has never inflicted.* He leaped up into Sardaî's saddle and looked over to the forest edge. Hundreds of the wild creatures were on their way, rushing to the aid of their queen.

Caphalor did not care how many they were. The greater their number, the more of them would die. He urged the stallion onwards with his heels and raced to the front line, swords raised.

His memories transported him to the past, to Shiimal, where, on his balcony at home he saw Enoïla standing with his daughter Tarlesa, who had saved his life. The idyllic picture vanished as the first row of srinks broke through the illusion with their claws, their muzzles and their nauseating howls.

I have lost everything I cared about, my dearest and my holiest possessions. What good is immortality now to me? "Forgive me for ever doubting what we had, Enoïla," he cried as he thundered through the enemy lines. "I shall be joining you!" Every thrust of his sword found a target. His blades wreaked death.

Chapter XVII

The Inextinguishables knew no fear.

They assembled their troops one mile off from the defense moat and placed themselves at the head of the army.

When the aberrant hordes of Ishím Voróo charged, Nagsor and Nagsar Inàste lifted the veils from their countenances.

Their beauty confounded their adversaries, robbing them of their minds. Driven insane, the enemy started to assault each other, grabbing former allies by the throat and killing them.

Not one of the älfar found it necessary to draw a sword or to release an arrow.

Epocrypha of the Creating Spirit,
2nd Book,
Chapter 1, 6–11

Ishím Voróo (The Outer Lands), älfar realm
Dsôn Faïmon, Radial Arm Wèlèron,
4371st division of unendingness (5199th solar cycle),
winter.

Sinthoras was already on his feet a second after the alarm went off. *It must be a mistake!*

A glance toward the forest showed him that that the mistake was his. The srinks were pouring out of the woods at the far side of the encampment and a lone älf was riding out to confront them, lightning flashes shooting out from his night-mare's fetlocks. Sinthoras thought he could hear the thundering hooves from his vantage point up on the tower. *Who would be crazy enough to take on the whole srink army single-handed?*

Sinthoras quickly realized, from the warrior's posture and the way he fought, who it was: "Caphalor!" *Why would he attempt such a suicidal move?* The älf was normally so level-headed and calm; he would never act like this without an exceptional reason.

The bodyguards and two sentries stormed up to the platform. "Nostàroi," one of them gasped, "what shall we do? Nostàroi Caphalor is attacking the srinks!"

"Why?"

"We don't know. He said he was going to meet their queen for a discussion."

Sinthoras gathered that the discussion had not turned out as expected. *It would have been better to accompany him. I should have gone with him instead of hiding away like this.* "Sound the alarm. The other garrisons must be alerted."

He had to make a decision. If he ordered the catapults fired, he would countermand the orders of the Inextinguishables. If he did not, the älfar would lose one of their greatest heroes. More importantly, Caphalor was bound to enter the lore and legends of the älfar with this solitary ride against the foe. There would be no combatting his reputation then.

The alarm sounded almost at once from the other islands, indicating battle readiness.

Sinthoras watched Caphalor sweeping through the srink lines, his night-mare trampling the enemy monsters under foot. *Without that stallion, Caphalor would have fallen long ago.* The srinks had nothing to pitch against the raging älfar warrior and there were so many of them that they were hindering each other in the melee.

"Nostàroi, your orders?" asked the soldier.

One of Caphalor's guards returned over the drawbridge and was brought up to the platform, where he gave Sinthoras his hurried report on events.

It was love, then. Up to a few moments of unendingness ago, Sinthoras would not have able to understand why anyone would ride to their death for love. He would have laughed at Caphalor's actions and thought him a fool for risking so much in pursuit of revenge. But since meeting Timanris, he had come to know this emotion in himself. It was a strong and wonderful feeling, and now he could understand. The mere thought that the obboona might have done the same thing to Timanris as had happened to Enoïla had him frozen to the core with fear.

Sinthoras took a deep breath and came to a decision.

Caphalor's mind and senses had shut down.

It was as if he were watching himself from above; seeing his night-mare Sardaî press ahead through the foe and his blades move of their own accord. Enemy blood spurted up and their claws lodged in his armor. Like the night-mare, he sported several wounds, but he felt nothing. *Perhaps my inner self is already leaving my body.* He imagined that his soul was flying along behind him like a child's kite pulled along in the wind—only the thinnest of strings connected him to the endingness, and soon that string would snap.

There was a swishing sound and Caphalor saw a bright yellow light fall on the faces of the srinks, intensifying in brilliance. Immediately afterward the fire bombs landed, burst open and released their lethal liquid flame to bathe the nearest srinks in a conflagration, reducing them to ashes.

A new sound was added: the rush of arrows and spears through the air, ripping great holes in the enemy ranks. It made Caphalor think of a gust of wind leveling a path through a cornfield.

The archers on the islands knew their stuff and were able to create wide corridors for him and Sardaî to plunge along in safety, leaping over burned and slaughtered srinks. The night-mare did not falter once, not even when galloping through a wall of fire.

The remaining srinks ran screaming for the woods. Caphalor reckoned there were not more than 300 of them left. Their formations had disintegrated into small groups that would make difficult targets at this distance, even for archers as skilled as the älfar. *300 left out of 2,000.* He had no idea how many of them he had killed himself. He was furious that there were any still alive at all.

Another army appeared out of the trees before the srink survivors reached the shelter of the thicket: Caphalor could see the banners and badges of the barbarians and óarcos.

Their intentions were clear. Following the bellowed commands of Toboribar and Lotor, the shield bearers charged the remaining srinks, their long spears holding off the enemy claws. The flight of the retreating srinks ended in an impenetrable hedge of forged metal spikes.

Shall today not be my last? Caphalor was back within his own body now, experiencing the world with all his senses and feeling the acute pain from his many wounds. His muscles screamed for release and his injuries needed urgent attention.

The largest wound was the one in his heart and it remained untouched by the blood of slaughtered enemies. Caphalor raised his head to the stars, whispering Enoïla's name. *The gods did not wish me to join you.* How he missed her. She was lost and could never return to him, cut out of his heart. Enoïla and their beloved daughter . . .

He lifted and lowered his sword in salute to the barbarians and the óarcos, who bowed their heads in respect.

Caphalor guided his night-mare toward the drawbridge and the island where he saw Sinthoras waiting for him. *I don't care what he says about this.* He reined Sardaî in. "I had no choice—" he began.

"Get your wounds seen to," said Sinthoras, sounding surprisingly gentle.

"I must go to the Inextinguishables," Caphalor responded, his throat dry. Blood was drying on his face and on his hands. "They have to be told what I have done. I shall offer them my life for having disobeyed orders."

"Don't be a fool, Caphalor," Sinthoras replied. "Get down. The Inextinguishables will—"

"I thank you for the support you sent, but I did not want it. My body should be lying between the carcasses of the monsters and my soul should be flying with Enoïla's." He rode past Sinthoras on his nightmare, dropping both his swords in turn. "It makes no sense," he muttered. "None of it makes any sense. They are dead, Sinthoras, so what do I want with eternal life?" Then Caphalor slipped out of the saddle and onto the planks of the wooden bridge.

"Take him to the tower and bring me a healer," commanded Sinthoras, picking up the bloodied swords.

I know how you are feeling. The thought that he might ever suffer a similar loss engendered a terrible fear in his heart.

Sinthoras acknowledged love's great drawback: concern and fear for the beloved. He would ensure Timanris could never go through what happened to Enoïla: he would kill any obboona he encountered.

Ishím Voróo (The Outer Lands), älfar realm
Dsôn Faïmon, Radial Arm Wêlèron,
1371st division of unendingness (5199th solar cycle),
spring.

In the gloom of the island guardroom, Caphalor sat staring at the wall.

A parchment bearing the seal of the Inextinguishables lay unopened before him; he was not interested in their decrees.

He should have been busying himself, like Sinthoras, with arrangements for the coming campaign against Tark Draan; he should have been meeting the commanding officers, poring over maps and making all the preparations needed for any operation of this kind.

For me it is over.

He sat alone in the darkened room.

He had been in the tower for ten moments of unendingness now, not eating, not sleeping. His eyes were dry from staring at the wall in the dark. He did not see the wall. He saw her face, Enoïla's face. And the face of his daughter. *Both lost.*

He would never take his own life, however welcome death might be. He had not been permitted to find his demise on the battlefield in combat with the srinks, and so must find another way to entice death. *By waiting and by doing nothing.*

There was a knock at the door.

Caphalor did not react.

Another knock came and the door opened. Sinthoras entered the room, halted, and stood watching him; then he picked up a chair and came to sit down opposite.

"You have not opened the letter," he said, his tone gentle but reproachful.

"Open it yourself if you want to know what they say. I sent them word that I resign as nostàroi," he said gruffly. It was a long time since he had used his voice at all.

"And why are you still here?"

"Why should I go back to the place where no one is waiting for me? I might just as well sit here."

Sinthoras sighed, reached for the sealed roll of parchment and opened it. "They refuse to accept your resignation," he read. "They insist on your carrying out the tasks of your office and they send their commiserations to you in your loss. You should use the hatred you feel and turn it against the elves." Sinthoras spread the letter out for Caphalor to peruse for himself. "You know everyone in Dsôn Faïmon is talking about you? Everybody is saying you did the right thing."

Caphalor looked up in surprise. "The right thing? We won't have the srinks participating in our invasion force—"

"Forget the srinks! The barbarians and the óarcos came to your aid of their own free will. They had always hated the srinks. Your people are mourning with you and are worried about you," Sinthoras cut in with feeling. "What you have done is already a legend, Caphalor."

"What would I give not to be a legend and have Enoïla by my side," he whispered, black tears coursing down his cheeks.

Sinthoras thought of Timanris and felt his heart grow heavy. Something stabbed him in the center of his body. "I would have done exactly the same in your place," he said after a while, swallowing hard. "Any älf would have done exactly the same, Caphalor. You must remain as nostàroi. Our troops admire you and so do all our allies."

Caphalor looked up. "Your tone of voice says you understand. I would not have expected that. What do you know about love, Sinthoras? Or the unquestioning love of a father for his child?"

"The emotion is new to me, I confess. And yet, know it I do," he admitted to his own amazement. He was not offended by Caphalor's words. "In the past I would not have been able to imagine your pain. Today . . ." He left his sentence hanging in the air.

Caphalor picked up the letter and recognized Nagsor Inàste's writing. "My downfall began with the whole operation against Tark Draan," he said. "It was a campaign I never supported. I did not want it and I did not understand it. I have lost everything because of it." He let the parchment fall to the ground at his feet. "It is more than ironic. Even Samusin would find no justice in this." He turned his face once more to the wall and fell silent.

Sinthoras did not know what to say. He looked down at the parchment roll. Anything that had touched the hand of the Inextinguishables would normally be treated with the greatest of respect, but here lay their missive in the dirt on the floorboards.

Sinthoras got up. "Pull yourself together, Caphalor. Get over your pain and ride into battle in Enoïla's name." He took his leave and went to the door.

"It won't bring her back," Caphalor answered somberly, without looking up. "To Tion with all thoughts of honor and fame and unendingness." He closed his eyes.

Sinthoras left the chamber with a sigh. He would try again when the next day dawned, and keep trying until he had forced his fellow nostàroi out of his black cloud.

While he strode—accompanied by his bodyguard—through the narrow alleys of the tower island, he thought about his letter to the Inextinguishables asking for mercy for Caphalor. That was another action that would previously have been unthinkable for him.

Timanris was changing him. *Is that a good thing?* He hoped that this new soft side would not mean that he would not be able to stand up to his political opponents. *I must appear harder. If they notice I have weakened they will give no quarter.*

Speaking to Caphalor had given him cause to think about his own immortality. He had never considered it before. Älfar lived forever; Inàste had made them superior to other races. A natural death was very rare if it did not occur violently. Extremely old älfar were said to long for death, but the question of suicide never arose. An älf lived forever, like the Inextinguishable Ones.

Sinthoras tried to work out how many divisions of unendingness the oldest älf he knew might have lived through. *Perhaps more than 2,000, but to look at him you would say 900 or less.* He was an art dealer in Dsôn. He was so old that nobody knew anything about his earlier life.

What would be the point of a life like that without Timanris? I shall do everything to keep her safe. His reason tried frantically to force him into marriage with Yantarai, but that voice of reason was growing quieter all the time.

He rode back into camp and headed straight for the green negotiation tent. This was where the charts of the area around the Stone Gateway and the plans of Tark Draan were to be found.

I had no idea we had so little solid knowledge. Rumors, half-truths, travelers' tales—no more than that. Constructing an invasion strategy out of these shreds of information was proving extremely difficult. *You might just as well send an arrow into the middle of the forest and hope it finds a deer.* It could happen, but would be very unlikely. *The groundlings keep a close watch. No foreigners get through into the mountains—whether their intentions are peaceful or warlike.*

Sinthoras dismounted by the massive tent. It needed to be that size to accommodate the giants, trolls and ogres. Inside he saw Lotor and Toboribar and he greeted the whole gathering with a nod. Servants unrolled the maps and charts. "The situation is as follows," he began. "We shall be collating your information today. We need to know what you know about the Stone Gateway. In particular the height and thickness of the containing walls, the nature of the surrounding rock, the layout of the Gray Range and any details of the gate itself, of course. Our scribes can record it all and we'll have it entered on the charts. *I want them to think we know most of the secrets already.* He pointed to the giantess. "You begin."

Gattalind raised her eyebrows. "Well, there's this Gate. And it's big. Bigger than us. Taller. Higher, I mean." She scratched her head. "And it's made of stone. That's about all."

Sinthoras smiled, but he was not pleased. *May the gods help us if we don't learn more than that today.* He tried not to let his disappointment show, "Toboribar, can you enlighten us with the knowledge the óarcos have gathered?"

A soldier scurried into the tent and came up to him.

"Nostàroi, there's someone waiting to see you," was the whispered message.

"Is there a further delegation?"

"It is a gàlran zhadar."

Sinthoras went ice cold. *What shall I do?* It could be the same gàlran zhadar they had stolen from—it was bad enough that he had survived. But why would he leave his sky fortress to chase a pair of petty thieves? "Is he alone?"

"Yes, Nostàroi."

"What does he want?" He glanced at Toboribar. "Carry on, please. The scribes will record every word you say," he said.

"He wanted to speak to you, Nostàroi. And to Nostàroi Caphalor."

He'll be here to demand the return of his vial, or to insist on compensation. This is not a good time. Sinthoras rose. "Excuse me," he said as he left the tent. "There's a new guest to be welcomed." He saw the curiosity written on their faces, but gave no further hints. In their eyes a gàlran zhadar outside of his sky fortress meant trouble—a whole world of it.

The gàlran zhadar was waiting outside the tent in full armor, his war hammers jammed right and left into his wide belt. He looked calm, rather than belligerent. Sinthoras breathed more easily. Behind the dwarf-like being stood three pack animals loaded with baggage.

The gålran zhadar made a point of looking around slowly as if he were on a spying mission and needed to remember every detail of the camp. "The Inextinguishables are putting their threat into action," he said, instead of a formal greeting; the dark voice made for an uncomfortable feeling in Sinthoras' stomach. "More or less every race is at your council of war." Now he turned his gaze on Sinthoras himself. "And you've been made a nostàroi, as I hear. That's a fine reward for a *thief.*"

Sinthoras put down the spear that had once belonged to the gålran zhadar. "There is nothing wrong with stealing from a robber," he replied, as nonchalantly as he could. "I don't think I need to accept criticism from one such as yourself."

"I assume I shall have my property returned?"

"No. Your soldiers already tried that. To no avail."

The gålran zhadar calmly laid his hands on the hammer heads. "I did not really expect you to say otherwise."

"So there's something you want from myself and Caphalor?"

"I want to know who was insane enough to give the vial to the demon creature."

"That is none of your business." Sinthoras was not going to confess to his own part in this. It had been an accident, after all. *I am innocent.* "What about it?"

Now the gålran zhadar was at a loss. "You must be trying to make fun of me, älf." He threw back his head and laughed loud enough to flap the canvas walls of every tent in the camp. "How could you not have known what it was you were stealing?"

As Sinthoras did not want to admit any complicity he evaded the issue: "It's nothing to do with you." *Go on, tell me the secret of the vial's contents.* He could not think of a way to entice the tantalizing truth out of the gålran zhadar without letting on that he was completely ignorant. *I'll wager he's already seen through me.*

"Well," said the other, wiping the tears of laughter from his eyes. "That's very funny. Disastrous for every single race and every single tribe on the face of the land, but a good joke. Yes, send him off to Tark Draan. Otherwise it means the end for the whole of Ishím Voróo. Including, of course, your Star Realm." He grinned while he was saying this. "Let's forget the vial. How are your war preparations getting along?"

Sinthoras could make neither head nor tail of what he had been told, but he had a very uneasy feeling about it. He was convinced the gâlran zhadar was not lying. "What is it that you want, given that you don't believe you will get your things back?"

"I want to put a proposition to you and Caphalor," came the prompt answer. "I know a weak point in the defenses for the Stone Gateway."

"You do?"

"The älfar are not the only ones who have a very long lifespan. Who knows, maybe I am even older than the Inextinguishables themselves?" He was obviously enjoying provoking Sinthoras. "I have had the opportunity to learn and do a great deal."

This is probably going to be of more use than the trash they're coming out with back in the negotiation tent. "What is this weak point you mention?" Sinthoras was being cautious. He knew his adversary to be extremely dangerous.

The gâlran zhadar rubbed his beard with his right hand. "You can see I look very like a dwarf. I sent one of my spies over to the groundlings. I thought it would be a good idea in case one day—I mean, one moment of unendingness, as you like to call it—I wanted to go to Tark Draan without being stopped. I could help you."

Don't believe everything he says. Sinthoras studied the gâlran zhadar carefully. "How do I know that what you are telling me is true?"

"The Stone Gateway is secured with five magic bolts that can only be opened with a specific incantation. I won't stop you if you want to go to the Northern Pass and check it out." He grinned at the älf. "Oh, and there aren't many who know the password, but guess who does, älf?"

"And you want what in return? A kingdom of your own in Tark Draan? Or here in Ishím Voróo?" Sinthoras saw the chance to gain an advantage. What with Caphalor's heroic ride and those rumors about Robonor, his own prestige had not exactly risen.

The gâlran zhadar burst out laughing again. "Do you know what, älf? If I want a kingdom or a piece of land, I take it. I don't need anyone's permission. To be honest with you: I'm getting a bit fed up with my

castle and I want to do something new with my life, but I know Ishím
Voróo inside out already." He leaned forward. "What I want is access to
Phondrasôn."

Sinthoras realized he was standing there with his mouth open like a
troll. *Phondrasôn?* The underground realm was something else entirely:
lawless violence ruled. If you went there, you were desperate to die in
combat, or you were fleeing some terrible fate. It was a kind of dungeon,
a place of banishment used by all the races. There were at least seven
entrances.

The gålran zhadar was delighted at the effect. "I know you älfar
send your young there to test them, so they may return either as hard-
ened warriors—or not at all. The other races send their worst criminals there."

"And that's where you want to go?" Sinthoras thought about the evil
nest of hideous creatures. Nobody had ever investigated it because it was
too dark and too deadly. The Inextinguishables would never entertain
the idea of sacrificing an army to explore and chart useless underground
caverns.

"The entrances to Phondrasôn are hidden and well-guarded, and
probably beset with countless traps. I admit I shan't be able to get there
without your agreement."

Sinthoras saw again the maze of caves and tunnels and ravines made
by the work of water and by the tools of banished hands. He had not
gone far in and had had to confront a hundred hungry óarcos and two
lizard-like monsters before escaping by the skin of his teeth to return, a
seasoned warrior, to his parents. "To Phondrasôn," he repeated incredu-
lously. "You want to exchange your life for certain death?"

"Let that be my concern. I want to exchange the boredom of security for the chance of constant challenge." The gålran zhadar rubbed his
nose. "What do you say? Are you going to give me access? I can arrange
for you to meet my spy beforehand: he can be at the Gateway the day
you arrive."

"It seems all a bit dubious to my ears." Sinthoras pretended not to
be interested. *In reality, it is an offer that would not cost me anything at
all.* It certainly meant a further option for conquering the realm of the

groundlings if the combined strengths of the giants and the ogres were to prove insufficient.

"Then I shall extend my offer," said the gålran zhadar. "The defenders have some unexploited gas sources in their territory that they have not yet discovered. My spy would be in a position to adjust the gas source so that it enters the tunnels where the groundlings live. This would cause them to fall ill."

Sinthoras pricked up his ears at this. "Is that all?"

"I'm practically handing you the Gateway on a plate, älf! You won't need to fight for it at all!"

"That's if what you say is true, and I'm sure the groundlings are tougher than you think; they may survive the gas attacks." *I'm sure you've got something else up your sleeve.*

The gålran zhadar pursed his lips. "A thief and impertinent into the bargain!"

"You're the one that wants access to Phondrasôn, not me." Sinthoras studied the end of his spear casually.

"My spy has a potion the fflecx brewed up. He can poison their water supply. By the time they've found out what's happening, the invasion should be over and done with."

Sinthoras smiled at him. "So there we have it."

All in all he did not get the impression the gålran zhadar was making the whole thing up. The reward he was demanding, on the other hand, was insignificant. "I will speak with my rulers. Wait in one of the tents until I tell you what they decide."

"Don't take too long. The demon is on his way here." He winked at Sinthoras. "They say that you are the one that controls him, but you've got the wrong end of the stick there. You broke the vial and you've let a vicious power loose, älf!" He laughed. "And you had no idea what you were doing. One of your gods must have been having a really bad day when he guided your steps." The gålran zhadar went over to the pack horses and slit open the sacks.

Out tumbled several fflecx corpses in various stages of decay and putrefaction; black stinking blood dripped out of their bodies. This was not normal.

"See what the demon has done with Black Gnomes."

"So he's killed them. What's new?" replied Sinthoras.

"He brings them back to life. His evil pervades the earth, poisoning ground, water, plants, and animals." The gâlran zhadar glanced at the cadavers. "The fact they're not moving yet means his power hasn't reached this far. That's good news for you, but he can make very quick progress. He has taken over all the fflecx except for Munumon and a handful of his closest followers. If these guys here open their eyes and rise up, you'll know how far the demon has traveled. Tell that to your rulers and get a move on. Neither they nor I can halt the demon. Not *any longer.*"

Sinthoras knew why the words had been stressed. *That accursed vial.* "The demon will obey me," he said stubbornly.

"No. He'll respond to your summons, that's all." The gâlran zhadar turned round and headed for the tent the älf had indicated. "Best get a move on," he repeated and sounded quite amused. *Schadenfreude* was the word—delight in others' distress.

Ishím Voróo (The Outer Lands), älfar realm
Dsôn Faïmon, Radial Arm Wêlèron,
4371st division of unendingness (5199th solar cycle),
spring.

Why is it taking so long? Caphalor had still not moved.

He was now only a shadow of the celebrated älfar hero. He had spent daystar-tides and moon-tides in his chamber in the island tower while Sinthoras had supervised all the campaign preparations.

Sinthoras sat with him again, as he did so often, reporting on progress. He told Caphalor about the gâlran zhadar, told him about their plans and told him how the Inextinguishables had responded to the latest offer. Caphalor continued to stare at the wall without showing any reaction. *Why was it taking so long?* He was waiting for death.

But death was not interested; it was as if it were avoiding him and wanted to prove that he did not have control. Caphalor lifted his arm. *No weakness even.*

Fury rose: anger at death itself. Death had decided to make a fool of him and was refusing him the chance to be reunited with his loved ones.

Then he heard something that made him stop gazing at the wall and turn his eyes to Sinthoras.

"We found out how the obboona got to Dsôn without being seen," said Sinthoras, flinching back when Caphalor's head suddenly jerked round. "The patrols had not checked a floating island properly. One of those reed mats had the obboona and a number of srinks concealed below it. That's how they managed to reach the other bank."

Caphalor clamped his jaws together. *The patrol could have prevented Enoïla's and Tarlesa's horrendous deaths! Samusin! See that they pay with their lives!*

"So it was sheer negligence that condemned my wife and daughter?" he croaked. His voice was husky with lack of use. "It's one of the duties of the island guards to burn off and sink anything found floating in the defense moat."

"I know. They did it, but they did it too late. We have punished the guards responsible."

"Are they dead yet?"

Sinthoras said nothing for a while, and then answered: "You have to understand—"

"How did you punish them?" Caphalor yelled. "Have you deprived them of whatever is dearest? Have you cut out their hearts and forced them to go on living?" *If they were here now I would strangle them with my bare hands.*

"They have been banished, Caphalor. There could be no harsher penalty for them."

"Yes, there could," he answered with sullen fury. "Tell me where their families live and I—" He stopped in obvious distress. "Do you see what the obboona has done to me? I am thirsting for the blood of my own people!"

"No one would reproach you. I can imagine how you are feeling."

For a long while they both sat in silence. Caphalor fought down his anger and looked at Sinthoras. "Why have the Inextinguishables not yet sent news of my release from office?"

"Why do you think they would do that?"

"Because I am doing nothing. Because I couldn't care less about this war and I'm leaving everything to you. Hero or not, I'm good for nothing at all." He noticed the flicker in Sinthoras' eyes and understood suddenly. "You're covering for me?"

"Let's just say I'm not necessarily keeping them totally in the picture . . ."

Caphalor gave a bitter laugh. "So that's where we are. Once upon a time we were bitter rivals and now you are protecting my status as nostàroi. Are you doing that to place yourself in a better light, or are you enjoying humiliating and outshining me for a splinter of unendingness?"

"If that was what I wanted," said Sinthoras, getting up, "I could have done it a long time ago. You should be up on your night-mare, setting off to war in Tark Draan, Caphalor." He opened the door. "And I think death is of the same opinion. Otherwise I would have found you lying here lifeless." He went out and closed the door behind him.

Caphalor stared into the gloom and waited for inspiration. *Or else the courage to commit the ultimate unspeakable act.* His left hand closed on the handle of his dagger and the blade glimmered, reflecting the half-light.

To take one's own life, abusing the immortality conferred by the gods, was a grave sin. His name would be inscribed in the hall of shame and remain there for all eternity, laden with curses and hated forever by every älf.

Even a hero such as myself is not safe from that fate. Caphalor balanced the familiar weapon in his hands. It had taken the life of many a foe and now it was about to cause his own blood to flow. *I wonder what you will do, Death*, he thought with a smile on his lips. *You can't avoid me forever.* He pressed the blade tip against his heart.

There came a knock at the door.

"Go away, Sinthoras!" he shouted. "I don't want to hear any more of your eternal reports!"

"It's not Sinthoras," said a female älf voice. "My name is Timanris. I must speak to you urgently, Nostàroi." *Maybe I should see her before mortality overtakes me.* Caphalor was curious to see what she looked like properly, this älf-woman who had bewitched Sinthoras and introduced him to the power of love—his earlier fleeting glance of her had not been enough. He lowered the dagger. "Come in, but keep it short."

The door swung open and she came in. "I won't keep you long." Her steps slowed when she saw the state he was in. She noted the long knife in his hand and her pupils widened for one or two heartbeats. "You don't look—"

"I know perfectly well what I look like," he interrupted roughly. "What do you want?"

Timanris bowed. "I am here to ask you to sell me your slave Raleeha."

He frowned sharply. "Why Raleeha?"

"I came across her by chance and caught sight of some of her drawings. For a human she possesses extraordinary artistic talent and despite her blindness she has created work that is unique in quality." She stepped forward and placed a thick piece of parchment on the table. It showed an engraved sketch of an älfar cityscape. The details were amazingly clear. "How many blind älfar do you know who could produce anything like this?"

In my pain I had completely forgotten her. He was ashamed. He was now in a position to help the girl. Caphalor did not betray the fact that Raleeha might one day regain the sight of one eye. "Not one," he agreed. "You want Raleeha?"

"Yes. Her talent should be fostered."

"She is a slave!" He laughed. "Why would you want to do that?"

"She is a human who, of her own free will, took up service with a certain älf. He passed her to you and I want to buy her now."

"If I follow your line of argument, I am being asked to sell a barbarian that I should not think of as my property in the first place," he said. She nodded. He understood why Sinthoras was attracted to her, but she could not compete with Enoïla. "Then ask Raleeha, I release her."

Timanris was surprised. "Nostàroi, are you serious?"

"Of course, she is free." He pulled the parchment over, took a quill pen and some ink and wrote that he laid no claim to Raleeha. "You are completely in the right. If Raleeha wants to go with you, you should take her in." He passed the parchment back to her.

She bowed. "My thanks, Nostàroi." Timanris indicated the dagger. "Do not do it. It would be more than one life you would be destroying."

Caphalor essayed a tired smile. "You think those few words will change my mind when I have spent so long making my decision?"

"Apart from your own people's disappointment at the loss of a hero, you would be punishing the wrong person by your death."

"Is that so?" He sat up straight. "I killed the one who murdered my family, but it gave me no satisfaction. Who should I slaughter now, in order to feel better? How many guilty can there be? When I die, my pain dies."

Timanris slowly shrugged her shoulders. "I cannot say, Nostàroi. I have no words of consolation or cheer. But do not do it; think of one thing that gives you the courage to live and cling to that thought until you find a better one. Or until you find a new love." She took the parchment.

"A new love?" He shot out of the chair and raised the dagger as if about to stab her. "How dare you speak to me of some new love? You never knew Enoïla. Nobody can replace her, nobody!" He pointed to the door. "Get out! Take Raleeha and get out!"

Timanris retreated, her eyes on the knife in his hand. She left the chamber without a further word.

If only I were already dead! Caphalor waited until she had left and then hurled the dagger at the closed door in exasperated fury: the blade buried itself deep into the wood.

He threw himself back into the chair and drummed his clenched fists against his temples. *Think of something that gives me the courage to live and then cling to that thought.*

My undoing, my misfortune—it all began with the whole campaign against Tark Draan. A war I never wanted. Then, all of a sudden, the saving thought occurred to him: *I will drown my fury and my grief in the blood of the land that took my consort and my daughter from me. Tark Draan must be exterminated. Every last old person. Every last child. They must all pay for the loss of Enoïla and Tarlesa.* He would cling to this idea: Tark Draan bore the guilt, Tark Draan and the cowardly elves that had hidden away there. Only after Tark Draan and the elves had fallen would he take his own life, should he not by then have fallen in battle. *Then Enoïla can rest and my soul can be at peace.*

Caphalor slowly let his arms fall and his hands relax. Getting to his feet, he went over to the window and opened the shutters to let in the starlight and fill his lungs with the cool night air.

With every fresh breath his resolve strengthened. He called for one of his servants, demanding food and drink. "And tell Sinthoras that I ride at his side on the morrow."

The älf put on his armor, feeling its familiar weight on his body once more. Life was returning, returning to let him bring death. *I shall be the cruelest, most relentless enemy of the elves and of any who shelter or support them. This is my solemn oath.*

Chapter XVIII

Our enemies served us in manifold ways.

We ground their bones into gravel for our pavements.

Their skin provided us with canvases and their blood was the binding agent for our paints.

We made ropes and cords and string from their tendons for our wind chimes.

Every part of our enemies was used. For art.

Exquisite and unsurpassable art.

Epocrypha of the Creating Spirit,
2nd Book,
Chapter 2, 12–20

Ishím Voróo (The Outer Lands), älfar realm Dsôn Faïmon, Dsôn, 4371st division of unendingness (5199th solar cycle), spring.

The high-ceilinged room where Raleeha sat was flooded with sunlight. She could discern the windows as bright rectangles with circular shapes at bottom and top.

My sight is getting better. Shadows had become vague shapes with more details. She could not yet distinguish faces, but could see faint ovals with indications of eyes, noses and mouths; colors were slowly returning. For the time being she was keeping the information about these improvements to herself.

As she waited for Timanris to return with her artist father, she let her thoughts stray at will.

A new house to get accustomed to. New corridors and rooms and halls. But Raleeha had consented at once when she heard of Caphalor's decision. Timanris had made eager promises about taking her under her wing and promoting her art. Freedom could wait.

Raleeha had another reason for wanting to take up the offer. She would be with Timanris and that meant that she would also be near Sinthoras, at least in spirit. The thought that she might come across him here—might hear his voice and catch his scent—delighted her. Together with the chance to draw and paint and the privilege of observing him at his art—perfection.

But whenever she thought amorously of Sinthoras, evil ideas concerning Timanris would creep into her mind. Thoughts about death and accidents, fatal accidents. Yet one more good reason to accept service with the älf-woman . . .

No! Raleeha struggled to suppress these inner voices, but part of her waited for the opportunity to remove her rival. Her common sense told her that it was madness to dream of Sinthoras ever choosing her as a mate rather than taking an älf-woman as his partner. *Yantarai is still in the picture. You cannot kill all the female älfar in Dsôn.*

But, countered the malicious voices, *he might take you back in his service and then he might see you as something he inherits from her.*

"I must not think like this," Raleeha told herself sadly as she smoothed down her gray slave attire, tidied her hair and adjusted the black lace to enable her to see through the blindfold. She heard voices in the corridor. The door opened and the two artists, father and daughter, entered the room.

Raleeha stood up and bowed to them.

"Pretty enough," said Timansor. For a male älf, his vocal range was strangely high and he spoke in an unusual way, emphasizing words differently. These were liberties an artist could afford to take. "So, what people say is true."

Raleeha kept her head bowed, but her eye flicked upward. She saw a white robe and the end of a yellow stole, which clearly rested over his shoulder. The ends of his hair were white and reflected the sunlight, or perhaps it was just part of the robe; her sight was not yet good enough to pick out the detail. *What should I say in reply?* She went for silent caution.

The two älfar walked past her over to a broad table, chatting quietly to each other; there was an occasional rustle as parchment sheets were shifted. *They are looking at my work!* Her heart started to race. She would never have dreamed of her drawings attracting the attention of an älfar artist.

"Come over here," commanded Timanris. "My father wants to speak to you."

"Yes, mistress." Raleeha moved to the table and stood in front of the älfar.

"You have a gift," said Timansor. "With your blindness and your talent you have created unique works. No artist in Dsôn could have done these. Of course, there are blind artists who are sculptors, but no one else can do what you have done, Raleeha."

"Thank you, sir," she answered, bowing once more. She was ecstatic. "Such appreciation is new for me and makes me all the happier." *If only Farron could hear what this artist thinks of my work.*

"Your oeuvre is extraordinary. I would like to exhibit your works and present them to my circle of friends, who are always eager to be shown something new," he went on. It was difficult for Raleeha to understand what he was saying; he had a flowery and extravagant manner of speech. "They will pay a fortune for one of these parchments." He tidied the drawings into a pile. "However, I cannot tell them that they have been executed by a slave."

Raleeha swallowed. "Sir, what—"

"We will say they were done by a blind älf who wishes to remain anonymous." Timansor wove a legend for her. "That will impress them even more. You will receive part of the money from the sales, but we won't let you have too much. After all, you are only a slave, Raleeha."

"Sir, your daughter said she would promote my talent and shelter me. I did not hear the word slave being used."

Timansor spoke with conviction. "It is your lot as a nonälf to live here in Dsôn without rights. That is the same as being a slave. But do not be downhearted, be glad instead that we will make your work immortal: your drawings will adorn the walls of our most significant citizens."

Raleeha realized what he was telling her. *I shall get no recognition at all!* She bit her lip to stop herself protesting. *It's the price I'll have to pay if I want to be near Sinthoras. And at least I shall be earning a few coins of my own.* The resentment, however, was a sharp thorn in her side, digging deeper in with each breath.

Timansor stepped back from the table and called for a slave to carry the parchments. He told the man to take them for framing, so that the precious drawings could be protected. Raleeha was forced to listen to the artist praising them as someone else's work. Then he left the room.

Raleeha continued to stand at the now empty table. She felt as though she had been robbed.

"That was not my idea," Timanris said quietly. She sounded unhappy. "Father is convinced we can't say that humans are capable of artistic creation of this standard." She came round the table and placed her hand on the girl's shoulder; for an älf to attempt to console anyone was a rare gesture indeed. "I tried to get him to change his mind because you deserve the recognition, but he is my father and I shall not dispute what he says. I trust his judgment. You shall have all the money, we do not need it."

"I am pleased to be able to help you and your house achieve increased esteem," Raleeha managed to say, her lips quivering. "I shall make even more of an effort with my next pictures." *You must get away from here,* her reason told her. *You can see how they treat you.*

"You are a good human, Raleeha." Timanris removed her hand from the girl's shoulder. "There's one more thing I wanted to say: my father called you a slave and everybody will think that you are my property, but you are free. If you want to leave me and leave the Star Realm, I shall not stop you. I shall write you a pass that guarantees unhindered passage to your brother. This was Caphalor's intention and I share it wholeheartedly."

"I shall stay, mistress," she said, bowing. *For Sinthoras, not for you.* "You are too good to me."

"I am glad!" Timanris sounded both relieved and delighted. "Have you been shown to your room yet? Are you happy with it?"

"Yes, mistress. Thank you. I appreciate having a chamber away from the slave quarters. Soon I shall know my way around the house and I shall be able to carry out your instructions."

"So you do not believe me? I tell you, you are not a slave and you will not be asked to carry out menial tasks, Raleeha. I want you to be able to spend all your time on your art." Timanris passed her, "I shall be telling Sinthoras that I have taken on his former slave. I wonder what he will say?" She laughed. "Maybe he'll want you back!"

How wonderful that would be! "I do not think so, mistress," she said, inclining her head. "He is glad to be rid of me."

Timanris left the room and Raleeha made her way to her new chamber. She knew what she would be sketching next: a miniature portrait of Timanris. Her mistress would be able to give it to Sinthoras in the form of a medallion. *I could put almost invisible lines in the etching to represent my own face. Sinthoras will wear the medallion over his heart and he'll never know it bears my likeness.* The idea pleased her.

Arriving at a steep stairway between first and second floors, she noticed the spears and banners on the wall.

She ran her finger experimentally along the four-sided blade. She gave a sharp intake of breath and a drop of blood appeared on the tip of her finger. A mere touch had been enough to make a cut.

What might that steel blade effect, whispered her inner voice, *if it were thrust into the tender body of a female älf? And what if that body were then pushed down these very stairs?*

Raleeha hurried past the weapons on the wall and made her way to her quarters.

Ishím Voróo (The Outer Lands), älfar realm
Dsôn Faïmon, Radial Arm Wèlèron,
1371st division of unendingness (5199th solar cycle),
spring.

As Caphalor strode into the assembly tent in full armor with his short swords on his back, Sinthoras observed a number of surprised looks. *They have noticed a change in him. His aura is darker and his features are somber. His presence is more terrifying than ever. It is hatred and a fervent death wish that have made him like this—he is not even employing our talent for inspiring fear.*

Sinthoras had been so convinced the other nostàroi would never leave his chamber that he was doubly glad to see him join them for the briefing. He indicated a seat next to his own at the head of the table.

Caphalor advanced, but remained standing, letting his solemn gaze roam slowly over every one of the leaders gathered there: beasts and barbarians alike. "I should like to apologize for the prolonged period of inactivity on my part," he addressed them. "I have been neglecting my task and have given you the impression that I have become indifferent to the outcome of our campaign. I give you all my solemn oath that from now on I shall show myself worthy of the high office of nostàroi. Tark Draan must fall to our forces and shall be subjected to your rule. It is for you to break up the human kingdoms." Dark lines of fury started to cross his face. "But the elves are to be left to us!" He sat down and took up a cup of wine.

Sinthoras could hardly believe his eyes, as one by one all the leaders, starting with Lotor and Toboribar strode over to Caphalor and bowed deeply before him, conveying sympathy and respect. *Is this possible?* He found himself unable to resist the strength of feeling in the gathering; he, too, stretched out a hand and pressed Caphalor's arm. The enmity that had driven him previously had vanished.

Caphalor looked at him and gave him a sad smile in response. The two nostàroi had buried their differences.

Someone pushed their way into the tent and a voice thundered, "I can't wait forever. What is the answer?" Heads swiveled in his direction as the gålran zhadar stomped in. "What have the Inextinguishables decided?"

Sinthoras took in the sight of the dwarf-like figure, his feet planted determinedly apart, horny hands aggressively on the hammer heads and nose boldly pointed upward. *He knows no fear. He's not afraid of the giants and he's not afraid of us.* He thought back to their clash with misgivings.

"It is a good thing you are here, gålran zhadar," he said calmly. "My rulers have notified me that they accept your offer. They are willing to take the risk of trusting what you say."

"And so they should, because it is the truth," he replied with a smile that would have made any lesser creature quake. "I will let my spy on the other side know what we want him to do. As soon as I have gained entry to Phondrasôn, I shall tell you the secret sign you have to give to my spy and then he will open the gate for you."

Hardly were the words out of his mouth before the delegates began to express their surprise. They had not been told that the gålran zhadar had access to such knowledge.

"Good," said Sinthoras, relishing the respectful and admiring glances coming his way. "I shall have the rulers' letter brought to you. I have ten warriors ready and waiting to accompany you to the entrance. Write down what we need to know."

"That is how it will be." The gålran zhadar grinned. "How did you manage to escape the effects of the lethal fflecx poison? You must have known that the parchment you stole contained the formulae for many vital antidotes?" He read from the expression on Sinthoras' face that this had not been the case and he gave a gleefully malicious belly laugh. "Oh, so you didn't know you were carrying the recipe for your own antidote?"

"Of course we knew," responded Caphalor coldly. "We deciphered it and were thus able to save our own lives. Would we be standing before you otherwise, gålran zhadar?"

Sinthoras was still battling with his astonishment. *So the obboona was tricking us then, too!* She had held the key to their recovery in her hands, but had pretended not to know what the writing meant.

"But of course." The gålran zhadar gazed round at the assembled delegates. "An illustrious gathering of mighty warriors. It will be easy for you to conquer Tark Draan, especially now you can call on the help of the demon." Again there was more than a touch of malice in his tone.

"Leave now!" ordered Sinthoras, expecting trickery from the dwarf-like creature on his departure, but the gålran zhadar did not do him that favor.

"You will find out," the gålran zhadar prophesied. "You will find out the *true* power of your new ally soon enough." He fixed his eyes on Sinthoras as if he knew that it had been him who had given the vial to the demon. "May your gods be with you." He turned and left the tent.

Farron Lotor got to his feet. "Nostàroi, may I learn what the gålran zhadar meant by that?"

Toboribar stood up as well. "You have had us plan a prolonged and complicated siege and all the time you knew how to simply open the gate? Is this an älfar idea of a joke?"

Sinthoras held up his arms in a commanding gesture as beasts and barbarians talked excitedly among themselves. "Quiet! I shall not make the mistake of relying on what he says. If the conventional strategies fail we still have the other possibility to fall back on." He did not go into details. *Really annoying that so many ears had to hear what the gålran zhadar said, but I could never have got him to keep it secret.* "My orders are as follows: we will cease all visible preparations for getting through the Stone Gateway. I insist that none of you, beast or barbarian, goes anywhere in sight of the gate." There was not a single whisper. All the delegates were hanging on his instructions. "We want to keep the groundlings in the dark—they must suspect nothing. In the meantime, the gålran zhadar's spy will carry out our plans to weaken the dwarves. Our attack will take them by surprise and the demon's participation will ensure we gain the upper hand."

Sinthoras carried on, speaking clearly and with an air of condescension, so that even the stupidest of the assembled leaders would know exactly what to do. *Far too many stupid ones for my liking.* He saw that Gattalind was struggling to keep up with what was being said.

Caphalor held back and followed the briefing details attentively. When the delegates were dismissed, he asked Sinthoras, Lotor and Toboribar to remain behind.

"I wanted to thank you," he said to the óarco and the barbarian. "Your people made the victory over the obboona possible."

"Glad to help," said Toboribar with a wide grin that showed his decorated tusks. "Srinks are scum; they've no brains."

Sinthoras reflected on a similar phrase that had been used in Dsôn when óarcos were discussed.

"Toboribar and Lotor, would you do me a further favor?" Caphalor asked. "For this, I will reward you and your soldiers with my share of Tark Draan."

"What do you want us to do?" grunted the óarco, curiosity in his tone.

"I have a feud with Munumon, the former king of the fflecx. Only he and a handful of his people are still alive. I want to make sure he pays for what he has done to Sinthoras and myself and I need a small troop to take me to where he is."

Lotor shook his head. "That's pure suicide. The alchemancers will still have enough poison to kill my men."

"I'm game," said Toboribar. "We won't give the stumpy button-heads any opportunity to get their blowpipes out."

Caphalor stood up, his expression both threatening and radiant. "Then let us make a start. The sooner we get back here the better."

Sinthoras thought of the dead fflecx that the gâlran zhadar had brought with him, and what he had been told about the demon's power. In his mind's eye he saw the entire land swarming with undead gnomes. *It was a mistake to tell Caphalor about that.* "Munumon will die anyway," he said, in an attempt to change Caphalor's mind. "It's not a good idea to split up and waste our energy on squabbles that have nothing to do with the main thrust of the campaign." He looked at him earnestly. "That's our own private quarrel, Caphalor."

The älf was silent for a while. "You are right," he said, after a pause for thought. He turned to the óarco prince. "I've decided against that plan. I don't need your services. But I will still give you my share of land because you were willing to follow me." He fixed his gray-green eyes on Sinthoras once more. "It won't take me long to locate them. You can look forward to my bringing you Munumon's head."

"It is too dangerous, we need you here to plan the campaign," said Sinthoras.

Caphalor dismissed this with a gesture of his hand. "I'll ride alone, I will not be noticed and Sardaî will get me there." He left the tent, his tone making it clear that his decision was final.

"Even I can see how deeply the death of his wife has affected him," said Lotor after a pause.

Sinthoras only nodded. He was worried. He was worried about so many things.

Ishím Voróo (The Outer Lands), thirty-two miles
behind the border of the fflecx kingdom,
4371st division of unendingness (5199th solar cycle),
spring.

Caphalor urged the night-mare through the vast expanses of the fflecx lands, away from the deserted royal palace; he was following recent vehicle tracks that could only have been left by Munumon—if the rumors about the destruction of the rest of the fflecx were to be believed.

Discarded objects at the roadside looked familiar and he realized the carts had been losing some of their freight in the fflecxs' hurried escape from the demon.

The last few miles had shown a strange alteration in the landscape. *This must be the mist-demon's work, the effect the gâlran zhadar spoke of. I had better take a closer look.*

He halted Sardaî at a small clump of trees and dismounted to examine them.

They were blackened, leafless, and looked dead, but on making a cut in the scorched trunk he discovered they were still alive, the resin transformed into stinking viscous oil, its normal golden color gone.

Caphalor took a piece of fungus and squashed it. Then he divided a small bush and pulled out a few grass stalks. Every living thing with roots in the soil had been affected by the demon's power: plants had withered away on shriveled stalks while others had mutated, the coloring of their flowers and leaves now dark. Even the grass under Sardaî's hooves had taken on a grayish hue. The entire landscape was odd. It was if they were in a different world.

I find these changes to my taste. He breathed death in and relished becoming one with the dead land. He liked the sound of it. *The Dead Land. And this is what will happen all over Tark Draan!* Neither elves nor magicians nor warriors would be able to withstand the allies' combined forces.

Caphalor swung himself back up into the saddle and continued along the tracks. He came across several headless corpses on the sides of the road. Mostly those of the fflecx, but there were also some barbarians. Perhaps the demon's power could only be stopped if the corpses were beheaded, or the skull crushed? Only then might the returning dead fall truly lifeless.

Toward evening he saw four carts on the road in front of him. They were being pulled along as fast as the bellowing oxen could go. The carts were piled high with boxes, sacks and crates.

Caphalor picked up his bow and selected an arrow. He could announce his arrival and it would put Munumon and his entourage into a state of terror. *I want them to realize they have no weapons to confront me with.*

He spanned the bow and aimed for one of the fflecx on the last wagon.

The soaring arrow took some time to hit home, but when it did, it pierced the fflecx through the breast, nailing him to one of the boxes. His companions did not, at first, realize what had happened, but then they started to yelp with fear.

Pitiful creatures! Caphalor laughed with satisfaction and spurred the night-mare onwards while he took out a second arrow from his quiver. *You don't even know what direction your death is approaching from.* A second fflecx soon fell dead, transfixed by his arrow. There was nowhere for them to seek shelter.

This was what the fflecx quickly realized after they had lost a third member of their troop to Caphalor's bow. They jumped down and took off for the bushes on either side of the road. The oxen rushed steadily onward with the carts.

Caphalor commanded Sardaî to gallop up to the first ox cart. *I can see you!* As he passed them, Caphalor shot two more of the unprepared fflecx foolish enough to pop their heads out of the undergrowth.

"Take me up ahead," he told Sardaî. That was where he thought he would find the former monarch. When he drew parallel to the cart-driver's seat, he could see Munumon hiding under the passenger bench with the reins in his hand, urging the oxen to increase their speed. Sardaî had no difficulty keeping up.

"Fflecx king," Caphalor called, hanging his bow on his saddle.

Munumon started and then tried to crawl back under the benches. "I'm not coming out," he shouted over the noise of the clattering wheels. He looked like a toad trying to hide under a stone.

"Don't you recognize me?"

The dark, warty face turned toward him.

"You are the black-eyes that I sent out to get my property back for me." But now he was surprised. "How did you survive my poison?" He swore. "Oh, I know! It was the demon. The demon has brought you back to life."

"No, I am properly alive and yet in my heart of hearts I am dead," Caphalor replied coldly. "You bear a great deal of the responsibility for that and you shall pay the price."

"Come a bit closer, so I can bash your head in!" Munumon wielded a giant ax and tried to look impressive.

Caphalor gave a short, evil laugh. "Your followers have abandoned you, King," he said spitefully. "They aren't going to come back and help you." He overtook the cart and used his native magic to make black streams of terror waft out toward the oxen, penetrating their simple brains so that they halted in fear, refusing to move on.

Munumon screamed and cursed wildly.

"Come back here, you cowards!" he yelled to his followers. "Come back here and help your king—you accepted my gold all right!"

Caphalor dismounted and laid down his bow. "Yes, do come back," he said under his breath. "Come back here so you can all die together."

The fflecx were feeling safer now that Caphalor's bow was not in his hand, and he suddenly found himself surrounded by nearly a dozen of them, armored and armed, their blow pipes already trained on him.

"Kill the black-eyes!" screeched Munumon, squeezing out from under the driver's box on the cart and whirling his ax. In his excitement he hopped up and down, the wooden planking squeaking and groaning under his ridiculous pointed shoes.

A shower of tiny darts was underway, hitting Caphalor in the face and penetrating his body between the plates of his armor. Burning pain was instantaneous.

With one hand he wiped the darts from his face and throat. Slowly, he pulled out his daggers from his belt; he held one blade pointing forward, the other pointing back. "Your deaths bear the name of Caphalor," he vowed, speaking in the älfar tongue. "I am taking your worthless lives. The Dead Land may keep your spirits."

At the sound of his voice the fflecx stepped back, unsure. The älf lunged forward.

I am a dancing shadow. He moved among them effortlessly, laughing. His daggers sliced through their scrawny necks and their blood spurted out in fountains, the tips of the blades piercing the fflecx armor and entering their hearts. Each blow was the end of a fflecx. *You can't even see me coming, can you?*

A few heartbeats later they all lay at his feet in a spreading pool of their own blood.

Munumon was trying to crawl back under the driver's bench, but Caphalor grabbed him by the leg and hurled him through the air to land in a puddle of blood. He stamped hard on the hand carrying the ax. The one-time ruler of the fflecx kingdom whimpered pitifully. "I can give you treasures, black-eyes," he sobbed. "And the antidote! Or otherwise you'll die! Do you want to die?"

"Your toxins no longer work on me," he replied, cleaning his knives and stowing them. "That was the one good thing about what you did to Sinthoras and myself." He bent down, took the gnome-like being in a stranglehold and rammed him up against the side of the wagon. With his left foot, Caphalor sent one of the fflecx's abandoned short swords flying into the air to catch. He jammed it under Munumon's collar bone, fixing the former king to the side of the cart. Then he stepped away, leaving his victim suspended in midair and roaring with pain. Blood poured down over the little creature's chest and back.

Caphalor sat down on a fallen tree trunk and observed the pathetic fflecx. "You scream too soon," he murmured. "When daybreak comes, I shall let you die." He plucked a blowpipe dart out of his armor and hurled it at Munumon, hitting him on the right cheek and eliciting a further screech of pain. "There's to be no release for you until then."

Ishím Voróo (The Outer Lands), älfar realm Dsôn Faïmon, Dsôn, 4371st division of unendingness (5199th solar cycle), spring.

Raleeha held her hand in front of her eyes.

She could make out her fingers now, even the details of the fine wrinkles and folds on the knuckles. *My sight is improving with every sunrise!* Near, she could see with the one eye almost as well as she had done before. It was only distance vision that was still a problem. However, she kept her remarkable recovery to herself and continued to wear her black lace eye band when not alone.

Her artwork was becoming more exquisitely refined and the etched pictures roused Timansor's ecstatic admiration. He assumed—as did the rest of the household—that these were the work of a blind woman. As he was prepared to cheat her of both prestige and profit, Raleeha had no compunction in deceiving him in this way. *Tarlesa cannot betray me now.*

Picking up the quill-trimming knife, she completed the last few touches on the tiny engraved portrait of Timanris. She had ostensibly studied for it by touching the älf-woman's face with her fingers and feeling its contours.

It would have been so easy to push your thumbs into the rival's hated eyes and kill her! said the reproachful little voice inside her head.

A shudder went up and down her spine.

But it would not have helped at all, answered the voice of reason. She, Raleeha, would be accused of murder, Sinthoras would despise her and her brother would perhaps have been made to pay with his life. No, it was important no suspicion fell on her.

"Be still!" She took a deep breath and her mind grew calmer. She laid the small knife down and brushed away the tiny fragments of parchment she had removed. It had worked very well. It was only the size of a coin, but exactly the älf-woman's likeness, even though it was virtually impossible to render the true effect of an älfar visage. Timanris would be thrilled with it and would give it to Sinthoras, of course. *He will wear it round his neck, next to his heart.*

Raleeha traced tiny grooves with the tip of her finger—the grooves that showed her own face. Nobody would notice—only she would know. She sighed, lifted the parchment and pressed it passionately to her lips.

There was a knock at the door. "Are you there, Raleeha?" *Timanris must want something.*

She put her work aside, then stood up and turned to the entrance. "Yes, mistress. Please come in. You do not need to knock or ask, I am your slave."

The älf-woman entered and smiled, although she thought Raleeha could not see her. "You know that you are no slave, even if my father thinks otherwise. You say this on purpose every time to make me angry and to show your resentment," she scolded, without really meaning it. She walked past Raleeha and studied the work on the tilted desk easel. "By Samusin!" she exclaimed. "It's perfect! You have captured my image more skillfully than anyone else who has ever attempted to draw me." She shook her head and laughed, picking up the parchment. "A blind human girl has trumped all älfar artists. If it ever comes out who has created these works we will have to invent some älfar blood for you, or whole swathes of our artists will be plunging to their deaths in despair. What disgrace! Defeated by a human girl!" the älf-woman laughed out loud again.

"No, I still have a long way to go before I can compare my work to älfar art," countered Raleeha—to her it was the truth. "I can draw simple things very well, but when I think about what I see—" She stopped. "I mean, what I used to be able to see, then my pictures are those of a child."

"Don't be silly," joked Timanris. "Come along." She hurried to the door and Raleeha followed her, hesitating slightly, to look genuinely blind.

They traversed the whole building, where works of art were on display in every available niche, on every wall, floor and ceiling alike: paintings, sculptures, collages—sometimes Raleeha did not really understand what they portrayed: abstract pieces adorned with the essence of transience and the spirit of beauty.

They reached the garden. Here, Timansor had spent a fortune and much effort imposing his aesthetic view of the world on the natural order. Bushes, shrubs, and trees had been trimmed into exotic shapes, dyed different colors and bordered by stones. Soft animal fur represented grass on decorative small islands on the ground.

Humans could never come up with anything like this. Raleeha was delighted to be able to see this splendor, but when she let her gaze sweep round to a delicate summerhouse structure with curtains at the semicircular windows, her heart stopped. *Sinthoras!*

"Come on," Timanris called happily. "I want Sinthoras to see who made my gift."

Raleeha felt as if she were pulled in two. She wanted to see him from close up, wanted to drink in the sight of him, but at the same time she feared she might lose control and betray herself. *My gods, do not desert me now.* Unable to hold back, she carried on walking straight up to her former owner and master who stood at the entrance to the arbor.

He stood up and greeted Timanris with a warm kiss, giving only a fleeting glance in Raleeha's direction. "Of course, you are her mistress now," he remarked conversationally. "Caphalor told me."

"She is her own mistress," said the älf-woman gently, returning his caress and holding the tiny portrait in her right hand.

I wish I was blind again! But she had to endure the sight of her former master sunk in another's embrace. It was almost impossible to stay impassive and not thrust herself between the two of them.

You could never take up the place she has, said her reason. *How do you know that if you have not tried absolutely everything?* argued the small voice in her head.

"Look," said Timanris, with love shining in her eyes. "See what she has engraved here. I want you to carry it with you at all times, Sinthoras." She handed him the piece of parchment. It is to protect you when you go to war and it is to bring you back home safe to me—safe and victorious!'

Raleeha saw her artwork changing hands, knowing her own face was going with it. *It will bring him back to me, not to you.* That thought served to appease the anger and confusion raging in her heart.

Sinthoras accepted the gift. "It is an excellent likeness, Raleeha. It seems you hid your talent from me. The pictures I saw in your chamber— you did not know I was looking at them—were nowhere near as good as this." Then he looked at Timanris and cradled her face in his hands. "My beloved, I need to tell you this: you make me complete! For you I ride to the ends of Tark Draan and home again. I shall crush the heads of all my enemies and bring them to your feet." He was singing the words more than speaking them.

Raleeha closed her eyes and luxuriated in the sound of his voice.

"As soon as I return from the campaign I want to take you as my life-companion."

Both girls, älf and human, took deep breaths: one in ecstasy, one in shock.

"What about Yantarai?" prompted Timanris softly. "I love you, Sinthoras, and don't want to stand in the way of your ambition. With her—"

"Life is monotonous, political, and without inspiration," he said, grasping her hands in his own. "I beg you, do not reject my proposal."

Timanris scanned his face, lost in thought.

Raleeha opened her eyes and stared at the älf-woman in horror. *She must not say yes!* She begged Tion to intervene, to prevent Timanris from uttering the dreaded syllable. But what female with any sense would turn down such an offer?

And then she heard Timanris say, "I accept from the bottom of my heart."

Again Raleeha was forced to witness their lips meet in a kiss. *Stop! Stop that now!* It was a scorching pain through her heart and she longed for the death of her rival. There was no guilt left now when she wished for Timanris to die. She had never asked her to be her patron. She certainly would never have asked for her own art to be attributed to someone else.

May the plague take you! Raleeha's burning anger increased until she could hardly breathe. Every part of her body was on fire. The conflagration scorched through all the reservations that common sense had imposed, searing through any remaining vestige of gratitude and reducing scruples to a blackened husk.

She was too taken up with her own distress to hear anything of the rest of their conversation. The tiny voice in her head was proposing sophisticated death plans for her rival and Raleeha paid eager attention. Finally she heard her own name and saw that Timanris had gone past her, so she followed her älf-mistress. But she was compelled to turn toward Sinthoras one last time: he was standing in the arbor doorway, one hand raised in farewell. She was convinced the gesture was intended for herself. *We shall meet again soon.* She managed to prevent herself from waving in response.

They went back inside the building and climbed to the first floor.

Raleeha noted the spears and pennants placed on the stairway. At each step she saw the promised instruments of her revenge, helping her to her heart's desire.

Don't do it, warned the voice of reason. *It will be your own downfall.*

Timanris stopped on the landing. "Don't tell my father about the proposal, should he ask," she said. "It must not be made known until Sinthoras returns from Tark Draan. My father is not overly fond of the warrior class, but he won't be able to refuse a hero." She sighed in the way of those deep in love, shrugging her shoulders playfully like a young girl. "May Samusin keep him safe. Samusin and your portrait, of course."

Enough! I can't bear your sentimental gushing any longer! Raleeha's hand gripped the nearest spear in fury. She could endure no more of this suffering! With a muffled scream of anger she plunged the four-sided blade into Timanris' side and pushed her backward to the top of the stairs. "You shall never have him," she hissed. "I sacrificed my sight, I put up with his contempt purely to be in his presence. I allowed myself to be exchanged and bartered like some animal and I gave up my liberty— only to be thwarted in this way!"

Timanris gasped at her open-mouthed, astonishment and agony in her eyes.

Raleeha ripped off the lace blindfold and stared her dying mistress in the face. "What use now your beauty, Timanris? I was sharper-witted than you. I was quicker than you. I was more devious. Are these not the qualities you älfar prize most highly?"

Timanris choked, raising her arm to touch Raleeha in a beseeching gesture.

"I had rather he took Yantarai than you," she hissed under her breath, as she pushed the älf woman out over the top step before releasing her hold on the spear.

Timanris snatched up one of the other spears and thrust it at Raleeha, catching her in the shoulder with the metal barb. As she fell, she dragged the slave girl down with her into the depths. They rolled down the stairs in a tangled heap, releasing more of the weapons as they passed. Step by step, they clattered down.

Raleeha screamed with pain. The barb tore at her flesh, making her unable to move her arm to free herself. Her anger turned to terror.

I warned you it would bring disaster, whispered the sad voice of common sense inside her head.

When she landed next to Timanris at the bottom of the stairs she went completely to pieces. The eyes of the älf-woman were alert and the spear had come out of her side, gouging a seeping wound the size of a fist.

Put an end to this! urged the high voice in her head. *Go on! Finish her off, or she will reveal your treachery and all will be lost!*

"Why don't you die?" shrieked the terrified Raleeha, about to grasp her rival's throat. Then she heard shouts nearby. She let go and racked her brain feverishly. *She must not survive or it will mean my death.*

She groaned at a new injury; Timanris had pierced her side under her ribcage with a broken-off spear point.

"Samusin," breathed Raleeha, sinking to the marble floor at her rival's feet.

Didn't I tell you what would happen? came the insistent voice of reason.

Chapter XIX

Once they had secured peace and beauty, the Inextinguishables sent out their scouts to find the deadly enemies of the älfar: the elves.

But however minutely they combed the lands of Ishím Voróo and investigated the remotest corners, they could locate no trace of the traitors.

There was an indication that they had left Ishím Voróo. Toward the south. Toward a land known as Girdlegard.

Epocrypha of the Creating Spirit

3rd book,

chapter 1, 1–10

Ishím Voróo (The Outer Lands), seventeen miles from the Northern Pass and the Stone Gateway, 4371st division of unendingness (5199th solar cycle), summer.

The two älfar nostàroi took their escort of forty warriors further up the pass to survey the extensive camp from above. "It was wise to make camp back at the base of the foothills," Caphalor remarked. "The ogres, trolls, and giants make so much noise and their voices carry quite a distance."

Sinthoras listened for a moment, then replied to Caphalor, satisfied that he could hear no sounds from the plain below. "That would have been all we needed: the groundlings warned of the attack by gales of laughter."

Their ban on going up to the Stone Gateway had also worked: they had not met a single beast or barbarian on their way up. The nostàroi were the first to set foot in the area for a long, long time.

The pass was steep, but it remained broad as it wound up through the mountains. This had not always been the case. During the few divisions of unendingness, when no beast had considered attacking the groundlings, there had only been occasional expeditions issuing into Ishím Voróo from Tark Draan. *The barbarians were keen to learn more about the unknown.* But after a time, invading óarcos and other monsters had flattened out the ground and widened the pass with pick and shovel, wanting to employ siege engines against the mighty stone portal. Sinthoras smiled grimly. *I think it is only polite to return the barbarians' visits.*

It was getting colder: they could see their breath collecting in white clouds in front of their faces and they could see hoar frost on the rim of each other's helmets. Sinthoras let his thoughts wander back over the miles to where his Timanris lay, badly injured.

The news of her accident had made him extremely concerned about his future companion's health and he was frightened for her. *Love does not only make us strong.* However, it was not possible to absent himself from the campaign for personal reasons, even if his heart was torn in two, and so he had been writing to her: countless letters, all sent to Dsôn by messenger.

I must find some distraction or my mind will be focused only on her and anxiety will overwhelm me. "Tell me what happened with Munumon," Sinthoras asked. "I presume you inflicted as much pain as possible?"

"Yes, more than I have ever tortured any creature before," Caphalor responded with a certain satisfaction in his voice. "I hope you will find a use for the blood I brought back?"

"I am preserving it carefully. Now there are no more fflecx, the life juice of their king is more valuable than ever." Sinthoras was disappointed. He had wanted to know the details. *Have we achieved revenge for the humili-ation Munumon imposed on us?*

But before he could inquire further, Caphalor said, "I am glad the pass is so wide. It is perfect for the size of our armies. We should get up there at a good speed."

"The catapults and storm ladders will be easy to transport, as well." As they walked, he saw the heaps of weathered bones, rusted and lichen-encrusted armor and abandoned wagons to the right and the left of the pass. Death had garnered many a prize. *Soon death can resume its work here.*

The night-mares had no problem with the altitude and the älfar soon arrived at the last platform before the gateway. The pass then led along the edge of the mountain for a further half a mile before disappearing west between the cliff sides.

"I have not seen any fresh tracks," said Caphalor. "It looks as if no one has been up to the Gateway for a long time."

"We'll leave some scouts here," Sinthoras decided. "There's always a possibility some of the barbarian kings in Tark Draan might choose to send out their troops just at the wrong moment, it would be too bad if they stumbled on our camp." He took a deep breath. Clear mountain air and a whiff of the empire he intended to conquer reached him. *The groundlings will only be the overture.*

"I can hardly wait," growled Caphalor, as if he were reading Sintho-ras' thoughts. "I want to see the cursed land of Tark Draan go up in flames. May its ashes calm my hatred."

Sinthoras nodded. "Indeed, my friend. Let them feel what you feel, you will see how your pain lessens with every elf trampled under your night-mare's hooves. In—"

Their heads shot round to the right: a dislodged stone fell down the slope.

"A barbarian," whispered Caphalor. "About eighty paces above us. He's looking out of a cave."

"How quickly can we get up?"

Caphalor pulled down his bow and was already loosing an arrow at the scout. The man fell out of his shelter and tumbled lifeless to the ground. "Not necessary," he remarked. "I've brought him down to us." He signaled to the troops to dismount and secure the area.

Sinthoras had been noticing the difference in the other hostáror's behavior for some time now. He conducted himself as befitted a warrior, a hero, not like some noble älf with a country estate who occasionally deigned to join the army. His new attitude won him the respect of his troops and the allies spoke of him with admiration. *No trace now of his softer personality. If he joined the Comets, that would be perfect.*

Not so long ago Sinthoras would have been green with envy, but today he remained relaxed: Caphalor was no longer an opponent or a rival and their political differences had been overcome. With the war going ahead and the whole Star State enthusiastic in its support, the leadership of two such experienced heroes would ensure victory.

From their mounts he and Caphalor looked down impassively at the dead barbarian. He was in a wretched condition, wearing animal skins over the remnants of uniform and rusty chainmail.

Sinthoras poked around near the corpse with the end of his lance, slitting open the man's bag of provisions. "He's got more than enough food with him. He must have belonged to some barbarian expeditionary force."

Caphalor gazed up toward the cave opening. "There will be others. We should deal with them before they see us and warn the groundlings." He gave commands to the troops; half the unit started to climb the slope. He followed them at a distance.

Sinthoras hung his spear over his shoulder by its strap and clambered up a steep path toward the cave. The remainder of the troop stayed with the night-mares, keeping watch.

Silently they entered the cave. There was a decided stink of barbarian and a simple encampment for two people: a bucket for slops, some old blankets, and animal skins on sacks of straw.

"A look-out post," Caphalor guessed, drawing out a knife. "The soldiers must have turned brigand. I expect there were waiting for some merchant to pass—anyone bold enough to still use this road."

Sinthoras nodded agreement. "Over there," he said, pointing to a tunnel behind them. The troop moved forward; they had no need of light.

The air was stale and they found a number of neglected lamps; the wicks had burned down and the canisters had not been refilled. The sides of the corridor were of natural provenance; the rounded edges of the rock indicating an earlier watercourse.

"We are going past the Stone Gateway," said Sinthoras.

"I wonder if the groundlings know it." Caphalor smiled. "I pray to Samusin that we have found something that will let us stab the bearded ones in the back."

A door loomed up in front of them showing a bar of light at its foot.

"We will leave one of them alive. The others must die." Sinthoras called up his power and he felt his spine tingle and grow warm in response. The black webs of terror hovered toward the door, slipped through the gap under the wood, locating and dousing the lamps. His victims were sitting in the dark, at a loss to understand what was happening. *Your death approaches.* When he heard the barbarians' startled shouts, he slowly opened the door.

They were mostly barbarian males: two ugly barbarian women were sitting at the back trying to calm the infants at their breasts. The babies had realized something was wrong.

They were so silent that nobody heard him or his troops as they spread about amongst the barbarians with their weapons at the ready.

Caphalor indicated the tallest man and made the sign for "leader."

Sinthoras studied the coarse face of the strong-smelling barbarian who was continuing to finish his food in the dark, with no idea of the mortal danger he was in. *You simple souls, it's a miracle you have survived so long.* The man was taking a hearty bite out of a sausage; the filling spurted out, smearing the sides of his mouth and covering his unkempt facial hair. He wiped his mouth on his sleeve and called out a command to relight the lamps; then he belched and felt for his mug of brandy. Sinthoras was disgusted. *I don't want to sully my blade with your blood.* He took the mug before the barbarian could grab it and he rammed it brutally into the man's throat.

This assault was a prompt for the others to attack.

The älfar killed the barbarians—man, woman, and child—within a couple of heartbeats. The leader was given a powerful blow to the temple to stun him. As the sound of the last dying gurgle faded away, Sinthoras permitted the lamps to shine once more.

The alfar were standing around the cave next to the barbarians they had each dispatched. There was a soft splashing sound as blood dripped out from gaping wounds onto the rocky floor.

Caphalor tossed the contents of a wine jug into the leader's face and smacked him round the head with the back of his armored hand to bring him round.

"Demons!" shouted the man, pulling back. He must have been twice the weight of the älf; muscular and powerful—but his will was shattered. "Ye mountain demons, I—"

"What are you up to here in the Gray Range, human?" Caphalor asked in a deep voice. "Who sent you here?"

Sinthoras knew that his nostàroi colleague was using the weapon of terror against the barbarian, torturing his soul. *His talent for fear is stronger than my own; is that because of his grief, I wonder?*

"We are soldiers from Gauragar. Our king sent us out to explore the pass, but we . . ." The human stopped speaking, unsure of himself.

Caphalor increased the terror in his aura. "The truth, barbarian!" Caphalor shouted.

"We are bandits now," the man replied, his hand pressed against his heart as if to still its pounding. He stared into the älfar face. "You did not even spare my infant sons," he sobbed.

"Why would we?" said Caphalor, amicably enough. "They are nothing but the worthless brood of criminals. Why not condemn a born outlaw to death before he can do any harm?" He placed the blade of his dagger on the barbarian's cheek. "Where do you get your food supplies?"

"We steal from the groundlings," he admitted quickly. "We made a tunnel through the rock they call false granite."

"And they have no idea?" growled Caphalor, pressing the edge of the blade harder into the man's face; bits of cutaway beard fell onto the barbarian's shirt. "No," came the whispered response. At Caphalor's insistence, the man indicated the tunnel's location, then he turned to Sinthoras. "Any further questions for him?" Sinthoras shook his head and Caphalor turned back to the quivering barbarian. "Then let us say that Caphalor is the name of your death."

His dagger severed the man's neck: only the vertebrae prevented the head from falling off completely. He took care not to get splashed by any of the spraying blood. "I take your life; your soul shall stand before Tion and be swallowed."

"Let's go—" Noises behind a second door cut him off before a groundling in full armor burst through it, a war hammer in his raised fist.

"Now I've got you, you thieving—" Noticing the corpses and then the älfar, he fell silent.

Sinthoras saw there were more small-statured sentries coming along the tunnel behind. *So they have picked up the robbers' tracks after all.*

Caphalor gave the order before Sinthoras could open his mouth to do the same: "Kill them. And be quick about it."

Ishím Voróo (The Outer Lands), älfar realm Dsôn Faïmon, Dsôn, 4371st division of unendingness (5199th solar cycle), summer.

Nagsor Inàste climbed out of the sunken tub where he had bathed in spiced milk and scented oils. A blind älf-woman proffered a soft toweling mantle, which he took and dried himself with.

What a wonderful feeling. He took a seat to allow the female and a second servant to brush and dress his hair with perfumed lotions and then to help him into a long black robe. Two more assistants approached to tie the belt of his attire and bring him shoes, jewelry and velvet gloves. They set the six-pointed coronet on his head before withdrawing. As always, they had worked together perfectly as a team.

Now I am ready to greet her. The Inextinguishable One left the bathing hall and went to find his sister, who was working on a sculpture to celebrate the new military campaign. He did not know any details: this was to be the first time he would be shown the completed work of art.

On the way to her studio, he was approached by a servant. "O, inextinguishable One, the gâlran zhadar has arrived. He is impudent enough to insist on being received immediately."

Nagsor Inàste could sense the fear the servant was experiencing. "His impudence is no fault of yours," he said to calm the servant. "If my anger is to be felt, it is he who will feel it. Go quickly to Nagsar and ask her to come to the Hall of Honor. She should be present when I speak with him." The servant hurried off.

The Inextinguishable ruler changed direction and strode calmly toward the Hall of Honor himself. *An insolent creature indeed.* Nagsor had summoned the gâlran zhadar to appear after his request for access to Phondrasôn, but the interview had been scheduled for after his meeting with his sister.

There have not been many opportunities in my lifespan for encountering a gâlran zhadar. The dwarf-like creatures were notoriously suspicious of others; they had magic powers and they had an effective army of followers around them at all times. He and his sister had always avoided confrontation with such difficult opponents.

Nagsor Inàste entered the ceremonial hall—but found no gâlran zhadar waiting. "Where are you?" he called out. "Keep your eyes closed. My beauty could be fatal for you."

"I'm here," came the response from a dark niche, and then the creature stepped out into the light that fell through the turquoise-colored windowpanes. The gâlran zhadar was slurping noisily from a beaker. His eyes were wide open. "You keep good wine, Inextinguishable."

"Where did you get that?" thundered Nagsor Inàste, drawing himself up to his full height.

"I found it in one of the chambers near here. I got fed up waiting for you so I gave myself a little tour of your Tower of Bones. It's a nice enough on the whole, but I think that as a building it lacks playfulness." He drank more of the wine and winked at the ruler over the rim of his cup. "It wasn't easy sneaking round your blind servants. Their hearing is very good."

At first the Inextinguishable One was speechless with indignation. Then he roared, "You are a guest here!" feeling the fury rise in him. "You have the impertinence, the impudence, no, you commit the blasphemy of taking my—"

His angry outburst was interrupted by the appearance of Nagsar Inàste. He wished now that his sister had not come. The deceitful expression in his visitor's eyes was warning enough. *This stunted freak has more in him than meets the eye. Considerably more.*

"You wanted to talk to me," said the gâlran zhadar, without making any concession to the entry of the regal sister. "Here I am." He pointed over to the window, indicating the sun. "Hurry up. I've got to get to Phondrasôn."

Nagsar Inàste stood open-mouthed at this lack of respect. "How can you—"

Her Inextinguishable brother raised his hand and came over to stand at her side. "It is in order," he said to reassure her. "Do not concern yourself with his lack of manners. He will not be with us for long; I merely want to learn the true reason for his wanting to leave Ishím Voróo. He has been living here for such a long time, his castle has proved totally impregnable, and I had understood from Sinthoras that the plan was to extend it." He regarded his visitor inquisitively. "So this looks like an enforced flight—what are you running away from, gâlran zhadar?"

The dwarf-like creature grinned. "So you want to find out whether there's something on its way that will put the fear of the gods up the älfar, too, if the gâlran zhadar are high-tailing it out of here? Am I right?"

Nagsor Inàste said nothing.

The gâlran zhadar laughed outright. "I was curious to know what you wanted from me, Inextinguishable. I thought that would be the question you'd come up with." He drained the beaker and chucked it over his shoulder. It clattered on the floor, causing an echo in the vast room. His face lost all trace of cheeriness. Suddenly his visage was suffused with hatred. "Your downfall is well deserved," he barked. "It's your own great heroes that have brought it about."

Nagsar Inàste stared at her brother in bewilderment. "I can't understand what he's saying. Do you intend—"

"Explain yourself, gâlran zhadar!" demanded Nagsor Inàste, no longer attempting to hide his anger. Black lightning flashes shot over his countenance. He did not understand what the other was hinting at and he was extremely concerned. "Otherwise I swear you shall not leave the Tower of Bones alive."

The creature uttered a long, loud laugh and seemed unimpressed. "One of your famous heroes—Sinthoras or Caphalor—stole a valuable possession of mine: a vial containing a magic substance concocted with the aim of intensifying the power of any demon and of binding that demon to one's own service—but only if used together with the right formula." By the expressions on the siblings' faces he knew that they had been unaware of this part of the journey the heroes had undertaken. He snorted. "Oh, I see the Highest Ones had absolutely no idea their heroes broke into my castle? They deceived you about that?" He was shaking with laughter, holding his belly.

Enough! "I am not going to permit you to—" began Nagsor Inàste.

"Silence!" growled the gâlran zhadar aggressively. "I know the extent of your envy. That is your motive for this campaign: you and your precious älfar were supposed to be the only immortal creatures, so you wanted to be rid of the harmless little demon who gives the dead a second life. You wanted to send him to Tark Draan, where he wouldn't be any trouble and that way you would continue to be the only everlasting creatures in Ishím Voróo."

"An end to this posturing!" commanded Nagsar Inàste and six armed servants rushed in to the hall; two further assistants brought the Inextinguishable Siblings their swords.

The gâlran zhadar was unmoved. "You don't frighten me. The vial was broken and now the demon is out of control; you have created a monster and let it out of its chains without the faintest of idea how to stop it. I predict that you will soon be having to serve this creature yourselves." He turned to the window. "That is why, Inextinguishable Ones, I am leaving here. Even my castle will not protect me from the power of this demon. I am off to Phondrasôn where I shall set up a new kingdom for myself from whence I can observe the demon engulfing Dsôn Faïmon." His voice grew quiet once more. "Pray to your gods that it prefers to pursue elves, dwarves, and humans rather than your own kind—or your realm will fall because *you* were jealous." He strode past, scything through the groups of blind servants as he went.

Nagsar Inàste looked at her brother. He breathed the order to attack.

The first servant aimed a sword thrust at the creature—a thrust as true as if he had been able to see, but his blade was parried by the war hammer; the gålran zhadar's second hammerhead smashed into the right side of the his face.

The visitor leaped to confront the second bodyguard, ducking under his sword and diverting it with a hammer blow to strike the belly of the third servant, while he used the other hammer to destroy both knees of the next contender. He quickly raised his weapon and smashed the hammer head onto the open mouth of the next älf. He took the sixth with a double hammer blow to the shoulders, snapping the collarbones and making the älf attacker double up in pain.

Then the gålran zhadar turned slowly round to face the Inextinguishables. An indefinable sound issued from his throat and the heads of his weapons were bathed in magic light. "If you wish me dead, Nagsar Inàste, I suggest you try to kill me yourself," he advised. "I wonder if you will dare. Whole races have called me their god."

Nagsor Inàste knew that his sister would be provoked into attacking. The magic power that emanated from the dwarf-like creature did not seem to deter her. *She must not be injured in any way.* He stepped swiftly between her and the gålran zhadar. "We still need the instructions from you about getting the spy with the groundlings to work for us, that is why we will let you live," he said, lowering his mighty sword.

"How very noble of you." The gålran zhadar gave a hollow laugh and the glowing light on the hammers faded. The weapons remained firmly, however, in his fists. "Noble and selfless." With these words he strode through the hall and out of the door, laughing fit to bust.

"You are really going to let him go?" Nagsar Inàste was at a loss to understand why the gålran zhadar should escape with his life. She raised her sword. "We have to kill him as soon as he's told us what we need! He must not be allowed to live after that unacceptable conduct."

Nagsor Inàste looked at the dead servants and the terrible injuries inflicted on them. *Their blood shall not have spilled in vain; they served me loyally and well. Perhaps I can use their shattered bones to make a sculpture, something on the theme of destroyed bodies and destroyed souls.* "You have forgotten one thing in your outrage, my beloved sister." He took the sword from her hand. "He beheld our features and he did not go insane. What do we deduce from that?" He kissed her gently on the lips before she could reply. Then he walked past her to call for slaves to bone the corpses and collect the blood. "It is best we let him go."

"And the enhanced powers of the demon?" she asked behind him.

"Don't worry," he reassured her. "We shall soon be rid of the demon." *I hope.*

Ishím Voróo (The Outer Lands), älfar realm Dsôn Faïmon, Dsôn, 4371st division of unendingness (5199th solar cycle), summer.

Raleeha rose from her couch with a stifled moan.

It was early morning and the sun was still on the far side of the crater's edge; light fell dimly, as if frightened, through the window. *A new day.* The first sight her gaze fell on was the wound in her side. The stitches were holding.

Unlike her älf mistress, she had recovered well from her injury and from the fall. Everyone assumed the slave girl had been hurrying to the assistance of her mistress when they both fell. Raleeha had not corrected this version of events.

Since the "accident," Timanris had been lying motionless in her bed, paler than usual and near endingness, unable to speak or to hear. Various healers had been consulted, but their opinions had always been the same: the impact after the fall had wiped all memory and all knowledge from her head. Her body, however, remained capable of the basic functions of breathing, swallowing, and excretion; this was why death had not yet stopped her heart.

I shall play the courageous slave girl one more time, concerned for the life of her mistress. Each day she spent long hours at the dying girl's bedside, talking softly to her about new works, and even showing them to Timanris, as if she were able to see them through her closed eyelids.

Secretly, however, Raleeha was consumed with fear. As soon as the älf-woman awakened, all would be lost. There would certainly never be another opportunity for her to kill her mistress. There were always nurses in attendance in the chamber. The voices in Raleeha's head kept giving her contradictory advice, driving her almost insane.

Perhaps I am already crazy. She dressed and went to her mistress as she did every morning before taking her first meal. *Is it my lucky day? Is she dead?* She entered the room.

She was surprised to see Hirai, Timanris' mother, at the bedside. Not a soul knew that her sight had been restored and so she acted as if unaware of the older älf-woman's presence.

"Wait at the door," she was chided. Hirai had letters in her lap; she had been reading them to her sleeping daughter.

"Forgive me. I did not know . . ." Raleeha bowed and remained standing, to listen.

"All right." Hirai continued to read aloud.

After a few sentences, Raleeha understood that the letters were from Sinthoras, written to his intended.

The words pained Raleeha, expressing as they did the deep concern the älf-warrior felt, so far away from Timanris on campaign and not able to hold her hand or plant a kiss on her lips. The phrases had an honest ring to them and they touched Raleeha's heart.

What have I done to him? What torture must he be suffering because of my actions? It was not long before tears began coursing down her cheeks. She wiped her face with her sleeve and withdrew from the doorway.

Her guilty conscience made her hate herself. Jealousy, greed, and those voices—these were what had driven her to it! *I shall not rest until I have confessed to Sinthoras what I have done.* It was not forgiveness that she craved, but she knew she must face his anger. What happened after that was immaterial.

The confrontation with Sinthoras, however, could not occur in Dsôn, not in Timansor's house.

I escaped from the realm of the älfar before—why should I not do it again? So many baggage trains were underway, bringing supplies and equipment to the troops, that she was sure she would be able to travel with one of them without exciting attention.

Her decision was made.

She returned to her chamber, packed a few items and wrote a letter to leave for Timansor, in which she stated that she was intending to return to her brother. *The safe conduct pass!* Raleeha remembered the note Timanris had written, liberating her and guaranteeing an escort out of Dsôn Faïmon. The safe conduct pass had not been dated, but it carried the appropriate seal and signature. It was difficult to accept that she must use the favor granted her by her victim. This was not helping to quieten her conscience.

Not delaying for a moment, she tossed down the farewell letter addressed to the head of the household, took the money that had accrued to her through the sale of her etchings, and hurried away from the house.

Fear and joy jostled with each other in Raleeha's head, adding to her agitation. She would ride out toward the south with a unit of soldiers in order to reach her master. If she were to die through his hand after making her confession, she would be content.

Do not throw your life away, said the small voice in her head. *You are too young to die and you are a talented artist. Come up with a different idea!*

Raleeha refused to listen.

It was not long before she found an expedition heading to the front with a cargo of ammunition for the catapults: spears and arrows. When she showed her safe conduct to the leader, he permitted her to find a space under a rough tarpaulin shelter on one of the ten flatbed carts.

Raleeha sat on the swaying cart as it juddered ever nearer to the frontier of the älfar realm. She was struck with nostalgia at having to leave the unique treasures of this land.

This is where you belong, not back with the humans. They never understood you, she heard. *The älfar admire your gifts. How can you possibly give that up?*

Despite her firm resolution to confess her crime to Sinthoras, it only took a few miles for her to come up with another plan: a plan worthy of a devious älf devoid of any conscience.

Ishím Voróo (The Outer Lands), seventeen miles from
the Northern Pass and the Stone Gateway,
4371st division of unendingness (5199th solar cycle),
summer.

Caphalor sprang forward, a dagger in his outstretched hand aimed at the right eye of the groundling before him. The thrust hit home and the dwarf collapsed as if struck in the heart.

If Caphalor had hoped to find the enemy in a state of chaos and confusion, he soon realized his mistake: the groundlings closed ranks and formed a high defense wall with their long shields, reaching from the tunnel floor to its roof. There was no getting past.

I could do with my reinforced arrows. They would pierce those shields easily.

His älfar troops stormed along in his wake, attacking the shield-wall with their swords, pressing the defenders back in an attempt to force them to a position where they would be more vulnerable.

But it was hard going; Caphalor and Sinthoras had taken on an extreme challenge. Again and again dwarf hands would shoot out of a sudden gap wielding a morningstar, a war hammer, or an ax, and the blows they dealt were expertly targeted. The älfar registered their first casualties, but Caphalor saw no enemy blood on the tunnel floor. *They are good.*

"They know what they are doing—it's home ground for them," Sinthoras remarked as he wiped the sweat from his brow. He jabbed his spear through a gap and a yell answered. He quickly activated the trigger for the secret adaptation and the yell turned to a scream that was suddenly cut off. Two älfar penetrated the gap in the shield wall and started laying about themselves, attacking the groundlings furiously.

Two further shields fell and the breach grew wider.

Show me what you can do, you stumpy-legged mine maggots. Caphalor was keen to learn more about the groundlings' methods of combat and so he pushed his way through his soldiers to the front of the melee, giving no heed to the warning shouts from Sinthoras. If he were to lose his unendingness now he would be with Enoïla all the sooner. But he carried within himself the strange certainty that he would not die here. *Not today, not tomorrow.* The main butchery was now taking place in a wider, higher part of the tunnel.

More room to fight in, at last! Caphalor saw a stocky, bushy-bearded dwarf wearing a densely woven chainmail shirt coming at him with a spiked mace. No normal knife would go through those tiny links, but Sinthoras' spear would.

"Whatever you are," roared the groundling, "I'm going to slice off your legs and cut you down to my size. Then let's see how well you fight."

Caphalor found it hard to understand what the groundling was saying. It was an excruciating dialect to listen to, but it was clear enough that these fighters were pretty sure of themselves.

With a rapid glance he assured himself that the shield wall had fallen and that all of his warriors were engaged in hand-to-hand combat with the groundlings. *Where are they trying to get to?* If he was interpreting the dark shadows at the end of the tunnel correctly, it looked as if at least four dwarves had taken flight. *If they reach their fellow groundlings our surprise attack is scuppered!*

But first he had to rid himself of the attentions of his bold opponent.

Three spike-set iron balls came toward him and Caphalor bent backward, kicking out at the same time to slam the sole of his foot into the dwarf's nose.

But the opponent, reaching only to Caphalor's hip, dodged the blow nimbly, if not with any degree of elegance, and then retaliated with the morningstar.

Two of the iron balls missed his pelvis, but the third, anchored as it was on a slightly longer chain, hit home.

Caphalor felt a dull ache; the padded undergarment beneath his black-plated armor had taken the full force of the blow, but it caused him to stumble to one side—directly into the path of a long-handled ax wielded by another of the groundlings.

Crossing his daggers, he fended off the ax, but was forced backward by the strength of the impact. The blade of the ax rang out as it glanced off of his armor.

Curses! The defenders of the Stone Gateway could not be underestimated. Their size was immaterial. *It would be easier to thrash an óarco than to overpower one of these.*

He separated his two knives and went for the dwarf's short neck, stabbing to the right and to the left of the groundling's raised arms. The dwarf fell, but the one with the spiked morningstar stepped forward, bellowing curses.

Caphalor dived over his assailant's head, swiveling round as he did so and slicing through the neck vertebrae from behind. The dwarf gave one stumbling pace forward and then slumped down.

Sinthoras jammed the heel of his boot down on a groundling's helmet, then reversed the spear and stabbed his adversary in the throat. He fended off a further attack with the flattened edge of his spear, skipping round his assailant to jab at him from behind. Then he thrust himself forward against a third dwarf and pierced it through the heart.

Sinthoras surveyed the scene. The dwarf he had just killed had been the last of them.

"Some have got away!" shouted Caphalor, pointing to the end of the corridor.

"After them!" Sinthoras ordered the remaining ten älfar; they had lost five warriors in the struggle.

The warriors set off in pursuit. When Caphalor started after them, Sinthoras held him back. "No, we need to go back and send reinforcements to check out the tunnels. Perhaps we can smuggle more of our soldiers in to Tark Draan this way."

Caphalor halted. "I don't know: the groundlings already know about the tunnel and the handful of dwarves that we have just killed can't have been more than the vanguard."

"Then we'll have to take it as it comes." Sinthoras ran back toward the cave.

Caphalor went with him reluctantly. He would have preferred to accompany the warriors and finish off a few more groundlings.

Soon they reached the night-mares and the waiting soldiers. Sinthoras briefed his troops: they were to confront and destroy the remaining dwarves and then push their way further into groundling territory. The älfar bowed to their commander and clambered up to the cave. The nos-tàroi were left alone.

"We'll lose our advantage if we are not careful," said Caphalor. "I don't doubt our own people, but the dwarves may be closer than we think." He looked at Sinthoras and pointed to the winding road leading down to the foot of the mountain. "The camp is visible from here. We should bring our attack forward."

Sinthoras studied the bright points of light down in the valley. "You think I should summon the demon? We still haven't heard from the gål-ran zhadar. We don't yet know how to contact his spy in order to get the gateway open."

Caphalor could understand the other's hesitation. *But it has to happen now.* "Did the demon not say that he, too, possessed the secret of unlocking the Stone Gateway?" He raised his eyes to the far distance. "I wonder how quickly he can get here. It is all so uncertain."

They remained silent, listening to the sound of the wind as it broke on the edge of the mountain range and delivered them a many-voiced and inharmonious song.

"You are right. We should begin the conventional attack without pinning all our hopes on the demon and the gålran zhadar," Sinthoras said suddenly. "Let's keep to our original plan." *Excellent!* Caphalor had been starting to doubt that his co-commander shared his view. The relief was considerable.

"The ogres have not arrived yet, but we've got enough beasts at our disposal to set against the gateway on storm ladders. It's no great loss if we sacrifice the óarcos. We won't deploy our own troops until the gate-way is open." He watched Sinthoras from the corner of his eye. "What about the demon?"

The älf took deep breaths of the cool mountain air and began to sing *Lay of Inàste's Tears* to summon the mist-demon to the Northern Pass.

Caphalor listened to the sad refrain and closed his eyes, moved to tears.

CHAPTER XX

But when the Inextinguishables thought everything was going according to their plans, Samusin, the god of Justice, showed them the power he extended to all.

Justice can take many forms.

Sometimes it might be an enemy's arrow, bringing endingness.

Sometimes it might be the kiss of a lover, after long periods of privation.

Sometimes it might be the forgotten ones, returning.

Epocrypha of the Creating Spirit,
Book of the Coming Death,
1–10

Ishím Voróo (The Outer Lands), seventeen miles from the Northern Pass and the Stone Gateway, 4371st division of unendingness (5199th solar cycle), summer.

The demon did not appear.

Several moments of unendingness had passed since Sinthoras had sung, but there was no sign of the mist-demon.

The älfar warriors Caphalor had sent to keep watch in the bandits' tunnel had not returned and, accordingly, the nostàroi had given orders to bring down the tunnel roof before any further groundling force could surprise them.

Sinthoras had arranged to have the first catapults brought up to the platform on the pass and he was discussing strategy with the leaders of the various allied armies, while Caphalor supervised final training exercises on scaling ladders at the cliff face.

Toboribar studied the model of the Stone Gateway and its environs. "I think it's too bold to go ahead and storm the gate before we've got any of the big ones with us," he said. "I agree we've got enough people, but if the groundlings start chucking molten pitch and burning coals down on us our losses might be greater than we can afford. We won't be able to bring up reinforcements fast enough."

"We've got that covered with the catapults. They'll swamp the parapet with liquid fire," said Sinthoras in an attempt to reassure the óarco leader. "You climb up, deal with the sentries and safeguard the gateway bolts."

"When is the demon coming?" Lotor asked. "Shouldn't we have him there from the start?"

"He is on his way." Sinthoras was getting fed up with all these negative voices. *Just do what you are told.* "He is gathering his strength so that he can be of optimum use to us when he arrives."

"Sounds good—if that is the case," responded the barbarian prince. "I'm not saying you're not telling the truth, but I'm never keen on trusting magic creatures. I'm afraid your demon might have had second thoughts in the meantime."

"Yes," came the voice of the giantess from above their heads. "But the nostàroi has promised that the demon is coming."

"He can promise till he's blue in the face if the mist thing is just going to do whatever it feels like," objected Toboribar. "We need him to break the spell on the portal and open the bolts, don't we?"

Sinthoras noticed that the mood amongst the leaders was turning nasty. They had been camped out at the foot of the Gray Range for far too long for their liking. They were eager to start fighting and to reap the promised rewards of victory. *Stupidity, greed and patience were unhappy bedfellows.* That was why he told them: "We have located the groundling traitor and have sent him a message. He can open the gate for us just as well." Everyone stared at him.

Lotor was the first to find his voice. "I'd be interested to hear more. How has the zhadar managed to smuggle one of his men in? I thought the groundlings were such a tight-knit community that a stranger would be noticed right away?"

Sinthoras was at a loss for an explanation at this juncture, but saw no reason to take refuge in a lie. "I don't know and I don't care. Just as long as their spy does what he's supposed to do." He hoped that the conviction in his tone would serve to quash all further objections.

Silence fell on the assembly once more.

Sinthoras sighed with relief. "To get back to—"

"So we have a demon who hasn't turned up and a planted traitor we have to trust but we don't need both of them in order to force entry at the gate," grumbled Toboribar. "If you ask me, Nostàroi, it's all starting to sound a bit different from our first talks about the campaign. We were sure, then, that the plan would succeed. Today," he said, indicating the model, "there isn't anything to be sure about."

"I swear we will succeed," Sinthoras countered firmly, staring the monster in the eyes until it dropped its gaze. "What is wrong with you? Since when did you turn coward? You've seen the army Caphalor and I have gathered here. Has there ever been a greater force assembled? Things may be tougher, but we will take the groundlings' defenses. Tell your troops they'll soon be plundering the treasure rooms and the corn stores!"

The majority of the leaders thumped their beakers on the table to signify their approval. Only Toboribar and Lotor exchanged skeptical glances.

"Now be off." Sinthoras remained seated and waited for all of them to leave. Then he uttered a curse as he surveyed the model of the gate they planned to storm. *Demon, what's keeping you?*

<I am very close.> The familiar voice coming from inside his own head startled him. That answer had been so clear, so loud and so sudden. <You do not doubt my loyalty, I hope?>

<I summoned you some time ago! The troops are getting impatient.>

<I wanted to flex my muscles and get used to the new powers you have endowed me with.>

The älf shut his eyes and concentrated on this strange internal conversation. <When will you be here with us?>

<Get the attack started, like you told them. I'll get there in good time. Look out for signs of decay.> The voice grew fainter. <And I shall bring you news of the spy.>

"You?" asked Sinthoras out loud, startled.

"Who else were you expecting?" came the reply from the tent flap—but it was not the voice of the mist-demon. When he opened his eyes he saw Caphalor standing on the other side of the table in full armor, a long white mantle protecting him from the cold. "Have I disturbed you at prayer?"

Sinthoras realized the demon had withdrawn from his thoughts. He told his colleague what had occurred. "What do you think?"

"The good thing is that he's coming," said Caphalor. "But how did he get to find out about the spy?" He took a seat next to Sinthoras. "No matter. We can attack very soon! The lower orders are getting restless. They want what we promised them."

"We can let them have it now." Sinthoras studied the model. "What's the situation with the beasts?"

"The óarcos have got the ladder scaling off pat now and they're not scared of heights. I'm worried about the catapult teams; they're still taking forever to get their eye in when they start shooting. But then, it won't be our own soldiers in the front line, so who cares? The óarcos have refused to let our people help them with the aiming."

Sinthoras listened and felt the tension ease. *From one heartbeat to the next, all the difficulties have resolved themselves.* "So all we need now are the ogres and everything's perfect."

One of the bodyguards entered the tent. "High Nostàroi, there's a slave here wishing to speak to Nostàroi Sinthoras. Her name is Raleeha."

Caphalor raised his eyebrows. "She's not run away again to find you?" he said, half in jest.

Sinthoras was not sure how amusing he found the situation. Memories of a certain night came back—the night when, in anger, he had given her away to Caphalor. "What does she want?"

"She has news from Dsôn, she says, Nostàroi. About Timanris."

Now his thoughts were somersaulting through his head, in turmoil between delight and terror. *Why is she sending Raleeha out to me at the front?* "Bring her in."

As Raleeha entered, Sinthoras noticed that her black summer mantle showed dirt and dust from the long journey. The familiar black lace blindfold covered the empty eye sockets, but her face was slimmer than ever, more like an älfar countenance. Her height completed the whole illusion. *If she had the pointed ears as well . . .*

"My greetings to you both, noble Nostàroi," she said quietly, bowing to them. She was shaking with cold. "I bring you news from Dsôn." She stepped forward, finding her way carefully with the tips of her feet to avoid any obstacles. "Master, it is not good news."

"I am no longer your master, Raleeha," said Sinthoras, afraid of what she might be going to tell him. What was she preparing him for? *I don't want to hear it.*

"From this moment of unendingness you are indeed my master once more," she contradicted, taking out a slim roll of script and handing it to him. "It was Timanris' last wish before she died." Raleeha held the parchment out.

Died . . . The word echoed and echoed round his head. Sinthoras stared at the rolled letter, staring so intensely that it might have burst into flame. Nothing could make him move to take the letter.

Died . . .

It was Caphalor who finally took hold of the parchment; as he did so his hand touched the slave girl's slim fingers, as it might be accidentally. "Sinthoras?"

"I don't want to read it," he said hoarsely.

Caphalor's face darkened with sadness. The memory of the loss he had suffered all too recently came flooding back and overwhelmed him. "You cannot make it un-happen," he said in a soft and sympathetic voice. "She is dead, Sinthoras."

"You read it," he groaned, picking up a goblet, pouring water for himself and swallowing it down. The liquid trickled down his constricted throat.

"It is addressed to you, master." Raleeha spoke up cautiously.

"Silence!" he roared at her. "I trust Caphalor." He swayed, grasping the edge of the table for support. The loss of his beloved was coming home to him, made manifest and gaining clarity through the words that Caphalor was speaking. *What shall I do now?* Sinthoras was in turmoil and could only understand small snatches of the writing.

Timanris had written to say that she loved him, but that the injuries she had suffered were too grave to permit recovery. Endingness was approaching for her. She wanted to exact an oath from him that he would never return to Dsôn where everything would remind him of her death. She wanted him to spare himself this grief. His future lay in Tark Draan where he should found his own realm. She was entrusting Raleeha to him. Raleeha had been a good friend to her. A sister.

"'Our souls were once as one,'" Caphalor read the message from the dead älf-woman, "'but now they must separate and I must let you go, beloved. Remember me, but do not chain yourself to my memory. Shelter Raleeha, whom I have freed, and she will be your faithful companion.'" He let the letter sink to the table and watched Sinthoras with sympathy, then turned his gaze on Raleeha, noticing the tears streaming down her face from under the black lace blindfold.

After a while he stepped over to Sinthoras and pressed his arm. "She is right. Listen to her words and do what is asked of you. I shall not be returning to the homeland either." He sought Sinthoras' eyes. "We are bound together by pain and grief. We shall let Tark Draan feel the extent of our suffering."

What else is there for me now? She is gone. Swallowed up by endingness. "We shall indeed," he croaked in agreement, fists clenched. With a loud cry he moved to the table where the parchment lay. "We shall attack. This very day!" He stormed past the others, roaring out commands until his voice was hoarse. Fanfares and drums sounded in response to his sudden pronouncement.

*   *   *

Caphalor took a deep breath and watched the former slave, who was standing at the entrance to the tent, uncertain what to do. "Were you expecting a different reaction?"

She bowed her head. "I am waiting to be told what to do. Even if I am free now, I still have to play the role of a slave when amongst others."

"Your task is clear from Timanris' words—to stay with him."

"I heard him make no oath," she said firmly. "He has not yet undertaken to carry out her final wishes."

Caphalor paid more attention. Her tone of voice indicated disappointment and yet there was the trace of a satisfied smile on her lips. *Because she is allowed to be back at his side again? Or is there . . .*

All of a sudden, the wording of that letter looked a little suspect. Concepts such as sister and companion were highly unlikely for an älf to employ in connection with a barbarian, artist or no. "How did this accident occur?" He did not take his eyes from her face and suppressed all previous feelings for her. *I shall remain true to Enoïla past death.*

Raleeha turned her face toward him as if she were able to see him. Really and truly see him. "What do you mean, sir?"

"I should like to know what happened when you and Timanris fell down the steps together." She looked surprised. *Surprised and something more than surprised.*

"I was walking behind her up the stairs when she slipped and fell. She put out her arms to find something to hang onto for support, grabbed a spear and pulled me with her." She shrugged. "That's all I can say. I hit my head and don't remember anything else."

"Very handy," responded Caphalor.

He picked up the parchment and pressed it into the slave girl's hand. Her fingers were shaking, so he closed them round the letter, holding fast to her. *She was keeping something secret.* He knew how obsessed she had always been by Sinthoras and his creative works. *How far would she go?*

"You know that Sinthoras will send a message to her father? He will want to express his sympathy? Perhaps they will meet, away from Dsôn, to share their grief?" The longer he spoke, the more she shook. "Or might it be that Sinthoras receives word from Timanris expressing her astonishment about his letter to her father?"

"Sir," she moaned. "No, that could not happen. Timanris is dead."

"I am sure that she is not." Caphalor smiled. "You know what you must do, Raleeha. If the truth emerges before you have unpicked your tissue of lies, you will have to endure pain such as you have never known and you will beg to be killed. Sinthoras can be cruel. Blinding you as he did was a kindness compared to the punishment he would inflict." He released her hand. "Tell him yourself: if it has to be me that tells him, there will be no mercy for you. Not even running away again will save you," he murmured softly before leaving the tent.

Stepping out into bright sunshine, he shaded his eyes with one hand to observe the hectic activity that had broken out on all sides in Sinthoras' wake.

Caphalor was looking forward to the battle and watched as thousands of their troops marched toward the gateway. Banners and pennants streamed out and snapped in the wind. The breeze carried the stink of the grease the óarcos used to coat their armor. By doing this, they hoped that enemy blades would slip and get no purchase.

Maybe it's no bad thing for the moment if Sinthoras believes Timanris is dead. His anger and grief at his loss would make him a single-mindedly fierce warrior, useful when storming the defenses. And for the invasion of Tark Draan.

Caphalor's own lust for destruction welcomed these developments and so he kept silent about Raleeha's lies. *It will come out one way or another. Raleeha will tell him, or there will be a letter from Dsôn, or it will be revealed quite by chance.* Sinthoras' joy then at having his beloved restored to him would be greater than ever.

He had to laugh. *It is amazing. I am starting to think in the same devious ways as Sinthoras used to.*

His gaze fell on the grass being trampled by bare feet, hooves, boots and wheels.

He looked more closely: *the grass had turned gray.* Every single blade of grass had lost its color.

Ishím Voróo (The Outer Lands), Gray Range, Stone Gateway,
4371st division of unendingness (5199th solar cycle),
summer.

The attack began in the afternoon.

From the saddles of their night-mares, Sinthoras and Caphalor dispatched the óarcos to the front line. The beasts lumbered along the thirty-pace broad pass, dragging heavy ladders and catapult parts to erect when nearer to the Gateway. Drums thumped out a repetitive beat and horns fired up the troops. The älfar warriors and other allies were under orders to hold back: the nostàroi wanted to establish how the groundlings would respond to the initial attack.

Grunting and roaring, the vanguard surged slowly forward, heading directly for the portal. The mountain walls reverberated with the clamor, magnifying the threatening noises.

With any luck these distorted sounds will penetrate the consciousness of the Gateway's defenders, thought Sinthoras. Their noisy mass of animal soldiery was sending out almost palpable waves of confident conviction, a groundswell of enthusiastic belief in their imminent victory.

"It's looking good," said Caphalor at his side. "And our attack comes at exactly the right time." He pointed out a mountain pine whose branches, within the space of a few blinks of an eye, had started to droop, the needles drifting to the stony ground. "See there! The demon's power travels ahead of him. He can't be far away now."

Sinthoras felt the same buoyant conviction as his attacking troops, but a corner of his heart remained stoney, unable to summon enthusiasm for the coming triumph. Timanris' name flitted constantly in and out of his thoughts like a ghost, even now, as he watched the óarcos erect their siege ladders at the portal and begin to clamber boldly up the none-too-sturdy contraptions; the archers provided cover with a steady shower of arrows.

The second unit of troops was assembling the catapults in order to support the attack with burning missiles. Loaded leather bags were set alight and hurled hissing through the air to burst on impact, spreading flaming petroleum wherever they landed.

For Sinthoras, the screams of the dying, the swish of the missiles and the sound of the bugles and horns sounded like an orchestral arrangement of *Timanris*, the name of his beloved. *If I had stayed behind she might still be alive. I was not even able to visit her as she lay on her sickbed.*

"Those idiots!" growled Caphalor. "I've trained them and trained them and they still can't do it right!" The initial salvos were too low, hitting their own óarco troops, but neither the hail of stones nor the hot bitumen raining down could dim the fervor of the óarcos rushing to replace those who fell. "Look how the beasts are fighting," he enthused. "Toboribar's creatures were made for this task." He raced off on his night-mare. "I ride to the eastern flank. The catapult teams need my help with aiming, otherwise they'll be sending our own forces up in flames."

Sinthoras was surprised by the amount of old bones the óarcos had to clamber over to get to the Stone Gateway. *So many have tried to get in and been destroyed by the groundlings: the living want to avenge the dead.* He observed the óarcos' efforts, watching them swing themselves up on to the battlements above the gateway to fight the groundlings.

But the stumpy defenders were presenting staunch resistance. They stood on fortifications designed specifically so that only a small number of guards would be needed to defend them.

Sinthoras kept glancing behind, looking for the mist-demon—but he did not appear. *That gate won't open without him. Hurry, demon!*

The nostàroi let the óarcos rampage until sundown in the hope of wearing out the defenders, and when darkness spread over the Northern Pass they had the retreat sounded. Bugles and trombones signaled a call to cease the onslaught. The creatures reacted obediently to the command.

Caphalor came back to join him and so did Toboribar. The latter was not in the best of moods. "What's happening, Nostàroi?" he complained. "My forces are already up on the parapet! The defenders' cauldrons of hot slack are empty and their supply of stones is running out. We're so close!" As he spoke, he revealed a missing tooth in his broad jaw.

"Close to what? What use to us are conquered parapets?" Caphalor interrupted.

Toboribar was not about to let himself be intimidated. "There are only a few dwarves, and we—"

"I want them to think they are winning again, as usual," responded Sinthoras. There was no way he was going to allow the óarco to take over the planning. "We'll wait a little and then make a renewed attack."

A rhythmic thumping sound was heard. Something very heavy was approaching. Caphalor looked over his shoulder. In the silver light of the moon he saw the impressive outlines of monsters four times as big and strong as the óarcos. Their ugly bodies were protected by badly made armor and the clubs they were waving in their great paws were young tree trunks. "The ogres and the giants have arrived—forty of them. They've got the grappling irons and chains I told them to bring. Perhaps they can force a gap in the gate."

"Tell the troops to hold themselves in readiness and explain it's a ruse; we are not really withdrawing."

Toboribar nodded and raced off as fast as his heavy armor allowed.

"We should not wait too long." Caphalor let his gaze sweep over the corpses and the shattered ladders in front of the gateway. "Otherwise we give the defenders too much opportunity to regain their strength."

"You heard what Toboribar's scum saw up there: they have no more warriors and they are running out of ammunition." He inhaled the disgusting aroma of the battlefield: shed blood, ruptured intestines, dust, petroleum, all mixed with the smell of fear, hatred and conviction. "Before the daystar reappears in the sky, we will be on the other side." He took out the medallion he wore under his armor and he passed his gauntlet over it. *For you, Timanris.* Then he turned toward his nightmare. "I'll go and tell the ogres and giants what we want them to do."

Caphalor commanded the second attack: a concerted mass of óarcos rushed forward, forming an alley. The ogres and giants were greeted with cries of delight as they approached. The two races were almost indistinguishable behind their armor; in stature they were equal.

Stop all that yowling and start fighting, he thought impatiently. *Your voices are unbearable, but not lethal enough to be weapons.* "Get yourselves to the front," he called out.

The huge monsters stomped off to the head of the army and prepared the grappling irons, each with four barbs the length of a grown barbarian. They pulled chains through the hole at the top end of each anchor and then whirled the irons round their heads and hurled them up in the air; with a rushing noise and a metallic clatter they shot through the night. In the meantime the óarcos took hold of the ends of the long chains

Caphalor was satisfied. The grappling irons sat securely in place on the massive outer battlements.

"*Now!*"

At his bellowed command, the waiting óarcos, together with the combined forces of the ogres and giants, pulled at the chains.

The metal links came taut, but that was all.

"Drive them harder!" shouted Caphalor, as he rode Sardaî between the troops, letting the night-mare snap his sharp teeth. He ordered the officers to use whips. *This has got to work! I don't want to wait any longer.* The chains were tightened and the creatures groaned with the exertion demanded of them.

Caphalor heard a slight crunching sound: the fortified gateway shook with the elemental energy of the monsters. "Keep going!" he shouted. "Pull down the parapet!"

Part of the battlements gave way and the grappling iron and pieces of stone hurtled down, killing ten óarcos and two of the ogres; fellow combatants were crushed and buried under their huge bodies.

"Send the grapple up again. Throw it up!" ordered Caphalor. The beasts did as they were bid. A few moments later the grappling iron was anchored to a different part of the wall. "They are retreating," he called out grimly. Up on the battlements he could see the groundlings' helmets as they scurried to and fro, positioning themselves behind the metal protection at the top of the stone doors. "Our first victory is at hand! Pull! Pull!"

The balustrade broke off and plunged down, clouds of dust rose as it hit the ground. The mountains shuddered under the impact: the monsters howled exultantly.

Sinthoras rode over to join his fellow commander. "Getting the gateway open would have been too much to hope for," he said.

"It might have worked." Caphalor studied the rubble that had fallen. "We'll have to get this cleared. It will be in our way." They rode forward together and gave the appropriate orders to the troops.

This time the complaining voices were louder. The óarcos wanted to get back to attacking and were not in the mood for heavy quarry work; rock-shifting was not what a proper warrior did. Even the blows from the captains' whips could not quash their inarticulate unrest. Stone after stone was passed back along their lines reluctantly and far too slowly to make way for the next attack.

On the wall, the groundlings had slowed, waiting for something, assembling new missiles. Caphalor and Sinthoras withdrew from the front line.

"Get a move on." Sinthoras told the óarcos. "I'll show them what happens when they go against the orders of a nostàroi," he muttered. Caphalor took his bow from behind his shoulder and notched a long reinforced arrow, his fingers resting lightly on the feathered shaft.

Some of the óarcos had turned away, refusing to take on a task so far beneath their dignity. Caphalor raised his bow. Three arrows left the bowstring in quick succession, sending three targets crashing to the ground.

The other green-skinned monsters understood the lethal warning and stumbled back to work with no further attempts at mutiny. Even the leaders and Toboribar kept their counsel and said nothing in protest. They were scared.

It took until dawn to clear away all the debris from in front of the gateway.

I have to keep my promise. Sinthoras was reminded of the deadline he had set for himself. "I cannot fail here." *Where have you got to, demon? Is this the way you show your loyalty?*

<You are expecting me.> He heard the demon's voice in his head.

<Yes,> he thought with relief. He did not want Caphalor to overhear him. <Keep your promise, break this gateway.>

<I shall show myself to the troops. They must see who it is they serve.> The mist-demon sounded much more insistent than at their first meeting.

<It is the Inextinguishables they serve—> He attempted to contradict the demon but was interrupted by the other's loud laughter.

<No. They serve me. You shall see how they bow their heads in obeisance to me. You and your friend, too, you will not be able to resist.>

Sinthoras decided to postpone this dispute. He did not want an argument now about who was going to obey whom. That could all wait until after the gateway had been breached. There were more important things. <How are you going to get the portal open?>

<I took the messenger the gâlran zhadar sent you. I know all his little secrets. The spy on the other side will do what he was told to.>

Sinthoras felt cold fingers sneaking through his mind and he gave himself a shake: it was worse than unpleasant. <Show yourself. At break of day we plan to go invade Tark Draan.>

<Look to the north!>

Sinthoras twisted round in the saddle. "He is coming!"

Caphalor knew who his friend was speaking of. He also directed his glance along the pass.

And while the eastern sky gradually grew lighter to announce the arrival of day, a broad bank of cloud rose behind them. In its interior there were shimmers of black, silver and red, the colors mixing and melding, the intensity flowing in waves.

"Tion!" exclaimed Caphalor. "Is that him?"

Sinthoras said nothing. That was not how the mist-demon had appeared at their first meeting. *And it is sending out a darkness, a malicious power that plants fear in my soul.*

"Is that him?" Caphalor repeated hoarsely, experiencing the same effects.

"Yes, I think so," Sinthoras stuttered, feeling small, worthless, and insignificant in the presence of the demon.

The demon moved over the heads of the monsters and floated—against the prevailing wind—directly toward the gateway.

The óarcos, normally so loud, fell silent at its approach, huddling together and trying to avoid any contact with the vibrant swirling cloud. Even the ogres and the giants retreated in fear.

It is . . . Sinthoras could not withstand the power that was stronger even than that of the Inextinguishable Ones. He and Caphalor both lowered their heads and offered a salute to this wraith, as befitted a sovereign lord.

The glittering bank of mist sank down to the ground in front of the älfar and remained there. <You see, I was telling no lie: you serve me. Now let us get ourselves some slaves.>

There was a lurch at the portal and the stone shook.

Sinthoras raised his head and heard the first of the five bolts sliding back. *The spy has spoken the password.* There was a rumbling louder even than the eager shouts of the beasts. Then the noises on the other side ceased.

The gigantic double gates moved slowly, jolting and resisting as they started to swing apart.

"Make ready!" ordered Caphalor at his side. "Assume your formations!"

Granite scraped on rock as the fissure became a yawning gap that increased to a wide opening. There was a final thump and a shudder, then the way lay open to the land of Tark Draan. *For the very first time in thousands of divisions of unendingness, the gateway is open.*

"Enjoy the sight, Caphalor," whispered Sinthoras. "No one before us has had such success."

"One of many great victories, my friend: our names will enter the legends of our people and the folk of Tark Draan will speak them with terror." Caphalor's eyes sparkled. "We are harbingers of a new age." He filled his lungs with air and bellowed the command: "Attack!"

Bugles and horns blared, the signal tunes clashing and drowning each other out—alerting the army's flanks and center. Óarcos, ogres and giants roared in response, waving their weapons in the air. Then they advanced—shields and swords, clubs and spears gripped fast. The tension could be felt in the air.

At the first insistent drum beats the army started to run, heavy boots thundering on the ground.

The squat and solid forms of the groundlings appeared, standing shoulder to shoulder to stem this tide, indifferent to their own fate. Forty of them against thousands. Sinthoras could not help but admire their steadfast courage, even if he could not understand it. "There is absolutely no sense in sacrificing themselves like that," he remarked to Caphalor. "They'd be better off going back to their tunnels—"

The two wings of the gate began to close.

"Hurry!" shouted Caphalor.

He aimed several arrows at their backs to speed them on. The óarcos grunted and moved more quickly to escape the nostàroi's fire. Those at the back pushed the ranks at the front.

"Get the ogres to hold open the gates! Take the grapping irons and the chains! Shove your worthless bodies in there to jam the gates, do you hear?"

The óarcos had reached the first of the dwarves—and died at their hands under hard and meticulously aimed blows. Greed had been making the monsters unwary; they were deceived by the defenders' size and had not reckoned with the enormous strength in those short limbs. Their axes shattered shields and the arms that held them; they broke open helmets, armor and the flesh and bones behind.

Sinthoras found it almost impossible to believe, but the first wave of attack was repulsed at the dwarf barrier. "Send a message back to the army: the gateway is open and the demon came to our aid. All units to make their way here," he called to a herald. "Tell our älfar warriors as well." Then, with Caphalor, he forced his way through the óarco lines and past the feet of the ogres and the giants, toward the opening.

The stubborn groundling defenders were starting to fall, one by one, wildly outnumbered by the invading force. Their tremendous stamina had its limits, but their tough stand had paid off. Several of the beasts had got through, but the main attack had been thwarted and the gate was almost completely shut again. Eight ogres were desperately trying to prevent the gates from slamming shut: the soles of their feet were slipping and scraping on the rocky path, taking off whole layers of horny skin.

Sinthoras was astonished. *Even their elemental strength is no match for the work of the dwarves.*

"What's the matter with you?" screamed Caphalor furiously as he jumped down from his night-mare. He shot his arrows into the backs of the house-high monsters to drive them on to greater effort. "Hold the stone back at all costs!"

<Be unconcerned.> Sinthoras heard the demon voice in his ear. <They have killed our spy but my power will bring him back to life. The formula is not lost.>

The älf glanced over to the glittering cloud and again was unable to resist its effect. He bowed respectfully and saw that his friend was beside himself with fury. "Caphalor! Leave them be. We'll get the portal open again soon. The spy will be restored from the dead. The demon has just told me." He dismounted and took off, spear in hand to seek out any groundling survivors.

This is exhausting. Dressed in armor far too big for her, Raleeha was trying to keep up with the barbarian army.

She had to find Sinthoras and there was no other way to reach him. She had joined her brother's unit, which was under orders to go to the front. When she had tried to make her way there in her own garments she had been held back by the sentries, so she was trying again in borrowed armor.

Raleeha could hardly wait to stand in front of Sinthoras and tell him the truth. *Caphalor was right: it will, of course, all come out sooner or later. It's far better I tell him myself and I can profess my love for him at the same time.* The unit was forced to a halt. The pass was thirty paces wide, but the army was so huge that it kept stopping. Some soldiers had fallen into the ravine when they tried to push their way to the front, and in other places edges of the road had crumbled away, sending dozens to their deaths. "Let me through!" Raleeha shouted, pushing others aside. She cared nothing for the verbal abuse she received for her pains and shook off any restraining hand. Gasping under the weight of the armor, she found the altitude was causing her problems as well and she was now perspiring heavily, her one good eye was burning in its socket with the sweat that trickled into it.

Raleeha got past the óarco rearguard, pushing her way through the pack and retching at the smell of the rancid fat on their armor. *He can't be far away now.*

She paid no heed to the óarcos' grunts of protest. As soon as she called out the words "Sinthoras" and "message," they let her through. Why else would a skinny lone barbarian want to get to the front line?

Drenched with sweat, Raleeha reached the platform and followed the pass until she saw the portal before her eyes, closing even as she watched. *Gods!* The battle had been fought and it looked to her as if it were going down as a defeat. *The gateway is closing, something must have gone awry.* In the first row between the beast cadavers and the rubble, she saw the älfar nostàroi dismount from their night-mares.

"Out of my way!" she screamed at the soldiers standing around. "I have to get to the nostàroi! I have a message for him." Raleeha ran toward Sinthoras, who was walking about between the bodies of the dwarves. Surrounded as she was by a stream of much broader and taller óarcos, it was difficult not to lose sight of him.

"Sinthoras, my master!" she shouted as loudly as she could, trying to resist the crush of huge bodies pressing her in the opposite direction. It was as if she were a piece of living flotsam carried on the tide of bodies. Had she not been wearing armor, she would have been squashed flat.

She managed to free herself from the densest part of the throng and saw Sinthoras ahead, bending over a groundling. Caphalor was moving up to him.

"My master!" she called out breathlessly as she stumbled over to him. She nearly fell as she clambered over the mutilated corpses of óarcos. "Timanris is alive!" It seemed to her as if she were breathing out the words so softly that they disappeared.

A movement she caught out of the corner of her eye made her swivel round. One of the dwarves had split an óarco in half and had grabbed hold of a throwing ax. He was looking round for new foes to slay. His gaze swept over Raleeha and fixed itself on Sinthoras.

The arm was raised for the throw.

"No," she whispered, realizing the dwarf had just selected her master as his target. With the last of her strength she sprang, just as the groundling hurled his weapon through the air.

The impact was as powerful as a fall from a great height. The blade pierced her leather armor, severing the chainmail rings and slicing through her left breast.

As Raleeha fell, her lungs collapsed; she could not speak. She could feel the blood pouring out of her side. Then new óarcos fell upon the groundling and his death cry resounded.

He has to know the truth. She lay rigid atop the corpse, groaning out the name of her master as clearly as she could. "Timanris awaits you," she gasped. She knew that death was not going to spare her. *This is my reward for my evil deeds, for all my lies.*

The gods have had enough of you, her reason spoke softly inside her head. *I warned you so often . . .*

At least she would die with the knowledge that she was giving her life to save her master: a good exchange. *May you become a hero such as Dsôn Faïmon has never known,* she thought, as her strength faded away.

Heavy steps approached. Three or four óarcos trampled over her unawares, and a foot trod the ax blade deeper into her body. Right through her heart.

Sinthoras spotted a wounded dwarf whose legs had been smashed, presumably by an ogre's club. *Here's one that won't be running away.* He twirled his spear and came up from behind. Let death come as a surprise to the stunted creature.

The groundling raised one hand to screen his eyes from the rays of the rising sun.

You'll not live to celebrate the closing gate. Sinthoras thrust the narrow spear tip through the rings of the dwarf's chainmail shirt and saw him go rigid. He stared in disbelief at the weapon sticking out of his chest as his breath began to fail.

Sinthoras left the blade in for a moment, then withdrew it and walked round his victim, crouching down by his side. He studied the coarse, weather-beaten features edged with a thick black beard. It must have taken a long time to braid the beard hair. It hung down onto his chest in braided ropes. The brown eyes shone with pain, bloody-mindedness and pride.

"Look at me," Sinthoras said in älfish. "The name of your death is Sinthoras. I shall take your life, the land shall take your soul." He could see he was not being understood. Caphalor, standing behind the dying dwarf, translated his colleague's words into the universal language of Tark Draan.

The dwarf coughed up dark blood and it ran from the corner of his mouth to trickle into his beard.

"Get out of my way! I want to watch the gateway close," he demanded roughly.

Sinthoras was fascinated to see this diminutive warrior refusing to die. *The injury I inflicted on him would have made any normal creature lose consciousness.* Instead, the groundling was attempting to drive him off with weakening blows of a bloody ax, which nearly slipped out of his grasp. His strength was ebbing away.

"Out of the way or I'll split you like straw, treacherous elf," he growled.

Sinthoras gave a cold-blooded smile. *Small in stature, but with an iron will.* He lifted the spear and poked the tip in through a gap in the chainmail. He was curious to observe the death process in this alien being. To put one of the hated mine maggots to death! *The first of innumerable such killings!*

"How wrong you are. We are the älfar. We have come to destroy the elves," Caphalor continued softly, torturing the dwarf with his words. "The gate may be closing now, but when the demon brings you back to life you will be one of us and you will open it again. You know the formula."

"Never!" contradicted the groundling, filled with renewed vigor. "You—"

"Your soul now belongs to the land," Caphalor interrupted. "Now die, then return and hand us the keys to Tark Draan."

Sinthoras wanted to give the death-thrust at that very moment, while the dwarf's life-force was surging back one last time. The sharpened end of the spear drove through the dwarf's flesh and the pain silenced him at last.

Applying pressure, the älf pushed the spear through the badly injured body for a second time. Sinthoras carried out the movement almost lovingly, full of joy. Then he awaited death's arrival and studied the dwarf's features in the final struggle, absorbing these unique impressions. *I am making you immortal, little man. When the battle is over I shall put you in a painting. Blood is here aplenty.*

Only when he was quite sure that the last spark of life had left the dwarf did Sinthoras stand up again.

"They die in a different way from the barbarians and the óarcos," he said to Caphalor. "More dignity and more defiance when their eyes glaze over. There is no fear. If they were not so small and ugly you might think they had something of ourselves in them." Then he gave a burst of dark laughter and his friend joined in.

The gate was closing more slowly now and the ogres and óarcos struggling to hold it open gave roars of relief. Countless hands pushed and shoved and the gates swung back.

<It's not them making the miracle happen. I got the traitor to speak the formula again when I made him undead,> said the demon to Sinthoras, speaking inside his head once more. <Nothing can stop you now. I can feel that the earth of Tark Draan holds the promise of immense power for me! You spoke true when we met that first time, älf!>

Sinthoras turned to Caphalor. "We should get to the head of the army, my friend. As commanders that is our place, not following behind." Sinthoras went over to his night-mare.

"I could have sworn I heard someone call your name just now," said Caphalor. "A woman's voice, whispering." He looked around, but as there was no woman to be seen, he thought his ears must have deceived him. "Battle noise like this is bad for sensitive hearing." He raised his hand and Sardaî trotted over to him. The älf swung himself up, sat tall in the saddle and looked to the Northern Pass. A never-ending stream of barbarians, óarcos and monsters was driving through the gateway. "They are the tools of my revenge; I will engrave Enoïla's memory into every inch of Tark Draan," he murmured. He uttered the vow: "Your death bears the name Caphalor." This solemn promise he made to all the inhabitants and creatures of Tark Draan. Then he urged his night-mare into a gallop.

Epilogue

*Ishím Voróo (The Outer Lands), former kingdom of the fflecx,
4371st division of unendingness (5199th solar cycle),
summer.*

Linschibog lifted his long nose and sniffed the soft evening air: it did not smell of óarcos or barbarians or of any other soldier in the nostàrois' army.

Good, good, good! He relaxed a little. As one of the very last fflecx, he had to be doubly careful if he wanted his race to remain alive—for that, of course, he would have to locate a female. So far, Linschibog had not come across another of his kind and he had gradually stopped bothering to pray. At least that made his existence a bit different from the norm.

The gnome-like creature got up from the long grass where he had been lying, adjusted his bright red tunic, shouldered his rucksack and continued to trek across the plain that was now covered in gray grass.

The power of the mist-demon had changed all living things. Whatever died returned as an undead horror.

And that was why Linschibog hated the älfar. *It was they who summoned the being from the northwest, woke it from its harmless slumbers, and aroused its insatiable hunger for more and yet more.*

Then there was Munumon, his king, killed by an älf: he had seen the body and the mutilations pointed to the älfar.

Somebody has got to destroy them! But they had been clever enough to drive all the strongest races out of Ishím Voróo and off to Tark Draan. *Who is left to threaten the black-eyes?*

Lost in thought, he trudged through the desolate stone-colored grass, but then the pointed toe of his right shoe got stuck on something that looked a bit odd. Linschibog bent down to pick up the leather roll that had been hidden under the long grass stalks.

He opened the folder and was amazed to see the drawings it contained: a city, fortifications, towers on islands, streets—pictures of the legendary center of the Star Realm, the city of Dsôn. At any rate, that's what people said it looked like, with that tower made of bones right at the heart. Someone had gone to enormous trouble to detail every bit of the so-called beauty of the älfar realm.

Linschibog could not find anything to like about the complicated buildings with their monotonous colors and all the fancy, cruel art on the fronts of the houses. "Garbage, load of poo, smelly donkey shit," he cursed, tossing the roll of drawings over his shoulder without attempting to refasten the ribbon. He stomped off. *There must be a mate for me somewhere.*

The breeze picked up the drawings one at a time and carried them off.

The gusts of wind made a game of whirling the pictures into the air: one would sail down again to land in the gray grass, or it might get stuck in the branches of a black tree, or float down onto the surface of a dirty-looking pond.

It was the drawing of Dsôn that stayed in the air longest, while behind it one sketch after another fell to the ground, like a strange paper-chase thought up by an eccentric artist.

But the picture of the Tower of Bones kept going—until an iron-clad hand grabbed it out of the air. Caught in that fist it looked small and forlorn.

The sketch was lifted level with the violet-blue gaze that stared out from a martial black helmet. An indefinable sound emerged, unlike speech, and the mighty fingers crushed the paper as if crushing the city itself. As if the fingers had no more fervent wish than the destruction of Dsôn.

The hand holding the picture lifted it high in the air and a mighty roar broke out from all sides . . .

Acknowledgments

Following on from the dwarves, the älfar now want to tell their version of the story. After the good ones, the evil take their turn—or is it only a question of perspective? This legend covers events preceding the storming of Girdlegard, as described in *The Dwarves*.

Sinthoras and Caphalor open the tale, and they will be given a further volume. Readers of *The Dwarves* know how that will end. But what they experience in the intervening cycles—at least the most dramatic events—will be coming to light on pages yet to be written.

The challenge I faced here was in changing sides and revealing the älfar way of thinking—to show them as they see themselves, how they conduct themselves with friends and the like. And how they initiated an entirely new form of art.

I do not dare to predict how many friends the älfar will find. But one thing is certain: the story continues.

Those who have helped me to keep this book going in the right direction include my trusted test readers, Sonja Rüther and Tanja Karmann, and the newcomer to the team, Petra Ney, whose comments and hints enhanced the novel.

My thanks are due also to my editor, Angela Kuepper, who always shows me ways I could improve, and Carsten Polzin from Piper Verlag, who at my request allowed me to design the German cover.

I'd like to say thank you again, this time to Tanja Howarth for setting the stage, Sheelagh Alabaster for the English translation, Nicola Budd for her work and our nice conversations, and, of course, Jo Fletcher— she has a heart for villains with style!

Markus Heitz
Germany,
2008